Sweeter with You

Endorsements

Thanks to Felkins's dynamic characters, I'm anticipating the rest of the series!
—**Beth K. Vogt**, Christy Award-winning author of the Thatcher Sisters Series

Mary Felkins has done it again! *Sweeter with You* is a charming romance that warms the heart in all the right places.
—**Kit Morgan**, *USA Today* bestselling author

Mary Felkins's second novel in "The Heart of Moreland Manor" series is a delectable treat of sharp wit, snark, and humor. But buried within, Mary has the ability to weave several complex characters with their fears and inadequacies, their conditions and their foibles, into understanding God's purpose and plan—to love unconditionally. A novel that will bring the reader into fits of laughter and as well as tears.
—**Claire O'Sullivan**, author of *Romance Under Wraps and Rules of Engagement.*

Mary A. Felkins has masterfully created characters that will make you laugh, cry, cheer, and jeer ... a wonderful supporting cast who will touch your heart. Throughout the story, faith in God will be a part of each person's journey. This book is a worthwhile read!
—**Bettie Boswell**, author of *On Cue, Free to Love, Sidetracked, Skateboarding*

Sweeter with You

Mary A. Felkins

A Christian Company
ElkLakePublishingInc.com

Copyright Notice

Sweeter with You

Cover and Interior Design: Derinda Babcock
Editor(s): Steve Mathisen, Cristel Phelps, Deb Haggerty

PUBLISHED BY: Elk Lake Publishing, Inc., 35 Dogwood Drive, Plymouth, MA 02360, 2023

Library Cataloging Data

Names: Felkins, Mary A. (Mary A. Felkins)

Sweeter with You / Mary A. Felkins

364 p. 23cm × 15cm (9in × 6 in.)

ISBN-13: 978-1-64949-784-0 (paperback) | 978-1-64949-785-7 (trade hardcover) | 978-1-64949-786-4 (trade paperback) | 978-1-64949-787-1 (e-book)

Key Words: Contemporary Christian romance; Contemporary romance Kindle books; Contemporary romance trilogy; Contemporary Christian romance series; Romance series for women;Christian contemporary romance for women; Trilogy of Christian romance for women

Library of Congress Control Number: 2022951831 Fiction

Dedication

To Margaret—a woman of influence who's learned the secret of being content and how to discern when it's time to move on from what we cannot change.

When I consider your heavens, the work of your fingers, the moon and the stars, which you have set in place, what is mankind that you are mindful of them, human beings that you care for them? You have made them a little lower than the angels and crowned them with glory and honor.

(Psalm 8:3-5 NIV)

Acknowledgments

Deb Haggerty, Editor in Chief, whose hands-on editing enables a novel to sing. Cristel Phelps, managing editor, whose keen eye helps prepare the manuscript for next steps. Steve Mathisen, editor, who strengthened readability, assured factual accuracy, and identified places where we could give the reader a deeper emotional experience. Derinda Babcock, senior graphic designer, who creates award-winning covers.

During the 2019 Deep Thinker's Writer's Retreat (DTR), the creative genius of best-selling authors Rachel Hauck and Susan May Warren inspired the idea of a cupcake baking NFL player. I scoffed. They were serious—and drew attention to two pro ball players who'd established a successful bakery in Austin, Texas. Brainstorming sessions and one-on-one chats with Rachel layered depth and meaning to my original story concept.

Pamela Snowden and Gracie Booth Wursthorn, creative members of the 2019 DTR brainstorming group who helped flesh out the story.

The staff of a New Orleans bakery who fielded questions about being a proprietor in the French Quarter.

Pattie Frampton, an invaluable craft partner who provided crucial objectivity throughout the construction of this story.

Beta readers and authors, Kathy Geary Anderson and Linda Jo Reed.

Along with Pattie, Kathy, and Linda Jo, I'm grateful to Dalyn Weller and Geralyn Beauchamp. These savvy authors in my MBT (My Book Therapy) Huddle group possess a wealth of writing industry experience and offer solid prayer support—oxygen for the writer's soul.

The ladies of Tuesday's prayer group at Corinth Reformed Church, Hickory NC. I'm grateful for their faithfulness to pray as I wrestled with these imaginary characters until they told the story God wanted to convey through the medium of fiction.

Chapter One

For a girl named after an iconic Parisian chapel built to offer peace, Serenity Chapelle Lewis was anything but serene. With the only remaining convection oven not in use suddenly on the fritz, hours before dozens of mini cupcakes were due to Moreland Manor B&B, peace would have to wait.

Again.

"Please tell me we've enough cash reserve to deal with equipment failure?"

Brooke, Serenity's former college roommate and part-time coworker, dotted her forehead. "Ask your sister Everley. She keeps the books."

"Let's hope she's got an affirmative on that. I'm worried."

"Because behind that well-crafted, cheery optimism, that's what you do, Serenity. Feed on worry like it's a pastry."

"Nothing a couple antacids won't fix."

"The first twenty-five dozen of these mini cupcakes are good."

"Then let's frost the ones we have and offer our apologies."

She hated to disappoint. Really hated it.

Soulful jazz piped from speakers and offset the clang and clatter inside her buzzing bakery, but it failed to lift her sagging mood. She navigated past a lineup of counters and equipment over to boxed inventory set on bulky shelving. "What if that stupid new bakery chain costs me more business? I'm struggling to cover this month's lease as is."

"Relax. Bakery World doesn't stand a chance against us. Our charming brick facade alone draws people in. Once they taste and see our products, they're believers."

Fact was, since Serenity opened The Pear Tree Bakery and Coffee Shop on Ursuline Street eight years ago, employing a modest, faithful staff, she'd enjoyed a slow and steady success. An impressive feat, really, considering the high-profile locale boasted a wide variety of eateries. That and parking availability in or around the French Quarter required strategy and tactic—no favors granted to proprietors, either. After having moved out of the upstairs apartment a year ago to her own place, she'd contended for a spot nearest her bakery each day she was open.

The recent decision to raise prices—yielding to Everley's accounting wisdom—had garnered irritated huffs from a few regulars and resulted in the slow disappearance of others.

Brooke assumed the posture of a lecturer. "But Bakery World isn't over there giving pastries to the needy. Everley has cautioned you about excessive benevolence. It's only eating at profits."

"I don't do cookie-cutter. The Pear Tree is like a fingerprint. It can't be duplicated."

Loved by patrons for its uniqueness, it also boasted a gallery containing the workmanship of various artisans— pottery, oil paintings, and handcrafted Appalachian soaps from a retailer in western North Carolina.

A bakery owned by a woman unafraid to be ... different.

Lettie Thibodeaux, head of product development, approached from the far side of the kitchen, hands parted in a show of irritation. "Miz Serenity, I can't do nothing with this oven. It appears to be giving up the ghost."

"You already gave it a swift kick?"

Pain wrinkled over Lettie's weathered face. "Nearly broke my toe."

Lettie had served as the faithful Lewis family house manager until Everley released her after Momma died a few years ago. Serenity valued Lettie's work ethic and baking finesse and hired her. But the beloved woman's capabilities ended at working miracles.

"The irksome look on your face tells me we're in a pickle."

"No more almond milk, neither."

"I just bought some."

"Spoiled. I tossed it."

Serenity marched past Lettie to the walk-in refrigerator and yanked it open. Tepid air raked over her arms. She stepped inside, wrinkling her nose at the assault of a rancid smell, and peered at the shelves.

The heat in the kitchen thickened, the vents sluggish to draw it out.

Lettie took a hard stance aside the door, drawing her hands to her waist. "Fridge on the blink too I's guessing."

Serenity's chin dipped to her chest, head shaking slowly as a withered sigh fell out of her.

Her phone rang. She slipped it from the front pocket of her apron. Envy kicked up steam at the screen image of Everley and her husband Gabe's unrestrained smiles from their wedding day two years ago.

Conserving the little bit of cool air that remained, she shut the refrigerator door. "Hey, Sis."

Please say the spring art festival was canceled.

"Quick reminder. The festival starts at 2:00. Artisans and guests will start arriving at 1:30. Any way you could get those cupcakes over here by 1:00?"

"The thing is—"

"I want to be sure we've got enough table space for you to set up."

At this rate, it would require a card table. "I'll do my best."

Loss. She hated it. But in a weirdish way, feeding on draughts of anxiety energized her.

A spark of an idea flared in Brooke's gaze. "I know just the person to help us out around here who'd make a huge personality splash."

"Who?"

"Owen."

The tick of silence. "Walker."

The formidable, unforgettable Owen Walker—a sternum crusher for the recently rebranded NFL team, the Kings, under new ownership.

Unwittingly, a heartbreaker.

His name in the moderate space of Serenity's bakery expanded the walls and allowed forbidden delight to feather her heart.

"Absolutely not," Serenity fumed, rallying her wits.

Untying her pink apron with a hard tug, Brooke bunched and tossed it onto the center island. "His influence, persona, and following is the one big somebody who has the power to turn this place around."

"The Pear Tree does not double as a football field."

"It makes perfect sense, Serenity. From the way you two interacted in college, he'd probably work for cupcakes and purchase an entire factory of industrial equipment. Just for you."

He might. She'd love that. *Needed it.*

"To set the record straight, Owen and I had no interaction outside of cupcake wars." Um, and maybe one passionate night of kissing that'd pushed limits, fogging the windows of his blue Chevelle.

"As aside, I think you two would be an ideal match."

Lettie's dark eyes ignited, playful and conspiratorial. "Hmm, mmm."

She pivoted hard and gestured to Lettie. "This is where you take my side, Lettie."

"You pay me to bake, Miz Serenity. Not tell tales."

Brooke's blue-eyed gaze lit up. "I mean, wow. Have you seen him?"

"Yes'm," Lettie said. "Big handsome fella. All smiley. A barracuda on the field. Runs faster than a jackrabbit."

Unbridled determination blazed in Brook's eyes. "It'd be a *crime* not to pass on his DNA."

Though Brooke lacked a certain tact under pressure, it hadn't stopped her husband, Justin O'Brien, from asking her out. One romantic proposal, a picture-perfect wedding, and two kids later, she'd procured a happily ever after with frosting on top.

Time to squash this wildly ridiculous suggestion. "Then lock me up and call me a felon."

And just how did Brooke make the unconscionable leap from getting a girl out of a jam to being a conduit for the replication of Owen's DNA?

"This is no time to stonewall, Serenity."

"Going to extremes is not necessary. I've got this art festival at Moreland Manor B&B today and a fairy princess birthday party order to fill by the end of the week. And then ..." She darted her gaze upward to recall. The ceiling suddenly gave the effect of lowering, a heated chamber threatening to press air from her lungs.

"As your scheduling coordinator, I'll tell you what you've got." Brooke winged a brow and tilted her head. "The inability to pay this month's rent. Maurice is hardly a sympathetic landlord."

"That's a fact." Kourtney Young, a university student and Serenity's part-time barista, breezed into the kitchen and interjected her unsolicited opinion. She let out a slow whistle, her auburn ponytail swishing with each hard shake of her head. "If you ask me, the man could use some laxatives."

Kourtney turned to Serenity. "I've gotta run. Mid-term paper due tonight." She gave everyone a parting wave and exited out the back.

Listlessness drew out Serenity's words. "I'll post more images on social media ... purchase ads or something."

"Consistency is key here," Brooke said. "In matters of vision and artistry and generosity and optimism, you excel. But administration isn't your strongest asset. It's a wonder God has prospered you this long. Maybe he's using equipment failure to pry you out of your stubborn independence."

"Why couldn't he have started with a shortage of napkins?"

The oven dinged. Serenity tapped the digital display, slipped her hands into thick, quilted mitts, and pulled the door. Steam walloped her cheeks. Concave, golden domes tucked in their casings stared back. One or two split open like baby bird beaks.

The little devils.

"I'm on board with the idea of asking someone to help get me through the next several months and reignite interest around here, but bringing in a personality like Walker? People will think I'm desperate. They'll suspect something's wrong."

"You kinda are, and it kinda is."

"It'll feel contrived. Artificial. I prefer a more organic approach."

One that didn't stir thoughts best left undisturbed.

Brooke's arms came up and fell against her sides. "Can't you just let down your drawbridge and envision this for a moment? The presence of the Kings wrecking machine endorsing your product, a bright pink Pear Tree apron strapped over his six-pack abs, would only result in a positive outcome. People will love it. You'll be scrambling to keep up with demand."

"It would be impossible for me to find an apron big enough."

"Ah. You're considering it. This is good."

"Even if I did agree to ask for a little help—for a short while, mind you—" Serenity speared a finger at Brooke. "How am I supposed to get in touch with the three-time Defensive Player of the Year?"

"Give him a call."

Serenity tossed mitts on the counter, curling a fist at her side. "Ha. Like I still have his number."

"You do."

She did. Hadn't deleted the contact since college.

"Add nosey to your many attributes, Brooke."

"I saw it the other day when I was looking for Maurice's number to tell him about the leaky faucet in the kitchen," Brooke seemed exceedingly pleased to announce, cornering Serenity as she strengthened her cause.

At the sound of fingernails drumming on the counter, Serenity peeked into the dining area. Her gaze connected with a woman whose expression held annoyance.

Serenity breezed over to the register. Big smiles. "May I help you?"

"You could have. But you didn't. I've been waiting here for several minutes. My GPS must have mistakenly routed me here. I'm actually looking for Bakery World."

"Oh." Serenity's shoulders slumped. "Bakery World is located a few blocks north of the Quarter."

Once the ill-mannered Broomhilda turned to go, leaving behind a noxious cloud of rejection, Serenity turned to Brooke, who pressed a palm to the counter.

Her Irish gaze bored holes in Serenity's resolve. "That does it. I'm making a call."

God didn't create perfect athletes, but in Owen Walker, he'd come close. Designed for the gridiron, Owen strove to make up the deficit. Six years playing for the Los Angeles Rams before he'd signed with the Kings provided empirical evidence of his record-breaking capabilities.

Walker's fans didn't care that he had other abilities and interests, even some unconventional for a guy his size. Because football was life—or so said Harvey Blanton Walker, his Hall of Famer dad, who'd hammered the mantra into Owen's brain as early as he could remember.

As for head hammering ...

It was all Owen could do not to tackle Dr. Liljeberg. The foolish orthopedic doc stood a mere two feet from Owen and had the audacity to suggest he retire after only eight illustrious years in the NFL.

Owen rolled up his sleeves and clamped his fingers under the exam table. "What are you saying here, Doc?"

"I realize you've still got two years on your contract and are enjoying hero status in New Orleans, bringing home the wins—"

"A team that earned a berth in a wild card game in postseason play—"

"A fact that, from my perspective, is inconsequential." Liljeberg turned toward an illuminated x-ray box on the wall and folded his arms. "It would appear your radiograph depicts what looks to be a lesion on your left temporal hemisphere." He turned slowly, darts for eyes. "More tests would need to be run—"

"To rule that out ..."

"Walker, face it." He unwound his arms. "Your body is reaching its limit."

Limits are meant to be broken.

Gale force winds moved into Doc's eyes, darkening them into a category 4 hurricane. "These hits you take on the field are measured in g-force. In addition to the two concussions you've already sustained in the space of three years, you've had surgery to repair ... let's see ..." He sat, swiveled in his chair, and awakened a laptop with rapid taps on the keyboard.

"I know, I know." The tissue crinkled beneath him as he shifted his weight. No one had to detail a pro football player's injuries. Unlike his stats, he'd chosen not to memorize each and every one. "Retirement leaves me with greater injury."

Dipping his chin, Doc peered over his glasses and wheeled his chair back to face Owen. "How so?"

"Being judged from the neck up."

Who was he, if not NFL's most recent Walter Peyton Man of the Year and three-time Defensive Player of the Year? He'd managed to successfully uphold league-wide respect. At this juncture, there'd be no stepping down. He'd retire when he was good and ready.

A reticent sigh drew Doc's shoulders down. "A guy who rushes to take down the QB even after he's lost his helmet is a risk for injury—far beyond the tibial plateau fracture you sustained a year ago that took you out for the season."

"Yeah. Bummer. I'd had a huge day against the Raiders. Three tackles, one for a loss, a pass breakup, and a touchdown."

Those games were always sweet. Energizing an already high-voltage crowd.

"Surgery, followed by aggressive PT sessions, will put you back in shape to re-enter. But don't make light of hits to the head."

Insidious, wicked rewiring of brain chemistry ... turning a man into a monster.

Retire. The word read like a bad CAT scan and quaked through his musculature frame.

When his six-year contract with the Rams ended two years ago, he'd signed a four-year deal to play in New Orleans, anxious to learn the town and establish himself among the fine folks of Louisiana. But the motivational fuel behind the move from LA had more to do with overseeing Dad's care. He'd set Dad up in a house restored by his friend Gabe Bellevue and outfitted for, well, wheelchair access, if needed.

So, no. Retirement wasn't an option. It held the tornadic force of a tiny black speck on a rippled gray horizon that threatened to morph into a sea monster and swallow him whole.

"Hear me out, Walker."

Owen blinked to awareness. He turned a wary glance at the good doctor.

"To continue in the game means putting yourself at great risk and causing angst for your loved ones."

Those who loved him amounted to Dad, his big brother Derek—a New Orleans cop— Jude Buchanan, his part-time driver and companion, and a vast number of fans whose names he didn't know and whose admiration rose and fell depending on his performance.

Standing, Liljeberg patted him on the shoulder. "There's an expiration date on that body of yours. I advise you to turn your attention toward non-impact activities and continue to pour your heart and soul into those sports camps for underprivileged kids. Or start a business that doesn't involve damage to your head."

He turned a hard stare at Doc.

"You'd once confided in me that you had a vision for going into a business with a buddy someday."

He'd let it slip?

"My plan is to retire injury free and at the top of my game, on my timetable. I've got plenty of years left in me."

"Owen, you've observed symptoms of CTE, Chronic Traumatic Encephalopathy, in your dad. Mild ones, but it's a darn shame they didn't have the concussion protocol back then. I'm not a gambling man, but I'll bet that's not a route you want to take."

Dad's route.

Having enjoyed an illustrious career, an essential element in Pittsburgh's Steel Curtain Defense, and a six-time Pro Bowl choice, Dad played in every championship game and enjoyed four Super Bowl victories. A brain pummeled by concussions, Harvey the Hammer had lumbered off the field and presently lived his days largely secluded inside that restored farmhouse, watching the only game he loved on a flatscreen.

Forever sidelined.

"I'm telling you, big guy." One hard pat. "Hang up your helmet."

"And what, bake ... or something?" Owen scoffed.

Doc's raised brow suggested he'd detected the renegade bubbles of passion in Owen's expression.

And, okay, he'd lied. Off the field, Owen loved to bake. A lot. Like football, he excelled at it. But life off the field held too much risk. He could lose himself. Would God be there to catch him? At times, his prayers turned into a holy tug-o-war to call it quits, but he'd let the decision simmer and negotiate with God later.

Days, weeks ... years ... later.

Leaving Liljeberg's office near an outskirt of less-traveled roadway, he drove the red, twin-turbo V-8 Ferrari rental to the NFL Network studio in Culver City, California, for a 2:00 interview before he'd jet back to New Orleans.

His phone rang. He slipped it from the console, set it to speaker, and spoke over the pulsing beat of his training playlist. "Hello?"

"Hey, Walker. It's Brooke O'Brien, Justin's wife. How are you?"

"Just ask my fans."

"I'm asking you."

"I'm perfect then."

"And prideful as always."

He'd let that go. "How's life with Justin treating you?"

"We're good. A boy. A girl. As rascally as their daddy."

"Your choice to marry that guy," he teased.

"Hey now, don't diss your best friend."

A friend whose back injury in college ended his shot at the pros and set him on a sure and steady course away from the turf. But Justin enjoyed a pretty wife, a couple kids, a retirement plan that probably stretched well into his early sixties, and good health.

"What's up?"

"I've taken a part-time job at a darling little bakery here in the French Quarter, working for this super sweet, charitable friend of mine—actually, no, she's gorgeous."

At that, the thrum of LA traffic receded to the back of his mind.

"She's been thriving until a well-established bakery chain opened up a few months ago and has lured clientele by way of lower prices and an easy, in-and-out parking lot."

Bakery? Now, really listening—though he knew next to nothing of anything darling and little.

"Why'd you take a job? You and Justin strapped for cash?"

"No, not at all. Justin's job is solid. It's just an outlet during the day while the kids are in school."

"All right, so back to the girl. How big is she?"

"You're one to talk."

"Seen my stats? Comes with the game."

"The girl—"

"Gorgeous, you said."

"She's struggling. Equipment failure, landlord slow to make repairs. Since you showed a bit of baking prowess back in the day, I'm wondering if you'd be willing to give some of your off-season time to help us out and give the business a boost."

"Yeah, but a bakery?" He palmed the wheel, the sun warm against his neck.

"You're a generous guy. I've seen your social media posts to help raise funds and awareness for Walker sports camps. You're always pictured with dozens of kids swarming around. Will you at least come check it out?"

Risk low. Injury free. And in more lucent and fleeting moments of late, Dad had prompted him to consider ideas for post-football careers.

Maybe this was the start of something ... different.

Chapter Two

From the beginning, Serenity had refused for The Pear Tree Bakery and Coffee Shop to be some substandard melding of the ordinary, common, and bland. It would not become a place where people snagged a muffin merely to stave off hunger, drink standardized coffee and be on their way. If her establishment didn't enable patrons to suspend reality for a bit or foster relationships ... if it didn't offer an experience unavailable elsewhere ... she'd failed. Over several years, she'd achieved—and, on some levels, exceeded—her goal.

Enter Bakery World, and her baby—her legacy—was losing oxygen.

As afternoon closing time neared, the bakery quieted from the bustle of the day. In the main dining area, she stood in front of the lighted display case and checked inventory. She considered the arrangement of chocolate ganache pastries and buttercream cupcakes.

"All is well." She dusted her hands and spun.

Thwack!

Staggering backward, her rounded gaze collided with the formidable body of Owen Walker, who stood significantly taller than she'd remembered. Took a lot to out-muscle thirty-one other players. But muscle he had in large volume.

"You. You're ..."

Years later and his presence still tied her tongue in knots.

He thrust his mammoth hand. "Owen Walker."

Right. Play dumb when she knew. Every faithful sports fan knew. The name alone communicated the impressive resume behind it.

Try as she might to ignore his stats, they rattled off in her mind like a sports commentator. Four hundred nine tackles during his career—currently the franchise leader with the Kings—a seven-time Pro Bowler, five times a first-team All-Pro. Enough sacks, interceptions, forced fumbles and recoveries, and defensive touchdowns to rival the fiercest competitor.

An unstoppable defenseman who'd demonstrated the ability to take off from the line of scrimmage and disrupt the game for a favorable outcome.

And now, the entirety of his six-foot, five-inch package was ... here.

In her bakery.

Stop staring at his chest!

Giving her head a slight tilt, she pasted a look of indifference on her face, mixing in a little bit of dumb blonde. Was it convincing? Because it wasn't heartfelt.

The media feasted on the multiple benevolent Walker Foundation initiatives, but the hallmark of the foundation was Walker's Sports Camps for kids, which offered multiple programs across the country. Add to that, Owen amassed an influential personality capable of raising nearly $40 million for hurricane disaster relief in the Gulf Coast region. Whatever he'd asked, his fans delivered.

Though the guy had much to brag about, he held it behind a wall of iron.

Enough about him. She had an order to fill. A large one.

Speaking of large …

"You want some coffee? A cupcake?" She nervously fumbled with the glass door that showcased the wonders of her bakery capabilities. A far cry from what his trophy case might contain, but we can't all be God's gift to mankind.

He stuffed immense fingers into his front pockets and roved a quizzical gaze over the chalkboard menu. His cedarwood and amber eyes narrowed in concentration. "I'd like something different. One of a kind."

No better time for a Serenity Special—if she'd had any to offer. The perfect cupcake recipe to outclass all others continued to dog her. She strove to create an impossibly scrumptious product harnessing the power to make people adjust their travel plans to taste and see.

"Those jumbo cinnamon pear muffins sound interesting," he said. "Give me three of those. Biggest you've got."

Naturally, and … interesting fell woefully short.

The way he held himself was an uncanny mixture of a cool, unruffled pro athlete who'd taken extra care with his appearance as though hoping to impress. He'd slicked gel through clean-cut, light-brown hair. His expression held a slight unease. An endearing nervousness even.

The thought of having the upper hand drew a sliver of a devilish smile.

She stepped around him in a wide berth to the opposite side of the case to separate herself from what amounted to a large shadow of the past. She pinched a muffin with her tongs and set it on a dish. Then another and another. "Want them heated?"

"Sure."

The burn of his stare sizzled against her back when she turned to warm the muffins. Had a flicker of recognition penetrated his thick skull?

He drummed his fingers on the counter to suggest twenty seconds was an inordinately long time to wait. No doubt he had private chefs aplenty who produced far greater wonders for him than she could and in a fraction of the time.

"I love what you've created here," he said. "You're not like all the others. Very ..."

She whirled around and drew a little gasp at the pull of his gaze.

"Unique."

A dash of euphoria fluttered over her heart, lifting her heels. She'd basked for far too many milliseconds in his hallmark Walker grin that'd propelled him into the hearts of millions. The victory smile after every sack, arms thrust upward, rousing thunderous applause. Ruggedly handsome in a veteran athlete sort of way. Far, far more alluring up close. Success looked good on the big guy.

If only it weren't a reckless decision to indulge in memory ...

"I mean, who names a bakery after a fruit tree, you know?" he said in a jeering laugh.

She had. *You big ox.* The comment thrust her rocketing brain back to earth, a literal free fall of disappointment deflated buoyant emotion. "I named it after the pear tree that flourished at my sister's B and B."

He returned an empty stare.

She splayed her arms on the edge of the counter. "You know, Moreland Manor. Down in Napoleonville?"

His failure to recognize her from their college days had been brutal enough. Now it seemed he'd lost all trace of memory, Owen an honored guest at Gabe and Everley's wedding last spring—Serenity, the maid of honor. Eight months before that, Serenity had an unwanted encounter with him at Moreland, the historic treasure Momma left to Everley.

Owen snapped his fingers. Awareness dawned by way of a brightened gaze and raised brows. "That's where we're hosting our foundation fundraiser end of the month. How could I forget?"

Because your brain is bordering on useless? "I guess we remember things that matter."

The slight notch at his brow suggested he'd felt the jab and searched his mental playbook for a defensive maneuver. She'd never forgotten him—wished he could. Instead, she'd memorized every nuance and detail as one might study a piece of art. Only to him, she was just another girl.

Indistinct.

Nothing special.

"Okay," came his cool response, poised to defend. "And what I remember is your sour greeting when I arrived at the community outpouring you pulled off to help them restore the place."

A masterpiece of human generosity tainted because … "I'd requested Redmon Callahan, the QB."

"Who was sick. Asked me to fill in."

A decision Callahan made that'd wholly pricked the balloon of her happy event to rally widespread support for Moreland, the house she'd loved, entrusted by Mom to Everley, who—up to that point—had despised it.

"Sorry to disappoint." The play of sarcasm fumbled what might have been a herculean effort to offer a sincere apology.

Crumbs of history settled in her throat. She coughed them out. "We went to college together."

A quizzical gaze registered in his eyes.

Quiet thrummed in her chest.

Straightening, he wore a pleased expression. "The cupcake girl. You played volleyball or something?"

"Soccer."

"We had those cupcake wars in our home economics study group. The other students made up our judges' panel."

Lights coming on, eh Sherlock?

Apparently, his memory of her ended at cupcakes. Their single steamy night in the spring of their senior year lay buried in an inebriated slumber of bad decisions. The fact that she'd styled her hair in a squared bob and dyed it a reddish hue then contrasted with today's blunt-cut blonde, length well below her shoulders. A distinct difference to throw off the most perceptive investigator.

Just as well. He'd unknowingly drawn an indelible line between them the moment he shared his desire to get married one day and have a house full of Walker kids.

Serenity and Owen were an impossibility.

He glanced at the vase of fresh, lavender roses on the counter and back to her, unimpressed, it seemed, by pear trees and uncommon flowers. Her appeal plummeted from what amounted to an already dismal rating.

"I understand you need help around here."

She slid the plate his direction and leaned on her elbows. "Help?"

"The girl that works here—Brooke, who went to our same college—called to say you could use an extra pair of hands during the spring and summer and …" He raised his palms and delivered a sly grin, a sheer spectacle of masculinity. "I got big ones."

Yes, the man was an exceptional baker. A delectable secret he'd managed to keep from the media's far-reaching grasp.

A wilted flower nourished by water, she perked up.

Because of Brooke's audacious intrusion, he'd come to breathe life into her troubled establishment. She'd just have to endure his involvement for a few months until she returned to solid financial standing.

"Guess Brooke didn't tell you who it was that needed help."

A smile tugged at his mouth. "She said you were gorgeous. There was no need to ask."

She felt her eyes flare and drew to standing. "She—?"

"Was correct."

At the uptick along the side of his mouth, tension tunneled between them. She sucked in a breath and cleared her throat. "An additional pair of hands would be great. Bakery World has been a thorn in my side. You'd only be needed for a little while until sales are steady. I couldn't pay you much."

"Pay me in cupcakes." He grinned, the memorable face—and glistening, shirtless upper body—of last summer's issue of Men's Health.

It's not like the man needed to be on payroll—or cupcakes, for that matter. She shrugged. "Sure. Eat all you want."

A spark of whimsy ignited in his eyes like she'd called him to huddle up for the winning play. He sidled around the counter and glanced toward the kitchen where Lettie clanged pots and hummed, "It is well with my soul," before a seamless transition to her own rendition of "Swing low, sweet Serenity."

But peace, she could use. And maybe God, utilizing a divine sense of humor, had delivered peace in an unforeseen—and immensely large—way.

"The most pressing problems are equipment failure and this month's rent is past due."

An ache of curiosity skated over his features as though itching to make a big play.

"Which piece of equipment failed?"

"One of my convection ovens—last Saturday, a few hours before I was due to deliver a large order to Everley at Moreland for an art festival. And a bakery missing an oven is like a body without a heart."

"Or a football player without a helmet."

Right ... though this one had no qualms rushing the QB after his helmet had been picked off. Unstoppable, Owen had sacked the defenseless player, taking an unbreakable grip around the QB's midsection and crushing him against the turf. Amazing game, that one. If a girl were keeping tabs.

"How much does one of those things run?" Then a laugh tumbled out, his broad shoulders quaking. "Not that cost matters."

"A single deck, full size, with legs, runs about two grand."

Pennies to a guy who earned that amount in a few minutes. She parted her arms wide, barely extending the width of his upper body. To come closer to eye level for the duration of his involvement, it might be good to switch out her athletic shoes for Everley's heels. Well into her first trimester and growing, big sis wouldn't need them.

"Just one oven?"

"One is good."

Um ... maybe toss in an industrial refrigerator?

Finger to the screen of his phone, he shot her a glance. "If you'll give me a link to what you need, I'll place the order and have it delivered the next day."

For all the effort she'd put into forgetting the guy she'd wanted desperately to love but could not—and who now filled the space of her bakery in delightfully close proximity—the rewards were well worth it.

Who knew the bakery girl in need of a boost would end up being Serenity Lewis? Owen had given to wonder what she'd done with her minor in business. But with the NFL in his sights, he'd forgotten about it—about *her*, a competitive type who'd carried distinct femininity inside a firm, shapely athletic build which, doing a once-over, she'd maintained nicely. Her shimmery, straight blonde hair fell loosely below her shoulders. A severe part down the middle accentuated an attractive symmetry. One thing hadn't changed. She still touted her baking sensations as superior to his. From what he remembered—an increasingly harrowing achievement as of late—the study group hailed his original recipe a winner.

His agreement to assist at The Pear Tree extended from March through the end of June, just before training camp. He likened the opportunity to a ball game. It began at kickoff, and then it ended. But the bakery gig didn't demand he suit up, take hits, and repeat.

Over and over and over again.

Dizziness overtook him. An ice-pick headache began a grinding throb at his temple. He gripped the counter, lids shuddering momentarily.

"Is something wrong?"

Awareness rushed at him as Serenity came into focus.

Worry lines crinkled aside her eyes. "Looked to me like you were about to pass out."

He shook his head, letting his gaze drift from the sting of her concern. "I'm good." A hard cough afforded him time to recover. "So, here's the deal. The Walker Foundation demands most of my attention in the spring when sports camp registrations open. I'll be managing aspects of the fundraiser end of the month, but I'll stop in here for a few hours at a time whenever I'm able."

"Any time you can spare is good,

Clarity pinged. Details surfaced in his mind. "Their wedding and reception last spring—the reason they couldn't host us last year—was an ideal springboard for managing large-scale events."

"In addition to overnight stays, Everley said she's booked weddings more than any other event. Their wedding pictures in the photo gallery of the website have been a strong selling point."

"It was unforgettable." He'd attended the lavish affair last year, Everley and Gabe's exclusive invitation a thank you for lending a muscle toward Moreland's restoration eight months prior. That and a generous financial contribution to secure its future.

He also remembered the scant interaction with Serenity, who'd begged off any conversation, claiming prime duty to her sister—though she'd held him at a distance as though he'd needed a shower.

Badly.

The bell dinged. A woman entered. Owen turned from the counter and waved. She halted mid-stride and drew in a little gasp, her eyes flickering in wonder. "Are you—?"

"Owen Walker. Welcome to The Apple Tree."

Serenity cuffed him on the arm.

He spun to face her.

Displeasure played over her tawny, sculpted brow. "For starters, big guy, you've got to get the fruit right. It's The *Pear* Tree." She made a chopping movement with the side of her hand against her palm.

Man, give that girl a black and white striped jersey and a whistle on a lanyard.

If Owen stood a chance of learning the complexities of bakery management, he'd need to start with fundamentals. Like exerting effort to remember the name of the place.

Agreeing to return tomorrow morning, Owen drove to the Foundation satellite office and greeted the director, Nina Jessup.

"How are things looking, your majesty?" He splayed his aching body on the leather sofa across from her desk and massaged his temples.

She stood to lean against the front edge of her desk and tapped at a digital note-taking device. "According to the website, camp registrations continue to pour in, my love."

An able-bodied Canadian, Nina carried a sophisticated air in a cleanly cut pixie do, pumps, and tailored suit. Her lithe, petite form operated like the rudder of a cruise liner.

"You think we need to expand the age, open camps up to kids as young as 8, or keep it to 10?"

"We'd have to hire more athletic staff, procure more scholarship funding. Requests for financial assistance continue to climb, almost double last year. We have nearly exceeded our ability to cover existing camps, my love."

He sat upright, planting elbows over his knees. Blast it. All that cupcake sugar rushed through his blood and coursed down to his toes. "I refuse to turn away an underserved kid because they can't afford registration. For most, one week of their sport of choice is a dream of a lifetime. We could be entrusted with tomorrow's Heisman winner or an NBA World Champion."

"Preaching to the choir, my love," she singsonged.

Aside from interacting with campers and making splash appearances, Owen loved to see kids try their hand at a sport of their choosing, coached by elite athletes procured across the country. Because no child should be form-fitted for football. He loved Dad—heart and soul—but Hall of Famer Harvey Walker had perpetually narrowed the path along which Owen and his older brother Derek were to travel. It was forever marked like prison fencing by a dusting of straight white lines over green turf.

"Since camps are being held in nearly every state now,

I think we need to secure more sponsors."

Nina tapped at her device. "We could collaborate with a local business wanting greater exposure."

"How about a bakery?"

"Marvelous idea. In fact, Bakery World would be perfect. Sugar goes hand in hand with kids."

He gave a tremulous laugh. "I was thinking more along the lines of—"

"Bakery World is a familiar chain, prolific across the country. Everyone is talking about it. Last I checked, their stock prices were soaring, a lucrative opportunity you ought to invest in, my love."

He held her pointed stare and broke it.

"No sense draining your handsome income on man toys, then one day wondering where it all went when you're facing retire—"

"Made your point. Invest in stock. Got it." He dipped his chin and clapped hands over his ears, then glanced back up. "The, uh, fundraiser?"

She set the device on her desk and crossed her ankles and arms. Gold bangles clinked along her wrists. "Want me to get your agent to contact Bakery World? See if they have interest?"

"Sure thing. Get Tommy involved. Whatever you think." He swept up a hand and let it fall limp. "Just keep it under wraps that I'm helping boost sales for another bakery in the area. A favor for the owner."

"Good luck surpassing Bakery World, my love." Ridicule slicked through her tone.

"You know me, Nina. I love a challenge."

The exchange with Nina reminded him to check in with Gabe Bellevue, who managed Moreland alongside his bride, Everley.

Serenity's big sis.

"Hey, buddy. It's Owen. How are things?"

"Never better, my friend. Business up and running again. What's up?"

"Just checking in on the fundraiser for the twenty-eighth. The board has taken care of marketing and confirmed vendors."

"We're good here. Blocked the day off months ago. Always happy to host a good cause."

"What's the contingency plan in case of rain?"

"The kids could run no-contact drills in the ballroom."

"And break all your valuables ..."

"Okay then, we'll just gather beneath the canopy and tell stories until the sun comes out."

No doubt about it. Marriage and the love of a woman who'd believed in him had been good for Gabe's soul.

"I realize this is coming out of left field, but would you be willing to allow a chopper to land on the place?"

"Huh. Got me there."

"My escort is a highly trained Marine, skilled in operating a chopper. I thought it'd be cool for him to give kids a lift." A rare opportunity Owen had been denied when an aviation missionary organization came to town because it conflicted with football practice and, well ...

Walkers play ball, son.

"There's plenty of open space out back. I think we could swing it but let me check with Everley." The scratchy sound of Gabe's phone against fabric, muffled voices, and then he returned. "Yep. She said that's no problem. She may be scarce that day, not feeling up to par since she's expecting our twins."

"Congrats, man!"

"What can I say? My wife can't keep her hands off me." A guffaw erupted through the phone, followed by, "Shut it, Gabe," and what may have been the sharp ping of a rubber ball against a wall.

"Hey now, dream girl," Gabe said, his voice ticklish and playful. "Beautiful things happen when me and you team up."

Team. That. Right there. A team made up of two people in love. Adding little Owen Walker boys and girls to the roster as God saw fit.

Mmmm. One of these days.

Chapter Three

"Sorry, Owen. My red-haired wife makes my brain dizzy. Hasn't stopped since high school." The sound of padded steps, shorter breaths, and rasps of birds suggested Gabe had walked outside. "Back to the fundraiser. What will you need from us besides space—which we've got an ample amount of?"

"Nothing, really. I'll have a board representative contact you to sort out details, but basically, we're doing a citywide promotion and shout-outs on social media. On the day of the event, we've secured the presence of corporate sponsorships and several elite athletes to represent our various sports camps. They'll meet and greet, sign autographs, and snap pictures. We'll handle setup, catering, and provide cupcakes."

Cupcakes?

"Cupcakes?"

"Yeah. Brooke O'Brien, a girl I knew in college, called me about a week ago, asked if I'd help out during the off-season at Serenity's bakery. Brooke is married to my buddy Justin."

"We know Brooke. She's the daughter of Bonnie Sue Gaudet, a good friend of Everley's mom, Marigold Lewis."

"Small world."

Gabe laughed. "From your vantage point, everything looks small, I guess."

"That it does, buddy."

"Everley oversees the accounting for The Pear Tree. She'd said things were precarious."

"Serenity didn't let on that degree of concern. Brushed it off a bit. I'm also unsure why Brooke didn't tell me it was Serenity's place that was struggling."

"Maybe she feared you'd refuse."

"I'm not one to turn my back on a good cause. Plus, she's paying me in cupcakes."

"That's a win-win arrangement for sure."

"She's hard to read, though. I don't think she likes me." Owen's voice swooped low.

"Give her time. She'll lower the drawbridge."

"Either way, my goal is to lend a hand and pray it benefits."

"Come December, that spitfire will have celebrated her eighth year in business."

"Sounds like it might be her last if something doesn't change."

"I'm confident your involvement will turn things around for the good."

"I'll do my best."

"An attitude that's served you well. Serenity's done a lot to help us out here at Moreland, particularly now that Everley is pregnant." His voice thinned. "I'd hate to see her shut her doors."

"Over my dead body." All six-foot, five-inches and two hundred eighty-nine pounds of it. The rogue call to champion a struggling business owner who'd bristled in his presence circuited through his thoughts. But he hadn't called Gabe to chat about cupcakes.

Or Gabe's gorgeous sister-in-law.

"How much are you looking to raise this year, Owen?"

"We've seen a growing demand for lacrosse and hockey camps. We need to ensure we can pay for training and staff to operate them. The waiting list for kids who can't pay is growing. I've fronted $100,000 for this year's baseline and want to see that doubled."

"God can supply."

Four years ago, he'd have scoffed at that. Or hung up. Because when a guy makes a god of his sport, he doesn't go looking for a replacement. Thanks to God's persistence in finding Owen amidst spiritual wanderings, he agreed with Gabe.

"Thanks, Gabe. Say hi to Everley."

"Will do."

With that, he ended the call and checked the time. 1 o'clock. Same time he'd promised to get to the bakery. Would Ice Woman kick up a fuss about his being late? All he knew was that his stomach was growling, and seeing a girl about some cupcakes sounded good.

He arranged for his escort, Major Jude Buchanan, to take him to The Pear Tree. He'd met Jude five years ago during Owen's USO tour with three other NFL ambassadors when the power team visited military bases throughout the Middle East. Point man on the ground that year, Jude hosted the players. After a conditional peace deal between the US and Taliban, Jude resigned his commission and followed a few of his brothers in arms to New Orleans—far from his family in Detroit. When Jude learned that Owen had relocated to play in New Orleans, he contacted him last fall in search of job leads.

"You a fan of the greatest game on earth?" Owen had said.

The stealthy soldier raised his glass and grinned. "What else is there, sir?"

And that was that. Owen hired Jude as escort and guard—a comrade and faithful friend off the field.

No price Owen could place on that.

Snug inside the passenger seat of his Bentley, Owen shared Gabe's confirmation about offering helicopter rides at Moreland. "Your willingness to pilot a chopper will be a huge hit, Jude."

Jude's uncharacteristic hesitation shimmied a wave of concern.

Owen angled his stare. "We'll cover fuel and operating expenses, of course."

Gaze concealed behind reflective shades, Jude set his stare ahead. A tick moved along his sharp jawline. His grip wrenched the steering wheel. "Being in the bird brings me back there, you know?"

"No, I can't say I do. But battlefields look different depending on who's standing on them and the war they're mandated to fight. Mine measures one hundred yards in length and is covered by turf."

"True, sir."

"Look, if the chopper idea is a bad move, I can come up with an alternative."

"No, sir. It's solid." He pulled up to the entrance. "Need me to park? Keep an eye out, sir?"

"We're not at the White House, I'm not the president, and you're not secret service—though if there comes a day when you aren't working for me, you'd be an ideal candidate."

Owen unfolded from the car and turned to lean into the open window. "I'll give you a shout when I'm finished here."

"Yes, sir."

In front of the bakery, Owen paused to take in the rich textures of the French Quarter. History oozed from the architecture. The buzz of jazz coming around the corner, fluted columns beneath balconies from which hung planters brimming with flowers.

The heady scent of a hosed-down pavement and manure moved him inside, where he drew in a large influx of bakery smells—butter, coffee, sugar—and noted the eccentric interspersion of color and textures throughout.

Something in him stirred and hugged his heart. Desire maybe? Where his future looked bleak, Serenity's was vibrant. An opportunity he wanted, a life he coveted.

A life Dad—nor his fans—would ever accept.

Hair cinched into a ponytail, Serenity—Frau Boss Lady—stood at the counter.

"You're late."

It did matter. "Got hung up in meetings. Sorry."

"My part-time barista just left. Mind taking coffee orders while Lettie and I bake?"

"That must mean the new oven arrived?"

"It has and is working wonderfully, thanks. She upturned her palm toward the coffee bar with a flourish. "So, barista?"

"How about I help bake, and this, uh, Lettie person does barista."

An older, stoop-shouldered, dark-skinned woman emerged from the kitchen wearing a flour-dusted, pink apron. She kept her dark hair, streaked with threads of gray, secured at the nape of her lean neck. The look of possessiveness readily flickered inside ebony eyes. She took a firm stance beside Serenity, balled a fist at her hip, and wielded a moistened wooden spoon in the other. "What you know about bakin' and such, chump?"

Did the weathered old woman pushing her midseventies who went by ... he peered at her name badge—ah, Lettie ... know who she'd just referred to as chump?

Turning to Lettie in a hard pivot, Serenity placed a gentle hand on her shoulder and smoothed a calm tone over a peeved countenance. "Lettie Thibodeaux, this is Owen Walker."

Jutting her chin, Lettie's nose wrinkled in thought. Her charcoal eyes grew cold.

"Number 91?" The lilting ring in Serenity's tone appeared to coax recognition. "Plays defense for the Kings?"

Awareness alighted on Lettie's face. She lowered her weapon and dipped her chin. "Pardon me, Mista Walker. I meant no disrespect. Darn if these ole' eyes aren't running out of they usefulness. Spectacles no good, no how."

"Earlier this year, Owen was awarded Man of the Year."

Instinctively, he squared his shoulders. "Three-time defensive player—"

Jerking a hard glance his direction, Serenity cut him off with raised palms. "I don't need you rattling off your stats, or we'll be here all day."

"Probably all week." He left Serenity with a grin as he turned to dip a finger into a nearly empty batter bowl, the bitter taste curdling his stomach. "I suggest easing up on the mocha, adding some cinnamon."

She worked up exaggerated irritation to match the testy stance. It only made her more irresistible.

"We're running short on Cherie's Red Velvet cupcake with cream cheese frosting and red sugar crystals. The priority right now is to mix up another batch of batter and frosting."

"I'll do one better. I'll also entertain clientele."

"Why does that not surprise me."

"I haven't achieved a successful career by sitting on the sidelines."

"A fact which I ..." She leaned to peer past his shoulder, rising to her toes, "... and the whole of New Orleans is well aware."

He turned to see a few women who'd formed a line. Several more sat at round tables, eager grins stilled on him. "Welcome to—" He turned Serenity's direction and flashed a wink. "The Pear Tree."

A crimson color flushed her cheeks. Gemstone blue and green eyes sparkled above a satisfied grin.

He turned back to the waiting women. "What can I do for you?"

Their sappy gazes suggested they wanted more than what was on the menu. Big man on turf would have to tone down the magnetism.

Taking their orders, he tapped hard strikes at the register, noting the need for an upgrade. One manufactured in the current century.

After two hours, a pleasing lull settled into the bakery, and a steady flow of afternoon regulars had come and gone. Clientele sat sipping beverages, nibbling on pastries, enveloped in the one-of-a-kind establishment. He walked through the main area toward an arched opening in the side wall at the back. It led to an adjoining courtyard that held paintings on mustard-colored brick and granite. Generous natural light streamed through a cutout ceiling, revealing a view of upper-level apartments, and fell over a trickling water fountain. Potted flowers sat aside wrought iron seating. A large window framed a view into the bakery.

Wandering back inside, hazy daylight pooled over a private nook in the corner near the front windows. Beside it, bar stools sat beneath a rustic ledge that jutted from the wall.

Crazy, but the feel of the place fit like a clean sports shirt fresh out of the dryer.

Returning to the kitchen, he found Serenity at one of the industrial sinks scrubbing a batter bowl. She'd gathered her hair into a loose hold. Strands of blonde like fell in creamy layers around her face. Heart-shaped and perfectly fashioned by what clearly was one matchless Creator.

Owen's brain went to strategy. He'd need to find a play that'd assure this fiery bakery owner would keep her doors open.

Her shoulders sank in a weary sigh as she nested a metal bowl into the overhead shelving. A quick glance his direction piqued awareness—she knew he'd been standing there, watching. She dried her hands with a dish towel, draped it over her shoulder, and moved from the kitchen to the front counter. He followed—eyes hooked on the pink ties about her waist.

In silence, she wiped the counter, evidently exerting immense energy to ignore him. He wasn't used to that in a woman. But it hadn't been Serenity who'd called for help. Most likely, the idea originated with Brooke. She probably protested.

Did it matter who came to assist her?

Would a trained orangutan have sufficed?

"Why don't we change things up."

She stilled her hand, blew strands from her face, and turned, taking on the look of a defensive coach on the cusp of spewing obscenities. "Why?"

Everything in him fought against the mounting urge to wipe that streak of flour off her pretty little nose and cheek. "You're struggling to keep this place afloat."

"Right."

"You're paying me in cupcakes to restore zing to your business, outclass Bakery World."

"Of course."

"Then I suggest a different angle. Let's add original offerings that can't be duplicated."

The play of annoyance in her eyes brightened them to a gemlike blue. Ah. He'd gotten under her skin. For whatever reason, he found it entertaining. Adorable. A challenge even.

She skirted the counter, took a stand beside one of two lit cases, and gestured with a sweeping hand. "Do you not think I can come up with a signature bake?" She sashayed into his space, raised to her toes, and poked a finger into his meaty upper arm. "Let's not forget, my cupcake won out over your Chocolate Wallop or whatever dumb name you'd given it."

She stepped back, folded her arms, and leaned against the counter. For effect, she crossed her ankles, stark orange athletic shoes now apparent.

Impossibly cute. One of a kind. A first for him, really. And he'd been heaven-sent for a small gap of time to help her keep the doors open. Not like he couldn't carve out time once training camp started. If she needed it.

If she wanted it.

If she considered him effective and useful outside of uniform.

"I say we create matchless offerings that Bakery World corporate headquarters has never considered." He waved a hand over the menu board. "Like Walker's Big Hit."

"Something tells me that idea didn't just materialize over the last few seconds, Walker. I think you've given this a lot of thought."

He had, actually. Years ago, while stirring some batter just enough to mix wet and dry ingredients before measuring exact amounts into fluted paper cups. Even allowed himself to envision what it might be like to do something insanely uncharacteristic and open a place of his own.

Ridiculous. Walkers play ball.

"Lower my prices? Forget it," Serenity scoffed. "At Everley's recommendation a month ago, I raised them. But I'll definitely give you wiggle room to come up with a new offering."

Because, stupid me, I could make room for you.

That trademark Walker smile increased the ambient temperature to a delicious warmth. It tickled the skin along her arms, swirling inside her middle. Easing steps her direction, Owen made it all too apparent how much pleasure he'd garnered by his teasing. "I won't let you down, bakery girl."

It took all her strength to refrain from noting he'd already achieved that years ago. The tender bruise on her heart bore evidence. If number 91 performed at his best and helped re-energize The Pear Tree, she'd rest in peace—and Owen would be on his way, adding another accomplishment to his unmatched resume.

The following morning at 6:00 a.m., Serenity unlocked the door, pulled the blinds to invite the full light of a blushing sunrise, and flipped the sign to announce she was open. Everley called a couple minutes after.

"Morning, Serenity."

"Are the babies all right?"

"They're fine. But for whatever reason, this morning sickness has become particularly wicked today."

"Sorry to hear that." Though she'd love to trade places, if only for a minute or so, and experience tiny limbs feathering her insides.

Gabe had wanted boys he could train to take over the business someday. In one pregnancy, God had blessed them with twice what they'd needed.

"You need me to sit with you, Evers?" Pretend I'm you, all glowy and expectant. "I've got full staff today, then Owen comes sometime later after Kourtney leaves."

"I'd love nothing more than your company, but I'm hosting a ladies' Lunch 'n Tour event here at noon. In preparation, I'd meant to go buy a box of—"

"Crazy talk. How many cupcakes do you need?"

"You sure you don't mind?"

"Not at all."

"Gabe is working a job in town. I'll ask him to pick them up."

"Okay. And thanks to a glorious and efficient new oven and repaired refrigerator, I can prepare as many as you need."

"Great. We've got twenty-eight guests registered. I've estimated they'll each eat at least one, so we'll need three dozen of whatever you think is best. I trust your judgment." That was Everley, the numbers girl. Tallying things in columns that all added up to one incredibly happy story.

"Just once, I'd love to hear you say, 'I don't know, Serenity. I hadn't thought that far ahead.'"

"But that would make me you. And there's absolutely no one who can do you as magnificently as you, Sis."

That loving sister bond they shared was as three cords, not easily broken. Hey, maybe that could be the quote of the day. Owen had suggested the idea to erect a free-standing chalkboard placard just inside the entrance, a means to greet clientele with an inspirational message. They'd compile a list of ideas and change it up every few days. Genius idea.

For the sake of an outdoor ladies' luncheon hosted on the lawn at Moreland, today's clear weather—radiant sunlight within an azure sky—was a blessing. But the rise of heat would do Serenity's cupcake frosting no favors.

At least the ones she'd been able to provide.

After Gabe texted to say he was on his way to pick them up, she called Everley to apologize. "Sorry I fell short of what you'd asked. I was sure I had enough cream cheese to fulfill the order."

"No worries. I'll have Gabe swing by Bakery World to make up the difference."

Terrific. Her insufficiency had created gaps. She hated gaps. Especially if she'd thought she was the cause of them. And now, she'd put her smarty big sister in the position of relying on an epically lame-sounding pastry chain. Nothing special about it.

Unlike you.

Me, God?

Yes.

Then help my unbelief.

At that moment, a wave of gratitude swelled at Owen's ability and willingness to provide for her immediate need. For the sake of her bakery, she'd have to shove all self-sufficiency aside, forget the fairest of months they'd shared while taking home ec class, and welcome the abundance God had delivered.

Brooke entered the kitchen, where Serenity had finished adding the chocolate shavings to a fresh batch of her signature cupcakes.

Perspiration gleamed over Brooke's forehead below a pink bandana. "I really like the change to your Serenity's Special recipe. Good to know your concerns about keeping this place open haven't sapped your creativity."

"Desperation fuels the inner artist, I suppose."

Brooke hooked her apron on a peg. "I thought of a way to reinvigorate buzz around here."

"More than bringing in an NFL football player?"

"In addition to that."

"Owen needs no addition. Barely fits into the kitchen as it is. You should have thought that through before you called him."

"And you'd still be without sufficient ovens or a functioning refrigerator."

A sudden urge to consume the entire batch of cupcakes clouded an otherwise sound mind. "Fine. What's your idea?"

"Submit that scrumptious recipe to Bryan J. Carlyle's contest."

She lifted a brow and cocked her head. "The celebrity chef."

"One and the same. He started soliciting entries a few days ago and limited them to citizens of New Orleans. Winner receives a cash prize and will be featured on his YouTube channel. Can you even imagine the benefits if you won?"

Bryan J. Carlyle, a California native with surfer dude good looks and blond hair cropped like choppy ocean waves, had amassed a huge following. Culinary ingenuity coursed through his cooking school and high-end restaurant, Ben's Seafood and Grille—named after his late younger brother.

Raising a cupcake to the light, she cradled it in her palm like a newborn and gazed longingly at the masterpiece. Delicate chocolate shavings dotted the white dome of swirled cream cheese frosting. "Do you have what it takes to be a winner?" she whispered.

Special it may be. But was it enough?

"It's got my vote." Confidence soaked Brooke's tone.

Serenity set the precious pastry on the counter and raised a hand at Brooke for a high five, followed by a hip bump like they'd done years ago. Back when their dreams were boundless. They'd laugh at silly things and memorize the football roster, circling the cute ones. Brooke had ogled Justin, Owen's roommate, a star running back and draft hopeful. Then she and Brooke would put the brakes on exam study and head to a pastry shop where they'd wash down a belly full of doughnuts with entirely too much coffee, which fueled an endless round of giggles.

"Give it some serious consideration, Serenity."

"I did. The answer is no."

"What harm is there in trying?"

"Losing."

But in the space of time after Brooke and her staff left and before Owen was due to arrive, she searched Bryan's website and listened to the YouTube announcement about the contest.

"A big hello to my fellow New Orleanians. Thanks for tuning into Carlyle's Cookin' Something Up. For the first time, I'm soliciting recipes from my faithful NOLA followers. If you've got a baked wonder you believe can outclass the others, let me—and the world—hear about it. My staff and I will select our favorite at the end of August and feature your creation on my show. For some lucky someone, this will be a game changer!"

"Never thought I'd envy a cupcake." Or fear for it. Because what if it didn't measure up? Then again, what would it mean for her entry to be picked *because* it was different?

Valued for the sheer fact of being ... odd.

To dream was one thing. To create involved risk—which Everley had at one time refused to do until Momma's gift of Moreland Manor. The 1846 antebellum treasure had snapped the chains that'd held her captive to the belief it was foolish to feed one's imagination.

The Pear Tree's future depended on Serenity's willingness to risk. She'd need this win to bolster the business once Owen took his magnetic charm and marketing ideas and dashed out of her life to return to the game he loved. Because, no sir, her heart had no business attaching itself to someone who held the power to deliver the greatest blow it would ever experience.

Following detailed instructions, Serenity completed registration and submitted payment, a pdf of the recipe, and portrait-worthy images of Serenity's Special.

"The outcome is in your hands, God."

And may it not crush me.

Chapter Four

The blush of Friday evening dusk fell in soft layers outside the bakery. Owen paused to peer through the front window at the coffee bar and found the scene before him wildly entertaining. Somehow Serenity had managed to get her head stuck inside the neck of a hoodie. Arms crossed overhead—she stood struggling to slip out of it.

He restrained a devilish laugh as he watched her fight for freedom near the register, that old piece of junk.

At least he'd gotten her refrigerator serviced and purchased a new oven. The hefty modern appliance added spark to her somewhat dated kitchen space.

Slowly, he opened the door and padded like a cougar toward the counter. Being that her head was stuck, she must not have heard the bell ding. Not much she could do to receive customers anyway. For her sake, it was a good thing there weren't any at present. The thought of her coming under a stranger's ridicule sped his pulse.

He'd spare her that.

Squirming in adorable helplessness, Serenity pivoted right, bumped into the counter, and bounced off it like a ping-pong ball. She stutter-stepped to the left, feet shuffling backward until she'd come within a few feet of his unmovable form.

He eased his fingers into his pants pockets to keep from wrapping his arms around this hilarious bundle, inhaling her scent of roses, sweet cream frosting, and sunshine.

Muttered frustration fumed behind the fabric. "This stupid thing."

"Need help, Miss?"

Arms like goalposts, she sucked in a sharp breath. "Tell me it's not you."

"At your service."

"I can think of plenty of things you could do to help, but one with fully functioning mental faculties would have already figured that out."

Opportunity overtook him. Hands to her waist, he lifted her moderate frame onto the counter and moved his middle to press against her knees. The restraint of his own laughter nearly suffocated him.

The old Owen would have found great advantage in the situation, the two of them—alone. They could lock up shop, draw the shades, and get to kissing. The new Owen had worked hard to crush such thoughts, contending against a relentless carnal nature.

She squiggled, squealed, and thrashed. Clinking utensils rocked on the counter aside her hips.

"If you'll just hold still for one skinny second." He belted out a laugh and took hold of the edge of her hoodie.

A hard huff punched at the fabric. She waited.

"Are you going to earn those cupcakes you consume and help me or not?"

"I'll be more than happy to help you out of this," he teased, eager to take a dip in the ocean of her eyes that sparkled like diamonds on the rippled surface.

Serene, to be sure.

"If it's all right with you, big shot, now would be a good time. I'm running out of oxygen."

Shoulders heaving, he pinched his lips against the onslaught of unbridled hilarity.

"Walker. Get this dumb thing off." She attempted to kick her legs while thrashing raised arms—to no avail.

He pressed his palms to the counter and leaned in, voice husky. "I don't know, Seren. Better do the toothpick test first and make sure you're ready to come out. Nothing worse than underbaked."

Another huff of heated irritation. Enough to toast a muffin. "I'd like nothing more than to shoot you right now."

"Not sure how you'd manage a handgun in this predicament."

"Never mind. I'd get greater satisfaction out of strangling you anyway."

"My lucky day since it doesn't appear you could do either."

"Dang it, Walker."

Rescue instincts overtook the fun. He tugged at the hoodie, slid it slowly along her arms, and plucked her head free. Amid a mass of golden hair, her eyes flared in utter relief and abject humiliation. Their gazes locked.

For the space of two heartbeats, she sat immobilized as if captivated by the pull of his stare. He drank deeply from her face, circling it with his eyes before her expression shifted. Unease fluttered all over her features. For a moment, he thought he might move heaven and earth for this girl and spend the rest of his Friday nights here. With her. Images of their time in college filtered effortlessly to the front of his brain, memories playing like a movie reel.

What felt like an awkward grin tipped the edges of his mouth. The rise and fall of her breath warmed his neck. He lowered her arms, massaging them. They had to ache.

He pressed knuckles on the counter's edge.

She squirmed.

He hemmed her in. "How's your day been?"

"Until you arrived, it's been great."

The blaze of ire in her eyes elicited more goading. "From my vantage point, I'd say I saved the day. Just sorry I wasn't here sooner."

"Which you should have been." She thrust her hips forward, attempting—and failing—to hop off the counter. Persisting in her effort to find a crack in the wall of his defense, he made way for her to wriggle past his rampart and plant her turquoise tennis shoes onto the floor.

The slightest hint of a grin sent a sliver of delight through him. She hadn't hated the whole affair as much as she'd portended. "Since you've mastered the art of convincing my customers to purchase far beyond what they've come for, I suggest you keep an eye out. In the meantime, I'll be in the kitchen recovering from my trauma while I check online orders and prepare products for tomorrow."

She breezed past him.

"If you get stuck again, give me a shout, Lewis."

She stopped and angled a smug stare at him over her shoulder. "You just stick to doing whatever it is that's worked thus far, Walker."

After what felt like mere minutes, twilight summoned the end of an atypical off-season Friday. He'd only planned to spare an hour, but here it was, time to close up shop.

The cursory obligation to help out poked at need, the environment painting Owen into the picture. Anxiety churned in his stomach at the thought of this arrangement coming to an end. Despite multiple hits to the head and surgeries to his back and leg, he'd always hated the inevitable end of practice or a game. When it did, he'd peel off the sweaty gear only to fill the vacuum watching game films over and over. Or buy stuff, search for property, date women. But all the recognition and awards he'd received over the span of an impressive career, earning enough money to fill an ocean, had only hollowed his soul.

Four years ago, during the third game of the season, Owen had incurred a particularly hard hit and found himself benched the rest of the game. Enter Pastor Donovan Crawford, Chaplain for the Rams. The man's gentle prodding, the offer of Jesus's complete forgiveness for the offense of sin, spoke to a need.

Possessing the heart of a lion, the gentleness of a dove, and the influence of an evangelist, Pastor Donovan detailed the disturbing trajectory for someone who chose to live for the world rather than surrender their will to the one who died to save it.

"Walker, the best play you'll ever make is to trade in your lust for things, take the free gift of salvation in a simple prayer of thanks, and let the Lord use your platform to leave a legacy that outlives your career."

From that point on, God had slowly, *very slowly* developed in Owen a distaste for shallow, temporary pleasures and instilled new motives. Investing in people and causes to change the world. Of prime importance, he'd enable underprivileged kids to find their sport of choice and, ultimately, their worth in Christ.

For Owen, it was different. Football was life. It always would be.

Saturday morning, Owen received a call from Ross Billings, a mild-mannered father of Eli, an eleven-year-old boy who'd participated in last year's football camp in Metairie, Louisiana.

Spunky kid. Great potential.

"Hi, Owen," Ross said. "We've registered Eli for camp again this year."

"Fantastic. Looking forward to hanging out with my hero."

While Owen loved each of his kids with equal fervor, Eli had taken up residence in his heart like no other. Desire to invest in Eli's hopes and dreams led to sharing his private cell number with Ross and his wife, Arlene, a privilege he'd never bestowed on a camper's family.

Aside from Eli's exuberant interest in football, his cocoa brown gaze ignited to life when he persisted in bold determination to one day beat Owen's record. Self-taught and racing ahead of his teachers, Eli was an adult packaged in a young boy's body.

"I realize this is a huge request, but Eli's twelfth birthday is Monday, and Arlene and I would love to surprise him. Would you be willing to pick him up at school—take him out for ice cream or something? As you know, he's got a sweet tooth like nobody's business."

Ideas sparked.

"With your permission, I'd like to make a day of it. Go kick the ball around."

You meant throw. Only you said kick. *Serenity's* game.

Darn if thoughts of the churlish, saucy, and spirited bakery girl hadn't seeped into the undamaged spaces in his brain. At times, emotion drizzled like a warm, chocolate glaze over his heart.

As for Eli, Owen would buy the kid as much ice cream as he wanted. He'd invite Serenity to join them. They could play soccer *and* football. Or croquette or tennis or marbles. Anything that'd give the kid an opportunity to explore alternatives—or reject them all.

"That would mean the world to him, Owen," Ross said.

"Pleasure's mine, believe me."

"I'll contact the school Monday morning and let them know you, er, *the* Owen Walker, will be taking Eli out after second period."

"And I'll bring him back home later that day."

The kid was none too sad for Owen to have made a splash in the classroom before he signed him out. They drove from there to a rec center near an ice cream parlor.

Beneath an oversized Kings ball cap, Eli's cottony soft, blondish-bronzed hair curled in gentle waves along his neck. The endearing, slight part between two wide front teeth and a dusting of freckles over his nose earned him a spot beside Owen among several other boys and girls for this year's camp promotional poster. Eli was a walking, talking encyclopedia of sports statistics, handpicking his favored players to nab titles and win playoffs.

Serenity had agreed to join Owen in the surprise outing and run soccer drills with Eli. She'd secured staff to cover the bakery for a few hours that afternoon. When she arrived at the field, he and Eli met her at her car. Equipment brimmed from the back seat—two goals, three balls, several cones.

Owen tugged one of the goals out of the car. "You weren't kidding about having everything needed to play soccer."

"I played intramural soccer in college." A tinge of regret for having never watched her play niggled through him. For not exerting energy to get to know her outside of home ec class. Blame it on football brain.

The fitting picture of a female athlete, she'd swept her hair into a high ponytail and wore a sweatband across her forehead. Black cleats, knee-high socks, and a coordinating orange jersey and shorts completed the look. Goals and cones in place, she jaunted to mid-field, her stride determined, smooth and practiced.

After she and Eli made acquaintance, she took a ball in hand and turned to Eli. "Toss the ball to me, and I'll kick it into the goal."

Eli gave the ball a swift fling.

Mid-waist, her foot connected with it. *Pop!* And the goal swallowed the ball.

He thrust two fists in the air. "Way to go, Miss Serenity!"

Taking a seat on the bleachers, Owen rested his elbows on his knees and propped his chin on interlocked hands. Staring, studying ... fitting this bakery girl into his life beyond a few fleeting months, imagining them side by side, stirring batter, and expanding the menu to include their originals.

In defense, the game of football shoved through his thoughts and sidelined ridiculous ideas. He considered the sports camps—the means by which myriads of youth were introduced to a wide variety of options. Like what Serenity was offering Eli now, effortlessly eliciting peals of laughter from a kid who, until now, hadn't showcased this depth of joy.

Eli had the heart, soul, drive, and determination for football but lacked the physical makeup necessary to take him beyond high school. Come to think of it, he hadn't registered for football camp this June.

He'd chosen soccer.

But Eli wasn't a Walker. Walkers play ball—the clear exception being Derek, who'd fallen short of stringent pro-ball standards and, instead, answered the worthy call to law enforcement. The protective instinct his brother possessed had been far better utilized in a para-military career.

Eli's receptiveness to Serenity's direction alighted in her countenance and sparked forcefully to life. The picture of a mother lovingly guiding her child. It warmed his insides and burned through his body. If he'd not been duly restrained by God's booming voice of conscience, his thoughts would have stepped out-of-bounds.

Just wow.

Keep to the playbook, Walker.

After an hour of easy drills and light scrimmage, they met outside Mon Cherie's Creamery. Eli sat on a bench, snug between Owen on his left and Serenity on his right. He took prominent front teeth to a solid mound of strawberry ice cream scooped inside a chocolate-dipped waffle cone. Ice cream dribbled down along Eli's fingers, past his wrist.

Serenity chose a mismatch of raspberry sorbet and chocolate peanut butter. He felt the deep V forming between his brows.

She turned a hard glance at him. "Think what you will, Walker, but my flavor preference outclasses your career stats."

Add mind reading to her list of attributes.

Wriggling her direction, Eli patted Owen's shoulder and produced for Serenity an astonished expression, his upper lip and nose coated in ice cream. "You are looking at one of only three players who are three-time winners of the NFL's Defensive Player of the Year, a career-high 372 tackles and ninety-six sacks, twenty of which were in one season alone. Named Sports Illustrated Player of the Week for his efforts."

"Another of the countless reasons I like you, pal." Owen tossed Serenity a victory wink.

As he'd predicted, she bristled and firmed her chin. "Wait just a minute, mister Eli. He's not that great."

It appeared she did her level best not to weaken beneath the mirth that'd broken free across Owen's lips, a maneuver to block the offense. The drizzle of glossy, sugary pink sorbet over her fingers did her no favors. The nibble of her lip to intercept the dawn of a smile suggested he'd gained yardage.

She rallied. "He works for me, you know."

Eli turned to Owen. Wariness filtered into his eyes and rippled over his brow. "You work at a bakery?"

Owen considered the bakery uniform. A striking pink— and entirely too small—apron.

Rush the tackle box and gain the advantage. He crossed an ankle over his knee and grinned. "My jumbo Walker's Big Hit recipe outclasses hers."

The heat of her annoyance burned his cheek.

Revolt inched over Eli's sunny face and turned it stormy. "You made a cupcake recipe?"

Fear snaked in. What if his biggest fan disdained this endeavor? Believed baking was for sissies, number 91 outfitted in a freakishly pink apron an utter laughingstock?

Had the enjoyment of being involved with The Pear Tree earned him a penalty?

A quick reminder quelled concern: his involvement with Serenity was only temporary.

When Owen told Serenity that he'd promised Gabe and Everley the Pear Tree would provide twenty dozen jumbo cupcakes for the fundraiser, it earned him a round of jet-fueled glowers.

"What were you thinking, Walker?"

"Two things. One, it'll be a huge turnout, and two, it'll increase your exposure, and three—"

"You said two."

"I thought of another." He leaned against the counter, arms enfolded across his chest, one foot lazily draped over the other. "You charge $4.50 for each of those things. Once they sell out, you'll have secured half of next month's rent in one single event."

The big guy did have business smarts inside that thick skull.

The hope was that Owen's involvement would offset the incoming storm surge of a rent increase and give her momentum to carry on once he returned to the field. His natural habitat. A bear in his den, a lion among his pride. And if she won Bryan J. Carlyle's contest, she'd secure her rightful place as a highly sought-after bakery and would eliminate the need to rely on him.

What Sports Illustrated hadn't captured on its cover were Owen's marketing superpowers and his ability to create original recipes. As to Eli's mention of Owen being the Player of the Week, she was well aware. Against better judgment, she retrieved the image in her mind—Owen's broad shoulders arched, a mean mug to rival any in the league, arms tightly rounded and barely covering the labyrinth of well-defined muscles and tendons hidden behind a smooth sheath of glistening skin.

At the splendor, tingles zipped up and down her spine, pulling her into a tipsy trance. If he discovered the copy she'd purchased, she'd never hear the end of provocation. Worse, he'd falsely presume she'd grown fond of the insufferable competitor. Worse still, he might see evidence of attraction in her gaze and come to the wrong conclusion that she cared.

Really cared. Wanted the impossible.

Because Mom always said physical beauty faded in time, and a wise girl developed the stuff on the inside, the home of the soul—God's playground of imagination and ingenuity and beauty. Her growing appreciation for Owen's fervor and genuine interest in her endeavor for her ultimate good had twined to her need. But she could not let his investment snuggle up to her heart. He was a perfect somebody for someone who didn't have ... missing pieces.

"We'll need another batch of cinnamon pear muffins. Recipe right here." Serenity tapped at the recipe.

"Gotcha." Giving the refrigerator handle a hard tug, Owen opened it. He retrieved the eggs, a block of butter, cream, and canned fresh pears, plucked from Moreland's pear tree. Stepping past him, she opened the pantry and pulled out the flour, salt, and cinnamon. At the subtle scent of his musky cologne, she willed the fuzzy fog over her brain to lift so she could think clearly.

One at a time, he cracked the eggs in his palm, tossed the shells, and whisked in melted butter.

The ease he displayed was uncanny, as though he'd found a new playing field and had determined to dominate it, too.

Yep. Good in the kitchen. *Real* good.

In a bid to remind herself of his sole purpose here, Serenity set her mind to task. Dry measuring cup in hand, she dipped it into the canister and leveled it with the flat side of a metal spatula. Overturning it into a large mixing bowl, she skimmed a peek at his smooth, confident technique.

Outside the prerequisite course he'd taken in college, the man had no other culinary experience, yet his instinctive ability to operate equipment and locate utensils baffled her. "I have to believe your comfort level in a kitchen hasn't come from one semester of home economics."

His cheeks flushed. An endearing dimple deepened aside his mouth.

"Who taught you to bake?"

"My mom."

His posture sank, chest caving in weighty exhale. "She died when I was thirteen. My number one fan."

"I'm so sorry, Owen."

He shrugged, tossing his head stiffly as though casting off the sting of memory.

There had been a time when Serenity endeavored to know everything about him—his family, values, interests, social life, favorite sports car—until struck by the realization that investing mental energy toward what she could never have amounted to a futile expenditure.

In the sweetness of this moment, she'd learned something about Owen that the public did not know. The key player, Connie Walker—adored mom of two strapping boys—had been the baking influence in his life. The reason he'd put his reputation on the line and risk being seen in a bakery.

Heaven praise the woman!

But amassing professional sports statistics allowed little to no room for rich backstory—that which had shaped the character of the man inside the jersey. To his fans and the league, Owen's exceptional ability to stir, measure, and bake didn't add points to the board. It wasn't the stuff that'd earned recognition during honors night, Super Bowl eve. But for Serenity, he'd added more value to her world in just one week than she'd experienced in a lifetime.

He caught her staring and held her immobilized as though he knew the effect he had on her. Gaze stilled on her mouth, he studied her face and showcased a full set of straight teeth. A smile that pretty much eliminated the need for overhead light.

Dear me, no.

She turned toward the pantry and opened it, angled a glance all around—looking at nothing because she needed nothing—closed it, drew in a breath, and returned to work beside Owen.

That smirk. He reached in front of her, wingspan blocking her vision as he slowly slid the canister of baking powder closer. "You looking for this?"

No. "Yes, thanks." She peeled off the lid and snatched a measuring spoon. "Tell me about your mom."

Divert focus off me.

"Her name was Connie. Whenever she'd bake something for the family or others, she'd invite me into the kitchen and instruct as she went. If I messed up, she didn't hesitate to correct me but exhibited an enormous amount of patience. A lot like how you interacted with Eli."

The satisfaction playing over his face suggested that her relationship with Eli held value beyond giving a kid a memorable birthday.

"I love that about her," Serenity said.

"So did I."

"I've always believed firm, but kind, instruction results in the best outcome for teacher and student." How God might intend a good-willed, loving parent to interact with a child. The way Serenity, a small girl of eight, had waited for Dad to show some sign that he'd delighted in her company. Benefited from her ideas.

Each time waiting.

Reticence claimed Owen's gaze. His mammoth hand slowed the pace of his work. "Mom and I used to make a game out of who could come up with the most original dessert. In the backyard, Dad attempted to chisel a professional out of my brother Derek. Fiercely determined to create an unstoppable Walker duo out of his boys, carry on his legend."

"How'd he let you off so easily?"

"I didn't say he let me off. Heck, he'd run me to the ground until I threw up. But I also didn't need to exert the same effort Derek did. Anyway, after an hour of Dad's ball toss and drills, he was satisfied enough to turn me loose." A guarded pain played across the sheen of Owen's eyes, dimmed them a dull brown, touched by pinpricks of overhead light.

"Baking, owning a bakery, is a lot like the rigors of football."

Letting the wild juxtaposition marinate a little, Serenity measured the salt, added it to the bowl, and stirred the dry mixture. "How so?"

"The repetitiveness required by the game allows you to come in and knock out a large order quickly and do it over and over to satisfy the fan base or, in this case, hungry, paying consumers."

"Without hits to the head."

An awkward laugh waved over his shoulders. "Guess so."

Begrudgingly, she admitted that his alterations to a few of her recipes improved on perfection and placed them prominently in front cases. Offering reduced prices resulted in greater demand.

Thus, sales.

Necessary oxygen.

What was it about Owen that held the ability to switch up a darn near perfect recipe and create more heavenly flavor? Maybe hidden inside his philanthropic heart and somewhere behind the matrix of muscle and a vast network of business savvy, he'd brought some of heaven to earth. The giver of dreams to kids across the country. A guy of immense stature who handled a rubber scraper and navigated the complexities of her industrial kitchen like nobody's business. Playing effortlessly in it like fresh, new turf.

The oddity was that the award-winning ballplayer hadn't loathed home economics class. He'd genuinely enjoyed it. Earned a solid A.

Who knew?

She did. Because he'd let her into a sliver of his world.

"I am grateful for all you've done, Owen. But you could have just written a check." Kept vulnerable hearts out of this conundrum.

"Guys in my position write checks all the time. I'm more of a cleats-on-the-ground kind of guy."

With the precision of a coyote pouncing on prey, he popped a cupcake in his mouth. Then another. With a hard swallow, he deepened his dimpled, irresistible grin.

What if he ate her profits? Kinda defeated the point.

"Walker, I'm going to dock your pay if you keep eating those."

"Trust me, Seren. I got your best interest at heart." The way he delighted in her name when he spoke it, the musicality of his tone, felt somewhat like the calming blush of sunrise over her bakery each morning, the arrival of a new day, expectant and hopeful.

Peaceful.

And then he gave a tortuous wink, and her brain went all wonky. Chills swirled in ridiculous circles through said heart, nearly unraveling her resolve. No doubt, many a girl had been the blessed recipient of his large package of charm.

And yet, of all the places this vast and seemingly immeasurable planet offered, Owen was here. This large and legendary man—in the modest bakery of an ordinary woman. Because he'd chosen to be here.

His decision to invest time here exposed his hidden capabilities and brought risk. Did he consider her worth it?

The fullness of his attention hooked on her for the briefest of seconds.

Her breath caught, coursing behind her ears. A hint of interest glinted in his honey amber eyes moments before it flickered out. But not before it sent an unsettling desire on a twisted path toward her heart in front of which she'd erected a sign.

Closed.

Chapter Five

Leave it to Owen to commit Serenity to provide for a fundraising event drawing more people than Moreland had probably ever enjoyed. The loyal supporters and the curious. Fans of what the Walker Foundation stood for in the community, throughout the country, and across the world. Without events like this, the heart of its hero stood to outgrow its wallet. Her presence here—entirely Owen's doing—seemed insignificant. Uninteresting, even.

What if the proceeds she raised to contribute to the foundation amounted to no more than a drop of water in the ocean?

But it was his ocean. And today's exposure could only result in good outcomes as The Pear Tree's sweet melodic voice was being drowned out by the cacophony of its gargantuan competitor. Today served two purposes: the sale of cupcakes beyond compare and a reminder of Serenity's presence and value to the community.

Amply shaded from the midday sun beneath the erected canopy, Brooke worked aside Serenity to drape covers over the three tables they'd arranged in a U.

"Whewee, Miz Serenity. Setting up for an event of this magnitude is no small task."

Kourtney ran the countertop refrigerated display case cable to one of the thick extension cords coming from the on-site generators installed for the occasion. She plugged it in and turned a glance at Serenity. "Did it work?"

Relief whooshed in as the inside light winked back, sounding a gentle whir. "Yes."

Once the component reached proper temperature, Kourtney, Lettie, and Brooke set chilled cupcakes on the shelves. Serenity placed the pastry risers on each table, covered in linen and tulle. She set several frosted mega-darlings in a careful display, tilting her head in assessment, chewing her lip until satisfied, while Brooke set out the signage noting the price of $4.50 for each, $8 for two.

Over the past several minutes, growing numbers of people spilled out of cars, squeezing the air from Serenity's lungs. "For all the grief I gave Owen over his promise we'd provide twenty dozen, now I'm concerned we'll run out. It's not even noon yet, and there are ... fifty-seven, fifty-eight, fifty-nine—"

"I welcomes that problem. 'Cause I sure don't want to be stuck with products we can't sell."

"Lettie, you know as good as I do that Serenity will donate what's left before the sun goes down."

Serenity set out business cards and brochures sporting a fresh new logo, menu, and catering options. "Kourtney, make sure everyone gets one of these."

"I will."

"And point out the website, contact and ordering info."

"Like I always do at the shop."

Serenity returned a sidelong grin. She turned to Brooke. "Think I should run into town and have more brochures printed?"

"Don't bother. Enjoy this day."

The day her business would get its needed mouth-to-mouth resuscitation—or choke to death.

Owen Walker's matchless voice drew her attention to the foundation booth erected several yards away in front of Moreland. Adjacent to the large black and gold canopy stood a slick raised vinyl poster featuring Owen and his sports-camp kids. Several men and women dressed in athletic gear and suits nodded as he spoke, giving pointed directions.

When her gaze connected with his, he broke away and jogged over. A short woman in dark, tailored pants and knit top skittered behind, yammering something at his back and clutching a tablet to her chest.

At his approach, the woman caught his arm. "This is wrong." She wound a glance at Serenity and lasered a stare along the booth's interior. "I assigned this prime location to Bakery World. She doesn't belong here, my love."

A knot tugged in Serenity's gut. Irritation simmered beneath her skin. Her mouth fell partially open in question.

"I canceled them."

Owen's cool explanation ignited an explosion of fury inside the woman's rounded gaze.

The woman raised and lowered her arms. "Now, why would you do that?"

"Conflict of interest. I'd arranged another, superior vendor." He gestured to Serenity. "Best there is."

"But this isn't what we invested marketing funds to advertise, my love. The public is expecting Bakery World, a known brand. Kids will be expecting to decorate cupcakes."

Defeat tightened a frayed rope around her heart.

"It was my decision, Nina. Let it go."

Ah. Nina she was. The victim of Owen's surreptitious maneuver. A curl of joy turned in Serenity's middle at the notion he'd strategized on her behalf, elevating her worth above the pernicious competitor.

"Does your alternative have the ability to meet the demand?" Nina jabbed.

"Meet and exceed it."

Unless she couldn't. At what point did having this guy in a girl's corner squeeze air from her lungs?

Angling away from Hurricane Nina—who'd likely hailed from some blistery cold province in Canada—Serenity schooled her voice, delivering words in a slow drip. "Owen, I appreciate your vote of confidence." Breathe, girl. "But I am really not prepared to—"

Owen's finger to her lips and a wink crushed all traces of concern to dust. "You have everything you need. I'll step in and help."

"This was entirely your idea, Walker. I'm the one who should be helping *you.*"

A flurry of kids and youth came toward the table and skidded to a stop. Gazes tipped in Owen's shadow. Awestruck stares encircled him like they'd stood at the base of a sequoia.

"Hey, there. How are my kids doing?"

The man loved kids. *Never forget.*

Relishing the moment, he bent to one knee, shook hands, tousled hair, and signed footballs, T-shirts, and ball caps. The giver of dreams. Layering joy and warmth to rival a golden cupcake fresh from the oven.

A girl in soccer cleats shouldered to the table. "Is this where we get to color frosting and decorate?"

"It is," Owen said.

"But Owen, I—"

"Walkers don't quit," he said, glancing down at her. "Let's give them some fun."

I'm not a Walker, you overstuffed circus clown.

She folded her arms. "All right. Fun, then."

Contemplation rumpled over his brow. He scratched his head as he turned to survey the product on display and inside the refrigerated case. Amusement blinked in his gaze. He slid the door aside and bent to glance inside. Stood straight. "All I see are your Serenity's Specials. Where are the Walker's Big Hits?"

Uh. She hooked a thumb over her shoulder. "They're back there."

"The objective is to sell, Seren. Put top sellers out front. Leave others for later."

"This is my chance to shine, not add to your overinflated ego," she groused.

His chin went taut. He spun to face his fans and forced a smile. "Hey, kids, instead of making a mess, I've got a better idea."

"You do?" Serenity said.

"Yes. I do." He did a double take, gave a look of hurried thought, and darted his gaze as though struggling to recall a play. "We're going to play ... a game."

"A guessing game," Serenity said, filling in mental blanks.

Brooke snickered.

Kourtney snorted.

Lettie clucked her tongue and thrust a fist into her hip.

"What are we guessing?" a young boy asked.

Owen wrapped an arm around him. "Which are the top two best sellers at Miss Serenity's bakery."

She fit a plastic smile to her lips and shifted a steely glance his direction, her heart a thin sheet of glass.

"Winner receives a—" Owen gestured a hand to Serenity. Intrigued stares alternated between them.

"A coupon." She clasped hands behind her and rocked onto the balls of her feet. "To my bakery, The Pear Tree." Assigning honor, she lifted a palm toward the signage.

Flat responses pummeled her chest.

"It'll be good for two, no, four of your favorite pastries." The lilt in her tone suggested desperation.

One kid scratched his head. Others winced or shrugged. Owen thumbed his chest. "And breakfast out with me." Rousing cheers erupted.

And just like that, the hero saves the day, exhuming cupcake wars better left beneath six feet of earth.

Owen raised a Walker's Big Hit to his lips, sunk his teeth into it, and spoke through pastry-stuffed cheeks. "Is it that you're unhappy they chose mine over yours?"

It took the strength of Job not to snort out a laugh when Serenity raised her hand, oh so desperately wanting to mash a cupcake into his handsome face.

"Winning by one kid isn't anything to brag about, Walker."

His smile disarmed her aggravation.

She dusted her apron and tilted her head up at him. "Don't you have a fundraiser that requires you to be the center of attention today?"

The way she wrinkled her nose shimmied something ... something sweet through him.

And yes, he did have a fundraiser to see about.

The vision to hold the annual event at Moreland Manor near Bayou Lafourche had come to Owen during preseason a year and a half ago, a day forever etched in his memory. One, because he'd been privileged to help restore the magnificent historical home—coveting its grandeur, size, and endless possibilities. And two, Moreland was where he'd become providentially reacquainted with Serenity Lewis, the owner's spirited younger sister who'd spearheaded the outpouring of support. The generous act resulted in enough funds and muscle to restore the historic estate.

A woman after his own heart.

Not sure why he hadn't dated her. Maybe, deep down, he knew she was one of those girls of substance. The marrying kind—for a guy whose head was screwed on right. A girl worth cherishing until death parted the two, not one to date until things got stale.

He'd been too much of a jerk back then. An unbelieving, faithless jerk. Dating a girl of Serenity's caliber would have inevitably added to his regrets on this exceptional day.

Nothing of sports camps nor the development of a philanthropic organization to meet the needs of underserved youth, the community, and those in the military—had entered his mind until he'd let his heart be ruled by that which ruled God's. Seeing people through new eyes was what made today's gathering so invigorating.

Past and present foundation supporters and vendor tents gathered on Moreland's property. A thick stretch of stately privacy trees ran along either side. Gabe and Everley allowed parking in the empty acreage behind the massive home.

During the first hour, Owen and several football players greeted guests, signed donated footballs, and posed for pictures. A life-size cardboard cutout near the south wing featured Owen ensconced by several of his sports camps kids, Eli on his right.

"How are you, Owen?"

Owen turned to see Ross and Arlene Billings, Eli beside them, ball in hand and dressed in the black and gold Kings jersey Owen had given him for his birthday and wearing a smile the width of the Mississippi.

"Great to see you." He took Ross's outstretched hand and dipped to hug Arlene before turning his attention to Eli.

"Hi, Owen."

"Hey, superstar."

"Can you and me play ball together today?" Eli's silky brown eyes sparkled. His hair had grown longer along the sides, trimmed neatly at the neck, and brushed loosely over the top.

In a surge of emotion, he hoisted the now twelve-year-old Eli to his shoulders—all five foot five and seventy pounds of him—and ran him across the lawn. Playing dad until God blessed him with his own. Children who'd carry the rich DNA of his smarts and athleticism and embody his mom's kindness and delicate features.

As the mid-afternoon sun eased westward, Owen and the players divided up to execute a friendly exhibition game. His team down by six at the half, he guzzled an energy drink, then high-tailed it into position to bring this game to a win. Blocking an offensive pass, he lurched to snag the ball midair and tucked it to his chest. He fixed his eye on the gravel driveway, a pre-determined endzone, hauled the ball the length of the property and proclaimed a touchdown.

Applause boomed over the lawn. Kids cheered in raucous *whoops!* He jogged back over, tossed the ball to Eli, and knelt to eye level. "That was for you, buddy."

The gleam of a never-ending smile dawned on Eli's face. Owen swallowed him in a hug. Man, he loved that kid. The feel of fatherhood soaked through his jersey.

Someday he'd clench the prize of a family.

A text from Jude alerted him to turn his attention skyward. A chopper hovered over the front lawn, rotors thrumming. Jude steadied the whirling bird over the house and then piloted it to a smooth landing behind it.

JUDE: All clear.

OWEN: Got your all clear.

Brandishing a mic, Owen lunged over the front steps and turned to the crowd. "Chopper rides out back!"

Jubilant squeals erupted.

Owen gestured for the youth to follow him past the stretch of vehicles parked within a taped area to the open field. Several of Jude's fellow Marines directed spectators and kids to stay within a safety zone. Taking two kids at a time, Jude secured them inside the chopper. He lifted the craft with ease and maneuvered it over the house, down the river, and back again.

On the final landing, Jude called Owen. "Any more takers?"

"I think we're good."

"Affirmative. Signing out, sir."

"Thanks, Jude. I appreciate you, man."

"Honored to serve."

In steady rise above the roof line, the chopper roared into the sky, blades spattering and whirling before it arced a hard right and shrank in the distance.

Three hours in, activity slowed, and the crowd thinned. Sauntering across the lawn in his blues, weapon holstered at his hip, Derek approached. The two leaned in and gave their customary two slaps across the shoulder.

Derek tucked his thumbs inside the front of his belt. "Hey there, big-little brother."

"Hello, little-big brother."

"Fantastic turnout today. Hope it'll raise what you need."

"Looks like it could exceed it. We drained scholarship funds from last year. I want to double that amount so we can reach more kids."

Derek turned to stand shoulder to shoulder and hiked his gun belt. "How's the bakery gig going?"

"Great. You should stop in. Check it out."

"I never miss an opportunity when I run the French Quarter. The owner gives me free coffee and product on hand."

"Ah. You're one of the reasons she's losing business," Owen jibed.

"Maybe. But that'll further your motivation to save the damsel in distress." Derek elbowed him in the ribs, tone suggesting false intention.

"My reckless days are behind me."

"Has there been measurable progress since you stepped in to assist?"

Stats. Talk stats. "Word has gotten out. Former customers are returning, sales have improved enough to spare her from having to close down. The goal is to turn things around enough to keep her afloat after I leave."

Come July, he'd trade his floured apron for a stretch jersey.

A wave of sadness rolled in, threatening to hollow his lungs. Because it meant he'd be staring down another grueling five weeks of training camp. Angst chugged up and beat against his brain. He tamped it down. No time for emotion to take him to his knees. What would fans say to a long-term decision to design baked goods for a living? The ridicule would be unbearable.

In the space of quiet, Derek's eyes roved the property. Looking for clues, looking for bad guys. Bearing the build of a pro ballplayer and yet, doing exactly what God had called him to do. Being who he was meant to be. The willingness to take a bullet to the head rather than a helmet. Vigilant and watchful.

The presence of law enforcement enabled guests to rest easy. Derek's career choice added supreme value to the event.

But what did Owen do to make people rest easy? The

question jarred him.

He built a wall out of his body, defended the lineup, sacked the QB, got battered … won games … received honors.

Year after year after year.

Owen trekked a glance around the diminished crowd. "Have you seen Dad?"

Derek jutted his chin in the direction of the front porch. "He's over there in a rocker, regaling Harvey Walker fans with his career highlights."

"Looks like he's managed to hold a good number of them in rapt attention."

A chortle sounded. "Probably recalling the glory days."

Stats. They make a man.

Owen clapped Derek on the shoulder. "Well, little-big bro', I probably ought to go run interference and leave you to policing everybody else."

Derek returned a two-fingered salute off his forehead.

The fan base clustered around Dad consisted of men and women in their fifties and sixties, most heads crowned in gray. Only Owen hadn't expected to find Serenity among them—a wildflower among mature oaks in her stylish, athletic wear and neon lace-ups who'd ditched her apron while Brooke, Lettie, and Kourtney tended the booth.

Fueled by collective drive, determination, and a boatload of ingredients, Owen and Serenity had produced the cupcake order he'd promised for today's event. The last time he'd checked, she'd sold them all.

Sure and certain, they'd made a terrific team.

"That's a heavenly bunch of cupcakes, Lewis," he'd said.

"Impossible without you, Walker," she readily admitted.

"With my creative ingenuity—"

"And my marketing finesse ..."

"Team Walker!"

They'd voiced the proclamation in unison like they'd practiced for hours and clapped floured hands midair.

Who knew planning and preparation could fill a man's soul? It'd been fun, exhilarating.

Incredible.

Any other woman would have been wrought with irritation, scraping seething glances down his frame in the limited space of a heated, boisterous kitchen. Not this one. She'd been in her element, his helping hands as water to revive a wilting flower.

An uncommon flower. Unlike any he'd ever known. She wasn't one to paint herself into a corner, confounded by career limitations. She'd freed herself to dream, risk, and create.

Dangerously attractive, mostly because she seemed unaware of the lethal nature of her unhindered beauty.

As Owen walked nearer the veranda, Serenity's countenance shifted to wild-eyed as though she'd deeply regretted her decision to engage Dad in conversation. Dad's animated gestures, baritone voice, and profanity broadened the space between them.

The monster awakes ...

What if horror over the grotesqueness of the disease overtook her?

Instinct thrummed behind his ears, rushing to his feet. A whistle blew in his head.

Move in, Number 91.

Chapter Six

Owen mounted the veranda steps and claimed space beside Serenity. "Hey, Dad. How're you doing?"

What damage have you done on this fine day?

"Good. Real good, in fact. Enjoying the unexpected pleasure these old eyes haven't seen in quite a while." His pithy tongue cluck spoke volumes.

Unease pinched the space between Serenity's sculpted, brown brows.

A man undyingly faithful to his wife of twenty years before Mom died, Dad must have kept private passions on lockdown. And now, it seemed, the unstoppable disease sought to unleash them all over Owen's employer.

The folks clustered in front of Dad parted to make space for Owen and shook his hand. Among them was Arthur McManus, CEO of Interstate Steel. "Great program you've started, Walker. You can count on our corporation to assist with promoting your camps." Enthusiasm saturated his voice. "I sure wish I'd had an opportunity like this when I was a young lad."

So did I.

It wasn't for lack of opportunity, though. Owen had tried other sports. And failed. Dad refused to let him forget.

Told you. Walkers play football.

"Anything you need, Owen. Say the word." McManus shook Owen's hand again, grasping his shoulder with the other.

"Much appreciated," Owen said. "Thanks for coming out."

When the event ended, his teammates waved goodbye, vendors broke down their equipment, and the lawn rested from vigorous activity.

Through the front door, Gabe appeared, toting a contagious smile. The man of the house with a heart just as big. Blessed to marry the girl of his dreams, he'd been providentially chosen to restore the house she'd inherited.

Fate sure knew how to create winning matchups.

Gabe wore jeans, an untucked plaid shirt, and boots. Layered brown hair framed his angular face.

"Hey there, Lord Bellevue," Owen said.

The corner of Gabe's lips inched to a smile. He sauntered over the dusty porch toward Dad, Serenity, and Owen. "Got any cupcakes around this place?"

Gabe winked at Serenity, who returned a smile, cheeks flamed pink.

Inside a rabid grouse, Dad spit displeasure into the air, fists wrenching the armrests. "Bakery girl says she ran out."

Serenity raised empty hands to verify.

"My loss," Gabe said.

Eli made his way over and stopped at the veranda.

"Hey, superstar." Owen gestured toward the steps. "Come join the party." Deflect attention off Dad's incessant jabberwocky. Captivated by his own imaginings, the aging hall of famer stared ahead in an intense study at what had to be game footage running through his mind's eye.

Owen bent to lift Eli to stand beside him and draped an arm around his shoulders. "Gabe, this is Eli Billings. He's my sports-camp boy wonder." He turned to Eli. "And that is the head of the house."

Gabe shook Eli's hand. "Pleased to meet you, Eli."

Awe and curiosity played over Eli's freckled face. "This is your house?"

"It actually belongs to my wife, who, at present, is losing her battle with nausea." He flitted a glance at Owen. "But when I married her, the house came with it. A package deal, if you will."

Eli traced an enamored gaze along the scale of the porch. "When was it built?"

"1846. Colonel Marshall R. Thompson needed a manor house for his sugar plantations and commissioned architect and Irish immigrant Howard Gallagher to build it."

Eli's gaze lit afire. "I love history."

Serenity moved to jab Gabe's side with her elbow. "Tell him, Gabe."

Gabe crouched in front of Eli. "In 1852, Colonel Thompson died of Yellow Fever. The care of Moreland Manor was left to his wife, Anna, and their only son. In 1855, she married a man named Edmund Bellevue who, I learned a couple years ago during our restoration, was my great, great-grandfather."

Eli's mouth fell open. His eyes rounded.

"In 1863, Edmund left Moreland to fight in the Civil War and rose in rank to Brigadier General."

Exuberance unmatched, the kid rotated an upward glance at Owen. "That's so cool!"

"Unfortunately, Edmund didn't make it back to his family." Gabe stood, leaned against a pillar, crossed his ankles, and entwined his arms. "But even in war, he ministered to soldiers who fought on both sides of the conflict. Died a hero's death on the field."

The day Owen first met Gabe, his reputable and thriving historic restoration business, sadly, had come to ruin. Crumbled by those who'd sought to tarnish his reputation, dredging up what Gabe had always assumed to be a long history of father failure. A heritage Gabe vowed to avoid.

To hear Gabe speak honorably of his ancestry and learn that he'd partnered with his father, Dalton Bellevue, doing business as Bellevue Historic Restoration Specialists, emboldened Owen.

"Hey, Eli," Serenity said. "Gabe played basketball in high school." She flitted a gaze Gabe's direction and turned back to Eli. "Come shoot hoops with us over on the drive."

"You play basketball?" Eli said to Serenity.

"I did in high school."

She played basketball, too?

"And Volleyball," she said. "But mostly soccer. Tried softball for a while, but failure to duck after a poorly directed fastball did me—and my head—no good."

Her unfettered laughter dripped like honey over the gathering. Owen tasted the sweetness of her adventurous spirit. It added color to an already intriguing and broadening canvas.

"Let's go shoot, boy wonder." Gabe nodded toward the drive.

Serenity followed Gabe and Eli, then paused to glance over her shoulder. When he didn't move, she journeyed an inquisitive stare over him. Right. What pro athlete would hesitate to participate in a harmless game of basketball with a little kid?

But the greater obstacle in his way was the difficulty of recovering from the tug of her smile—bewitched by her many facets. He returned a nod and prolonged his stare as she skip-walked to the drive.

"I see that look." Dad's bass timbre splintered Owen's thoughts.

He gave his ball cap a tug and rubbed the back of his neck.

"Still hankering to try a different sport." Contempt blazed over Dad's tone.

"How about you come cheer me on?" And drop the rebuke.

"I'm content to watch from here while you give it a shot."

But he wouldn't. His beefy frame was built for speed and strength, a body designed for one game. Within those boundaries, he'd excelled.

Leaving Dad to engage in conversation with his inner demons, Owen joined Gabe, Eli, and Serenity at the top of the drive, where he stood out of the way to observe the threesome.

Gabe exhibited the only refined skills among them, and Eli barely reached his midsection in height. At about five foot six and full of energy, well, Serenity just added another layer of appeal to the whole picture. Pump fake, dribbling, pivoting like her life depended on it.

Owen loved the way she engaged Eli. It stirred his longing to be a dad.

In one unique package, she was auspiciously uncommon and good and agile and spirited. The kind of whimsical soul he imagined waking up to each day. Unlike other women he'd taken into his arms back in the day, Serenity possessed physical discipline and strength of character.

With each interaction, his interest grew in intensity. A brutal test of his resolve.

Objective: Help her out.

Once training camp started, Owen would be forced to untie those apron strings and stuff his beat-up brain back inside his helmet.

Two weeks after the fundraiser, Owen received an email from the foundation director to its members reporting that the monies raised from the event garnished nearly triple what he'd prayed for.

"Praise God," he said. Conviction fisted inside. "No, no. Praise You, Almighty God."

He'd asked Nina to schedule a board meeting for the following week. He wanted members to weigh in on current financial standings and to develop strategies to broaden corporate support base.

"We need to close registration end of April," Nina said. "I'll publish scholarship availability on the website and compose an email to subscribers. Your social media manager will post a spotlight about the camps during prime-time viewing to solicit more registrations. Last I checked, you'd reached well past a couple million followers, my love."

Numbers had soared. Platform extended its reach.

"Bakery World declined sponsorship, given your rash decision to cancel."

He gave a sappy puppy dog expression.

The haughty jag of her brow festered inside his gut. "Since you seem to have a rogue interest in bakeries, I sent first-quarter Bakery World earnings to your inbox for consideration. Their stock value might be of interest."

He'd already considered it. Coddled the idea even. Because a good player knew the value of aligning himself with greatness. Wise matchups won games. And if Bakery World was soaring, it'd benefit him to consider the investment. If it wasn't meant for him to have a place of his own, he could profit from those who did.

The next Saturday, Owen left the bakery after only two hours. He owed his brief stay to a prior commitment with Dad and Derek, particularly as Dad's symptoms had become more pronounced over the last year. When Derek and his wife Marianne moved from Pennsylvania to be closer to her family, he'd put in for a transfer to the New Orleans Police Department. Concern for Dad being alone prompted Owen to purchase the farmhouse close to Derek and contract Bellevue Historic Restoration to restore it.

Not since Mom's death had they lived in the same city. The trio —Dad, Derek, and Owen—were an antithetical mix of regret, vigilance, and muscle.

In that order.

Thanks to Mom's relentless endeavor, the common bond of love for each other held the odd mix in its unyielding grip. That and an undying love for the game.

All three Walker men gathered in Dad's airy main room, Derek in uniform at shift's end and Dad, at present, facing the paneled wall, banging his forehead against it.

Disparagement marked Derek's gaze. "That sure gives new meaning to a Harvey Wallbanger," he murmured.

Dad turned from the wall, spewing obscenities at the screen in a funnel cloud of sorrow and fury. "C'mon, ref! Completely missed the call on that face mask. That's *not* football's fault." Caged and wild, Dad set to pacing, fists curled, stiff arms swinging at his sides. "An egregious call?!"

"Need some Vodka for that Wallbanger, Dad?" Derek smarted.

No response.

The furnishings of Dad's house and the mental status of its occupant dulled the luster of what had been a magazine-worthy space when he'd moved in.

A swift wind rattled the opposite window that framed a clear view of the back acreage. Several panes of splintered glass were precariously held together by duct tape. Owen trailed Derek as he rose from the sofa and drew the sheer aside. His interrogative gaze peered left and right. "What happened here, Dad?"

A grunt, absent stare. "Steelers lost a game they should not have. I was unhappy about it."

Wearing his wrinkled, gray T-shirt and saggy sweatpants that smelled as though they'd been worn for several days, Dad shrugged and ambled in his slippers—one black, one brown—to a recliner. Remote in hand, he aimed it at the screen and crossed his ankles on the footrest.

Gaze locked on the screen, he surfed channels.

The cushion of a threadbare, sagging sofa pinged when Derek eased into it. He uncapped a beer bottle and set it on an end table.

In the adjoining, open kitchen, Owen grimaced at the sink brimming with dirty dishes. He opened the pantry. A bag of chips yawned open, expiration date marked two years ago. He trashed it, opened a fresh bag, and dumped the chips into a bowl.

When he tugged the refrigerator open, a caustic stench assaulted him. The culprits were two tubs of outdated dip, a tray of ashen deli meat, a block of moldy cheese, and an open container of potato salad. He bagged the tainted food and stuffed it in the outside trash can.

Far from a banquet, Owen brought the chips and three bottles of water into the family room and sat beside Derek. He set the water and bowl on the only available space atop the coffee table, covered end to end in sports magazines.

Dad hadn't stopped surfing. "Derek, what's new in your world?"

"Not much. Just the usual. Foot chases, domestic violence. A near-fatal shooting in a drug bust gone bad two days ago."

That shift nearly cost Derek his life but hailed him a hero in the eyes of a grateful community. The timely interdiction resulted in a lengthy write-up in the paper and became the focus of social media buzz. But through Dad's eyes, it mattered not that Derek had chosen an equally honorable career after a blown knee in training camp cost him a shot at the pros.

But incarcerating bad guys, bearing the weight of the badge, rising in rank, and being esteemed by peers weren't football. Dad had no mental receptors for things outside pigskin, turf, and goal lines.

In the barren expanse of the off-season, Dad was as irritable as they come.

"That uniform you're wearing. The pistol and all the gear around your middle ... You in law enforcement or something?"

"Yeah, Dad. Joined the force eight years ago." Derek released a hard sigh, confidence sapped as he drew long from his beer. "Promoted to Officer IV last year."

Countenance vacant, Dad returned to surfing sports channels for several silent minutes, searching for the all-American game.

"Dang it," Dad spit out. "Draft doesn't start for another week."

"PGA tournaments are going on," Owen offered.

A grunt.

"Major league baseball is in full swing," Derek said.

A guffaw. "Guys whacking a ball with a wooden stick, running in circles around what they call a playing field."

"I know a lot of gifted pro athletes who play in multiple pro sports leagues, Dad."

"You're just not one of 'em, Owen."

Like he needed reminding of his inability to measure up as a well-rounded athlete, limited by divine design.

Not liberated.

But the body had an expiration date. The inevitable fact of it tightened his muscles and threatened to tear tendon from bone.

May arrived like a fierce storm warning. Serenity subdued the threat with a full month's rent paid to Maurice—before the due date. To have resuscitated the place she loved swirled ethereal relief inside her.

Maurice relented on shutting her down, though his email response was wrought with finality. "No further delinquencies will be tolerated, mademoiselle."

She had to keep the bakery open.

She *would* keep it open.

She refused to cave to desperation.

To snuff out a smoldering wick.

Serenity bent to peer inside the display case and rotated baked wonders every which way until satisfied with the presentation. She stood and turned to Brooke. "It's too late to change the name of my signature cupcake for the Carlyle contest entry, but maybe around here, it would be better just to call it Serenity's."

"But I love the name Serenity's Special."

Toting a large coffee urn, Kourtney set it gently on the counter and turned. "You should definitely keep it. I mean, you gave your stamp of approval on my signature coffee blend, named it Special K."

Serenity slid the glass door shut and dusted her palms together. "But I get all tongue-twisty when I say it. People might think I'm saying Serenity is special."

A gentle smile played in Brooke's eyes.

"Don't you think that's a bit weird, Brooke?"

"Whatever it takes for you to embrace that which makes you unique."

Or for others to invest a millisecond to know the essence of Serenity—the stuff behind the colorful veneer of a bakery shop owner. But what if they didn't like what they saw?

Living in a shell of uniqueness had its price.

As for price, thus sayeth the mighty Owen Walker, hers were too high. Exorbitant, in fact.

In all his grandeur, Owen appeared at the door, his ability to be obscure as effective as a Special Forces commander in full gear at a little girl's tea party. The dining area measurably shrank as he navigated through it. Stares fixed on his forward stride. It struck her anew that Owen Walker bothered to lend support to a place that represented a sliver of sweetness in a giant of a planet. On the one hand, it made zero sense. On the other, it made all the sense in the world, considering his baking capabilities and genuine interest.

In one large package, the sturdy athlete amassed physical strength, ingenuity, and business finesse. During her season of struggle, he represented a walking, talking—handsome—billboard who'd come in her favor.

Thank you, God.

Yesterday, Owen reported that April's fundraiser had raised nearly $300,000 for the foundation. No surprise, really. Take Owen's magnetic personality, place it in a magical location, toss in an exhibition game played by next season's starters, and offer free helicopter rides piloted by a highly decorated Marine. Mix in his power of persuasion, and hundreds more Walker kids will have a shot at their dreams.

"Hey there, Lewis," he said.

"You're early."

"And you sound irritated."

"Add mindreading to your résumé."

"I can go grab some Cajun if that'd bounce me out of bakery shop jail."

"No. Don't pester the locals." Serenity snatched his special order XXXL apron and handed it over. "Just get to doing whatever it is you do, which, at present, has four, no—" She leaned around him, bobbed her head counting, then drew back. "*Five* women ogling you in guilty pleasure."

Curiosity and a wolfish grin ravaged his gaze. He twisted at the waist and waved. "Hi, ladies. Welcome to The Pear Tree."

At his rapturous greeting, one woman floated a hand to her neck and slunk into her chair. The woman beside her gave her a playful pop on the arm, giggling as she leaned in. "Could you be any more obvious, Jillian?"

The others were too mesmerized to do much but hold a coffee cup to their mouths and stare. All fine and good. But once his short stint here was over, no way could Serenity nor her meager staff sustain his same level of energy. She knew exactly what effect his unmatched charm had on that gaggle of women.

So long as number 91 was in the house, it'd worked magnificently. Even those in commerce had come sniffing, looking to study her methods. Several new patrons frequented her bakery. They'd become hooked on her unique coffee blends, the addition of a matcha latte, and, yes, the increasingly requested jumbo chocolate fudge cupcake Owen all-too-proudly named Walker's Big Hit like it was his firstborn son.

He slipped his head through the neck strap of his apron. The ties curled on the floor.

She made a rotating motion with her finger.

He turned a practiced one-eighty, and she fastened the ties into a simple knot against his taut lower back. In a bakery oozing with delicious scents, she experienced only one—the unmistakable essence of Owen Walker.

Raw power, capable hands, sheer determination.

Disarmingly cute wrapped in that pink apron.

Hands to his waist, she pivoted him to face her. Rather than step back, he moved closer as though forming a huddle out of the two of them.

"How's business today, Seren?"

Good gracious! The way he spoke her name caused her breath to short-circuit. Delight sparkled in his eyes each time he uttered her name as though it brought him pleasure. She blinked, stepped back to break his ability to watch the play of emotion in her eyes—anything to subvert his ability to detect the uptick of her heartbeat. He might assume his hypnotic stare had an effect on her.

It hadn't. None at all.

We're an impossibility.

"I paid rent yesterday. The morning's been steady, picked up strong at midday, and then slowed some."

But when Owen arrived, it'd attracted a trail of women eager to gaze long at her part-time employee. An NFL player in a bakery wrapped in pink was not the average sight. So long as his presence—however temporary—met the need, she'd summon the strength to share her kitchen space and listen to his unsolicited counsel about her business and marketing methodology.

The topic at hand—her prices.

"In order to sustain the upward swing, your next move would be to bring the price down on your cupcakes. Buy one, get one. That kind of thing."

"I can't afford to lower prices further."

Arms folded at his chest, chiseled biceps expanding the ribbed cuff of his white shirt, Owen's look turned serious. "Then, for starters, stop handing product out to homeless people."

"Gabe started it. Comes in every Friday morning, tells me he's run across another person in need, and we offer warm muffins or cupcakes."

"Then let him continue being Good Samaritan at his own expense. And second, add a new coffee blend or pastry of the month—at a fraction of the cost to you. Promote a coffee-pastry favorite combo deal. Provide your loyal base with punch cards where they'll receive a free menu item after, say, six purchases. It's a powerful marketing tool. That'll bring in more clientele, get them hooked. When profits roll in, hike your prices up again."

Speaking of clientele, several entered as if his charm and finesse had seeped through the door and effectively lured a string of new and eager faces.

Captivated, hook in nose. Seeking something special.

Didn't matter if number 91 knew how to bake or not. He was Owen Walker. He could have just as easily sat in the corner, checking his cell.

Inside that thick skull, he also possessed bakery magic enough to draw in an army.

An army she'd needed.

Among the next round of new faces that'd found their way to The Pear Tree was Mrs. Beasley, a former faithful customer. Evidently, she hadn't died, as Serenity had concluded in an effort to console herself.

Though pushing her early seventies, Mrs. Beasley's gaping stare hadn't moved since Owen took her hand in a wallop of a greeting, his overwhelming personality rendering her somewhat catatonic.

Heaven help the dear lady.

Okay, the facts. Owen's involvement enabled Serenity to cover rent and overhead expenses for a few months and boost business. According to Everley, income had been procured enough to stave off closing the shop and give a wink to modernizing equipment. But Serenity had not—no, not ever—intended for Owen's involvement to stir up a hot mess of fanatical feminine gushing.

She gave thought to renewing her CPR certification should she need to revive a fan.

"Care for a Serenity's Special, Mrs. Beasley?" Serenity stooped and slid the display case door aside, chilled air tickling her skin.

A geriatric giggle drenched in absurdity.

Serenity stood.

Mrs. Beasley's gaze kindled into diffidence. "I prefer the jumbo ones. Walker's Big Hit. You can't lose."

Owen took the space beside Serenity and flashed a smile. "And neither can you." His apron, fastened over his barreled chest, morphed into a superhero getup.

Hands bracketed on the ledge, he leaned toward the breathless woman, drawing a rosy blush over her cheeks. Her stance wobbled.

Curds formed in Serenity's stomach.

Unquestionably, the big guy had parted an ominous cloud of concern for the place and poured a nourishing spring rain over it.

But when the whistle blew to hail the start of another season, would The Pear Tree continue to breathe on its own?

Chapter Seven

The first Saturday in May brought a seasonal parade in the Marigny district, adjacent to Serenity's bakery. She closed a few hours early because parades of this magnitude drew spectators who frequented Cajun bistros, bohemian bars, and jazz clubs. The cacophony of brass bands, sidewalk musicians, and club activity often turned into one big block party and rarely translated into paying customers.

But the real reason behind her decision to close early was that she'd challenged Owen to a soccer match—if only to put an end to his incessant mouthing off.

"Football is the favored sport over soccer, Lewis. It's the all-American game."

Number 91 had said one thing too many.

The front door key clutched in hand, she whirled within inches of his solid chest, an impenetrable wall of defense that'd brought grief to many an opposing player, and tipped her gaze. "No way you're better than me."

"There you go, smack-talking, stirring up the competition, Lewis."

"I'll have you know I was team captain for the women's intramural soccer league in college."

Did he know?

The distant look in his eyes substantiated her fears. He set his hands low on his hips as though struggling to retrieve some fragment of a memory. Apparently, there hadn't been much in his mental hardware with her name on it.

Just because she'd clandestinely watched his exposition of muscular athleticism didn't mean he'd shared any inkling of interest in her. She was the forgettable, ordinary girl who'd baked for their study group.

"Show me what you got, Lewis."

He called his escort. "Hey Jude, we're finished up here. Could you give me and Seren a lift over to, uh ..." He angled a glance her direction. "What field?"

"McDougal, youth league ball field."

He gave her a nod and returned his attention to Jude. "McDougal field."

A steely voice of authority sounded through the phone. "Reason, sir?"

"A friendly showcase of one-upmanship."

In a matter of minutes, a sleek silver Bentley— compliments of a handsome salary—stopped outside the bakery. The fearsome driver with close-cut hair held a familiar profile.

Demeanor, stern and commanding, as though on special assignment.

"Is that the helicopter pilot?"

Owen nodded. "Major Jude Buchanan."

"He's somewhat of a serious type."

"He served in the Corps for over a decade. Highly decorated."

"So, an incredibly dangerous, serious type."

"I trust Jude with my stuff, my life. Marines are trained to speak in a singular language. My inability to interpret hasn't hindered our friendship."

"You ever see him smile?"

"The man has seen a lot."

"I guess war doesn't leave a person with much to smile about."

Owing to the car's tight compartment, Serenity wedged herself into the back seat behind Jude, leaving Owen to ride shotgun—the only reasonable option. Enveloped in a rich scent of premium leather, cool against her skin, Serenity shimmied against the middle console. She set an elbow to it, working to still the trembling in her arms and behave like this was an everyday experience.

At McDougal field, Owen opened her door and tugged her to standing. The sun hung as an orange orb in a vast stretch of blue sky pinned in dollops of white and dove-gray clouds.

Jude stood guard aside the car like it held highly classified intelligence. Or explosives.

"Text if you need something, sir."

"Will do," Owen said.

Taking center field, Serenity popped the ball from palm to palm. Hair secured in a ponytail—the ends swished against her neck.

Owen's lazy stride carried an overabundance of self-assurance. "All right, Lewis, show me some stuff."

Stuff. The makings of a pillow. But show him she would. What other girl in the entire universe had been granted an opportunity to outclass the iconic athlete? She pressed the ball to her hip and summoned him with her curled finger and a smile.

He followed her to center field, where she dropped the ball at her feet. "First, you position the ball just inside your feet and move side to side to roll it along, tapping at it, controlling speed, advancing in quick strides as you maneuver the ball left and right to protect it from—"

Owen stepped in, interjected a forceful kick, and sent the ball in a high arc across the field. It spanked the cement steps running between the metal bleachers and tumbled in a succession of pings on a sorry descent before it rolled to its death. "Ah. Missed."

"A little bit, yeah."

His posture wilted. He shook his head slowly. Leaning on one leg, he splayed hands at his wide hips, thighs as trunks above his black and gold athletic shorts.

"The aim isn't to tackle the ball."

"Yes, ma'am. Carry on, Coach."

She dropped the ball at her feet. "I'll stand at one end, and you attempt to block my pass as I approach."

"Blocking I can do."

"Remember, though, I'm not wearing pads, so no bull-rushing."

Delight cascaded through her at those dimples and his photogenic smile.

In swift and practiced movement, she manipulated the ball along the grass using the insides of her feet, positioning herself several yards away. She turned and found him as she left him—waiting and staring, a partial teasing smile—casting a long shadow.

"I can be pretty tricky, so keep your eyes on the ball."

She readied her stance, then skip-hopped and tapped the ball side to side, knees bent just so, hips pitching ... rolling it forward ... pacing herself ... moving in ... closer. Two feet from Owen, she drew her right leg back, swung it forward, and ... *splat!* Colliding against the unmovable mass of his chest, she staggered backward.

In a swift lunge, he secured his arms about her waist and hefted her over the wide perch of his shoulders, where she dangled like a limp rag doll. He jaunted across the field toward the netted goal. She pounded her fists against his back. Wasted effort. He probably couldn't feel it. "Dang it, Walker, I'm not ... a ... football," she hollered over a fizz of effervescent laughter.

Setting her on her feet, he sported a satisfied grin. The slippery slope of desire blared a warning. She turned from the allure of his gaze and needlessly brushed the front of her jersey. "You've got a long way to go before mastering the basics of soccer, Walker."

"Actually, I think I've accomplished a lot today, Lewis."

Seconds ticked endlessly. The heat of his stare intensified.

She glanced away and chewed on her bottom lip. An impish idea bubbled up. She sounded a horrified gasp and cupped one hand to her mouth, pointing with the other. "What is *that?!*"

At the force of her voice, he followed the direction of her arm.

She assaulted the ball with blunt force and sped toward the goal, propelled by the high octane of sure and certain victory.

In mere seconds, Owen's shadow loomed at her heels. The full stretch of his arms encircled her middle. He took her to his chest like he had no intention of letting her go and spun her in dizzying, happy circles.

Elation skittered along her spine, turning her insides into swirls of cream cheese frosting.

"No one gets past the Walker Wall, Lewis," he said in a playful tone.

Deviant giggling slipped past her guard.

He slowed the last rotation and gazed at her as though admiring his prize. Sluggish at first until shifting into something more. He looked deeper, indulging, maybe? The beguiling hues of brown and green in his eyes enticed her to get lost in them.

Their gazes locked, bodies fitted together like puzzle pieces that completed the whole picture. Affection sizzled over his features to convey he somehow enjoyed the closeness.

Enjoyed ... her.

He eased his hold in a tortuously slow downward slide along impressive engineering of toughness, rigor, and determination. Once he had her at eye level, he tightened his grip and halted her descent. Her feet hovered near the turf. The warmth of his breath, the rapid influx of air, his masculine scent—musky and wonderful.

For a millisecond, she wondered if he'd gifted any other woman with that same look. Because this felt in every way like the gush of a man's first experience.

His brows lifted in question. He peered harder, circling a searching gaze over her face, settling on her lips. Vulnerability, eagerness clouded his eyes.

Waiting for permission?

How unlike a man. How unlike what she knew of *this* man.

With millions to his name, Owen could change the world with one social media post to solicit support for any cause he chose to get behind. And yet—the sun serving as a holy witness—the cupcake-baking ballplayer was embracing ... her.

Engulfed by the strength of his arms, she answered his unspoken entreaty and parted her lips. He lowered his head and connected with them as she indulged in the magnificent sweetness of Owen Walker's mouth on hers. Soft and hard and delicious. His hands pressed against her back in what felt like desperation. The taste of salt tingled as she moved in rhythm with his kisses, feathery soft and sweet.

Galaxies beyond what she'd imagined years ago.

Slowly, he withdrew and caressed her with an impossibly sexy smile. His voice swooped low. "I was wrong."

I was a disappointment. Nothing special.

"You've got great skill, Lewis."

Warmth crawled into her neck. Her pulse thudded behind her ears. Because, *no, no, no*. Those kisses were absolutely not supposed to happen.

They could not.

Love held the potential to grow in unexpected, craggy places, but it stood no chance of flourishing between them. She'd already walked these arid places after Dad's accident. And witnessed Everley's suffering when her first husband didn't return from deployment, relegating her to a predictable and passionless existence crunching numbers in Chicago. But when Momma chose Everley as Moreland's heiress and Gabe the one to restore it, a happily ever after was born.

The stuff of romance novels.

Limited to those without missing pieces.

So, no. Dating Owen was a bad idea. It meant sure and certain heartbreak and would expose Serenity to public scrutiny. Dating him put her business—her very soul—at risk. Hence, romantic involvement defeated the whole point of his helping her out.

"Let's take a walk," he said.

Yes, let's abandon this ridiculousness.

He took her hand as they strolled through trails beyond the field. The brief *stupid* kisses had limited their verbiage to shallow observations—the mild temperature and scurrying woodland creatures.

At the trail's end, they emerged near shady sidelines and sat in camp chairs. Sunlight fingered through encroaching cloud cover.

Owen recovered his voice and transitioned to fervent talk about wanting a house full of Walker kids to pass on his DNA.

This had to end.

This shouldn't have started.

If only she hadn't asked … "So, what's your vision for the future? I mean, you can't play forever."

He shirked off the comment. "Maybe I could father the front five. Establish the Walker Power forward."

A soft ring of light circled that enchanting mix of color in his gaze and deepened the kaleidoscope of enigmatic hues.

Stop swimming in his eyes.

Easing back in his chair, he drew a slow glance across the field. "I'd love to have at least one girl to carry on Mom's legacy, her beauty, wisdom, and industrious spirit." A whimsical moan sounded in his throat. "Dad called her Lady Constance."

"She must have been pretty special."

There she went again, acting like she'd not watched every online interview about Owen's mom, including the one where he'd shared about her tragic car accident on the way to one of his games. Seated across from the interviewer, he'd hailed Connie's praises. He'd worn a sleek, black athletic shirt … like the one he was wearing now. The studio lights illuminated his fine lines … like the way the sun broke through passing clouds and highlighted his features.

The subject of his mom always elicited a glint of emotion in his eyes. Rightly so. Crazy in love at 17, Connie Martin married 22-year-old Harvey Blanton Walker at the conception of his career. A woman of strength who knew what she'd signed up for.

"Mom never missed a ball game. Rarely missed practice."

Serenity remembered doing the same in college. But unlike those laughable groupies who'd clustered like lovesick puppies on the bleachers, snug white tank tops lacking ample coverage, she'd dressed appropriately to observe the Owen Walker showcase.

Not that he'd noticed. Nor would it have made a difference if she'd made a spectacle of herself for the hope of his attention.

Serenity held the loaded question, cocked and ready, her heart caught in its crosshairs. "What are your thoughts on adoption?"

Wariness claimed his gaze over the strain of a grin. "Not a fan."

"I think it's a loving option for couples who can't have children."

He shrugged, rotating the heel of his shoe left and right. "But kids aren't like something you can return to customer service if you're dissatisfied. I've known couples who firmly believed God had called them to adopt, but it wrecked their marriage. Why bring in a child when you've got no idea what degree of trauma they've been exposed to?"

Elevating the beauty of adoption would exhaust her, but she had to try. And if no one had had the guts to challenge his beliefs on the subject, now was the time. Because to be a Lewis was to dream big and live life unafraid. At least, this one had.

"We're all created with a need to belong. It's an inseparable part of our design. Why deny a child the opportunity to be made whole again, to find security? Introduce them to a loving God?"

"I don't disagree, but, for me, Mom's memory deserves to be carried on. It's my aim to see that it does."

Her vision pinholed. A jet ripped through the sky.

"It takes an incredibly selfless individual to graft a kid into a family with a different biological design than his parents just so they'll have a place to belong, receive the full right of inheritance," he said.

"What makes you certain you'll be able to father children?"

"I'm fully operational, I assure you, Lewis." His pithy laughter and wink turned her insides into a river of molten caramel and made mush of her need to upend his substandard reasoning. As to whether or not he was—as he'd so gallantly alleged—fully operational, that knowledge would fall to whoever had the pleasure of becoming his wife. In either case, it would never be Serenity's guilt to bear.

It wasn't the explosive kiss Owen and Seren shared that'd turned his mental gears nor the way she'd feverishly matched his passion. Wow. It was the reticence he'd detected in her gaze when he brought up the subject of kids.

For someone devoted to family and a champion of its value, Serenity hadn't expressed any interest for herself.

Why?

Jude returned to the field minutes after Owen called. He opened the door, pushed the seat forward, and stood beside it. Owen placed a hand on Serenity's back as she climbed into the seat like a hand inside a tight glove. She glanced up, pleasuring him with that beautiful face.

He'd encountered countless beautiful faces.

Serenity's was sweet. Her features were delicate, distinct, and her complexion clean and fresh. The makings of a china doll. A powerful feminine charm and self-assurance. Both helpless and independent, like she wanted him desperately but had no need of him. The slaying combo drove him wild.

That or past hits to the head were coming into play. At least his mental gears were turning, reasoning things out. That was good.

He bracketed an arm across the open car door and stared. Too long, maybe. Gaze transfixed, he fit her into a picture framed by family. He conjured an image of a free-spirited, blonde-haired little Walker girl.

Like Mom.

Like Serenity. Geez. Was this the one?

He leaned in to kiss her again.

She drew tight.

"Something wrong?"

"No, no. I'm good." Her smile stopped short of her eyes.

He acquiesced and folded himself into the front seat, Serenity behind him to the left.

As Jude pulled out of the parking lot, the roar of the engine filled the hollowed silence. Owen's thoughts rose above the thunder of horsepower. The mantra he'd once lived by was to take from women what he'd wanted—or what had been freely given. But these relationships always left his soul dark and shallow and threw him into a pit he'd struggled to climb out of. Had kissing her been nothing more than a habitual response to feminine flirtation? Kissing for the sheer pleasure it promised? An impulsive reaction he'd learned from women who'd made it all too evident they desired him? Had his old self muscled in and run amuck over newfound principles?

Maybe Serenity's demeanor dulled because he'd broken employer-employee rules. That had to be it. The arrangement was temporary. He was subservient to her, payment in the form of all-you-can-eat pastries. She'd struck him as one who erred on the side of ethics. A good girl.

Waste no time on girls you have no intention of marrying, Walker.

Pastor Crawford's weighty oratory came after they'd lost a playoff game in overtime, which resulted in Owen's reckless night in LA.

Serenity was different. She came with a wildly different manual. The rogue kisses had upset the cart.

Regret balled in his stomach.

He drew his voice low. "Hey, Seren. Sorry things got out of hand back there."

She whipped a faraway gaze from the window and looked pointedly at him. "Out of hand?"

"Kissing. That was the wrong move."

Jude didn't flinch—a man trained to focus on his mission and go ghost when needed.

"I crossed a line," Owen said. "It won't happen again."

Her level stare only hinted at offense. Beneath the surface, beyond her slow-blinking gaze, she communicated an unrelated concern as though it hadn't been the out-of-bounds kissing that'd bothered her.

And ... she did kiss him back.

But it didn't matter that he found her insufferably difficult to read. Where she was concerned, he didn't need to be reading anything. Beyond these next few months, there wouldn't be anything to hold them together. When she'd started fishing for his thoughts on adoption, it'd raised a wall. He'd always loved kids. They were God's good gifts—all races and abilities and status and income. But he remained fiercely determined to have his own and leave adoption to other folks. It made no sense for God to create him the way he did and give him a fierce passion to pass down his abilities to his own kids yet deny him the very thing his heart desired in the context of a God-centered family.

Her gaze flickered, returning from the gloomy place it'd roamed. "Consider it forgotten."

Easy enough. He'd done it with women before, and he could do it again. The thing was, no woman had ever asked him to forget his kiss.

Jude returned to the French Quarter through a matrix of sluggish streets narrowed by cars parked aside meters. He navigated through jubilant pedestrians to Ursuline Street and pulled into an open spot, two storefronts down.

Owen twisted in his seat, barely able to stretch his body to face her.

"I'd hoped to hang out here a little longer, but I've got foundation emails to answer and camp issues to discuss with Nina."

"I understand. You're under no obligation."

Not sure why that razzed him. Or why she felt he needed to hear the obvious.

"I don't mind it a bit." *Miss it.* "Would love to give more if I could."

She wrinkled her nose in a smile and patted his arm. "Thanks for helping out earlier."

Her gaze darted to the driver's side door, her expression registering confusion. A caged bird. She glanced rapidly between Owen and Jude.

"Sit tight. I'll let you out," Owen said.

Engine idling, he felt himself staring. Thinking. Strategizing.

Considering the next play.

She gave him a side-eye. "Were you thinking you might let me out sometime today or ...?"

Jude drummed his thumbs alternately against the steering wheel. Probably playing the Marine Corps Hymn in his head while he awaited orders. His unwavering display of calm suggested he'd wait an eternity if duty called. The embodiment of loyalty, bravery, and sacrifice.

Owen's thick upper legs mashed against a wide console. He scrubbed a hand along his jaw. Twisting again, he peered back at her. "Would you be willing to teach a soccer clinic one afternoon the second week of June? Eli is participating, and I think he'd get a kick out of it. No pun intended," he said, amused at his wit.

The murmured laugh didn't reach her eyes. "Teach a clinic?"

"Sure. It'd give you the freedom to exhibit your soccer skills without my play-by-play commentary."

"Or tackles?"

He laughed.

"That's a promise, Walker."

"How long were you thinking?"

"One hour. Two tops. I'd have to contact the camp director, see what time slots are open in their schedule, and let you know."

"Does this pay?"

"Name your price."

Contemplation claimed her face, chin and lips taut as her gaze momentarily drifted upward.

One second followed another in a drawn-out silence, the thrumming of his heart a sonic boom behind his ears. "Lewis, this isn't rocket science."

"Give me your secret to Walker's Big Hit."

"Forget it," he spit back.

"Then no deal."

Knees jammed against Jude's seat, she squirmed and strained to reach the door handle.

"All right, I'll tell you."

Her wrestling to exit stilled.

"But not until after the clinic."

"Before."

He playfully cuffed her shoulder. "After."

The set of her jaw firmed. Her jeweled eyes went ablaze to warn him he'd pushed her to the limit. "Before."

Silly girl. Limits merely incited his inner bull rusher to trample through them.

"After. Or I ... quit."

It'd been no more than an attempt to razz her, but the struggle to cough up the ultimatum wasn't lost on him. Maybe not on her.

She wriggled her slim hand to unlatch the door, still out of reach, and sat back in a huff. Consternation rang in her countenance. "Okay, keep your stupid secret recipe. Mine is superior anyway."

"Which is why you asked for mine."

Reaching again.

Extending his arm, he placed a gentle hand on her arm, massaging the warm skin. "So, clinic?"

She lolled a surrendered glance at him, all trace of haughty mug erased. In its place, her soft and buttery smile. The face of an angel and the smell of sunshine, lavender, and roses.

His gaze stilled a little too long on her perfectly sculpted lips. Wanting another taste.

"I'd be honored to conduct a clinic. For Eli."

Team Walker for the win.

Chapter Eight

Serenity's bakery presently held a sorry sum total of four customers who sipped designer coffees, nibbled on pastries, or sat in deep concentration in front of screens. May brought flowers all right, but along with it came a persistent urge that wouldn't let up.

Surreptitiously, she slipped out her cell and clicked on the app.

Top ten defensive plays in the last six seasons. Owen Walker, the phenomenon. "Yes, that's the one," she whispered.

Thus far, she'd watched the video montage enough to have memorized every move, the line of his body, the crouch, snarled expression, right hand steepled as he awaited the snap. Several games would have had a different outcome if it weren't for his bull-rushing ferocity, punishing tackles, and the signature Walker dominance. Opposing teams had little to no answers against his double-team offensive lineups, where he scrambled through to sack the QB. He'd customarily bob his head to rouse accolades, mighty proud of his play.

Who wouldn't be? He was Owen Walker, her blessed counterpart—for now.

In mid-July, he'd return to the sport he was meant to play, and his flexible schedule would return to its rigidity.

He'd reconnect with teammates and reactivate those God-given abilities out on the field. A whale back in his ocean rather than confined to a fishbowl.

A very fragile thread wound Serenity and Owen's vastly opposing worlds together. Pressure at either end threatened to snap and end in disaster.

"Go, go, go ..." She thrust a victory fist into the air. "Yes! Seventh sack in a single game."

The weight of a stare, accompanied by a lead-heavy sigh, plucked her attention from her cell to a waiting customer whose expression suggested he'd reached his limit. His fingers tapped on the counter. "If it's sports that's captured your attention, you might ought to go to Bakery World. They've got flat screens in every corner. I came here to get away from all that racket."

This was no time for a haughty rebuttal. It might cause her rising Trip Tips ratings to plummet when they'd swooped from 400 to over 800 since April. Customer reviews were positive, even enthusiastic. She bent to snag the Serenity's Special requested by the paying customer, placed it in a decorative box, and bagged a dozen mini-sized cinnamon pear muffins. "Sorry to keep you waiting, sir. Coffee's on the house."

A strategy taken right out of Owen Walker's "How to save a girl's bakery" playbook.

Over the next twenty minutes, she served clientele while Brooke managed the coffee machine in Kourtney's absence and whipped up special orders.

An austere gentleman entered and trekked his gaze around the interior. Grave concentration skated over his defined features. Dressed in a crisp, tailored suit, he bore the look of someone who'd singlehandedly funded the whole of New Orleans.

He approached the counter. "Give me a Red Eye brew and three dozen of your jumbo-sized Walker's Big Hit cupcakes, please, ma'am."

A nervous giggle bubbled up. "Three dozen? That seems a bit much."

"Not for one who needs three dozen."

"I mean, have you seen the size?"

Clearly, the man hadn't considered his troublesome order would nearly wipe out her inventory mere hours before closing.

"Aren't you in the business to *make* money?" he chided.

Brooke jabbed an elbow into Serenity's ribs and pinned a frozen smile to her face. She capped the steamy coffee he'd ordered and set it on the counter.

Mr. Austere sounded a disgruntled huff, leaned in, and concentrated his gaze. "Miss ... uh ..."

"Serenity."

He nodded acknowledgment. "Name's Warren Murdock of Murdock Enterprises."

Said like she should know.

"Now, if you please. Three dozen Walkers." He glanced at the silver Rolex encircling his wrist. "I've got an investors' meeting, and, well, they're a hungry bunch."

"Where'd you park?"

"It's a challenge, to be sure, but luckily, I was able to find a metered spot on Ursuline."

Gratitude at his good fortune buoyed her tone. "Wonderful. My team will deliver them directly to your car."

Brooke took payment, and Serenity slipped to the back to collect nine specialty-size cupcake boxes. With Lettie's help, she inserted the jumbo cutout liners and deftly assembled them. She'd leave the four remaining Big Hits in the display case out front and package those he'd prepared and refrigerated yesterday.

Once the boxes were eased into Mr. Murdock's car, she and Brooke waved him off. Questions nagged. Was he a safe driver? Would he do everything possible to ensure those creations were well cared for? Did he appreciate their value?

Will those babies be loved just as they are?

Afternoon had come and gone. No sign of or word from Owen. Not that Serenity needed him. She and her team had handled the unexpected order seamlessly, and when Kourtney had come in for her shift, she'd managed the coffee bar and served patrons.

The ripple effect of the interest Owen had generated since March was palpable. The Pear Tree had been resuscitated and thrived in his absence. That was the whole point. Nothing more. If Serenity repeated the mantra with enough frequency, it'd crowd out the space she'd stupidly made for him in her heart.

Dumb, reckless kisses.

And yes, today went remarkably well. It fortified her ability to bear up when Lettie became short of breath. Serenity turned off the mixer when the precious soul placed a tentative hand on her heart and leaned over the counter near the walk-in refrigerator. Concern filtered into Lettie's blackening gaze. Deep creases formed on her brow. "Miz Serenity. My heart, it's a flutterin' extra much today. I best go home and rest up awhile."

Serenity placed a hand on Lettie's thin shoulder. "Sure, sure. It's been a crazy day. Let me drive you to the doctor."

"Naw, naw. I'm just feelin' a might woozy is all. You needs to be here." The authority in her tone belied her small frame.

With effort, Serenity yielded to the woman's demands, though she insisted on walking with her the several blocks to a residential parking lot where she'd parked.

Four hours later, Lettie called—her voice barely above a whisper. "Miz Serenity. I's letting you know a call into the doctor landed me at the hospital for a few tests. I'm here at home now. I'll be okay. Just feelin' puny."

Shock seized Serenity's insides. "What happened?"

"Mild heart attack, they think."

She tugged off her apron and tossed it onto the counter. "I'll be right over."

"No need to fuss over this old woman."

But fuss she would. Because Lettie was family. Lettie was special.

Brooke and Kourtney had already left for the day. She called Owen. Clanking metal and muffled music sounded through the phone.

"Hey, Owen. I've got a situation here at the bakery."

"What's up?" His breath was labored, voice punching through the din of what sounded like a crowded fitness center.

"According to doctors, Lettie has suffered a mild heart attack."

"Oh wow. Sorry to hear that."

"Me, too. Right now, she's at home. Alone. Brooke and Kourtney have already come and gone, so, if possible, I need you to close up today."

"I'm finishing up a workout at the athletic complex over in Metairie, but I could be there in about a half hour or so."

"Thanks, Owen. I appreciate it. You're a big help."

Very big.

Once she had Owen in play and reviewed the closing procedure with him, she accepted his engulfing hug. The compassionate strokes along her back diffused her fear. His prolonged hold suggested he needed reassurance as much as she did. She'd successfully dodged the hint of interest playing in his eyes before leaving her place in his capable care.

Outside, the moist warm air clung to her face. She drove to Lettie's housing unit in New Orleans East. Redevelopment of the region after extensive hurricane damage years ago still lagged despite the increasingly affluent population that'd returned to the area.

In all the years Serenity had known Lettie, she'd owned little, lived marginally, and loved big.

Inside the quiet of Lettie's dimly lit bedroom, she tip-toed past dark paneled walls over to the bed. The faithful soul rested on her back. Her fingers curled over the top edge of a quilted coverlet she'd drawn to her neck.

Slowly, her lids blinked open. The drag of a weathered smile crept across her mouth. "Hey der, Miz Serenity. Sorry to be such a bother."

"You're never a bother, sweet lady."

A corner window gave a smudged view of the outside. She took a nearby chair and moved it to sit beside the bed. Outside, cicadas buzzed as a shaft of sun moved in across the room, blanketing the coverlet. "I'm very thankful you're okay."

Serenity's voice withered. She drew a faraway stare to the ceiling. A tear slipped into her ear.

The scramble to keep the bakery open had required an all-hands-on-deck effort. Serenity hadn't stopped to consider the effect the additional hours might have on Lettie.

Serenity took Lettie's folded, gnarled hand in hers and stroked it, caressing protruding veins. "Am I working you too hard, Lettie? Is that what's strained your heart?"

Mischief and a hint of guilt rose in her countenance. Her lips thinned into a mile-wide grin. "I gots a long history of heart problems, Miz Serenity, but it could be I stared a might too long at Mista Walker."

Serenity chuckled, amused at Owen's ability to take up space in a room he didn't even occupy.

"Maybe all the glory that man radiates weakened this ole' heart."

Disconcerted huffs chugged up. "He's hardly your type, Lettie."

"I guess so, but if a woman's reaching the end of her days, she oughta be looking at somethin' desirable."

A fuzzy fog landed over her heart. The vision of a million tomorrows with Owen assaulted common sense.

"Never you mind me anyways, Miz Serenity. I'll leave the lookin to you."

"I have no need to look. At him or anyone else."

"Hogwash. I seen it coming. Something about the way he looks you over."

"There's nothing unusual about Owen Walker looking at a woman."

"This lookin' is different. He's been scrutinizin' you. Sizing you up for something. Now I knows what it be."

"What's that?"

"He wants you for his wife."

"Oh, for pity's sake, Lettie. You know his past."

"That was way back when. What I see today is the clearness of the Lawd in his eyes, an old soul hollowed out and made clean. Restored to its original design."

Serenity had detected evidence of such in brief video clips on social media, Owen rallying people to be bold and unashamed of their faith in God. To live with intention—a driving force for change in their sphere of influence, however large or small.

Lettie gave Serenity's hand a couple tugs. "I say he be NFL's *New* Man of the Year."

No argument there. The commentary of today wasn't the Owen she'd met in college. Although he'd always had a kind heart, an eye for those in need ... delivering Christmas gifts anonymously to underprivileged kids over winter break. Throughout his career, he hadn't taken advantage of the opportunities his wealth afforded him. The first evidence of heart change was spearheading a fundraising campaign for hurricane relief. To jump-start the effort, he'd given a generous $100,000 of his own money, soliciting double that.

For his unbridled selflessness, the league had eagerly awarded him the coveted Man of the Year.

The one unmistakable common denominator about Owen is that he loved kids—only now he knew their value and worth could be found in God.

Owen Walker was a rare and precious find who'd unabashedly said he thought she was all kinds of wonderful, sealed it with a kiss. But he didn't know everything about her. A swell of tears hazed her eyes.

Most couples spent a lifetime discovering each other, unearthing treasure, and keeping the flames of romance alive. But if one of them had a condition that made a happy union impossible, then what?

A breakup. A very *painful* one.

"If you would, Miz Serenity, read to me from the Psalms. These spectacles are of little use. Them pills they gives me must have changed the pressure behind my eyeballs."

Taking a finger to the bridge of her nose, Serenity dotted her watery eyes and sniffed. She took Lettie's worn Bible in hand. The weight of it felt like something of great worth.

"I likes Psalm one thirty-nine," Lettie said. "Jes flip open to where the ribbon hangs out."

Serenity tugged on the silky, burgundy place marker and opened the treasured book. The pages were wrinkled in ink, multiple passages underlined with notes and dates scrawled in the margins.

She angled the book toward the open window. "You knit me together in my mother's womb. I praise you because I am fearfully and wonderfully made. Your works are wonderful. I know that full well."

She blinked over the text, letting the truth diffuse into her pores.

"Maybe God moved me out of the way for such a time as this so you'd see something, Miz Serenity."

In the years Serenity had known Lettie, the woman's rasped words didn't always fit together in a sensible way. But Serenity had learned to take them into her heart and whisk them around awhile. More often than not, clumps of truth eventually blended into her thoughts. In this moment, it created a clear picture of a deeply conflicted woman haunted by inadequacy.

Unfit for anyone.

Different.

Lettie's lids lowered, the effect of any manner of pain relief. She turned a hollowed, angular cheek to her pillow and succumbed to peaceful slumber.

She took Lettie's hand, stroked it gently, and worked up a whisper. "Oh, Lettie, my heart just can't bear to tell him."

Each day Owen had been involved in the bakery strengthened a dormant desire. He'd have to perform at a consistently higher level to match Serenity's standard. To develop the stamina for the rigors involved in prospering the place.

But with sports camps in full swing across the country throughout the summer—and the onslaught of league training camp in July—he questioned the wisdom in coaxing it along. If only images of the interior hadn't persistently invaded his head space ... the favored courtyard that functioned as somewhat of an art gallery bathed in natural light on sunny days ... its beautiful owner. Sometimes he viewed thoughts of Serenity and the bakery as an intrusion. Other times he relished it.

On days when Serenity had scheduled him for a couple hours, he'd stayed three or four. Days when she'd insisted that he wasn't needed, he'd stop in anyway—if for no other reason than to meet and greet patrons and slip into ownership role and wear it like a custom-tailored jersey.

He'd let himself play the part of a man free to pursue a different career.

With greater frequency, she'd run short of his cupcakes. On those days, she'd bless him with a look of relief, wave a hand toward the display case, and say, "Aptly named, Walker. I'm about out of your Big Hits again." Then she'd grace him with a smile, one cheek hitched in irresistible helplessness, and beg, "Make more?"

"You bet," he'd say, tweaking her nose.

Then she'd drizzle a sweet sigh of gratitude when he'd slip on his apron and get to work. Because The Pear Tree required perseverance, self-denial, hard work, sacrifice, and dedication to excellence.

Like football. Like life.

Lettie being on injured reserve—God bless and sustain that precious woman—afforded him the freedom to run around on a vastly different playing field.

Owen and Serenity had developed a rhythm. They'd learned each other's strengths and weaknesses and worked as a team that'd outclassed competitors. In greater measure, he'd grown to like the idea. More so, he believed in it. The two of them together, in business and in life, could be a supremely successful venture.

Owen didn't engage in opportunities he didn't believe he could win.

Team Walker had winning written all over it.

A yearning to step off the field gripped like a new pair of defensive gloves. Even on days like today when he'd joined Serenity at 4:00 a.m.—two hours ahead of opening—and stayed to meet demand until closing.

"What in the world are Level 10 meetings?" She'd bristled at his suggestion.

"It's a framework to help business leaders execute strategies and meet goals. We'd keep it to once a week, starting and ending on time. The team identifies the most important issues to tackle, and everyone participates in decisions and solutions. We'd repeat the plays that worked and ditch those that didn't. At the end of the meeting, we each rate the success of the meeting on a scale of 1 to 10 and walk out with a clear resolution."

"Spoken like a defensive end."

Her playful smile set off a fiery passion. He took her arms and stroked them, the feel of velvety skin shivering through him. "Spoken like one who cares."

Disquiet moved across her face like a thundercloud drifting in front of the sun. Hesitation collected in her gaze. Intuition blew a whistle inside his brain.

It was a brutal test of fortitude to refrain from lifting her off the ground in one swift movement to face him, feathering a succession of tender kisses over her lips. To remember again the taste of her kiss, draw out the unabated passion caged inside her.

Offsides. Regroup. Wait for the go-ahead.

In the second week of June, seasonable heat smothered the first day of camp. Overcast skies hinted at late afternoon rain. Jude took several days off to go fishing which left Owen to drive to Matt Savoie Soccer Complex on the west side of City Park. Orleans Canal bordered the park to the west and Bayou St. John to the east. Four raised brick columns marked the entrance to the soccer pavilion that shaded several picnic tables on either side of a common area. Activity buzzed over City Park's athletic fields.

Since Hurricane Katrina ravaged the massive acreage in 2005, aggressive restoration efforts returned the park to its former glory and enticed hundreds of daily visitors. The smell of moist earth emanated from the turf as Owen exited his car. He'd conducted his usual visit to greet his camp kids throughout the various athletic fields—baseball, lacrosse, volleyball, and rugby.

Owen saved the best for last.

The foundation had secured a well-rounded soccer coaching staff comprised of players on the New Orleans Jesters, a pro soccer league. He could have lined up any number of them to conduct an hour-long clinic. So why Serenity? Maybe kissing her bore evidence of a lapse in mental judgment. Crucial games were lost that way.

Was his involvement with Serenity dulling discernment? This morning's verse on his Bible app taught that abounding in the knowledge of God's love resulted in greater discernment. Pastor Crawford had often drilled into him that scripture was a living, breathing thing, able to judge the thoughts and attitudes of the heart. Once he'd gotten hold of that, he'd viewed the Bible as a holy playbook to assist him as he maneuvered through the field of life. Though progress had been sluggish over the last four years, he committed to memorizing God's word.

Temptation had been his greatest opponent. It assigned beauty to what God had clearly labeled wrong. His passion for the game, a family of his own—a huddle of kids that looked like him and played like him—weren't godless desires. But had his utter refusal to consider life without them become an object of worship?

A harsh whistle rent the air.

From his place of quiet observation near the bleachers, Owen turned his attention along the sidelines to Reidland Jones, greater New Orleans's sports-camp director.

Wearing dark track pants and a dark blue golf shirt bearing the embroidered Walker Foundation logo, Reidland gathered over one hundred ten-to-fifteen-year-old boys to center field. An array of pro soccer players stood in arced formation behind them. Eli, the golden child, sat front and center. His toothy smile and rapt attention set him apart.

Grab that kid a halo.

Positioned behind Reidland and to his right, Serenity waited for an introduction. She held a soccer ball out front of her and shifted her stance left and right in readiness. Unruffled. Confident and eager to assist.

Outfitted in a white jersey and shorts, pads snug beneath knee-high gold socks, Serenity fastened her hair in a tight ponytail and sported a turquoise sweatband.

"All right, listen up, boys," Reidland said. "We've got a special guest for you this afternoon."

At that, Serenity moved in beside him.

Eli's hand shot up in a wave. She returned a grin and jutted her chin at him.

"Serenity Lewis played intramural soccer in college, and she's a friend of Owen Walker."

Cheers erupted.

"At his request, she's here to show you guys some killer skills. Please give her your undivided attention."

Reidland stepped back and gestured to Serenity, who moved to the front of the group.

"How's everybody doing this afternoon?"

Enthusiastic responses floated over the group.

In stealthy footfall, Owen moved from the bleachers and crossed her direction, crushing underfoot a fit of envy over her exceptional skill at this foreign sport.

"I'm going to demonstrate passing, shooting, dribbling, and ball control drills for you guys. Sound like a plan?"

Eli cupped a hand to his mouth. "Yes!"

"That's the spirit, superstar," Owen whispered as he approached Serenity to her left, avoiding her direct line of sight.

"For starters, dribbling. In order to beat your opponent down the wing, it's an essential skill to master. Dribbling through cones develops the ability to control the ball through close quarters."

As Owen neared Serenity, several players took a hard influx of air. When he touched a finger to his lips, they sat as granite boulders.

He shadowed her, inhaling her scent.

With a jerk, she turned her gaze upward and squinted to meet his eyes.

"Well now, look who's blessed us with his presence." She worked haughty tease in her tone.

Like trained seals, a few boys on the right called out, "Owen!" Others on the left readily answered with "Walker!"

Serenity's gaze darted left and right while they pinged his name back and forth for several rounds.

Her crystal blues dimmed and took on a severe cast.

He shrugged. "They're excited to see me."

At her glower, he faked injury, doubling over.

She turned to the campers and raised a stiff hand until they quieted down.

"Listen up, guys. I know your hero is here but keep the focus on me."

A flurry of masculine snickers pecked the air.

She turned to Owen and leveled a peeved stare. "Did you come to learn from the best or demonstrate your ability to become invisible?"

"Me? Invisible?" He raised brows of mock outrage.

"Right. That's an impossibility." She shook her head stiffly, the electrified white gold wires of her hair brushing along her neck. "Then how about you make yourself scarce while I conduct the clinic?"

His wink resulted in her adorable, wrinkled frown.

A little goading had elicited a smile. He'd goad more often.

He turned to the boys. "What's your call? Should I do the lady's bidding?"

"For the good of the relationship, you'd better get outta here," Eli said.

"Then I'm out. Love you, guys."

He'd shelve his routine pep talk for later—the one where he addressed the importance of being unafraid to try things, to find the sport one was created to play, slipping in a call for godly integrity on the field. Because God had given him a platform, and he'd speak on it unashamed until his last breath.

Back at the sidelines a few yards behind Serenity, Owen turned to see her glance over her shoulder as though she'd waited to gift him with the fullness of her one-of-a-kind smile before she gave undivided attention to the group and morphed into coach mode. "Now then, passing ..."

For the duration of the clinic, she taught technique and maintained their rapt attention. She'd conducted herself fearlessly and showcased natural agility. The makings of pro-league professionalism and grace.

Beautiful. But not in a striking, gorgeous cover model way. Serenity owned an unfettered, innocent beauty. Simple and pure, as though unstained by the world's trappings. Downright refreshing to the thirsty.

Again, he found himself staring, immobilized by her finesse.

Wrong play, Walker.

"Next, shooting." She popped the ball onto one knee, sending it up a few feet, then performed alternating knee touches several times in seamless motion before clutching it to her side.

Lucky ball.

He placed a hand aside his mouth. "Show off."

She whirled to face him, blue eyes blazing. She thrust the ball at his chest.

He caught it. Barely. "You're quick, Lewis."

"And you're determined to disrupt my clinic, Walker."

Laughter bubbled up over the group, warming his insides.

He flitted a gaze at Eli, who embodied one very happy kid. Giving soccer a try this year—because he could.

Ball in one hand, Owen drop-kicked it back to Serenity, who sprung to the left and retrieved the ball on its way past her head.

"You done causing a ruckus?"

"For now."

As he stepped back, he swept a hand in an underhand motion and let her have the stage.

"All right, eyes over here, guys. Back to shooting. When you receive a well-weighted pass from your teammates, this skill is far easier if attackers create space ..." She gave Owen a side-eye and returned to the group. "As for headers, you don't always have to make contact. Sometimes closing down the opponent's angles is enough for them to make a mistake."

Another of her pointed glances, coupled with an exaggerated head tilt. "A good defender knows when to pressure and when to back off."

"Point well taken, Miss Lewis."

"Good."

Next, she directed the coaches along each of the four corners of the field to arrange cones and conduct drills. Following a succession of roll-overs and scissor kicks, she instructed campers to work on dribbling through the cones using the insides of both feet.

Owen itched to join in, imperceptibly moving his feet according to her instruction. "Outside, inside and outside of the right foot, inside and outside of the left," he mimicked.

No. Not his turf.

But a girl like that could almost convince a guy to hang up his helmet and consider protecting what was left of himself to give her a life free from what Dad currently suffered.

To dissuade that guy, such a person would have to be really special.

That determined girl over there, ponytail forever swishing, engaging his kids, spiking the ball toward the open goal?

She was special.

One of a kind.

Chapter Nine

A *hmmm* noise rose in Owen's throat. He left Serenity to do her thing on the field and made customary rounds to each group. Typically, showering the campers with pithy words of motivation—his favorite part—came easy. But his limbs went heavy, bearing the weight of a sinking stomach. A headache pricked at his temple.

"So, yeah. Fight to win, listen to your coach ... be good to yourself and your teammates, and, you know, keep your eye on the goal."

Lame. But how could he motivate them when his brain whirled in dizzying circles?

A distraction, that's what Serenity had become. She'd inadvertently blurred his focus on clearly established career goals.

Girls had come and gone. He excelled at forgetting them. Not this one.

He'd told Derek about last month's kiss and how, ever since, thoughts of Serenity had continued to intrude. As unforgiving as a Sharpie marker.

On the way back to his car, he rubbed a hand through his hair. His muscles tightened. He tilted his head side to side, rolling the tension out of his neck.

Perspective was in order.

That evening, Owen met Derek at a favorite sports bar. Being a cop required the skill of an objective, cool-headed individual. Derek exceeded this capability. Touted as Harvey Walker's Pro Set when they were growing up, the two brothers formed somewhat of a side-by-side, split-back formation. A visual to ensure Dad's legacy would be manifested in his sons. The pressure of public attention thrust them into a spotlight neither had asked for.

Derek shrank from it. Owen stood taller.

They'd had their share of fights over stupid stuff, but once Mom got wind of it, she'd step into threat space, fists swinging to pry them apart. She'd made them sit shoulder to shoulder on the sofa until they'd reconciled.

Sloppy apologies never met her standard.

They'd maintained regular communication through it all—Derek's injury in college that clipped any chance at playing pro and Owen's relocation to LA as a first-round draft pick for the Rams. Mom's death when Owen was thirteen had drawn them close, and Dad's worsening symptoms had tightened them into a knot.

The Walkers had also excelled at hiding the ugly truth about their financial devastation after Harvey's income dried up—the spoils of war. In the public eye, they'd upheld the picture of a wealthy NFL family when really, they'd increasingly relied on the church, charitable handouts, and thrift stores.

Owen had entrusted the truth to Pastor Donovan and Blitz, the family dog.

Minding Derek's bulky utility belt, Owen took him in a swift hug. "Hi, little-big brother."

"Hello, big-little brother."

"Hungry?"

"Starved."

They sat near the front entrance so Derek's ever-vigilant gaze could surveil the surroundings. Contemporary music strummed through corner speakers. Flashy flat screens lined a far wall beyond the bar and broadcasted games. Track lights ran alongside a vast network of metal cylinders within the warehouse ceiling.

The waitstaff, who went by Evan, delivered their order—a heaping platter of glazed wings bearing the heady scent of garlic, teriyaki, and barbecue. "Let me know if you need anything else."

Answers. He needed answers.

"Thank you, sir." Derek pinched a wing between his fingers.

From Evan's pale coloring and flatlined response in Owen's presence, he must have just come off a boat from Iceland or some equally remote location that lacked access to the internet.

Owen piled several wings on his plate and brought one to his mouth.

"So, about Serenity—"

"That's telling." Derek welded his stare on Owen.

Let the interrogation begin.

A hard swallow bobbed at Owen's throat. He squeezed his eyebrows together. "What's it telling?"

"You like her."

"Not to shoot holes in your investigative skills, but I'd already told you that over the phone."

"Even if you hadn't, I'd already detected it."

Turbulence rumbled through him. Owen shifted in his seat. The table's edge pressed against his middle. "How so?"

"That look."

Owen sat upright. Heat moved in waves around his neck with a fierce intensity that exceeded the seconds before NFL draft announcements. His brain throbbed. "Look?"

Lids hooded, Derek pierced a finger at Owen. "That one, right there."

Busted.

"I didn't advance in my career without mastering the skill of pressing a person of interest until he spilled, Owen."

"A well-deserved promotion." Owen gave a low laugh. He clasped jittery hands on the table. "Serenity isn't anything like the women I've always been attracted to. She's good, you know?"

Severe disapproval captured Derek's countenance. He sat ramrod straight, eyes firing rounds. "You didn't."

Owen shook his head in rapid succession. He waved his hands as if subduing the snarling menace of a Belgian Malinois. "No, no. She's good in the true sense of the word. Her character, the stuff she's made of."

Derek's shoulders eased. He sipped his drink and set it down. Elbows on the table, he folded his arms. "Given your track record, I suspect you think you're unworthy of a good woman."

"No. Not really. I mean, as a Christian, my understanding is that I'm fully redeemed from past mistakes."

"But do you believe it?"

"I'm trying." Transformative thinking had come slowly. Drips of water over a rock, eroding the past. "Serenity's got this crazy attractive innocence about her."

Unmarked by the world and yet the intoxicating tease of a hard-core romantic throbbed behind her crystal blues as though she'd unleash reckless abandon if the right switch was flipped. She all but challenged him to search for it.

If only he could recover his innocence, taste its sweetness. Serenity was the closest he'd come. She was like that one cupcake behind the glass that said, "You've never enjoyed anything like this before. Just try to resist me."

"What confounds me is that we knew each other in college, but she never really blew my hair back. I mean, she looked entirely different then—short, blunt haircut, tinted this weird shade ... I don't remember."

A steeled gaze. "Is memory becoming an issue?"

"No." Maybe a little. "We reconnected at Moreland over a year ago for the restoration effort. She'd modernized her look, but none of our interactions left a lasting impact."

He blew out a shaky breath. His stomach bunched. "Serenity dissed me when I showed up at the place instead of Callahan, left me feeling like my presence was offensive. But now, I can't see anything but this beautiful, intelligent woman."

Unforgettable.

"God gave you a new set of eyes."

He let the truth settle and penetrate the guard of his heart. "Problem is, my reason for being at the bakery is strictly business. And it ends when training camp starts next month."

"You could still help out, right? I mean, camp isn't a death sentence."

Owen swiped the grease off his fingers and fisted the napkin in his palm. "Schedule's tight. I'm focused. At that point, I've got no mental space for anything outside of the gridiron."

"Then why date her?" Derek cleaned the meat off another wing. The question was delivered with a lidded stare and inflection that suggested Derek knew the answer but prodded Owen to shoulder the weight of discernment.

"She's incredible."

"Detail that for me." Derek rotated his sweating mug between his thumb and forefinger.

"She's fun. She's creative. She's generous. All of which I love in a girl, and she looks like and reminds me of Mom."

The truth came out in a whoosh of heated breath.

Derek stilled a wing at his mouth and caught Owen's gaze. Held it. He dropped the bare bone onto a plate. Then he did that thing where he balled a fist inside the palm of his other hand and massaged it like a boulder he'd inevitably grind to dust until he achieved satisfactory answers. "Looks fade. Our bodies fail."

He refused to consider it and held fast to the possibility of outsmarting longevity. To be that one guy who'd played past his prime and continued to impress.

"If I start dating Serenity, I'd like to have your blessing."

"Does she love God?"

"She's generous."

"So was Al Capone."

"Be serious, Derek."

"I'm very serious. In addition to his crimes, Capone opened one of the world's first soup kitchens, serving 120,000 meals to the poor and needy in the Windy City. I repeat. Is she a believer?"

Dang.

"All right, officer, lower your weapon. I'll ask."

Derek's shoulders shook in restrained laughter.

The untimely injury Derek sustained had shielded him from the temptations that came with being in the big leagues. He'd remained devoted to his wife Marianne, his high school sweetheart who, today, was a social media influencer and manager of a non-profit organization. They didn't have children, but according to Derek, they were in no rush and simply enjoyed the process of trying.

"Consider this, big-little bro. On those days when we're looking in the mirror and don't like what we see, it's essential to know we've married a girl who loves God first and will, in turn, love us for what's inside without exacting conditions."

Conditions. That. Right there. Over time, outward appearance faded, but God looked at the heart. Given Owen's hits to the head over the course of eight years, he could justifiably ask that Serenity place no conditions on him. But could he equitably offer it?

Love endures all things.

Derek's gaze went ruthlessly level. "Let me get this straight. You have feelings for her, yet the two of you aren't even dating."

"Crazy, I know."

"And you kissed her."

"She kissed me back."

His lip went into a grim line as though he'd shirked off a comeback and returned to fact-finding. "You have no idea if she's a Christian, even though you know it's essential to hook up with someone who is in order for there to be any merit in the relationship or a shot at going the distance—"

"She talks about God, church."

"Aw, c'mon." Derek slapped his palm on the table. Plates shifted, clanked, and rattled. "So does the devil." He shook his head and chewed vigorously on another wing, then dropped the bone onto his plate. "I suggest you circle back and establish what foundation you'd both be building on. From there, determine whether or not it'll hold. Otherwise, the relationship is apt to crumble when things get tough."

The wisdom scrambled into formation behind a virtual line of scrimmage in Owen's head.

Derek's voice hovered low and direct. "Because I'm detecting something more here."

The ticking seconds of quiet expanded the booth.

Above the thudding of his pulse behind his ears, Owen registered shrill whistles and squeaking shoes sounding off flatscreens.

"You're falling in love with her."

Owen glanced away and rubbed his forefinger and thumb over his scruffy chin. Turning back to Derek, the answer rushed to his tongue. "Yeah. Maybe I am."

A week ago Friday—the last day of Serenity's soccer clinic—she'd thought Owen might offer for the two of them to go out. To recap. A purely platonic wrap-up of how things went. But he'd made plans to meet his brother Derek at a local brewery. Last week, he'd had multiple obligations and spent sparse time at the bakery.

"Today, I'm all yours, Seren."

In the confines of an oven-warmed kitchen, Serenity worked alongside Owen to pipe frosting over the last cooled batch of lemon cupcakes. Every now and then, he'd lean her direction, study her technique, and give it a try—or suggest a better way.

"If you use this flatter star piping tip with narrow slits and hug the case of the cupcake as you squeeze the buttercream, working it toward the center, it gives you a nice ruffle swirl."

She examined his design. A fresh new look. "Oh, I really like that."

The affirmation seemed to square Owen's shoulders, an expression awash in pleasure.

"I've also found that if you let the butter melt on its own and stir it, you get a thicker batter. The cupcakes stay moist longer when you brush a sugar syrup over the tops when they're still warm."

He was on a roll.

She welcomed it.

Her mouth opened in wonderment—mind drained of all concern. Weightlessness flushed glowy sensations down to her feet. Her body went slack. He could have spent an hour teaching the elementary mechanics of measuring flour, and she'd have happily played the apprentice.

But at what point had she let the jagged edges of renegade euphoria rip open possibility?

At this juncture, he'd already spent an hour longer than he'd claimed he could afford and offered to prepare baked goods for tomorrow. Today, however, he displayed an unusual restlessness. She might even label his behavior ... nervous.

A man of his notoriety nervous? Around her?

Cute and adorable and vulnerable—nothing the media had ever seen.

She detected very little of the veteran athlete's easy confidence and charm—the secret sauce which had attracted many new and committed patrons to her bakery and, admittedly, her own fragile soul when Brooke and Justin's romance blossomed, and she'd let her mind conjure an impossible dream.

The kind of quirky, awkward behavior a guy exhibits right before he asks a girl out on—

"Hey, Seren." He set the piping bag down and turned to her. "Would you like to go out for coffee?"

Thoughts swirled like leaves caught in a vortex of chilly air.

But, uh ... "Coffee?" She gave him a side-eyed smile.

He squeezed his eyes shut and sheepishly shook his head. His dimples deepened inside a crooked grin, cheeks a slight shade of pink.

His shoulders shook in easy laughter. "Okay, that was stupid."

Adorable.

"How about we take a picnic lunch over to City Park on Sunday afternoon, rent kayaks, and ride the carousel."

A thirteen-hundred-acre park featuring two football stadiums, multiple athletic fields, and a museum, and the big guy suggested they ride a carousel. It hadn't escaped her notice that he'd given this outing some thought despite his effort to pull off the guise of spontaneity. A man of his caliber didn't reach his level of success by thinking on a whim.

"Is this a date?"

He took a step, the awkward movement of a novice. The feel of someone whose approach with women didn't involve a prolonged, respectful, step-wise approach to asking her out. The appearance of one who feared her rejection worse than being cut and released. "It could be."

The vagueness had her all elbows. "That's not what I asked. Is this a date?"

"Persistent little cuss, aren't you?"

In one flicker of a second, Walker's inner hero rallied, cape and all.

Waiting, she hitched a brow.

"Yes, Seren, I would like to take you out on a date. No coffee shall be consumed. And as large as City Park is, we could make an entire day of it. How's that sound?"

"Heavenly, Walker."

Stupid heart. Ah, but a happy one. What harm could come from suspending disbelief for a day and feasting on fantasy?

When Owen arrived at her door, he wore athletic shorts and a charcoal gray, crew neck T-shirt that traced the lines of his defined upper body. He offered his arms. She stepped into them. When he drew her against his chest, she let the hug linger as though it'd been more than three days since he'd asked her out. The silky, cool feel of him suffused her pores.

Heart, this is madness.

And this was Owen Walker. Hugging her.

Choosing her.

No better time to revisit her list of reasons why this was an insanely bad idea. Trying her best not to inhale his sandalwood scent and melt at the feel of his strength, Serenity dug deeper to add to the list. Because they were an impossible pairing. And she was the reason why.

She glanced up to find his endearing eyes shaded by a ball cap. When he leaned in closer, she unwound herself from his hold—narrowly dodging his attempt at another reckless kiss—and directed her attention to his Bentley. "Where's Jude?"

The sleek lines of his car extended the breadth of her cracked driveway. "I gave him the weekend off."

When Owen opened the passenger door, the smell of leather wafted from the elegant interior. He placed one hand on the rim of the window, the other on the small of her back.

Wait, where were they going?

Picnic.

She pivoted hard and bumped into his sturdy chest, giving a little grunt. She tipped a glance at him. "Food. We'll need food."

"It's in the trunk."

"What about—"

Finger to her lips, he winked. "I've taken care of everything, Seren."

At City Park, Owen found an open spot on a paved road beneath a long stretch of overarching trees near Big Lake, located on the north end of the massive property beside the New Orleans Museum of Art.

They followed the honk and screech of ducks gliding over the lake. Reedy grasses whiskered the embankment. Sparrows and warblers flitted and piped birdsong overhead.

Tucked inside the double-seat kayak rental, they paddled for an hour, effortlessly dipping oars into the slate surface of the water, directing a course around the perimeter. Ripples reflected a white sky and mirrored the swell of desire across her heart.

Worry slithered in. Why had she agreed to this? She had no business being here—with him—or with *any* man of interest. But he'd chosen her. Gone to great effort to plan this date, executing the play perfectly. What was he really after?

And why didn't I turn your head years ago?

Trudging the modest embankment together, they hauled the kayak back to the rental house, Owen letting her believe he'd needed her muscle to help carry it.

He patted his abdomen. "Time to fill the tank."

From the car, he hefted a wicker picnic basket, handling it as though it weighed a feather, while she grabbed the quilted blanket. "Lettie made this quilt."

He gave the artwork a cursory glance and nodded.

"Momma once shared that she and Daddy had enjoyed snuggling on it out on the lawn at Moreland."

"I'm thankful to see her strength returning after that heart attack."

"Me too. It scared me."

"She's an asset to the bakery."

They strolled toward the massive trunk of the Singing Oak adjacent to the lake. Her senses soared at the pinging and pitches of wind chimes strung from branches. The soulful sound freed her to forget Maurice's rental increase that'd jabbed like a hot poker. She'd kept the news from Owen. He'd simply transfer the money and rob her of the struggle to find God's purpose in it.

I've always believed hardships should be embraced for the gift that they are. They are the substance of the stories we tell the world about what we believe is true of God.

Sure thing, Momma.

Serenity sprawled the quilt over the patchy grass and sat cross-legged beside Owen. Basket open, he set po' boys, chips, and fresh-cut fruit on sturdy paper plates. He placed two cupcakes—his and her recipes—between them, handling the container like a baby carrier.

He placed his elbows on his knees. "Do you pray before you eat?"

"Definitely." She lowered her po' boy and attempted to dust crumbs off her clammy hands. *Owen Walker wants to pray.* "That'd be good."

"Good because I suggested it, or good because you believe in it?"

"Both."

His gaze rang in satisfaction. Dimples deepened aside his mouth.

He opened his palm.

She slipped her hand in his. What amounted to no more than a gentle hold shot a high-voltage charge beneath her skin. Following his lead, she dipped her head. The birdsong and children's squeals faded beneath the power—and simplicity—of his words.

"Dear God, thanks for this day, this food, and amazing company. In Jesus's name. Amen."

Amazing? No one had ever considered her amazing— or given voice to it. No one except Jesus, whose powerful presence Owen evoked just then and whose presence he'd invited to sit among them.

"Thanks."

"For the prayer or the part about you being amazing?"

Somehow he'd mastered the art of telepathy. "Both."

"I'm two for two."

He'd kept score.

"No way! Is that Owen Walker?"

At the sound of his name behind her, Serenity followed Owen's glance over his shoulder to see a young couple approaching them.

In a gesture of joyful disbelief, the guy slowly shook his head. "Man, I'm a huge fan." He proffered his hand.

Graciously, Owen stood and shook the guy's hand, then the girl's, pumping with less force while a bedazzled expression overtook her face.

The Owen Walker effect.

"Name's Gregory. This is my girlfriend, Lauren."

"We've never missed a game," Lauren, the bedazzled, said. "Followed your career from LA to New Orleans."

Gregory scratched at his head and shook it. "Man, that touchdown, eighty yards after a tip-off. Something else."

Still seated, Serenity let herself disappear amid the three-way revelry. She certainly was not the reason they'd stopped.

Owen offered Serenity his hand.

In slow motion, she took it, and he tugged her to stand beside him. In an unabashed show of ownership, he slipped his arm behind her back and tugged her to his side. The warmth of his body melted through her like rich chocolate fudge.

"This is Serenity Lewis. She's the owner of The Pear Tree bakery."

Absent glances marked their expressions.

"It's in the Quarter," Owen prodded.

Still unfamiliar.

"The best bakery and coffee shop in town. Outclasses any other. You should come try it out."

No other rating in the world could surpass his endorsement.

"For sure. We will."

"Where's it located." Lauren tilted her head, gaze foggy—a bit on the starstruck side.

If only to break the spell, Serenity interjected, "On Ursuline, between Royal and Chartres."

Ah, the bedazzled Lauren, self-appointed president of the Walker fan club, had regained consciousness.

"Parking, though," Gregory said in crusty lament.

"Who doesn't like a challenge, huh?" Owen centered a stiff knuckle punch on Gregory's upper arm.

"Good point, man."

While Gregory nursed his arm and smothered a wince, Lauren spoke into the cavern of her purse and produced a cell. "Can we get a picture with you, Owen?"

Serenity dismissed the sting of Owen's apologetic glance and turned to Lauren. "Here, I'll take it." She stepped back and directed them to huddle close.

In seconds, they flanked the iconic ballplayer. All smiles.

No doubt they'd post the image and include a peppering of savory hashtags. The world would never know Serenity had been present among the gathering.

Owen broke from the lineup and turned to Serenity. "I want you in the picture."

"That's not necessary."

A touch of sadness filtered into his compassionate expression. "Why?"

"The media will make something out of us that's nothing."

"You and I aren't nothing, I—"

"It's okay, Owen." Her lungs sank in a belabored sigh.

Gregory peered around Owen. "Is she your girlfriend?"

Seconds ticked. He drew his lower lip into his mouth in a contemplative stare, struggling to answer, it appeared.

None came. Speaking volumes.

Of course. Owen Walker had no business being involved with her. She'd known that. Maybe the inevitable had socked him in the gut, too.

The date was a mistake. The kisses had to stop. This unsurpassed, bull-rushing, benevolent, defensive end of the New Orleans' Kings needed to return to the turf, bask in the adoration of millions, and, in the off-seasons, continue to deliver opportunities to kids and communities all over the country.

Leaving her heart out of it.

Angst wrinkled over his brow.

Stroking his arm, she massaged the anguish out of him. "It's you they're interested in." The words whispered out and fell on soft breezes.

He opened his mouth and shut it.

Playing coach, she moved her hand to his barreled chest and patted it. "Go on, Walker. Your fans are waiting."

Chapter Ten

A pinkish wonder and promise filled Serenity at the aroma of baked, sugary pastries, robust coffee, and the delightful thrum of chatter in The Pear Tree.

Her reenergized bakery had survived another month. July's rent had been paid with income enough to invest in upgrades and a marketing push. As hoped, Owen had helped turn things around, garnering top ratings on Trip Tips' online advisory site. The fact that he'd encouraged an expansion of the catering menu shouldn't have surprised her.

She'd even nurtured his idea to redesign the logo and create a fresh, new color scheme. A brazen suggestion, honestly.

"C'mon, Seren," he'd said, head shaking. "The pink is a bit overdone."

"It's not my problem that you dislike pink," she'd said in rebuff.

"I'm not a pink kind of guy, no, but there's a point where people start to associate our place with Pepto-Bismol. Not what we're going for here."

Maybe the big guy was onto something. Anyway, she certainly hadn't missed his hint at co-ownership.

"Welcome back to life, my precious Pear Tree."

Minutes before closing, Serenity's gaze caught the familiar form of a haggard woman and her two small children drifting past the front window.

She filled a paper bag with several mini cinnamon pear muffins and scampered past Kourtney at the coffee bar. Outside the door, her gaze landed on the threesome slumped beneath the awning of the tattoo parlor two doors down. She strode over and stooped to make eye contact. "Hello. I'm Serenity. What's your name?"

"Lynette. These are my children, Hudson and Ellie."

Their filthy faces returned weak smiles.

Serenity offered the warm, sugary-smelling bag. "Somehow, I miscalculated today. It'd be a huge help if you'd take these off my hands."

Lynette took it, fisting the top like she'd fall off the planet if she let go. "Thanks, miss. You're so kind. God bless you."

"God bless you, too."

And please, don't tell Owen.

Scrambling back to the kitchen, she reviewed the inventory. "Need more Serenity's Specials."

Thank you, Jesus.

As she re-stocked the display case, Kourtney tugged off her apron at the register. "That's it for me. See you Wednesday."

"Bye, Kourtney. Thanks so much."

Soon after Kourtney left, Brooke arrived and sailed into the kitchen to join Serenity. She wore an eager smile to complement skinny jeans and a bakery T-shirt. She gathered her strawberry-blonde hair into a tight knot.

Lettie hadn't recovered enough strength following her heart attack to return full-time. Two or three half days of baking, and she'd get to feeling as though she'd run a marathon.

"Thanks for helping out today, Brooke, and adding one more half-day a week."

"Happy to, but I really can't spare more than that. Which reminds me, Justin and I are taking a two-week anniversary cruise in July. You'll want to ask Owen to fill in."

"Doubt he could. He's been traveling for several days, checking on staff and campers before training starts. He's got foundation meetings, speaking engagements, podcast and media interviews. As it is, I've already taken advantage of his generosity."

"Ha. Like he really hates being there." Brooke glanced at the daily order fulfillment list and stood aside Serenity. "Baking, greeting, serving, marketing, checking with Everley on the accounting end. From day one, he's never so much as hinted at feeling put upon. If I didn't know otherwise, I'd have guessed this was his establishment."

"It's crazy, really. But it's working."

It'd worked all right, creating a dependency on one individual who'd created a vacuum only he could fill. Taking his Big Hit recipe with him.

Stubborn man.

"We're running low on my Specials."

Serenity took a bowl of eggs from the refrigerator and set it on the prep table. She assembled dry ingredients and several boxes of dark chocolate-covered cordial cherries. She gave the block of butter she'd set out an hour ago a tender squeeze. "Just right."

"Overly soft butter makes for an oily batter, right?"

"Yes. If it's too hard, it doesn't allow for even mixing."

"And creates air pockets."

Serenity nodded. "I'm doing something different with my recipe."

Intrigue washed over Brooke's countenance. "Different from what you'd submitted to Carlyle's contest?"

"Yes, but if it flops, I'll go back to the original."

"What'd you do different?"

"Well, at Owen's suggestion—"

"Uh-huh." A playful tease worked up the edges of Brooke's mouth.

"What's that supposed to mean?"

"I didn't say a word." The comment trailed into a chuckle as Brooke fastened her apron.

"You said plenty. Owen just seems to think I need to up my game is all."

"If anyone knows how to up the game, it'd be him."

"Once these babies have cooled, we'll place a chocolate-covered cordial cherry on top before we frost it. I'm also tinting the buttercream a pale lavender—using a different piping tip. The candy will be hidden inside."

Serenity took a package of white, polka-dotted purple liners. "And I'm switching to these. Aren't they the cutest?"

"Owen's suggestion?"

Maybe. Okay, yes. "No. My idea."

How on earth had Owen fit himself into her kitchen when he wasn't even there?

Serenaded by seventies classic rock, the two got to work. Brooke prepared the batter, and Serenity mixed the buttercream.

"How did your Independence Day date go with Owen last Saturday?"

Owen again.

Their fourth date—breathlessly wonderful. Sparks flew ... "Pretty good. We went to Crescent Park and watched fireworks over the river. Then we ate from vendors at the Mandeville Wharf and watched a performance by The National WWII Museum's Victory Belles." Moving in motion like two ordinary people, Owen had blended in beside her, the dusky evening and a ball cap masking his legendary status.

The soothing whir of the industrial mixer churned buttery memory. Their second date back in June had been a serene stroll through the Sculpture Garden behind the New Orleans Museum of Art. No kisses. The voltage of emotion between them had sparked heat enough to fuse her soul to his. Hand in his, they'd ambled along, stopping to pose like the sculptures, judging who did a better job.

She'd laughed until her sides hurt. Days later, they'd still hurt in a blissful sort of way.

In its most elemental state, the experience was ethereal. Their prolonged stares nearly seduced her senseless. His pursuit of her felt too perfect for this world. *Her* world. Which was why agreeing to the third date the very next day had been certifiably insane.

"Let's take a passenger ferry at Canal Street, cross the river, and watch the city skyline at sunset at the levee," he'd said.

His tone was provocative, inviting, and held no question. The determination and eagerness that'd filtered into his enigmatic eyes melted her resolve into a puddle.

The proverbial 'just one more and I'll quit' mentality that kept many an addict in bondage had held her captive. She'd blamed the willingness to continue the madness on two things: the undeniable swell of feelings she'd developed for him—the new Owen Walker of restored character, love for God and people—and his insistence she was more than she really was.

The fantasy tasted irresistibly decadent.

Despite Serenity's effort to minimize the depth developing between them—the entrusted secrets, recreational companionship, and inclusion of God in conversation—guilt hammered hard. Because she'd still not told Owen all there was to know.

As long as she refused to let him bite down hard enough on their relationship, he'd never discover the secret surprise inside her.

Once cupcakes were prepped and orders filled, Serenity and Brooke entered the main room. Brooke dumped coffee grounds into a special bag for customers to repurpose as compost for their gardens. "Can you imagine pastries delivered by Owen Walker?"

Imagine she did. Customers would surface—like that heavily jeweled woman peering through the front door, undeterred by the closed sign. A repeat customer whose constitution bore sophistication and wealth.

That's right. Repeat patrons would scrutinize the interior ... like this woman had done moments after Serenity ushered her inside like it was the start of the business day and she had enough energy to rocket to the moon. They'd turn toward the counter, and hope would gather in their eyes, undoubtedly looking to interact with the muscled hero. Inspired by Owen's size, they'd purchase more than intended as his playful conversation and dimpled smile turned their insides into cascades of melted chocolate.

Serenity had always smiled at patrons when they'd entered. Only it hadn't been enough.

When Ms. Sophistication approached, she drew in a wisp of a breath. "Is Owen here?"

Oh, the whimsy in her voice, the coy tilt of her head.

Think, think. Was this Pamela or ... Pauline, maybe?

"I'm sorry, no, he's not."

In a hard swallow, Serenity squared her shoulders and reminded herself she'd thrived for eight years apart from the Kings' blue-chip player.

"I'm Serenity. The owner."

"Oh. Guess I got my wires crossed. Somehow, I thought Owen was the owner now."

"He's just a friend of mine who, believe it or not, asked if he could help out during the off-season."

Okay, she'd twisted the truth a bit. A girl can't honestly assign friendship to a guy who'd dropped her from his memory.

"Last time I was in, I'd asked him if you cater weddings. He'd said no, but that he thought it was a great idea and wanted to discuss it."

"Did he, now?" She hadn't meant for that to come out sounding crass.

"Yes. My daughter Carmen is getting married in December ..."

The woman's name surfaced ... Prissy or, no, Priscilla!

"Carmen discovered The Pear Tree recently and hasn't stopped raving about it. At her insistence, my women's league visited, and, I have to agree, it's wonderful." This purveyor of extravagance glanced around the bakery. "The eclectic interior, cozy courtyard, and superior products. Trendy, delicious. It's the whole package and worth every penny."

"Glad you like it." *It's my baby.*

"My husband, Warren Murdock, and I would like to offer The Pear Tree brand cupcakes for the wedding."

"Where's the wedding?"

"The Mandeville Ellipse, at Crescent Park, adjacent the river."

Serenity took a Moreland Manor Bed and Breakfast flyer near her and hovered a pen over a blank space. "Number of guests?"

Fifty minimum. A hundred. Please?

"Our initial list includes only 500, but we're actively broadening our reach."

Serenity drew her head back. Her mouth fell open. "We can do that."

The fulfillment would take an army. Make that every military branch and one big visionary football player who amassed business smarts, and—wonder of wonders ...

The man loved to bake.

Before returning to New Orleans on July 3rd, Owen had made a short stopover in Houston to speak at an annual banquet for an international Christian athletic organization. While he was back in town over the last two weeks, he and Serenity had enjoyed a few more dates.

When apart, they'd texted, called each other nearly every day. He'd asked about the bakery. She'd asked how his camps were going, how he felt about the upcoming season. The conversation flowed seamlessly and organically, their two worlds melding into one.

Romancing Serenity was effortless, a source of joy. At this point, he considered her his girl.

The most crucial qualification being—she loved God. It could only get better from there.

Into the mix of a growing interest in Serenity, Owen added more time with Dad, who needed to be frequently removed from the dark cave of his existence—a diversion from a raging mental war. Hours ahead of visiting a lacrosse camp at City Park, Owen took Dad to his neurology appointment.

As Owen feared, the doctor uncovered evidence of disease progression. The news moved him to involve Dad in Owen's scheduled activities. Because once the season started, his attention would be funneled toward football.

Leaving the medical complex, they journeyed to City Park, where Serenity had agreed to meet them at the lacrosse field at 3:30.

When they arrived, Owen panned the field and spotted her on the sidelines with an open box of cupcakes. The players closed in, popping them into their mouths. She engaged with his kids effortlessly as though they were her own.

He'd been around enough women to know when they were playing the role, attempting in not-so-subtle ways to lure him. Her interactions held nothing contrived, the interest in his kids genuine. The provision of cupcakes was a sweet addition.

A keen realization awakened. In greater measure, he'd fit Serenity inside the frame of his life and envisioned relational gameplays. What if the two of them ran the bakery together? Jointly, they could sell products at foundation venues. She could conduct soccer clinics and provide pastries. A mutually beneficial, double-team effort to bless kids all over the country. Together, they'd make the world better. More colorful.

Far, far sweeter.

His attention quickened back to the present. He tamped down the urge to kiss her and, instead, took her in a casual hug.

"I missed you," he whispered near her ear.

She tipped her gaze and blessed him with a smile. "Missed you, too."

The scent of lavender roses, sunshine, and a million tomorrows took possession of him. She empowered and propelled him beyond isolated moments of greatness to take his talent to the highest level of achievement and execution. To be the best Owen Lane Walker possible.

Sure, he'd pray about it, but he'd stop at nothing to pursue the heart of Serenity Lewis. In the end, he knew more now than ever ... *She's the one.*

"Gabe and Everley invited us over to Moreland for pizza night."

"Sounds wonderful. Four boxes enough?"

"Sure. But that leaves nothing for the rest of you."

"You're funny, Walker." She poked a finger at his chest.

"You're fun, Lewis."

You're mine.

Schoolgirl shyness claimed her cheeks, dusting them a rosy pink. His pulse raced. He'd nearly forgotten about Dad, who sat on the bleachers near center field.

"Mind keeping Dad company while I interact with the kids and coaches?"

A hint of resignation claimed her blue gaze, the sheen of her eyes now dull. Her brows wrinkled in consternation as though mulling over the decision. "Okay."

He bent to kiss her temple. The impulsive move drew the attention of players who, he turned to see, stood gaping. Evidently, one with raised cell had captured the interlude.

Serenity stiffened and wriggled out of his hug. "Catch you later."

Once the media learned of Owen's love life, he'd coach Serenity on how to achieve a comfort level with the heightened interest it would inevitably bring.

She traversed the field over to Dad. The steel gray, smoldering seriousness of Owen's former high school coach was minimally shaded by a ball cap that covered a head of shaggy gray hair. Dad made jerky little movements as though inner voices had him assessing gameplay.

For the next half hour, Owen stole glances at the misfit pair. Elbows on her knees and leaning in, Serenity looked to be entertained by Dad's ramblings. It wasn't just any girl who could engage the formidable Harvey Walker. He'd bet none could, and those of recent years had boldly refused.

This one scored.

After eliciting updates from staff on camp status and suggestions for improvements, Owen waved them off and jogged back over to Dad, who now sat alone.

"Where's Serenity?" He reached for his cell and looked for a missed call. A text.

Nothing.

He grunted. "Said she had to go."

"Why?"

"Didn't give a reason. Looked like she was going to throw up."

Disquiet gripped like a vice.

"Dad, did you say anything to—"

"Too bad you couldn't hack lacrosse. Studying the game up close, it looks to be a credible sport."

Owen had zero interest in exhuming a blundered attempt to try out for the team. He stepped away and called Serenity. No answer. Why would she disappear without telling him? If she was sick, he'd want to be there for her. Their pizza date with Everley and Gabe could wait another night.

He phoned again. No answer. Worry slithered in.

OWEN: Dad said you're sick. Please call me.

He called Gabe. The thrum of machinery sounded in the background. "Hey, Champ. Sorry to hear our plans fell through."

"You and me both. I can't get a hold of Serenity. You heard from her?"

"Everley said she didn't feel well. That's all I know."

"All right then. Rain check. Thanks, Gabe."

In a feverish attempt to uncover any missteps, he rehearsed everything he'd said or done from the time he and Serenity met up on the lacrosse field to his request that she keep company with Dad. She'd seemed genuinely pleased to see him, engaged in banter, and returned his hug.

The kiss on the temple? Couldn't be.

Was it ... Dad?

"Pass it, you moron!"

The object of Dad's corrosive correction was an offensive player who'd cradled the ball and rushed toward the goal, weaving in and around a three-man defense.

Since tonight's plans went up in smoke, Owen patted Dad on the shoulder. "Let's get you back home. Take in some football. Just you and me."

Enfolded inside his Bentley, he and Dad closed the remaining hours of the day watching highlights of last year's Super Bowl.

Three times over.

"Fourth down and one. The fake, the rush, and ... what!?" Utter bliss played over Dad's countenance. He shot to his feet and targeted the screen. "Picked off by Perry, coming through ... unstoppable ... and score! Tremendous stamina, right there."

Dad shook his head in awestruck wonder. With that fractured window at his back, he turned a sidelong grin at Owen. Balmy, moist air whistled through the room. "As phenomenal as that play was, it doesn't match your skill. Never will." He jabbed a finger at him, voice gruff. "You're a Walker. Keep at it, son. Make me proud."

Right. Walkers play football. Football was ... life.

But just how risky should a guy be with his health when football was all he knew?

Within the dimly lit room that held an intensely flickering flatscreen, Dad's repetitive mantra had sentenced Owen to life in a mental prison. Maybe all his ramblings were brain injury talking. What would Dad say if he were of sound mind? Could he even accept the idea of Owen off the field, pursuing a different passion?

But really, owning a bakery? If his worst fear were realized and he could no longer play, would he lose Dad's favor?

And why did it matter so much?

In the midst of listening to Dad spew profanities at the players, Owen managed to dislodge anguish over Serenity's disappearing act earlier. If she needed space, he'd give it to her. If she asked for the world, he'd give her that, too.

If she cuts me loose, I'll fall apart.

Serenity's explanation the following day was weak. "Sorry I didn't return your calls, Owen. It's just … without Lettie here full-time and the others working part-time, I'm exhausted."

"You mean sick."

"Yes. Nothing serious."

"Serious enough to leave without telling me, refuse my call. Not return texts."

Irritation simmered to a low boil. Remembering her need for grace—that free gift of God had lavished on his own sorry soul—he turned the heat down.

"Listen. I care about you, Seren. I drove by your house to see if you were okay, but the lights were out, and I didn't see your car."

A labored sigh sounded through the phone. "I ended up going to Moreland and binge-watched Rocky movies with Everley. Needed sister time. And I fear she's overextending herself."

One call to Everley would substantiate or dismantle her story. Either way, he had no claim on her. A beautiful, creative, and smart girl like Serenity, packaged in wildly attractive innocence, had no need to settle for a battered athlete who'd taken far too many bites out of the world's offerings.

Doubt seeped in. Pain throbbed at his temples. Was she seeing someone else? Disinterested? Given the romantic tension that'd intensified between them since their first date at City Park—and sizzled hotter ever since—nothing about that presumption made sense.

He kneaded the back of his neck and massaged the tightness out. "I thought I'd done something wrong or offended you. It had me in knots all night."

"I'm really sorry I caused you a sleepless night. Forgive me?"

At that, he melted, though he hated not knowing if she was playing games or stringing him along. It was the equivalent of being at the line of scrimmage, fourth and ten—blindfolded and without knowledge of gameplay. "Of course. Forgiven."

Timidity marked her words. "Everley's doctor threatened bed rest if she didn't slow down. I'm fearful for the babies, and I'd like to ease the load, take calls, and manage the office. Is there any chance you could come in today?"

The request to handle the bakery jarred him. Not because he didn't want to join her in her world but because he did. Desperately. Because ... wasn't it time to make himself scarce and let her manage without him? Planned obsolescence?

"How much do you need me to cover?"

All day?

"Just a few hours."

"I can do that."

Her relief whispered through a heavy sigh. "Great. When could you be here?"

"Mid-morning. I've got to respond to emails first. Want me to bring you and the ladies some lunch?"

Way to make yourself scarce, Superman.

"That'd be great."

"Shrimp po' boys sound good?"

"Yes, if you don't mind."

"Glad to. See you soon."

Inside The Pear Tree, a plethora of scents drizzled over him. More and more, he wanted to stay. More and more, he hated to leave and loved who he was when wrapped inside this place.

In the kitchen, a noticeably weaker Lettie had joined the scant but happy staff while Brooke managed the register and Kourtney served coffee. They'd made a great team. Serenity was the icing on the cake.

When the bakery reached a lull, Serenity left for Moreland, followed by Brooke and Kourtney a half hour later. It was good to have Lettie back, but there wasn't enough staff for the bakery to thrive.

In the kitchen, Lettie made good work of clanging bowls, whirring the mixer, and humming, "It is well with my soul."

He hummed along, only the lyrics didn't penetrate his heart. Because training camp loomed in two and a half weeks, and his soul revolted.

In slow motion, sadness seeped in … several feet shy of the endzone … tripping over laces, heat bearing down. The collision of helmets, head thrashing, his body one big sore, twisted mass on the field.

Exhaustion, excessive thirst.

Shooting pain bored into his temples. Another headache, this one intense and relentless. He tilted his head left and right. Was it always this loud? Heat suffused the kitchen, drawing the walls in tight.

Spoon in hand, Lettie jabbed him in the side with her elbow, whisking his thoughts to the present. She'd spared him from slumping against the wall. "That's it for me, Mista Walker. You good to close up?"

"Yes, ma'am. It's good to have you back."

"Nothing a few heart pills can't fix. Sure appreciates you helping out, especially allowing for Miz Serenity to visit Mo'land. Those two sisters I've known since they's babies. Thicker than thieves." Her gaze drew up and caught overhead light, her chin drawn in the stretch of a smile. "A wildly different pair, but they sure do love and accept each other."

The subtext hadn't been lost on him.

"I can see that."

Her spindly hands squeezed his wrists. She fixed a slow, nodding gaze on him, boring past his exterior on a winding path to his soul. "Good."

Hailing a cab out front, Lettie left him alone in the bakery.

Serenity's bakery.

After batter had been labeled and refrigerated and pastries placed on designated shelves for the following morning, he drew in one final exhale. Eyes shut, he banked memories of the place inside his brain.

Gratitude coursed through his veins and landed on his tongue. "God, thank you for these last several months. For the opportunity to assist. For the gift of Serenity. Please bless her, this business. In Jesus's name, Amen."

He secured the front door and turned to see the free-standing chalkboard near the entrance. At his suggestion, Serenity purchased it to promote her products. Written with deep pink chalk, the signature swirly script read, "Today's Favorite Pick, Serenity's Special."

An idea sparked.

Taking his thumb, he erased the apostrophe and the s. Then chalked the word "is."

If he hadn't done enough to make Serenity feel special—and if she didn't already know—when she arrived tomorrow, she'd know.

Serenity is Special.

Chapter Eleven

Early Monday morning, Serenity unlocked the front door and stepped past the placard inside the entrance. Her mind took a quick snapshot, noting something amiss. She spun and rounded to stare at it. A subtle gasp sounded in her throat.

"Serenity is ... Special."

Ah. Brooke. A thoughtful gesture. If it weren't 5 o'clock in the morning, the sluggish plum sky awaiting the light of dawn, she'd text her thanks.

Serenity's phone pinged.

OWEN: Like it?

He was awake? *Thinking of me ...*

SERENITY: Were you the one?

OWEN: You're the one. You're Owen's special.

She typed her heart's response, released a long sigh, and deleted it in exchange for the safe zone.

SERENITY: You're sweet.

Owen's sentiment had stroked satiny fingers across her soul, stirring an unexpected heart longing. Because no guy had ever expressed his devotion so unreservedly. According to Harvey, Owen's search was over.

He'd said as much at the lacrosse field before she'd tucked tail and ran.

The crusty ex-ball player had cornered her with bold assumptions. "Yup. I expect you'll make him a wonderful wife, be a good momma to his kids."

Hardly, sir.

Gaze on the field, Harvey had threaded arms across his chest. "Lord knows, he's wanted a slew of them for years."

To be precise, Owen wanted a daughter to add to a power seven and carry on the beauty and kindness that was the hallmark of his mother. The adored, loyal, and reigning queen of the male-dominated Walker household, Connie amassed wealth from the bond of love, particularly when—as Owen had privately confessed—Harvey's reckless spending and bad investments ran the well of their income dry.

A doting and faithful wife Serenity could easily be. But she had nothing to offer a man who'd wanted to keep the legacy of his mom alive. Guilt and dread churned in her stomach. The time had come to let Owen know.

And lose him forever.

"I've completely and hopelessly fallen for you, Owen Walker."

The realization wrapped around her soul like a cotton blanket warmed by sunshine. She let the temporal fantasy whisk its magical spell throughout her entire body until it rendered her partially hypnotic.

Over the next two weeks, Owen devoted the last of his summer to country-wide camp visitation. He'd called her each evening, their conversations sometimes stretching for hours, the lateness of nights of no concern.

"I was contacted by a production company about doing a documentary on my career and what's around the corner."

"That's great, Owen. You going to do it?"

"I'm not sure."

"Why wouldn't you?"

"I don't like the way they pitched it to me. Made it sound like I've come to the end of the road."

You have.

Everything in her wanted to scream. Instead, she held her breath and stood in his corner. "Being the subject of the film, you have creative control regarding the content. Make them angle it in your favor or tell them there's no deal."

"I love the way you think."

"What do you want people to know about you?"

"That football is my life. It's who I am."

"But it isn't."

"It is."

"Football is what you do. It's not who you are. Your identity is defined by God."

An uneasy quiet severed the moment. She could almost hear the wheels in his head turning, gathering defense.

"God created me for this game, Seren."

"And you've done what he created you to do throughout the time he's given you to do it. At some point—sooner than you might want to admit—he'll call you to expend energy elsewhere."

"I'm not giving it up."

Once he'd erected the Walker Wall, it was impossible to break through.

God, please give light to his eyes. Enable him to see Your purpose and strength to follow Your direction.

"It'll be hard to leave the bakery." Owen's voice went noticeably low, whimsical.

"Hearts will break after you're gone."

"Yours is the only heart I care about."

His heated and velvety seriousness swooned down her spine.

A response landed on her tongue, close enough to reciprocate the sentiment without going in too deep. "I care about your heart, too."

The Monday after Owen's return to New Orleans, Serenity got a call from Everley.

"I could use some company."

"You mean you need someone to hold you accountable to keep you off your feet."

"Guilty. Plus, who could refuse a visit to Moreland?"

"At the rate you and Gabe charge for a day tour, I couldn't afford it."

"Perks of family."

Serenity arranged for Brooke to manage the bakery through mid-afternoon and drove to Moreland. She'd thought of asking Owen to come in, but to do so would oppose her need to transition him out.

And pretend he hadn't turned her world upside down.

Shaded by stately pine and oaks to her right, Serenity exited her car. She traversed the lawn to the front door, shaded by an expansive balcony. It was here where Gabe Bellevue had swept Everley off her feet.

Literally.

Last spring, on their wedding day, Gabe stood on Moreland's veranda—looking blatantly handsome in his black tux—and simply begged pardon of their guests mingling on the lawn. He'd scooped Everley into his arms and whisked her over the threshold.

Bride in tow, he cradled his treasure up the staircase to the master bedroom where—according to Everley—they took advantage of all the rights and privileges afforded a husband and wife.

Fate—and maybe Moreland—played a part in pairing these two unlikely mismatches. Prior to Mom's death, Everley worked for a prestigious CPA firm in Chicago where her supervisor had pin-pointed her as partner material. When she'd received the splendorous estate as an inheritance, it was Serenity who'd championed its restoration. Bound by obligation, Everley did right by the house and responded to Momma's letter, which specified she was only to hire Gabriel Bellevue to complete the restoration.

Nothing about Momma's dreamy ideals made sense to Everley. When MidDay Media's production company wanted to film the project to create a sizzle reel to pitch to the H2H network, she obliged. But only because it granted a financial advantage.

Beyond the majesty of its Greek revival exterior, Moreland was a functional house with multiple rooms, each crisply decorated. The north and south wings offered common areas for dining and sizable gatherings.

At the threshold of the master bedroom, the coveted chamber of generations gone by, Serenity found Everley resting on her side, burrowed beneath a cottony, white sheet. In addition to mild contractions, Everley battled latent morning sickness.

A shaft of sunlight streamed through angular glass windows framed by translucent curtains and brushed over the pinewood floor and poster bed. The antique furnishings and plastered walls were bathed in soft, yellow light and held yesteryear's secrets and echoes of laughter.

Everley stirred and opened her eyes. A complexion typically rosy to match russet hair now bore a gray pallor.

Side effects of pregnancy, Serenity presumed.

"Hey, Sis." Everley elbowed the pillow and sat upright. "Thanks for coming to visit me in my misery."

The subtle moan was not convincing. Cinderella lived in a palace with Prince Charming, who'd never met a fixer-upper he couldn't fix.

Hardly a miserable life.

"The October due date feels like it's six years away," Everley said.

"If you don't slow down, you'll never make it that long."

Everley fluffed and patted a pillow beside her. "Come sit."

Slipping out of her flats, Serenity crossed over a sculpted rug to the bed. With her legs outstretched, she bunched the pillow at her back and leaned against the mahogany headboard.

"Is Gabe taking calls in the office?"

"No. He's overseeing the restoration of several houses in town. I left it on voicemail."

The abandoned French Victorian in Napoleonville rustled through Serenity's thoughts. Rich in charm, history, and style. The asymmetrical architecture with a wraparound porch and four-sided mansard roof—a place conjured out of her dreams—begged to function as a bakery. Presently, the nearest bakery required the people of Napoleonville to trek forty-five minutes north.

No matter. The cost to obtain and convert the property was beyond her means.

"How'd you break free from The Pear Tree?"

"I asked Brooke to stay a few extra hours."

"Why not Owen, your secret sauce?"

"He just returned from being out of town for two weeks. On one of his stops, he spent the day with a sixteen-year-old boy with a rare blood disorder who'd told the Make-A-Wish Foundation he wanted to meet Owen Walker. Going all out, Owen met the family, took everyone out to eat, got pictures, and conducted an impromptu football clinic."

"He's so generous."

"And then ... training camp begins in two days." Her voice withered. Their impossible romance shrank and faded in the rearview mirror of her mind.

"You don't sound happy about it."

"I'm not. He's crazy to keep at this game. But there's not a doctor on the planet who's willing to ground him. The warnings about how precarious it is for him to continue to play have landed on deaf ears—including his."

"Why does what he does with his career matter to you?" The lilt in her tone prodded confession.

"I love him." The admission felt like a silken strand on her tongue before it thickened into a rope and knotted around her traitorous heart.

A cheeky laugh erupted. The barest smile tugged at Everley's lips. "I've known for years." She wagged a finger. "You're no good at hiding your feelings."

"And you excel at it," Serenity chortled.

"Point well taken."

"This calls for some Lewis sister time on the balcony."

"Yes, it does." Everley untangled her pale legs from the sheets and crossed to the window. She wore denim shorts and the oversized T-shirt Gabe gifted her that told the world, "My Wife is Amazing."

A special order granted out of a fairy tale and written for girls who were desirable.

Everley effortlessly tugged the sash and slid it upward.

"I thought that window was hopelessly stuck."

Stooping, Everley stepped gingerly onto the balcony and turned to Serenity, who joined her to stand in a wedge of sunlight. "Gabe restored it."

Intricate lattice work graced Moreland's deep balcony built above massive ionic columns. The elevated location enabled a wishful type to invite dreams.

Big *impossible* ones.

Two white rockers sat on either side of double sash windows. Everley eased into one, and Serenity took the other. Birds rasped from the sprawling, knobby branches of the oak shading the far edge of the lawn. The whole scene coaxed make-believe.

As a little girl, Serenity strategically tugged Dad's attention away from Everley, the older, methodical of the two. She sought reassurance that he loved her just the way she was—carefree, colorful, and quirky. Different. When Dad and Mom purchased Moreland in *as-is* condition, it'd been abandoned for a decade. Surely Dad's love and acceptance of his daughter exceeded that of an old house. But his untimely death left the needed affirmation unsatisfied.

"Remember when we pretended to be princesses trapped inside the palace?" Serenity said.

Everley chuckled and summoned the sing-song voice of a theater actress. "We'd waited for our chivalrous Prince Charmings to arrive, riding gallantly across the lawn on white horses."

An unnatural stillness overtook Serenity. Her gaze dropped, tone deadpan. "Yours finally came, Evers."

"Yes. But it took my stubborn heart far too long to recognize the obvious." Everley touched her on the arm. "I believe your prince has come."

Breaking the spell of Everley's logic, Serenity tilted her gaze toward an indistinct white sky. Wished she could paint the desire of her heart, step into the scene, and let it whisk her off her feet.

"Are you worried about what will happen between you and Owen once the season begins?"

"Not really. Disruption and travel come with dating a pro ballplayer." Serenity upped the speed of rocking. "I just wish he'd quit while he can and spare himself for those he loves."

A lone car whizzed along the highway, disrupting the frothy, distant chimes of St. Anne's church.

"As far as I know, not one medical professional has ever strong-armed him about it."

"Would he be forthcoming if they had?"

"Of course."

Because love was truthful, right?

Everley placed a hand on her abdomen and winced as she readjusted her widened hips in the rocker. "What concerns you then?"

"You know from keeping the books, the business is bolstered enough to sustain me through July. I submitted my Serenity's Special recipe to this contest put on by Bryan J. Carlyle, the celebrity cooking show host. If it's chosen, the exposure will be like winning the lottery. If it's rejected, I won't be able to sustain The Pear Tree. Bakery World die-hards have come looking for *him* and *his* cupcakes, not me and mine."

Everley probed like a neurosurgeon. "These are not insurmountable problems. There's more you're not telling me."

Serenity hugged her middle. "He wants kids, Evers. Lots of them."

Anguish drifted in dark shades across Everley's face. A sympathetic murmur fractured the fragile silence.

"I didn't open a bakery just because I thought it would be fun."

Feet pressed to the railing, Serenity drew a breath, rocking slowly as she released it. "In part, it was to appease Momma."

"How so?"

"When I first mentioned the idea, her enthusiasm was so fierce I was doggedly determined to invest in it, fiscally and emotionally. The Pear Tree speaks of my willingness to move beyond my imagination and take a risk rather than stay stuck in a dream."

"I love—and envy—that about you."

Hollowness slashed at her heart. She chewed on her lower lip and sighed. "But I suspect Momma's true intention was that I find a viable way to bring life into the world."

Sympathy rumbled over Everley's countenance. "No matter her reasons, you've done well by it, blessed so many. Far more than I ever could or would."

Serenity returned a feeble smile.

"What does Owen think about the fact that you can't have kids?"

"He doesn't know."

Everley gripped the armrest and shot her a hard glance. "You've got to let him know."

"I'll lose him."

"That's not a deal breaker. You could adopt."

"I know that, Evers. It's a perfect solution, except he's opposed to it."

"But if you're willing to love each other through—and because of—your differences, God will make a way."

In the months Owen had invested in propping up Serenity's business, he'd developed greater knowledge of the inner workings of the establishment. Initially, he'd assumed it would be nothing but a kitchen on steroids. But he'd made himself a student of its complexities—painfully early mornings, inevitable equipment failure, stringent health department standards. Inventory, purchasing, demand for products, and strategic marketing.

Since March, he'd studied every aspect of the industrial kitchen, the flow of clientele in and around the seated area, the interior design, sales items, and menu offerings. Unwittingly, he'd signed on as a virtual co-owner.

Serenity's place.

I love Serenity.

He'd developed resounding gratitude for Lettie commandeering the kitchen, Kourtney tackling barista duties, and Brooke greeting and serving.

It was no small wonder The Pear Tree had done well for so long. Only God knew what predicament Seren's bakery would be in if Owen hadn't intervened. In an indelible way, the place, its owner, had taken hold. He'd no sooner disregard it than he would his own child.

What had begun as an easy in-and-out favor to assist had turned into a voluntary obligation that'd flipped his heart inside out. Because someday, in the far future, the need to give serious consideration to retirement would begin to claw at him. And when it did, he'd gracefully bow out of a decorated career and consider owning his own place.

Nothing about his career was ordinary. Life after football wouldn't be any different.

Save one thing. His place—his life—would include Serenity.

For now, Owen would tackle the emptiness wrenching his heart and soak up every second on this, his last day. He went about inhaling the fragrance, essence, and nuance of the place and tucked them in his memory for easy retrieval when everything in his bruised, sweat-drenched body begged him to leave the game. Because it would. But over time, he'd mastered the ability to ignore the urge and push past exhaustion, fatigue, and sleeplessness.

At the coffee bar, Kourtney whipped up a custom order. Lettie had already left for the day, and Brooke cut her time short to take one of her kids to the doctor. Earlier, Owen had inventoried stock supplies and placed an ingredient order.

Turning attention to products, he assembled, baked, and frosted four batches of his Big Hits, working at a ridiculously slow pace as if to still the hands of time. After shelving most of them, he set half a batch inside the display case.

When the bell at the door jangled, Owen broke from talking ball with patrons to see Serenity, who'd gone to Moreland to help Everley again. Beside the chalkboard, she paused forward steps and gazed long at it.

For the second time, the sentiment he'd written flooded her eyes with light. It'd done something to her ... the beautiful, kissable, pure, and inventive girl he wanted to clutch to his chest.

The one standing right over there whose awed gaze was locked on the placard.

He stood in the center of the tables, lifted his arms at his side like a helicopter, and circled the eating area. "Well, look who's here." He swept a hand in her direction. "The real Serenity Special."

Guests twisted in their chairs. Her cheeks blossomed pink inside a sheepish grin. She cupped them with her hands and walked over to him.

"If you were looking for a way to entice me to pay you in cupcakes again, it worked."

"Good. Then I'll take two dozen of yours."

The grin she gave held a mix of passion and playfulness, neither overriding the other. A perfect blend. Enough to pluck him away from starstruck clientele and follow her into the kitchen.

Owen draped a cozy arm about her neck and pulled her close. "How was your time with Everley? Did you talk about pregnancy and babies and all that?"

All right, dial it down.

"She's hanging in there, considering she's got twin boys."

"Score. Two for one. Knowing Gabe, he'll put a tool in their hands as soon as they're born."

He continued to mine for truth, curious about her vision for family. Being a visionary, surely, she had one.

"You ever see yourself having twins?"

Another booming non-answer. Her gaze flitted over the kitchen, gaze twitchy as though uncertain where to focus as she demonstrated her keen ability to deflect his questions.

He waved a hand in front of her frozen gaze. "Hey. Seren."

Stance easing a bit, her lids shuddered. "Uh, thanks for being here this morning. You're free to go if you need to. Or stay. Whatever."

Don't make me go.

Behind her lonesome exterior, she'd sheltered a tinge of hurt. His phone rang. It was Ross Billings.

"Hey, Ross. How's my superstar?"

"Not sure, Owen. We're here at Children's Hospital. Eli has been admitted for tests."

Concern seized Owen's chest. He pinned his cell to his ear and turned from the whirr and clatter of appliances. "What's wrong?"

"We don't know. A severe headache this morning had him vomiting. He's complained of blurry vision and couldn't walk without difficulty."

Angst slithered through.

"They're ruling out a tumor. In his brain."

The muscles in Owen's legs tightened, his stomach clenched. He turned to Serenity, lowered his phone and mouthed, "Eli. Hospital."

"He's one sick young man, Owen," Ross rasped out. "And he's asking for you."

"Be right over."

Owen ended the call. He reached for Serenity, who readily let him sink into her arms. The kitchen went cloudy. The feel of her slowed the speed of his thoughts enough to infuse a small measure of peace.

"Go be with Eli," she directed. "I'll close up early and meet you there."

He leaned back, letting her see the mounting pressure of tears behind his eyes. His need for strength. Compassion gathered in her blue eyes and soothed his nerves. Need swept in. He drew his lips to hover over hers and kissed her intensely. She tasted like everything that made her wonderfully perfect. An antidote. Her tightened hold infused strength he didn't have. She returned his affection openly and readily. A murmur hummed in her throat.

Wrong time to start a fire he couldn't put out—or use her goodness to pretend darkness didn't exist. He eased out of her arms, tipped her chin with a finger, and leaned down to kiss her forehead. "I can't defeat this component without you, Seren."

Stuck in a clog of snarled traffic on Hwy 90, Owen wished Jude were available to pilot him over the mess in his helicopter. But his faithful escort was conducting self-defense instruction and couldn't break away.

At the hospital, Owen raced to the elevator and rode it to Eli's room on the fourth floor. Somber air shrouded the artificially lit room. A mid-sized flat screen broadcasting a major league baseball game hung on the far wall above the end of Eli's partially raised bed. Facing Owen, Ross stood on one side of it. With her back to Owen, Arlene hovered over her son and stroked healing fingers through his soft curls, combing them in that soothing way mothers did. The way Mom did when Owen had taken a hit during high school and spent a night in the hospital.

He hated hospitals.

He took a step and halted. A wallop of sorrow sucker-punched him in the gut. He gripped the door jamb to steady himself. Eli angled his gaze at Owen. Instantly, his ashen pallor brightened.

"Owen." It was evident from the tinny sound of his voice that his boy had struggled for strength.

So weak. Fragile.

With effort, he waved a hand. Forced a grin. Emotion balled in Owen's throat. Misty tears fogged his vision. But he'd come to deliver hope, not let sorrow throw him to the turf.

He clenched his jaw, filled his lungs with a heap of air, and swaggered toward the bed. "So this is where the superstars bunk."

Turning to Ross, Owen took his hand in a firm grip. He bent low to give Arlene a gentle hug. She muffled the thunder of a cry into his shoulder. He shut his eyes and prayed. *God, please strengthen them to face whatever this is.*

And then—crush it.

She drew back, bracketing his arms with her hands. Gratitude flickered in her weary gaze. "Thanks for being here. It means so much," she eked out.

"You start camp tomorrow." Eli made football the centerpiece and dissipated the dread trying to claim the room.

Arlene moved aside, creating space for Owen beside the bed. "You'd make an excellent head coach, kid."

Or a Nazi commandant.

"I'm bummed I can't go. I had to give my tickets to one of the guys I met at soccer camp."

Just as well. Leaving bakery life to start camp soured his stomach. Made him question if he had the guts to show up.

"How about if I assure you and your parents never miss a home game this year?"

Gaping, Eli levered himself upward. The network of tubes hanging off his arms rustled.

"That'd be awesome!"

"Can't let my best buddy down."

His eyes were lit like stadium lights. "Can you get tickets for Serenity? She's so cool."

Seren. At some point, Eli had made a couple out of him and his boss. "Sure thing. But listen. I need you to do something for me."

"Anything but eat broccoli." He slumped into his pillow, arms folded in mock defense.

Welcome laughter expanded the walls, unwinding the knots in Owen's neck. Almost offset an incoming headache.

"I don't know what you may be facing here, Eli, but I'm praying for you to do whatever it takes to get well. Go into this challenge like it's the toughest game you've ever played."

Eli dipped his chin and fidgeted with the tube that snaked along his arm. "It will be."

Malignant fear weakened Eli's words, but it coursed fresh resolve and determination through Owen's veins. He targeted Eli's glistening eyes and spoke in hushed strength. "God's fighting for you, buddy."

Ross stepped near and touched Owen on the back. "The doctor wants to talk out in the hallway. I've authorized you to listen in if you're willing."

"Sure." He bent to pat Eli on the shoulder. "Love you, superstar. I'll come see you tomorrow."

"You've got camp."

"It can wait."

Owen joined Ross at a nearby nursing station. A dark-haired doctor with coppery skin lumbered over, looking like he'd seen better shifts. Sweat darkened the neck of his scrubs. Darkened, puffy circles underscored a beleaguered gaze.

Ross's hallmark optimistic demeanor had gone missing, his expression bearing equal weight. Traces of Eli's angelic countenance grew less apparent in his angular features.

After a quick glance at Owen, the doctor's face ignited in recognition. His mouth curved into a minimal smile as he offered his hand. Owen shook it.

"Hello. I am Doctor Amin. You are Owen Walker. Player for the Kings?"

"That's right."

"Good to meet you."

"Wish it were under better circumstances."

"How do you know Mr. Billings?"

"Eli is one of my camp kids. He'd asked for me."

"I understand. The tests I have conducted confirm Eli has glioblastoma."

Anguish gathered at Ross's brow. His chin firmed beneath a quivering lower lip.

Terse tones and scuffling medical staff droned. Owen rubbed at the clot of heat in his chest. "That sounds bad."

Dr. Amin alternated his attention between them, gesturing with his hands. "Glioblastoma, also known as glioblastoma multiforme, is the most common and aggressive type of primary brain cancer. Glios can be remarkably difficult to treat."

Muscling through the darkness of his thoughts, Owen chased slivers of sunshine. "Prognosis is good, though?"

"It depends on the molecular profile of the tumor. Once we confirm the grade and type, we will assess the location to determine whether it is favorable for removal."

More sunshine. *I need Seren.* My touchstone. The center of gravity when life started to spin ... like it was doing now. Nausea roiled. "Surgery is an option?"

"We're still running tests to assure Eli is a candidate. Assuming there are no contraindications, yes, an image-guided craniotomy can be performed. Initially, he will receive chemotherapy to shrink the tumor. Whether or not we use radiation is determined by the type of glioma, and it is typically used post-operatively to eliminate any remaining malignant cells and treat unresectable tumors."

Still looking for the open pocket, chasing down a win-win. "And then?"

"The goal is simply to alleviate symptoms associated with the tumor and to extend survival and life expectancy."

Seren. *Now.*

Excusing himself, Owen found his way outside to the outskirts of a garden courtyard and collapsed onto an empty bench. Emotion bubbled up. Tears stung his eyes and threatened to break through his exterior. He swiped at them with the pad of his thumb.

He tugged the brim of his ball cap and leaned forward, pressing elbows to his knees. He hated for Serenity to witness the weakness, but he needed her presence to sustain him.

If grief was going to gain yardage, she was the only woman he wanted by his side.

Chapter Twelve

Serenity drove past sections of manicured foliage on either side of a curved drive and passed the illuminated signage outside the imposing Children's Hospital that held the welcome of a witch's castle. Inside its walls lay one very special boy.

From the parking lot, she walked along the curb toward the looming entrance and scanned the property.

Owen called her on his cell. "I see you. I'm in the garden to the right of the hospital."

He'd watched for her.

His voice cracked. She'd stay strong.

His unmistakable form rose sluggishly from a bench beneath a sprawling tree. Lumbering her direction, he emerged into the weak light of dusk. His face was grave. Eyes reddened.

His silence slashed at her heart.

Tears glazed her eyes.

He bent and clutched her to him. The weight of his head pressed against the crook of her neck, an unstoppable defensive end crumbling in her embrace. His breathing slowed at their gentle swaying. It was difficult to tell who held who. At his muffled sniff, she smoothed her hands along his upper back, working out the hardness of what felt ominous.

Because wasn't this the proper response to reassure a troubled soul that all was well?

Daddy, do you think I'm special?

"You're here," he finally said.

"Who's with Eli?"

"His parents."

"Do they know what's wrong?"

He eased out of her arms, drew a knuckle to his eyes. Doubtful the human fortress had ever entrusted this vulnerable side to anyone. Pinpricks of waning light caught in his haggard gaze. "Eli has a brain tumor."

She took a half step back, clapped a hand to her mouth, and drew a hard breath. Emotion constricted her throat, pricking her heart. Sorrow bled through.

The depth of Owen's connection with his kids was crystal clear. When they lost, he lost. When they won, he won.

If they died, he did too.

"How serious is it?"

"Too soon to tell. They have to do a biopsy and a bunch of other medical stuff."

"Let's not lose hope."

He gave a pitiful laugh. "You're way further along on the hope journey than me. We're stronger together."

She loved being his strength, the voice of reassurance to speak truth into the hardness of his struggle. To meet a need where football and coaches and fans fell short. A man whose training included overturning tractor tires needed her assistance to bear up under sadness.

His large hand grasped hers as they plodded toward the entrance. The gesture caused her to consider the cost of loving a guy who, it seemed, doggedly refused to put his health—his love life and future—above his passion for the game.

At some point, she'd need to ask Owen the million-dollar question.

A velvety muse played in his gaze. "For whatever reason, I love Eli like he was my own kid."

Yes, she knew. She opened her mouth to speak and closed it, giving room for God to open Owen's heart and mind to see what he currently could not.

Or would not.

There was a vast difference.

Beneath the columned portico, a set of glass doors swished open and led to an expansive atrium. They took the elevator and followed a colorful tiled hallway to Eli's room.

At first sight of a pale, listless Eli, she inhaled slowly, emptied her lungs of heated breaths, and managed a smile. When they entered, Eli's father stood from a corner chair. His haggard expression belied the appearance of calm as conveyed in neatly trimmed hair, pale yellow shirt, and pressed khakis. Eli's mom turned and switched her gaze between her and Owen. The simple, fitted dress with scooped neckline matched her genteel smile.

Their dark hair and olive coloring bore minimal resemblance to Eli, whose round, fair-skinned, freckled complexion was crowned by blonde, cottony hair.

Between Eli's weakened state and the effect it'd had on Owen, Serenity wasn't sure where to direct her sympathy.

The father extended a hand. "Ross Billings. You must be Serenity."

She nodded and took his hand. "Yes. Nice to meet you, Ross."

"Thank you for taking time out of your busy day to be here. It means a lot to me and my wife, Arlene, and to Eli."

Eliminating the awkwardness of unfamiliarity, Arlene took Serenity's hands and squeezed them. A weathered smile tipped the edges of her tawny lips. "You must be the special lady Owen has talked so much about."

Serenity drew a cautious glance at Owen, whose mouth quirked in half-grin, deepening those trademark dimples.

Lifting the mood, Eli began to rattle off Owen's stats, including a few she'd not known.

A knock on the door drew heads toward an ebony-eyed doctor in blue scrubs, skin tone a light caramel color. "How is Master Eli feeling?"

One thin shoulder lifted—and sank. "Like a pin cushion," he muttered.

"What can you tell us, Doctor Amin?" Ross said, voice timorous.

The remains of a weak smile faded. Concern deepened the lines around Dr. Amin's eyes. "Without a biopsy, I cannot confirm, but the scans suggest we are dealing with a malignant, grade 4 astrocytoma. It is an aggressive tumor that grows into normal brain tissue. The goal of surgery is to remove as much of the tissue as possible."

"Why not all of it?" Owen challenged.

"Scans suggest complete removal will not be possible. The remaining cells can be treated with chemotherapy and radiation. I have referred Eli's case to a neuro-oncology, multi-disciplinary team for a complete assessment and treatment plan."

A guttural moan rumbled in Arlene's throat. She cupped her mouth, chest wrenching at the onset of a sob.

Serenity placed a hand on Arlene's shoulder.

Arlene took a few stumbled steps and raised limp arms to Serenity. "My son," she whispered.

"Would it help if we found someplace to talk?"

Sniffing, Arlene nodded vigorously.

Gently, Serenity drew back and turned to Owen. "Call if you need me."

Aimlessness claimed his expression. He returned a minimal nod.

The ink-black sky filled the windows of the atrium in the lobby. Serenity and Arlene found a quiet alcove and sat in cushioned armchairs. A small lamp table between them held a box of tissues.

Arlene curled her fingers into a fist at her knees, voice barely above a whisper. "I shudder to think God would find it good to take our only son."

"That would be hard to bear."

"This is something I never wanted to walk, a test I never wanted to take." Her shoulders sank in exhale. "No matter how they come to us, children are a gift from God. But, I guess ... they must be held loosely."

Truth rustled across Serenity's heart. She tugged two tissues, handed one to Arlene, and swiped at her nose with the other.

"Ross and I were married three years when I found out I was unable to have children. I wasted no time considering options to adopt and—"

"Eli was adopted?"

"Yes." Zeal electrified her tone. "God's grace visited me through the vessel of another woman's body."

Would God's grace visit Serenity?

"Eli was born at a county hospital in LA to a girl named Crystal. She was nineteen years old. The father had no intention of marrying her or caring for his son, so Crystal made her way to New Orleans, where she lived with an aunt. It was an open adoption. After we met her, we completed paperwork for home study and, in two months, Eli was ours." Her shoulders shook in pained laughter. "Initially, Ross resisted the idea, but once he'd held Eli in his arms ... considered the alternative for that baby boy ... God moved mountains in his heart."

Oh, kindred spirit. A woman who'd inadvertently furrowed the hard soil of barrenness and moistened it with raw authenticity, creating a fertile place for Serenity to share her own struggle.

"I understand infertility." When the truth shot out, it ripped a gaping hole in her stomach. Her chin quivered.

A long look of empathy and compassion softened the sheen of Arlene's eyes to velvet.

"No one knows that except my mom—who's passed away—my sister, and now you."

The fact that she'd thrust a dark secret into the light, entrusting it to a mere stranger, both unnerved and delighted her. A sudden urge to curl inside the warmth of her bakery nearly set her on a wild dash to the elevator.

"Not Owen?"

A weighty exhale left Serenity's lungs. "You know his love for kids. I can't ... Fact is, I'm not ... enough." Her voice was gravelly, crushing her words to little bits.

"I once believed that hooey. A counselor helped me rewrite the narrative. She said the problem wasn't my inability to bear children but to see myself the way God sees me. Complete. A masterpiece. Designed exactly the way he wanted and that he'd made no mistake."

Two opposing positions stared Serenity down. To protect her heart, she'd reject Owen if he divulged medical evidence of progressive brain injury—which he was powerless to change, but when and if she shared her limitations, she'd demand grace. Otherwise, he was no Christian.

The hypocrisy stung like a swarm of yellow jackets.

As people entered and exited the hospital, the cooler air of a summer evening breeze passed through the sliding doors. Inclining her heart to God's direction, Serenity gazed intently through his lens.

You must tell him.

I don't have the strength.

I am your strength.

The world and its brokenness faded into the background, delineating a portrait of a woman who'd reached the precipice of avoidance. Guilt pressed and shallowed her breathing. She clasped trembling hands across her knees.

Arlene placed her hand on Serenity's knee. "Don't give up on him."

Returning to Eli's room, Serenity paused at the open doorway to see Ross dozing in a corner chair, an open newspaper across his lap. Her gaze trekked to Eli, who'd fallen into an angelic slumber. Beside the bed, Owen had lowered his broad, muscular upper body to one knee. Head bowed, he'd shut his eyes and moved his lips.

Looking small against the enormity of God. A giant of a man defeated by a diagnosis, seeking divine intervention on behalf of his buddy.

The squeak of rubber tread alerted her presence. Owen shifted and glanced over his shoulder. When their gazes connected, he rose and dusted his knee. A wan grin fit his lips. "Hey," he said, voice froggy and tenuous.

Ross stirred and blinked to arousal. The paper fell to the floor. Yawning, he stood and gave his pants an upward yank. "Sorry. Must have nodded off." Arlene returned to the head of Eli's bed in the manner of a sentinel.

The posture of a mother where her child was concerned.

"Ross, I think it would be good to let Crystal know," Arlene said.

"Yes, I suppose she'll want to come see him." Ross took his cell in hand, excused himself, and left the room.

"Who's Crystal?" Owen said.

"Eli's birth mother."

In a heartbeat of mocking silence, Serenity detected the whirr and blip of medical machinery. Serenity watched Owen work his jaw back and forth. His expression hardened, and his eyes narrowed. A grim line drew across his jaw.

"I didn't realize Eli wasn't yours," he finally said, somewhat abruptly.

"Oh, he's ours." Arlene stroked fingers through Eli's hair, gracing him with rapt adoration. "I just didn't give birth to him."

Notably gobsmacked, Owen's shoulders sank in a slow exhale. He traversed a dismayed gaze between mother and child. Prior to returning to Eli's room, Serenity rashly let hope rise in her heart. Now it swirled like vapor before it vanished. Because this was not the response her heart needed.

Over the next half hour, the athlete and his number one fan filled the sterile room with therapeutic doses of playful banter while watching YouTube videos of remarkable Walker plays on Owen's phone.

"Where's that one where you intercept a pass, take it eighty yards for a touchdown," Eli begged as Owen lay next to him on the woefully small medical bed, his white athletic shoes extending several inches beyond the end of it.

"You mean the one where I leave a disgruntled running back in my rearview mirror?" he laughed, thumbing the screen.

For a benevolent guy who used his platform to rally people to dig deep and love well, why couldn't he extend the same kindness to himself?

Retire, you big, dumb jock. *Retire!*

As a veteran, Owen didn't attend camp to have his ability evaluated. He'd come to round back into form. He'd continued to maintain a minimum workout schedule, hitting the gym when he'd traveled. But months of endless cupcake consumption had left its mark, weakening muscle tone, strength, and agility. The next several weeks—two-a-day training, meetings, and pre-season games—promised to be brutal.

At night, he'd ingest sick amounts of food, take scalding hot baths, endure rub downs, and hit the sack early. The next day, he'd repeat the beating.

The anticipation—grueling drills, weight training, heat stroke, dehydration ... possible blows to the head—held the thrill of a root canal. Thus, the reason Owen returned three days late and had dragged his cleats every day since.

But camp separated the men from the boys. He was a man.

Which is why Dad's insistence that they talk outside the doctor's office yesterday had rattled his cage.

"What are you saying, Dad?"

"Contrary to what it may look like, I'm not enjoying any of this."

Outside the medical complex, the door had closed behind them, shutting disease and bad CAT scans inside. "I sure wish I'd listened to your mom when she begged me to turn in my helmet. For all its fancy engineering, the darn thing never did keep its promise to protect."

"Wait. Mom asked you to quit?"

"Many times."

"I had no idea."

"Never told you. Warned her not to talk you out of it either." He'd pressed fingers inside his pockets and kicked at a chunk of broken granite. "Just 'cause I got banged up, I saw no reason to side-swipe you from an illustrious career. And that handsome salary you've earned? You got someone to help you invest it. Helping poor kids and rebuilding the community. You've darn near changed the world. Lots of good things I never did."

A player whose career ended in his early thirties—Dad couldn't touch his pension until he was forty-five. As a result, the Walker family was hurting for cash following poor investments, prodigious spending, and mounting medical bills. The generosity of churches and local ministries kept them afloat.

Owen had scanned Dad's countenance, looking for signs of lucidity, distinguishing between truth and nonsense. Dad slapped him twice on the shoulder and squeezed. The way he'd done when he'd coached with clarity, fully convinced it would crush Mom's heart to see Owen leave the game.

Dad really was losing his marbles. Because if Owen's number ever came up for trade consideration, the public would conclude he wasn't serious about the game. His value would tank.

He'd tank.

The first of four highly anticipated pre-season games in August stared Owen down. He blamed last week's lack of vigor on concern for Eli, who'd undergone a craniotomy a week ago Friday and now faced the rigors of chemotherapy. But if Eli was called to suffer, he'd suffer right along with him.

Like a superhero, he squeezed into his uniform. Bulky, weighty pads pressed against his chest. Sweat sealed fabric to his skin.

As previous years had proven, every trace of mental meandering—fantasizing about life off the field—would halt in September when the regular season hit. Stadium light would flood the field, and he'd race over the turf, pumping his arms, showcasing a vicious mug for the cameras.

At the first feel of his arms coiled about the midsection of an offensive player, his spirit would soar again. That powerful, unstoppable resurgence of passion for the game would fit the truth back into its proper place. This was football. No other life for number 91.

The warmth of the overhead sun settled over Owen as he sat in his Bentley in front of the Metairie practice complex. He'd kept his hair closely shaved, a little longer on top and combed over, fluffed in places, because, fingering through his hair one night, Serenity had said she preferred it that way. He'd drawn her closer, and they'd kissed. A lot.

Man.

Since their providential encounter at the bakery, that amazing girl had taken up a great deal of space in his mind and heart. Thoughts of her had crowded out love for the game. Where was his zeal? The fire that used to burn inside and enable him to slam through an offensive lineup like they were paper dolls and sack, yet another QB?

A harsh command shocked him to attention. "Walker! Your job post-snap is to diagnose the blocking scheme and defend the gap!"

With fingers dug into the rough turf, he crouched in readiness. Shrill whistle … lunge forward, attack, and slam!

Repeat.

The past five months with Serenity stirred a mix of ingredients into a perfect product—the saucy girl with moves worthy of pro soccer, comfortable around his camp kids. Her soft blond hair that smelled of baked sugar framed the sweetest, most beautiful face he'd ever seen. He loved the way her long, fluttery eyelashes curled at the sides.

Yep. He was a wreck.

And what would happen to The Pear Tree by month's end? Had he done more harm by drawing clientele and then disappearing? Could she keep up the pace without his direct involvement?

A shrill whistle. "Walker! Get your head in the game! We're not all gathered here this afternoon in full gear to watch the grass grow." Defensive Coach McNamara's face matched the color of a stewed tomato. He wasn't being paid to boost a guy's ego. "This time, shoot the B-gap and attack the opponent's side of the line of scrimmage from the interior."

To this, there was no defense. Owen's bruised brain, presently tucked inside the swarming heat of a rock-solid helmet inside a stifling recreational facility, had succumbed to envisioning life after football.

So long as it included Serenity.

Side by side, the two of them inside a heated industrial kitchen. A happy, well-paid staff buzzing in and around the establishment.

His business smarts and her spunk and creative ingenuity.

Mmmm.

She was like a lone flower, sitting pretty out in a field. The uncommon, overlooked lavender rose among a dozen reds. Complicated and intricate in its design, intriguing and a little chaotic—in all the right ways.

He'd memorized that subtle mingling of fragrance at her neck—airy, flirtatious, with a sensual scent of flowers and honey.

The vision of her felt as real as the sun beating down overhead, sucking the breath from his burning lungs.

Bam!

A clunk echoed between Owen's ears and slammed against his head, twisting him into a knot on the field. In a hard thud, he rolled onto his back, arms splayed to his side. Sweat trickled past his face mask and streaked down his cheek.

A thick shadow moved in overhead and smothered. He peered through slit lids.

"Walker, what's gotten into you?" McNamara bit out. "You've got the attention span of a rock out here today."

Mr. Sensitivity, he was not.

Owen lolled his gaze upward, forcing eye contact with Coach, and raised a limp, gloved hand. "Yeah. Wasn't thinking, Coach."

"At your salary, you'd better be thinking."

He managed a nod.

"If I may remind you of the elementary rules of engagement, your job is to focus, dismiss potential distractions, and forget mistakes. Now get your butt up off the grass, take your position, and let's run this drill again."

Again and again and again.

Three hours in, wooziness crept into Owen's head and crawled past the shell of his helmet like a legion of ants. His cleats dragged over the turf, and lungs chugged for air. An aggressive shove from a fullback buckled his knees, slamming him to his side, arms and legs limp. Useless appendages.

Impotent and unfit.

Passion for the game ... drifting out of reach.

One torrential wave of pain traveled from his head down the length of his body.

"Sideline it, Walker. You're out for the day. Maybe longer. I'll have medical take a look."

He struggled to sit upright and draped his arms across his knees, waving a dismissive hand. "No, no. I'm fine."

"If that's fine, the NFL is wasting an astronomical amount of cash. I'm invoking the concussion protocol. See if they can figure out why you're training like a girl."

Actually, one girl, when handed a soccer ball, trained at least this hard. In life, in baking. In love.

Yeah. I love Serenity.

The hit was hardly just cause for a medical evaluation. He'd only been out for a few seconds.

"Three minutes, Walker."

Okay, off by a little.

Sheesh. A lot.

Seated on a round vinyl swivel chair, team doc Victor Blair rolled near. Gravity filtered into his gaze. The unnerving—familiar—look of a medical professional who bore unpleasant news.

"Back at it?"

The hitch in Doc Blair's voice, the steadied gaze tinted by pity as though he knew Owen had no other place to go.

He flashed a light into Owen's right eye. Held it and murmured. Flashed it left. Held it. Then pocketed the light, lips bunched into a tight circle.

A laptop on a rolling cart displayed Owen's medical chart. He glanced over his shoulder at the wall behind him, on which hung an illuminated image of Owen's brain. The tight network of gray and white and hazy markings—God's design under attack. But what would he know of medical tests? Radiographs? What did he care?

You need to care.

"First day in full gear, and you've already taken a hit?"

"I'm not a water boy. Hits come with the position. It's what God made me to do." There he went sermonizing, lugging God into the defensive lineup.

With his stare glued to the jarring, marbled x-ray image, Doc Blair's heaving sigh drew long. Slowly, he tilted his head as though seeking a different angle.

"I aced the cognitive test, right?" Owen curled his fingers under the exam table.

"No changes from last time. No improvement, either." He turned from the creepy visual. "How've you been sleeping?"

Fitfully. "Well enough."

Missing his girl. And those dreams had come more often. After he and Serenity had talked on the phone, he'd dozed off thinking of her. She arrived in his dreams, curled beneath his arm, her head pressed to his chest.

She'd clung, fitting against him perfectly ... hand in glove ... her breathing hitched and shallow.

"Walker?" Doc waved.

Owen blinked. "Huh?"

"What I see here concerns me. My advice is that you bow out before football drastically alters the course of your life."

Response clogged in his throat. His shoulders shook in a salty laugh.

"I know what could develop for athletes whose rads look like yours. The problem is, you're Owen Walker. The league won't cut you loose, and I'm not making this call." Doc rolled his squeaky chair close, voice grave. "The decision rests on you."

He stood and snagged his jacket. Wooziness filled his head. "Then we're done here."

Doc stood and unleashed a defeated exhale. "Guess so."

The heat of Doc's exasperated expression burned against his back as Owen exited the exam room.

Back in his car, discordant echoes of Doc Liljeberg's words last spring crackled through his brain like a welder's gun, soldering truth to his mental circuitry. He turned the ignition. The restraint of power roared beneath his seat. He pulled onto the main road, his thoughts a calamity.

Go forward and potentially end his career, incurring damage on the way out, or quit on his own terms and pursue the heart of the woman he loved.

Man, they'd make a winning team.

As he cruised south, he conjured the dream again. They'd have two boys on offense, two on defense, a QB, and a blonde-headed mirror image of Serenity.

But for all his hustle, Owen had yet to penetrate the defensive wall of Serenity Lewis. She had the impressive—and equally maddening—ability to both invite him in and refuse him entrance.

They shared a love for God and a desire to help the underserved. Lettie ratted her out that she'd persisted in giving free pastries to the homeless outside the bakery.

Sweet. Costly but sweet.

When it came down to it, the bakery was Serenity's ministry.

Back home, Owen toed off his shoes. The gaping quiet rattled through his brain. From his custom-built, modernized kitchen, he walked to the main room, trod over a sprawling area rug that lay over hardwoods, and trudged upstairs to his bedroom.

Lights on, he tossed his keys on the dresser. He sank against the edge of his king-sized bed, then threw the weight of his body onto his back. Fingers laced behind his head, he shut his lids. The pillow felt stiff against his neck.

Talk of hospitals and illness and surgery—blitzes. It all gave Owen headaches. Or maybe the headaches he'd experienced had nothing to do with being in the sterile environment for the sick and everything to do with something inside his brain.

Insidious and progressive.

Nausea and light-headedness niggled in. Sheesh. He texted Tommy Caplin.

OWEN: Symptoms again.

TOMMY: Name them.

OWEN: Headaches, nauseous. Weak. Forgetting things. What should I do?

TOMMY: Go see the trainer.

OWEN: He'll report it upstairs and put it in the file.

TOMMY: If you don't come forward, you won't get healthy and play your best.

In this league, the suggestion of injury was a death sentence.

A voicemail from Coach McNamara stung his senses. "I've seen the rads, today's performance. Time you and I had a talk."

Chapter Thirteen

Owen's power of persuasion stopped at McNamara. The effort to bring calm inside the inner sanctum of his office was as effective as slowing the advance of a funnel cloud with a grin. McNamara's demeanor was murky, thick, and furious in its velocity.

Designed for destruction.

He spun and raised a finger. "I didn't just crawl out from under a rock, Walker. Convince me there's no concern here."

"It's nothing. I'll push past it, give it everything I've got."

"I don't want one hundred percent," he sniped. "I want twice that."

"Yes, sir, Coach. Just got a lot on my mind right now." Like death.

And Seren.

"If anything inside your head isn't thinking blitzes and going after big uglies, get rid of it."

Three days after Eli's initial diagnosis, Owen visited Eli in the hospital—a promise he'd made to his buddy before they prepped him for surgery.

Fear of poor prognosis crept along his skin, dominating his thoughts. Hours spent researching brain tumors—like the one Dr. Amin said had found a home behind Eli's skull—fueled more concern.

Dr. Amin's quiet, articulate tone, skilled hands, and sturdy reputation for performing craniotomies should have been enough to slow the speed of Owen's pulse. But this wasn't just another kid with a tumor. It was Eli.

A boy he loved like his own.

Owen had researched the potential complications to brain tissue and nerves—memory, thinking, speech, behavior issues ... deafness, blindness, double vision ... paralysis, balance, and seizures. It all felt so unfair. Here was a kid who might become mentally and physically debilitated and couldn't blame the diagnosis on a hard-hitting career.

But like Owen, Eli's fate was in the hands of Almighty God.

At a water fountain in the corridor outside Eli's room, Owen took a small vial from his pocket and palmed two pain relievers. He bent to sip, popped the pills into his mouth, and swallowed. He rapped on the partially opened door and peered in to see Eli's languid, glassy eyes roving over the small, suspended, flat screen. Plastic tubing and clear bags of who knew what hung all around.

A profile that he'd always assumed bore the image of Ross and Arlene now held a genetic mystery. It turned out that Eli was the product of a girl named Crystal and some coward who, Ross had said, split after he learned she was pregnant.

To think the fate of an unborn baby boy—*his* Eli—had been left in the hands of an unwed mother.

Thank you, God, for preserving and nurturing his life. And bringing him into mine.

His chest tightened. The sensation reached behind his eyes and stung. No. He didn't come here to cry. Crouch to position, eye on offense.

He gulped the air, squared his shoulders, and entered with a cool saunter like the kid was merely having a mole removed. "How's my superstar?"

Eli turned his attention to Owen. A measure of surprise played in his haggard gaze.

In the space of only three days, Eli looked markedly thinner, his cheeks sallow. Owen sidled over, doggedly determined to deliver happiness in a place the size of a blue tent.

And just as unpleasant.

"I got about thirty minutes before I head to camp. Don't want to be late."

"It started at six this morning. You're already late. By *three* days. And made a buttload of fans righteously angry."

Okay, so the little man had his guns loaded.

"You ever consider going into investigations, pal?" Owen snagged a chair, spun it backward, and sat hard on it. "I think you've got a bright future."

"Do you know how many people stayed up all hours to stand in line, paying ridiculous amounts of money to see you?"

And suddenly, faster than a fake punt, a role reversal had taken place. Shame niggled in and tugged at his shoulders. "Ever consider what it feels like to fear heat stroke while getting hit on for six hours a day, and some of that in the form of verbal abuse from defensive coaches? They can really hurt a guy."

"What's the real reason you've been a no-show?"

"Investigations?" Owen inched a brow. The attempt to deflect failed.

"C'mon, Walker." Eli interlaced his fingers at his middle. "I'm waaaiting." The lilt in his tone rattled down Owen's back.

Eli the Conqueror dug his bony little elbows into his pillow and concentrated his stare.

How could Owen tell his number one he'd wrestled with the beast of apathy and wasn't sure he could carry on? That the amount of fervor he had for the game would fill a thimble? That he'd grown to hate being pinned between the turf and three offensive linemen—struggling for oxygen. Fearing the game he'd loved could kill him, ruin his shot at the girl he'd come to—

"I just ... It's that—"

"You love her. That much I know." Eli tapped his temple.

"Wow, kid. Seriously, investigations." He extended a hand. "Let's shake on it."

Eli shook Owen's hand, then, maneuvering the network of tubes, folded his arms. His lips pinched to a little round circle. "Own up."

"Yes. I love her."

"What does she say to that?"

"I haven't told her."

Eli's cute, round face was quickly morphing into Judge Judy's.

And, honestly, Owen had no good reason for not telling Serenity. Figured he'd done for the bakery what was asked, and she had no more need of him. Maybe stoking the fires of romance had been the wrong play. One that could cost him the greatest game of his life.

"Can't be harder than telling a twelve-year-old kid who's dying of brain cancer that you've got weaknesses." He raised a practiced, three-finger Boy Scout salute. "I promise to take your secret to the grave."

His jaw hardened. He balled a fist inside his palm. "You're not dying, Eli. They can fix this. Remember how it goes, 'I may win, and I may lose ...'"

"But I will never—"

"Be defeated."

"Emmitt Smith."

Owen touched his knuckles to Eli's. "Smart kid."

"Back to Serenity. She's pretty. And she likes you, too. That sappy look you both have when you're around each other is indefensible. You got the bakery thing in common. I seriously doubt she'd say no. So I think your greatest play would be to retire and go after her."

How could he even suggest—

"You'd hate it if I stopped playing, kid."

"Doesn't matter if I would or not. You're already my hero. The question really is, can *you* be okay if you stopped playing."

With the stretch of a yawn, Eli's lids shuddered closed. The question of the century was left hanging, thick in the air between them.

Owen leaned in, patted the superstar on the leg, and padded out the door.

Interrogation sure had a way of wearing a little body out.

Minutes after Serenity's sports app notified her of Owen's sidelining, the solemn news had reached the smattering of bakery patrons—the faithful few who'd favored Serenity's Special.

The interview depicted a conflicted man—showered and wearing street clothes. Owen's closely shaved head angled down, eyes shaded by the brim of a ball cap. When pelted with questions about his future, he gave no more than an occasional, indifferent shrug.

Owen clasped his hands and circled his thumbs in wild rotation. "Comes with my position. Not worried a bit. Medical has cleared me. I'm good to go and ready for another winning season."

And then he gave that enigmatic Walker smile that'd found its way into Serenity's heart and took up residence in her soul. At his parting comment, a barrage of cameras flashed against the banner behind where he sat, the issue dropped.

In a heated whisper, she mouthed at her phone. "Retire. R-E-T-I-R-E."

A tongue cluck drew her attention to Lettie, who'd come in for a few hours to bake several batches of cinnamon pear muffins. "I don't buys it that you don't love the man."

"Who could possibly love that stubborn fool?"

In a slow movement, Lettie drew her gaze upward, jut a chin. "Another stubborn fool."

Serenity's cheek twisted into a grin. "You're one wise and wonderful lady."

Lettie cracked an egg on the edge of the silver mixing bowl. "I's just one fool to another, blessed beyond what I deserve."

Inventory to par level and prepped on metal trays on the racks, Serenity left Lettie to her artistry. In the dining area, she drew in the heady scent of blossoming lavender roses she'd purchased and set near the register. The bell over the door pinged. Everley entered, a belly round and full of life beneath a baby blue maternity shirt. Trepidation fell over her features. She paused her wobbled steps and drew a slow gaze around the room like she'd boarded the Titanic.

"Hi, Evers. Doctor freed you to drive?"

"No. Gabe dropped me off. Had to pick up some supplies from his warehouse."

"Good man. Taking care of my nephews." Serenity drew her into an easy hug, Everley's abdomen taut against her own. One teeming with life, the other dark and void.

"You decided on names yet?"

"Getting close. We're thinking Dalton after his dad and Peter after Dad."

"I love it!"

"You free to talk? Somewhere private?" She clasped both hands over her protruding abdomen. "It's important."

Everley's ominous tone rankled. The sound of impending doom. Entering behind her were two women dressed in professional attire and pump heels.

"I'm going to say hi to Lettie. Be right back." Everley excused herself and waddled into the kitchen.

The women approached the loaded display case, stooping to peruse the pastries.

"I don't see any," one of them said, her brow notched.

The other produced a punch card. Owen's idea—buy ten pastries, get one free.

The first woman straightened. Disappointment soaked her tone. "Are you out of Walker's Big Hits?"

"We are." Really out.

Tweedle Dee and Tweedle Dum exchanged disappointed glances and shook their heads.

Tweedle Dee leaned a hand to the top of the case. "We drove all the way down from Baton Rouge to taste and see what all the fuss was about."

"Anything associated with Owen Walker has got to be golden," Tweedle Dum said, slipping the punch card back inside her wallet.

"I should have called first." Tweedle Dee paused in thought. "Will you expect more today?"

"Sorry, but those were a seasonal offering." Came and went. No promise of return. Her gut wrenched at the thought. She rallied, bobbed on her toes, and arched a brow to incite interest. "But I've got a fresh batch of Serenity's Specials. Frosted within the last hour."

A shrug. "Sure, I guess."

"What choice do we have?"

Their reluctance shivered down Serenity's spine. She served two lavender-frosted cupcakes with a cordial cherry tucked inside, then prepared their order of Special K blend and a matcha latte. Pleased with the alternative, the pernicious pair paid and sat in the nook by the window.

Everley returned, a hand pressed to her lower back. Her breaths were short and shallow. "Free to talk?"

"I've got all the time you want."

"Maurice called to say you hadn't returned his call."

Angst clutched her chest and twisted the screws. "Now I've only got two seconds."

In the eight years since Serenity opened the bakery, Maurice had called three times. The first was right after she'd moved in, a robust welcome to assure everything was suitable, the new front door key a proper fit. The second was last January when she'd been late on lease payment, the early symptoms of Bakery World's infestation. At that time, his call had come with a kind warning, unable to abide delinquency. Today's call was the third. It likely held bad news.

Frustration had Serenity sweeping an arm over the dining area. "As you can see, The Pear Tree is not quite booming. It won't be long before word travels that Owen is no longer in my employ to bake his winning cupcakes and regale customers with career highlights."

A mix of sympathy and level-headed reasoning reigned over Everley's expression. "How about we take this conversation to the courtyard."

"Serenity's Special on the house?"

"I'd love nothing better."

Plating the cupcake, Serenity turned toward the courtyard. The absence of happy chatter, along with chairs all askew around empty tables, resounded discordant notes in Serenity's head. Not long ago, clientele made sport of finding an open table.

Rainfall earlier in the day left a muggy, earthy feel. Thick, hazy sunshine filled the courtyard. Choosing a table along a wall that held one of Momma's oil paintings, Serenity inhaled the musty smell of moist pavement, cigarette smoke, and manure.

With care, Everley lowered herself into a chair, grimacing as she curled her hands around the table's edge for balance. Serenity reached a hand to her arm and guided her descent.

"As to your unspoken question about why I haven't returned Maurice's call," Serenity said. "I've been distracted."

"How so?" Everley peeled off the cupcake casing.

"Owen's injury during a camp scrimmage, a *scrimmage*, mind you, has my insides quivering."

She'd given herself points for having felt even the smallest dose of compassion for the stubborn athlete. An untrained eye could ascertain he hadn't played to the best of his capability.

"And then we found out Eli has a brain tumor."

Sorrow waved over Everley's brow. "So sorry to hear that."

"Me, too. I've gotten close to him and his mom, Arlene. He's such a special kid. Means the world to Owen."

Gaze intent, Everley sank her teeth into the frosting. "How serious is it?"

"His tumor was diagnosed as grade four, the worst ever. That … and Owen …" Bullheaded jock. She sniffed. "I hadn't realized The Pear Tree was a sinking ship."

A murmur of sympathy rumbled in Everley's throat. She took the napkin to her lips and nodded. "Gabe and I would loan you the difference, but most of what we bring in as B&B proprietors goes toward maintaining Moreland, and it'd only compile debt on top of your outstanding bank loan."

"That's okay. I'd hate to ask that of you anyway."

"Maurice says he won't renew the lease and has other plans for the space. It kills me to say it, but you'll have to vacate by the end of the month."

Which meant one thing. The Pear Tree was gasping its last breath.

Dying ...

The place people frequented for its uniqueness. A cozy, eclectic vibe and signature offerings at fair pricing. At its heart, The Pear Tree was not a bakery but an experience—a world apart from the world. Here, lucrative business deals had been made, patrons found solace, the hungry were fed, and relationships reconciled. One time, a proposal took place here in the courtyard and garnered feverish attention from social media.

"Kourtney has graduated and taken a full-time job, and while that cuts costs, you've lost your best barista. You've still got Brooke and Lettie, but they don't work for free."

The odds were mounting against Serenity—stacking up like bricks.

"Back in March, your net profit over the first week equals what August has brought in."

Owen.

"But quite simply, accounts payable are greater than receivables."

Owen, Owen.

"Believe me, I've looked at this from every angle." Everley gave the metallic, uncompromising tone of one who worked with numbers.

Serenity raised a staying palm, waving it rapidly. "No need to say more."

The glacial reality slicked down her spine, icy shards slashing at her heart. Was this how it felt for a mother to have her child plucked from her arms or lost to miscarriage, its heart beating one second, life snuffed out the next?

"I know you've had your eye on that Victorian in Napoleonville," Everley said. "Maybe God is doing a beautiful new thing."

Hope sprang to life. Serenity rallied her wits. "I'll tell Maurice about the recipe contest and ask him to hold off on his decision until the winner is chosen. Because if I win, I'll be in solid financial standing for several months."

The prize money and media spotlight would propel her up and out of this pit and breathe life apart from relying on the Kings' favored defensive lineman who'd persisted in having the life beat out of him.

"Your optimism, as always, is admirable, but Maurice has extended all the grace he's willing. I seriously doubt—"

"Please don't layer logic and reasoning over this. Let me dream." She sniffed and clutched Everley's knee. "The Pear Tree is *my* child."

Everly's gaze softened. She cupped a hand over Serenity's hand. Envy seeped into her tone. "For what it's worth, I've always admired you for having the courage to chase after your dream. Unafraid of the risk involved in creating a beautiful space like this. I wasn't given the unhindered spirit you and Mom and Dad have."

"Thanks, Evers. It sure doesn't come without cost."

When Gabe returned, van idling out front, Serenity draped an arm over Everley's shoulders as they walked to the curb. She embraced Gabe in a quick greeting and ambled back inside. Her cell pinged a voicemail notification from Maurice, his message peppered with a French accent and directive clear. "I give you two weeks to vacate de premises, Meese Lewis." A stiff laugh held derision. "Unless you can produce a miracle."

The man believed in miracles, did he?

Today called for one.

Chapter Fourteen

An idea erupted through the thick shadows threatening to engulf Serenity's soul. What if she could convince Owen to work for her? It was no secret he loved being there, and he'd performed admirably. The numbers proved he could bring in business. Inside that fissured skull, he possessed valuable marketing smarts. If he sold sticks, people would come for miles to buy them.

He was Owen Walker—the force behind The Pear Tree's success over the past five months.

After closing the bakery, Serenity drove to the athletic complex in Metairie, the location of the Kings' training camp. In the location where athletes exited, she spotted Owen's Bentley and waited.

Within fifteen minutes, players began to emerge. She concentrated her gaze and spotted Owen's sturdy gait, his thighs like trunks. A sliver of hope resided inside that muscular frame.

Key fob in hand, he lumbered toward his car wearing track pants, a black T-shirt, and athletic shoes, the gait of a soldier returning from war. His car sounded a chirp. When he met her gaze, a slow smile broke across his handsome face.

Hello there, Mr. Hope.

Leaning against her car, she raised a hand to wave. "Hey."

"Aren't you a sight for sore eyes and one heck of a sore body." He enfolded her to his chest, kissed her head, and inhaled. As they swayed side to side, a weary sigh left his lungs.

"I heard about your mishap on the field today."

One cheek inched in a grin. "It's nothing."

"I've got a proposition for you."

A wide grin rose on his face. He drew his gaze down her front and circled it back to fix a foxy stare on her.

"Not what you think, Walker."

"That's too bad 'cause you're my person."

One hand behind her neck and the other at her back, he kissed her, mouth urgent and achy and wanting. His sporty, fresh, clean scent shivered through her, swirling like frosting down to her toes.

He picked me.

"What do you think about working full-time at the bakery?"

He straightened, taking half a step back. An awkward smile claimed his face, signature dimples lacking impact. "I can't."

"But you could."

"It's not who I am."

"Neither is football."

"You're wrong. It is."

Exasperation shimmied down her spine and firmed her stance. "Why doesn't someone in that almighty league have the guts to get in your face and warn you against carrying on?"

His stare faltered, lids flickering. He jerked a glance away and sluggishly brought it back, lips thinning in resolve.

They'd reached an impasse. Offense against defense. Now wasn't the time to tell him she'd been desperate, that if she didn't win Chef Carlyle's contest, he'd be her only hope, but he had pretty much trampled it beneath his cleats.

With one hand fisted at her leg, she refused pity. He'd merely write her a check and save the day, leaving his heart out of it.

Defeat slumped her shoulders. Her chin quivered. She removed her gaze to the spectacle of an early evening sky. Shades of orange took on a sulphuric glow. Her heart sank in somber dusk.

Sorry, Pear Tree. Momma tried.

It would be nothing short of a miracle for her to afford the Victorian she adored in Napoleonville—to have Gabe restore and outfit the house as a bakery and coffee shop to service a community without one.

Owen cupped her jaw and tilted his chin to target his gaze. "You okay, Seren?"

She gave a feeble nod.

"That's my girl." He gave her shoulders a squeeze. "I've got good news."

You'll quit and work with me.

"I've secured six tickets for the season opener on September 10th. Three for Dad, Derek, and Julianne. You could go with Gabe and Everley. Or Brooke and Justin. Whoever you want."

He's who she wanted. Seated beside her, cheering from the safe zone. Out of harm's way.

Another season. The phrase rankled like a bad CAT scan. She turned her gaze upward, let it linger, and slowly winged a brow. Giving ample opportunity for him to register the gravity his decision had on her.

The way he deepened his dimples and pasted a proud smile to his lips suggested he hadn't computed.

Any other girl would've raised her arms skyward in a hallelujah at the coveted gift. She was not now—nor ever would be—any other girl. As his select person, she'd been privy to personal time with Harvey Walker and what it could mean for Owen to staunchly forge ahead, still believing he was invincible.

But the truth was, stars did fall from the sky. He could be the next.

A sigh filled her lungs, threatening to rip through her chest. She released it in a jagged breath and nodded an obligatory thanks. Further attempts to convince him to give this game up amounted to talking to a brick wall.

"What's the update on Eli since his first chemotherapy?" she said.

Reticence claimed his expression. Tension ticked along his jaw. His gaze dulled to pewter. "Ross said his first round went pretty well, considering how weak he is."

"I've been praying for him—that he'll make a full recovery."

"Me, too." He leaned in for another kiss as if he'd drawn strength from her essence.

A warbled vision came into focus—the two operating as a power duo to help sweeten the world. Just as quickly, she shut her eyes against it, hating herself for liking the idea of them so much.

The world spun, jumbled her thoughts.

"Pretty crazy to learn that Eli was adopted."

At her effort to prod a response, his eyes turned flinty and hard. He shifted his stance like he was unsure what to do with his feet. "Makes me sad for him."

"Why? Ross and Arlene are wonderful parents."

"Yes, they are." He rubbed his chin, staring absently. "But for all Dad's faults, I get this incredible satisfaction when I look at him, study his mannerisms. The size of his hands, shape of his fingers, and his stature and brute strength. Even the way he walks and processes information. I love the fact that those aspects of him are manifested in me and Derek."

Callahan, the QB, whizzed past, honking as he waved at Owen out his window.

"I can't imagine how disconnected a kid must feel to be unable to see a likeness of himself in another person. It'd feel like standing in front of a mirror that's been blacked out. And what if they get sick and have no way of knowing if it was a genetic thing? I'd hate that for my kids."

Forever conjuring little Walker people.

Her ribs grew tight, restricting her breath.

He lifted his brows a bit, inviting her to agree.

She couldn't. She wouldn't. At best, he'd be annoyed. At worst, it'd be all over.

The best strategy was to lead him to the water's edge of truth and invite him to drink.

"Eli gives no evidence he feels slighted by being raised by two people who aren't his biological mother and father. They are the parents God gave him."

Contemplation moved like clouds over his eyes.

"As much as you love kids, I can't understand why you wouldn't consider adoption. You'd be giving a child a loving home, raising them to know Jesus and that he loves them more than you ever could."

He leaned in and tucked hair behind her ears. His lips feathered hers as he spoke in a breathy whisper. "I've got you."

Disquiet rolled in thunderous waves along her neck and thickened in her throat. The truth simmered on her tongue, no—burned. She stepped as close to the precipice as she dared. "Owen, what if I can't have children?"

Incredulity claimed his expression, nearly collapsing her lungs.

A heartily amused laugh shook his upper body. "You, Seren, can do anything."

Almost anything, big guy. Almost.

Serenity refused despair's attempt to engulf her, a feat worthy of an Olympic gold medal. Since Owen's incident four days ago, he'd called her every night, regaling her with play stats, minimizing the grueling nature of each morning's required rehab with the team trainer. Being Saturday—and one of the three days off allotted in August—he'd committed to spending the day fishing with Harvey and Derek on Derek's boat while Serenity broke the bad news to Lettie and Brooke about Maurice's decision.

"I'm afraid The Pear Tree's closing is imminent and binding."

Tears were shed, and hugs exchanged. Optimism bubbled up. "We could give the remaining baked products to the soup kitchen in Napoleonville or New Orleans' Second Harvest food bank," she said.

"I know a church that might want to purchase some kitchen equipment," Brooke said.

"Great idea. I'll call the artisans and have them pick up unsold paintings and pottery."

"And all those books?" Brooke motioned toward labored shelving.

"With the exception of the signed copy I got from my romance author friend in North Carolina—which I treasure—I'll donate them to a library or school."

Eyes ringing red, Lettie clasped hands in her lap and sighed. "I's shore gonna miss this place. Gots to find me another job."

Sitting straighter, Serenity grasped Lettie's hand. "You should talk to Everley and Gabe. They could use your help at Moreland."

The split of a smile showcased large, pearly teeth. "Truth, Miz Serenity. Come October, those rascally boys will demand attention."

"Everley maintains a full schedule of overnight guests, which requires meal preparation and service and housekeeping, and she hosts luncheons and philanthropic events."

At Serenity's attempt to spread sunshine, Lettie's eyes went silky. Daylight streamed warmth over the courtyard.

"We've still got nine days. Let's make the best of it."

The next morning, a lone customer sat near the front window with his $2.00 order of black coffee. He turned from his laptop. Confusion rang in his tone. "Did y'all change the Wi-Fi password? WALKER FAN isn't working."

"Yes." Serenity crossed over to his table. "It's B-U-L-L."

Tap, tap, tap, tap.

Face slightly screwed and fingers hovering over the keyboard, he waited.

"H-E-A-D-E-D."

Tap, tap, tap, tap, tap, tap.

Mouth partly unhinged, he turned a perplexed gaze her direction. "Is that it?"

"Number nine and then one."

Tap, tap.

He shrank back. His complexion shifted a degree toward chalk. "Bullheaded nine-one."

"Did that work?"

"S-sure."

Two days before the end of August, Serenity arranged for Gabe and his crew to empty the place. Once hollowed, she left The Pear Tree to grieve in private before Maurice posted signage on the door.

At the precise ticking of God's timetable, the bakery's final day arrived. Realization alighted on Serenity's thoughts and kept her sinking emotions above water. The Pear Tree had been a gift—a very good one. A place to express her own brand of uniqueness, birth new pastries, and bless the community. A conduit through which, two years prior, she'd met Gabe Bellevue. His Friday morning visits to buy products—for himself and the downtrodden—ultimately led to him being a player in God's sovereign plan, whereby he found Everley, his forever girl.

At what point had Serenity adopted The Pear Tree as her child? She didn't know. But the fact that she had made it all the more difficult to let go.

Staring at the interior brick wall—the bakery now a gaping hole—a lament of yesterday clanged through her soul ... a flashback to the day she, Gabe and Everley, and Brooke and Justin had painted and hauled in equipment, seating, fixed countertops, and display cases. Preparing a nursery of sorts, anticipating new life.

Serenity was a unique combination of many intricate parts. Owen had been the only man in her life who'd been industrious and interested enough to discover what they were.

Owen. Her bakery needed Owen. *She* needed Owen. But Owen had chosen football.

Anguish sucked the air from Serenity's lungs. Slumped against the brick wall, her knees buckled and drew her to the floor. Her heart lay in crumbled little pieces.

After several minutes, she rose and fell momentarily dizzy against the wall. Leaving the scent of sugar, pears, and dreams behind, she shut the front door. She turned the key in the worn brass handle and tugged. Impulsively, she gave the handle a turn.

To enter now would be trespassing. A federal offense.

Sagging clouds outlined in stark granite cloaked a pale dusk. Gaslights glowed inside halos of foggy air.

Garbled sounds drifted from open bars. Atypical quiet exploded from nearby Jackson Square. She started at the ping of an email notification on her cell.

Bryan J. Carlyle's name popped off the screen. The subject line read, "Contest winner announced."

She clicked on it, reading the perfunctory greeting. "Thanks for entering your recipe."

Her gaze skimmed the first few lines, then skidded to a stop.

"Unfortunately—"

Her stomach took a downward dip. The sting of tears built a force behind her eyes.

A young couple ambled past and stopped just past the entrance. Serenity recognized them as Gregory and Lauren, the enthused couple at City Park who'd wanted a picture with Owen.

With *Owen*.

She stepped into the shadows and made herself small, leaning a shoulder to the brick and gazing down at the pavement.

"Oh, wow. Out of business?" Gregory said.

"The bakery with the courtyard, wasn't it?" Lauren said.

"Yeah."

"It wasn't all that great."

"Especially since Owen Walker doesn't work there anymore."

"And it's next to impossible to find a place to park."

Objections to the bakery swirled above their head like air pollution from an oil refinery. A turbo-charged counteroffensive scream fired up and lodged in her throat.

Through a blur of tears, Serenity watched as they continued on their way, the caustic review entangled by the jarring screech of a jazz player.

Chapter Fifteen

Seated inside the Mercedes-Benz Superdome, the roar of the crowd banged against Serenity's chest. Justin sat on the other side of Brooke to Serenity's right, offered his thoughts—as though Serenity had asked.

She hadn't.

"I started playing football when I was yay high." Justin extended a hand a few feet from the ground. "It's tough to sit from this vantage point and realize all I've missed out on. The thrill of the game." Slowly, he shook his head as if that were the worst news in all history.

No good would come from debating the negative aspects of said game. Certainly not with Harvey squeezed in beside her on the left, grumbling in low tones. Every few seconds, he'd interject his play-by-play to Derek, who sat on the other side of him—his wife Marianne snuggled in beside Derek—and bellow at the refs, who were—according to Harvey—complete idiots.

"Few people really understand a guy's passion for football and the hardship of being denied the opportunity to act on it," Justin added.

The sentiment pinpricked Serenity's heart. Brooke gave Justin a pat of sympathy and leaned in to kiss him on the cheek. "I love you, J."

He managed to remove his gaze from the field long enough to return a smile and wink. "I love you, too, babe."

And Serenity loved Owen—the guy who *wasn't* denied the opportunity and fueled an inner vow to keep his cleats on the field. NFL's prize possession. A commodity paid millions who was—currently—at great risk.

Not to mention a supreme baker with marketing savvy and kisses hot enough to smelt iron.

Her gaze fixed on number 91, crouched and hungry at the line of scrimmage. Serenity's admission fizzed like effervescent bubbles and rose to her throat, constricted by emotion.

While Justin kept a slit-eyed gaze ahead to suggest he'd lasered the entirety of his focus on the remaining minutes, Serenity touched Brooke on the knee.

"I love him, Brooke." The words eked out in a raspy whisper.

Brooke turned to Serenity, the angle of her brow soft and agreeable. "Then tell him how you feel."

"What's the point? It's reckless to love a man who wants what I can't give."

"It's a greater wrong to deny him the privilege of choosing you. He'll respect that."

Then he'll walk, no, *run* away.

"You've had a few solid proposals in the past and turned them down for no good reason, Serenity. I *know* you want to get married—raise kids."

Over what had been deemed a bad call, the crowd rose and spewed obscenities—Justin among them. "Ah, c'mon, ref! Screw your head on straight!"

More whistles. Serenity strained to see around fans who'd stood and blocked her sight. The Tigers had possession of the ball. They desperately sought to gain yardage and penetrate the Walker Wall, the Kings' prime weapon of destruction.

Good luck with that.

Brooke nudged Serenity. "Fight for him."

A soul-deep realization awakened. For far too long, Serenity lived in fear of disappointing others. Namely Daddy. When he'd sustained a tragic fall off Moreland's south wing roof when she was eight, he'd taken his honest assessment of his youngest daughter to the grave, leaving her to guess. To daydream. To conjure fantasies of Daddy assuring her he loved her exactly the way she'd been designed.

For years, she'd wrestled against the belief that God had made a mistake. That he'd stood at a holy assembly line and gaped in frustration at the way *this* one turned out. Mom's pithy answer had only muddied the picture.

"Your sister hides behind a safe and predictable life, in need of someone—or something—to nudge her out of it," she'd said. "But you, Serenity, are a free-thinker. Unafraid to dream big and open your heart in love. You are your own unique and wonderful self. What could possibly be wrong with that?"

A lot, Momma.

Was she worth the effort? What if she turned out to be one big disappointment?

Fear had enslaved her. Kept her from fighting for what she most desired—the love of a good man, the hope of a family. On the whisper of her heart's confession, it was time to put things to the test.

Did Owen have smarts enough to love a woman who was incomplete?

At game's end, she'd know. As planned, she'd wait with Brooke, Justin, Harvey, Derek, and Marianne until Owen emerged from the belly of the Superdome, showered and satisfied and kissable. She'd congratulate his accomplishment and welcome his embrace and let her heart do the talking.

Week after agonizing week under a blazing sun, Owen endured the grueling drills. Often, he wanted to vomit. On one occasion, he did—after taking a wild dash toward the trees bordering the field. Then he'd rallied, forced a smile, and delivered his practiced reassurance to a lineup of concerned staff that nothing was wrong.

"Just needed to catch my breath," he'd said.

Two-a-days had been torturous. Technique, play execution, full-speed drills. Daily lifting sessions. Meetings and endless practice films. Today's sweat mixed with ointment spread over yesterday's bruises. His brain and body felt like they'd been in a car accident. But he'd push through the stiffness, strained back, and bruises, an ongoing goal of catching the eye of the coaching staff. A heroic effort to give credibility to their decision to keep him on the field.

How could they not?

He was Owen Walker.

Walkers play ball.

It'd taken a few scrimmages before he'd acclimated to game speed and shook off lax technique. Following today's pregame warm-up, fans clustered throughout the stadium for the season opener. Cheers thundered as more filed in.

He was ready.

The thought of Serenity here to watch him play had the effect of a full day's workout. Invigorating, empowering. Dad and Derek were icing on the cake.

Speaking of cake, he'd chosen to rectify what, on the surface, was a lucrative financial move on his part but amounted to a thoughtless and hair-brained decision.

"Sell my shares in Bakery World, Nina," he'd said.

"I don't advise it, my love. Their value surged. You've gained another two grand."

"Good, funnel those gains toward The Pear Tree."

At season's end, he'd focus his attention on his relationship with Seren. Take a long look at a future together.

If she wanted him.

For now, head coach Griff Wagner barked orders in the locker room to gather 'round.

Fantasies muscled in, daring him to shed the burden.

Quit, Owen. Quit while you can. Before it's too—

He tamped the idiocy down to his cleats and crushed it. A well-trained body now constricted inside pads and stretch pants, Owen was here for those who'd come to see him play. To add depth to the team and bring home a win.

"Play for Seren."

In step with his teammates, Owen's nubbed cleats clicked on the paved, shadowed tunnel. A circle of sunlight at the end of it widened as they strode toward the stadium and onto the field. Spectators cheered in resounding thunder. Adrenaline dumped into his muscles.

A rustle of nerves fired down Owen's spine as he huddled mid-field under the direction of wide receiver and team leader Christian Russell. Fingering the Q-collar at his neck, he circled his head and eased tension by bouncing on his toes.

"Let's fight for each other tonight!" Christian said.

The steady thunder of energized fans boomed behind his chest pads.

"We control our process, not whether we win or lose, so just give it all you got. No matter what it takes."

No matter what.

Don't let me down, son.

No, sir, Dad.

Fist raised in a battle-ready war cry. Christian elevated his voice over the huddle. "Let's go get this one!"

Forefingers jabbed the air in a synchronized cheer. "One, two, three!" Following a hard clap, the huddle broke into position.

The shrill whistle splintered the stadium and cracked through Owen's brain.

Owen jogged toward the thirty-two. First and ten for the Tigers. Crouched in a three-point stance and right arm cocked near his thigh, he'd ensure they'd gain little to no yardage. The turf tingled through the steepled fingers of his left hand. His heart drummed behind his pads. He locked a concentrated gaze on the lineman as power surged through his limbs, ready to rush.

Watching, Seren?

Throughout his years in the league, no woman had ever flickered through his mind in the heat of play. In no uncertain terms, Owen loved Serenity something wild.

Up by fourteen at the half, his unstoppable rushing and two QB sacks called for a triple-team. Making him more vulnerable to friendly fire from linebackers and safeties. To start off the second half, he rushed through an offensive wall, lunging for the QB for his third sack.

In the fourth quarter, Coach Wagner switched Owen out for number 99, Antonio Tyson. He blamed his substandard performance on a bout of wooziness and mild dehydration. He hailed the water boy, who dashed over and handed him a chilled bottle which he drained in seconds. The glaring lights aggravated a prick of pain at his temples. Gulping the ever-thinning air, his chest hitched in and out. Sweat drenched his neck and face, helmet a vice around his head.

Play. At all costs.

Huddle up. Determine strategy. Focus.

Next play, holding the QB in his line of vision, he dug through a triple-team offensive wall and crushed a player whose gaze rounded in shock.

Success!

Owen scrambled to his feet and bobbed a head in victory. Did she see it? Was she proud?

I love Seren.

Again, ready stance. Watch for the snap and take aim.

The clock ticked the remaining minutes of the game, the Kings up by twenty-one—a comfortable, unbeatable margin. Coach McNamara slapped him on the butt. "Walker. You're up. Let's secure the win!"

Mmmm. Snug inside the skin of who he was.

The heat inside his helmet intensified. Air sawed in and out of his lungs.

The Tigers broke their huddle and established formation. The QB prepped for third down. Glancing left and right, he called the play and took the easy snap. He shuffle-stepped backward and scrambled to dodge a sack. The ball connected with the receiver.

Targeting the handler, Owen powered past the linebacker. He clipped a towering, stocky guard and stumbled, nearly sliding beneath the weight of what would have amounted to an aluminum can being crushed by an eighteen-wheeler.

Regaining momentum, he pumped his arms and sped toward the receiver. Head angled to intercept his opponent, his helmet collided with unyielding chest pads.

Slam!

His neck jerked and twisted.

Two milliseconds passed. Stars flashed. The space in his brain gave way to silent blackness. A widening mental hole flattened him onto his back, and his arms went limp and splayed against the turf.

Immobilized ... head spinning.

He registered discordant whistles and a rush of footfall around his head. Figures overshadowed him. One crouched at his side, leaning in.

"Walker. It's Doctor Blair. Can you hear me?"

"Yeah. Of c-course."

Another voice. "Owen, it's Steve. You know who I am?"

"Trainer. Right? You ... train .... Or something, I think."

Muddled, snarled thoughts tightened into knots. He was dizzy, buoyant, flying upward.

She's watching.

Get. Up.

His helmet felt like lead. He scrambled to his knees and stood. Attempted—and failed—to wave it off.

The crowd responded in generous but cautious applause and emboldened his forward motion ... *c'mon, man* ... one foot in front of the other. The world spun, blurred.

He staggered, unable to walk a straight line on his own. Steadying his stance on both sides of him was Doc and ... *Steve, was it?* He winced, squinting ahead.

Murmurs, disgruntled moans, and gasps scraped over the stadium, his ego in shreds.

God, wake me from this nightmare so I can get back on the field.

Tick, tick, tick. Serenity's heels bobbed nervously as the insufferably long game dragged on. Her heart thudded wildly. *Ba bum, ba bum, ba bum.*

Her mental meandering ended abruptly at another one of Harvey's edgy rebukes. At this point, the Kings had broadened their lead to twenty-one. The Tigers' offense lumbered to the line.

First and ten.

Owen's prowess hadn't slowed. New records were broken and added to his stats. Indisputably, God continued to protect him. Her desperate need for him to quit pulled against God's good purpose for keeping him in the game. A purpose beyond what either she or Owen, for that matter, could envision.

Despite the absurdity of it, a delicious thought snuggled inside her brain, the idea that maybe, *maybe*, he'd played his best because he knew she was there, watching him? A body weighing in heavier and performing better than last season because he'd experienced a sweet summer of cupcakes and—*smile*—romance?

Game analysts Adam Gannon and Bill Haverty delivered their spirited assessment through the Jumbotron. "Once again, Bill." Adam's cheek pinched in a knowing grin. "Walker in on the tackle, an absolute wrecking machine. A guy who remains, in my opinion, the best defensive player in the league."

"I have to agree, Adam. Last year, the man led interior defenders by twelve total pressures and looks to surpass that this season."

"So long as he remains injury free, I honestly think it'll put the Kings in the running to clinch the title come February."

Fourth quarter. Three minutes, seven seconds. Whistle, snap, and ... Owen sped like a freight train and tackled the receiver in the endzone, popping the ball out of his hands.

Brows lifted, Bill turned a rounded gaze on Adam. "Good gracious, if I hadn't seen it with my own eyes, I'd never have believed it."

The crowd cheered. Several players rallied and landed hard slaps against Owen's back and helmet. When they broke away, Owen tipped his chin and jabbed a finger heavenward. He paused, lowered a knee, then jogged back to the line of scrimmage. The new and improved Owen Walker. An irrefutably humble move that neither Serenity—nor his followers—had witnessed in years past.

Amid the roar of the crowd, she retrieved the memory of him in that ginormous pink apron, making himself the centerpiece of her bakery. Looking both out of place and perfectly suited. Spreading pixie dust of arresting charm everywhere.

She recalled his demeanor throughout the summer. He'd been content. Unashamed. Nothing contrived in his enthusiasm or work ethic.

For four amazing months, he'd turned her place right side up and baked wonders in her kitchen, whisking a magic spell over her. Her bakery.

Longing reverberated in her chest. Her breathing shallowed. The right time to tell him about The Pear Tree's demise would come soon enough, but tonight would be about them. She'd not let the sad news ruin his victory because he'd probably tear up like a little kid.

Two minutes, thirty-two seconds. Second and sixth.

Nerves jangled. "Game almost over, game almost over ..."

At the snap, Owen raced toward the offensive receiver who'd managed to catch the QB pass as he sliced it through the air. Head dipped like a snorting bull, Owen wound his arms around the receiver's waist in an attempt to sling him to the ground, a hallmark Walker move. In the rush, he was crushed between two offensive linemen who'd barreled in and intercepted his defensive move from opposite sides. The multi-player collision downed the receiver but left Owen's stance unsteady. His head precariously swayed before he crumbled to his knees and collapsed onto his back.

Out. Laid low like a felled sequoia.

Serenity gasped hard, stood, and clapped a hand over her mouth. "Dear God, no." The heat of her angsty prayer moistened her palm.

The whistle blew. The clock stopped. A flurry of staff raced over. She released the breath she'd been holding. Her lungs chugged air. Tears pooled and burned. Brooke wrapped an arm around Serenity's shoulders and tugged her close. Saying nothing.

Owen's unresponsiveness had said plenty.

Get up, Owen. Please, get up!

"That's a sight no one wants to see," Justin rasped out, his face drained of color. He bellowed out a battle cry. "C'mon, buddy. Got a whole season ahead of you. On your feet!"

Players took to their knees on the sidelines. Heads all around shook in disbelief, mouthing a collective "*No!*" Murmuring shrouded the icy stadium, all waiting for their hero to hop up and shake out his cape.

Owen's heels lay pinned to the turf. Slowly, he moved his feet from side to side. One knee bent a little. He writhed as if in terrific pain. Privately, he'd confessed how he hated for fans to witness him in a helpless state. If this were avoidable, he'd have shaken it off by now. Early in his life, a "stuff the pain behind your chest pads and carry on" mantra had been deeply embedded into his neural circuitry. In present circumstances, it'd done him a disservice.

To fill the agony of waiting, she took long drags of air—inhaling, exhaling—infusing strength where, apparently, he had none.

Amplified whispers sounded as staff eased him upright. Owen nodded, lips moving—most likely responding to a slew of concussion protocol questions.

What's your name? Where are you? Who's ahead? What was our last play?

She'd add another. *When are you going to put an end to this madness?*

With assistance, he managed a few steps. Sweaty, ashen. No trace of a smile. He raised a hand. Cheers and whistles boomed over the field and scattered tense clusters of horrible murmurs.

He stopped. A hush settled on the anxious crowd. The Jumbotron image magnified the look of one held captive by confusion. He conveyed a supreme struggle to follow directives. Staff hemmed him in on all sides like he was the Ark of the Covenant and guided him toward the blue pop-up tent on the sidelines.

No.

"Is that bad?" Brooke said, hands clasped beneath her chin.

Harvey had been deathly silent thus far. He mustered up a tinny tone. "It ain't good."

"Dad, you ought to go see if they'll let you in," Derek said.

A beefy harumph. "The sacred blue tent? They wouldn't let God inside that thing."

"But you're—"

Harvey's rigorous head shake intercepted Derek's rebuttal and suggested he refused further notoriety, burying it long ago. His granite features softened. His jaw steeled against what could be a sinister medical report. Had the wicked display of crushed athlete enabled Harvey to come to terms with his condition?

A little too late in the game.

"Nothing I can do, D." Harvey's piercing gaze smoldered concern. "Any long-term damage to that rock-hard head of his will be evident in time."

Confusion, fear, and uncertainty blanketed the stadium in ominous stillness. Serenity ached to rush to Owen's side, grasp his hand, and reassure him she was there. Being Owen's most unlikely girlfriend and someone comparatively insignificant in the eyes of the NFL, she had no sway against their regulations. Even head coach Wagner was forbidden to enter the blue tent.

Maybe Harvey was right. God may not have been permitted inside.

But a prayer ... Serenity's desperate petition stretched beyond the stratosphere, breaking through every barrier. "Fighting for you, Owen. Pull through," she whispered through clenched teeth.

A man popped out of the tent. Then another. When Owen appeared behind them, they moved to his side and took him by the upper arm. This time, he didn't raise a hand. He did nothing. Unaware, it seemed, of what had happened.

Though Serenity couldn't fully register his expression, she felt it deeply. A weighty foreboding.

For several minutes, her mind suffered a wallop of rabid, pinging thoughts. Would Owen be okay? What would they discover? Had he dodged another bullet?

Why hadn't anyone had the gumption to tell him the truth?

"He'll be fine so long as they don't take him to the locker room," Justin said.

Adam's update amplified in black waves, drowning Serenity in dread. "Well, folks, looks like Walker is headed to the locker room and will likely be pulled from the game."

Chapteen Sixteen

In isolated, sporadic milliseconds of coherency, Owen remembered being helped to his feet, guided along. A canopy of sulky blue masked his ability to see the field. Doc Blair stood over him on his right, an unaffiliated doc on his left. Both were studying him like scientists examining a specimen. Looking far too close.

"Why am I here?" he managed to ask.

"You got your bell rung out there. Film replay shows gross motor instability, mumbling, and confusion."

"I got up."

"Not without effort."

"You know the drill, Walker. We're here to look for no-go features. Headaches, numbness, difficulty with speech, changes in vision."

"I want Serenity."

They exchanged glances and shook their heads. Doc Blair laughed. "Don't we all."

"No, no. Serenity. A girl."

"Tell us about Serenity, Walker."

Serenity Walker? Sounded perfect.

The emergence of an image fogged his brain. He squinted and tried to focus his mind's eye before it faded to black again. He rubbed at his forehead with his thumb and fingers. "I ... I'm not sure. No one, I guess."

"Tell me what you remember about what happened."

"I was after ... the receiver. I hunted him down. Hit his chest ... I think."

"That it?"

"It went dark. Linemen piled on top."

"Okay, right."

Coherency rustled. "No, wait." The pieces were coming together. Words filled in the blanks and enabled him to articulate. "I rushed the player, suspected he'd go right but hit him square on. Then the blockers came at me from the sides." Their bodies were a cement wall.

"Somewhat accurate. Now, can you tell us where we are in the game?"

"Superdome."

"No, what quarter."

"It's the second half. Um, fourth quarter. Getting close to the end. Second and sixth."

"Who scored last?"

"We did."

They nodded in synch. "Did we win?"

More gameplay surfaced. The scoreboard came into focus.

"Don't know—the game wasn't over. We're up by twenty-one."

More nodding.

For several more minutes, Owen endured a focused neurological exam. "There's no head bleed, but I'm not ruling out inter-cranial damage. Let's run the cervical check, range of motion of the neck, conduct pupil exam." Stiff, cold fingers palpated the back of his neck, followed by a series of head rotations.

Soreness crept into his neck. Old wounds or new, he couldn't tell. Next, a jarring light lasered each eye. His temples throbbed. Outside the tent, he heard the anxious rumblings of the crowd.

Put me back in. Can't let them down.

"All right, Walker. Stand up for us, and let's check your gait."

With minimal assistance, he sat upright, his head a cinder block. Feet planted, he exhaled, then walked slowly from one end of the tent to the other. "See that?" He pivoted to face the jury, swept his arms aside as if pronouncing judgment, and flashed a smile. "Perfect."

"We've seen and heard enough."

He reclaimed his helmet. "Then I'm good to go."

A staying hand pressed against his shoulder. "SCAT test suggests concussion. We'll conduct an extensive evaluation in the locker room."

The place where he suited up to win games—to show the world who he was and give fans what they'd expected— had been converted to a chamber for postmortem viewing.

"But the game isn't over." He thumbed over his shoulder, moving forward.

They stood and blocked the tent flap. "Neither are we."

Dipping his head for clearance through the flap, he emerged into the light and basked in a thunderous roar. Cameras flashed. Players scrambled near, quickly restrained by coaches. "You're the reason, Walker! You're the reason!" his teammates cheered.

He managed to raise a hand, masking signs of injury.

See, I'm fine.

Once engulfed by an elongated tunnel, he trudged down the corridor to the locker room's blindingly bright common area encased in white walls.

In step with his somber entourage, he passed empty gear cubbies, stainless steel ice baths, and massage tables and entered the private physician's exam room. A thousand miles away.

The crisp, cold air chilled the sweat over his body and prickled his skin. He ached for Serenity's warmth and reassurance. How had this affected her? If he could just get to his cell and call her ...

I'm okay, Seren. You okay?

The two doctors alternately checked his reflexes, all five senses, and his muscle strength. All good until he failed at balance, his coordination scoring that of a toddler.

Dang.

Doc Blair called Coach. "We're done in here. I suggest a team meeting. Get everyone up to speed."

Steps shuffled within the hallowed hall outside the room. The door to this inner sanctum banged open and screeched shut behind the threatening form of Coach Wagner, who doubled as the Gestapo.

Gaze steeled in defense, Owen balled fists at his side. *That's right, try and take everything I have. All I am. Just try.*

"Walker," Coach Wagner said. "I need you to take this seriously. You're to be reevaluated by a provider and go through the return-to-play protocol."

Doc Blair stepped into the circle and directed his gaze at Coach. "The truth is, he shouldn't step onto a football field again. That's my call."

"I second that," the other doctor said.

Coach Wagner's posture went rigid. "No way we're releasing him. We'll put him on reserve until after he's had time to recover and cleared to return."

Owen clenched his teeth, flared his nostrils, and gripped the edge of the exam table. "I'm on IR?"

"Yes." Coach Wagner's voice went throaty with emotion. The discipline of a good father. "The decision will remain non-disclosed, of course, but it's the best for you, the team."

"You can't bench me."

"We can, and we are. Face it, Walker. We need you healthy. You're not at your best."

"What do you mean?" he barked. "I dominated the game on defense."

"Until you got crushed."

"I'll look for another team."

"Contract won't allow it. Besides, no team is going to touch you."

He needed Seren. Where was Seren?

God, where are you? Why did you let this happen?

A blue-chip player's name on an injury report was the tip of the iceberg. Because the full medical story lurked beneath the surface where only a few understood the magnitude. The few, as it were, stood shoulder to shoulder in solidarity in front of him. Gazes bleak, disgruntled.

"The only people who can know about this decision are right here." Coach Wagner circled the room with his finger—his chin taut, tone gravely and abrupt. "The owner, GM, Coach McNamara, Doc Blair, you, and me."

Soon enough, the world.

Dad.

"If the league suspects something is awry, we'll have the VP of communications contact our media relations director. If that's unsuccessful, they'll target the GM. We can't let this out."

Owen's throat clogged. His heart tore along the edges at the gut-wrenching blow. Now he felt what his opponents on the field had always felt—the unmatched vice of Owen Walker, who'd squeezed a player, rendering him nearly incapable of breath, before he slammed him onto the field.

The news wouldn't stay contained for long. The media would sniff it out. Tweets would go viral. Degrading disillusionment would spread among his fans. Would it harm his reputation? The Foundation? Would he lose sponsorship?

If he chose to retire and partner with Serenity, the burden of proof that he had enough smarts to run a business rested on his shoulders. Did he have value out of uniform? Could the pro-ball nation accept him as an aproned baker who had the chops to compete for market share?

How could he prove what he didn't believe about himself?

How could he continue to walk on water?

His mind scrambled for comfort and circled back to Serenity. Because if he lost football, he still had her. She was wonder, swirled inside pure sweetness and frosted with generosity. The thought of the two of them enjoying an awesome future together sped his pulse and heightened his senses.

The stunning contact of their kisses—her lips soft, firm, and warm—made his knees buckle. But beyond that, she instilled the courage to step off the field. They were better together. She strengthened him where he was weak. He emboldened her where she was afraid.

Team Walker.

Man, he really loved that woman.

Two hours later, the trainer ... *Steve, right?* ... released Owen with the gentleness of a probation officer. Coach Wagner tackled a slew of post-game questions at the press conference held behind the partitioned area on the stadium's lower level. The Kings' victory should dominate today's obligatory Q&A session, but the media would undoubtedly localize their interrogation around Owen's status.

As usual—and as promised—Coach would minimize the extent of his injury. He'd assure the reporters that they'd reserve further judgments about his condition until next week's practice played out. Basically, he'd shrug the unfortunate incident off when really, the medical staff's observations had rattled them enough for Coach to exact the punishment of putting Owen on IR.

Owen wasn't woozy beyond the ability to know tonight's hit bore definitive significance.

He pressed splayed hands against the slick tile of the shower and let the wall hold him steady. The spray of hot water pricked at his neck and sluiced down his back. The final minutes of the game looped through his thoughts, the gravity of the play a vice on his brain. The clash of helmets against his sternum, the years of head trauma ... all to carry the Walker legacy ... walking in his identity.

Football is what you do. It's not who you are.

Steam coiled around his lungs. *Enough!*

He shoved away from the wall and wrenched the faucet. The stream trickled to a slow drip. He had plans after the game to meet his girl. Recall flickered, faded in and out to reveal her pretty face whose name momentarily evaded him.

Seren.

That's right. He had plans after the game to meet Seren, Justin, his wife, er, Brooke ... and Dad, Derek, and Marianne.

No better time to celebrate a win.

Serenity dodged the counterflow of fans spilling out of the stadium. She chewed on her lower lip as she glanced around the expansive, starkly lit walkway. The air held the acrid smell of cigarette smoke and stale alcohol.

As she stood with the rest awaiting word from Owen, her limbs tingled, and her insides quivered. She swallowed past a dry throat.

"It could be hours before they release him," Justin moaned with a hard sigh.

"Either he's been withheld by medical or become fodder for media." Harvey gave his saggy jeans a yank. "I warned that stubborn cuss. Suggested he quit and take heed of what the docs have said, but you can't stop a train."

Serenity bored a stare at Harvey. "He's been warned? By medical professionals?"

"Bad rads."

Ire churned in a low squall and throbbed behind her lids. "He never told me this."

"Wish he had. But men in our situation don't cough up that info. Not even for the ones we love the most."

Her need to mentally process—*alone*—began to engulf her. There was a proper time and place to draw energy from people.

This was not it.

The discordant whine of incomplete closure mocked loudly. Or maybe it'd been the haunting cry of her bakery seeking reassurance like a momma comforts her dying child.

Or maybe her soul had taken its last breath.

An inescapable urgency fired from head to toe.

She turned to address the group. "I thought of something I need to do at the bakery."

Bewildered stares answered.

"But it's empty," Brooke said. "And locked."

"No need to state the obvious."

She spun to go.

Derek impeded her exit with a touch on the shoulder. "Dad and I will walk you to your car."

Up against an impregnable Walker fortress—and strength too sapped for a fight—what other choice did she have but to relent?

Dressed in black jeans, athletic shoes, and a snug cotton T-shirt, Owen slipped out the back and texted Serenity.

OWEN: I'm done here.

He called her. No answer. Went to voicemail.
He left a message.
"Hey, Seren. I guess you saw the whole thing. Just wanted you to know I'm fine and headed to the parking lot. See you soon, beautiful."

Outside, Dad, Derek, Marianne, Justin, and ... ah ha, *Brooke* ... stood waiting, their expressions fit for a funeral.

"Way to bring 'em down, Champ," Dad said, giving Owen a nod, but his voice lacked its usual resonant timbre.

Marianne managed to stop cataloging a play-by-play on her phone long enough to turn a pointed glance at Derek, who gave Dad a mild grin, then turned to Owen. "You had us worried, brother. That was quite a hit."

"I'm all right. A little foggy, but I'm okay."

Badly injured and benched.

Thick dusk hovered overhead. A moist sky bore angry, burly clouds. Stadium lights limited his visibility. Were they always this bright? He felt for his keys and glanced across the starting lineup. "Where's Serenity?"

"About time you asked." Brooke's forehead wrinkled in disdain.

He shot her the look.

"She took off before the game ended," Marianne said. "Said she had some unfinished work to do at her bakery and might meet us later."

"Might?" That didn't ring well. "I'll go see about her, then she and I will meet you at …" He circled a finger. "The, uh, place where we're meeting."

"Ben's Seafood and Grille." Derek's punctuated tone knifed at Owen's ribs.

"I knew that."

Head foggy, he'd forgotten where he parked, but that was a responsibility he'd often left to Jude anyway.

Dad's rusty chuckle clawed beneath Owen's skin.

Derek placed a hand on Owen's shoulder and pinned a stare. "You're not right."

"I'm fine. Just concerned about Seren. This is the second time she's gone ghost on me."

"Did they clear you to drive, Owen?" Brooke said.

"Warned me not to. Clear enough."

Feet parted, Derek placed hands low at his hips. The cop in him closed in for closer inspection, his expression fraught with concern. "Believe me, brother, you don't want to add a careless and reckless citation to what's happened today."

Dad's thick silence descended. For all his fumbled short-term memory, he knew the fix Owen was in. Once a player confessed to a problem, it was game over.

"You still have that Marine in your employ, don't you?" Justin said.

"Yes."

"Then call him to take the wheel," Derek said.

Drilling, drilling.

"There's no need for that. Anyway, he was at the Marine support facility earlier today, and he'd asked for the night off to spend with some fellow Marines who are in town."

He squeezed the keys in his palm. "I'm going after Seren. Save us a seat."

Chapter Seventeen

Cloaked in the waning light of dusk, the deepening oceanic sky spread over the Quarter. The space once known as The Pear Tree had lowered its lids, its entrance perceptible only by the translucent glow of gas lamps erected along the storefronts.

Serenity's custom-made signage had been plucked from its chain, leaving a cavern of nothingness above the door. Only ten days ago, her sign invited the hungry and curious to her cozy, trendy world to enjoy the product of her artisan soul. She found comfort in the memory of Owen's suggestion that they design a new logo featuring crisp, neutral colors and rebrand the business anyway.

"The Kings did it," he'd playfully goaded. "We should give it a go."

We. Sigh.

She peered through the window. A lonesome blackness stared back.

Countering a sudden ache, she pictured the bakery as she'd remembered it on opening day. Eager for a new and unique experience, expectant clientele formed a line that trailed out the door. Inside, the earthen color palette she'd chosen coexisted with a vibrant vibe, the walls veneered by stone-washed brick.

No other place like it. Wholly irreproducible—the way God created each of his people.

Hope had soared that day.

To materialize her dream, she'd kicked risk to the curb and achieved what the conservative and cautious Everley had always feared.

"Think you're special enough to live unafraid?" Dad had said.

"Sure do, Daddy."

Saying nothing, Dad had tousled her mess of knotted hair. He'd drawn a wry grin across his lips, leaving the ache for approval unsatisfied.

Something is inherently wrong with me.

She flattened her hands on the icy window. Her breath fogged the glass. "I fought for you."

She tipped her gaze. Moist air clung to her face. "Dear Jesus, thanks for blessing the bakery. For bringing Owen here to help sustain it." Emotion balled in her throat, threatening to shred her heart and squeeze the air from her lungs. "But I don't want to do life alone anymore."

Tears gathered strength behind her eyes. She sniffed them back.

When she stepped back, any remaining joy she possessed drained out of her. Thoughts of Owen filled the empty space. Surely, he'd see the wisdom in retiring after today's game. Because there was no way the Kings would release him. It would be his decision.

A wisp of peace drifted in. Renewed purpose and vision alighted on her soul, scattered sorrow. Optimism circuited through her veins.

Ideas bubbled up.

She'd support Owen and nurse his wounds as fans fixed their attention elsewhere. She and Owen would cheer for Eli throughout chemo and radiation treatments, reassuring him of God's faithfulness.

Did the kid even have a relationship with God? If not, now was the time to share the crucial invitation.

They'd scout out new foundation partnerships to expand their reach. They could bake up wonders together in that cute Victorian house ... or his kitchen ... and donate to charitable organizations. Utilizing the unlimited power of God, they could achieve the impossible and add numbers to God's kingdom.

A raindrop pinged off her cheeks and yanked her to the present.

She felt for her phone. "Shoot, I left it in the car."

For the very last time, she turned from the property and paused mid-stride, squinting at the approach of an immense, shadowed figure across the street.

"And they say *I'm* losing my memory."

The unmistakable—unforgettable—voice of Owen Walker. Husky, confident, lovable—all together desirable.

Her breath caught and her feet froze in place.

He prowled forward, a cheeky grin now evident through the mist. He thumbed over his shoulder. "Ben's is about four miles west of here," he said in tease.

He took two steps closer, standing within reach now. His gait showed little evidence of injury or mental impairment. Was the man superhuman? Had she died and gone to heaven? She pinched her arm.

Ow!

"What task is so urgent at the bakery that you skipped out on me again, Seren?"

Clearly, his cognitive abilities stopped at the ability to discern the deathly silence inside the bakery, still oblivious to the gaping dark space behind her.

"How are you?" A lame and weak question, given what she'd witnessed hours ago and the brutal assault of Harvey's revelation.

"I'm all right. I left you a voicemail and sent texts telling you that."

"Oh. I left my cell in the car."

He maintained a neutral stare as though unsure which play to make, assessing the line of scrimmage. He roved his tongue along the inside of his cheek.

"They took you out of the game. I was worried sick. We all were."

"Sorry you had to see that, but you'll get used to it." He slayed her with another enigmatic grin, his dimples pronounced and purposeful.

She stepped back and knotted her arms at her chest. "Wait. You're not going to keep playing after what happened—the first game of the season." Dark sarcasm saturated her flatlined tone.

"I took a hit and things hurt inside and out, but that's football. We're warriors. We're *supposed* to love this thing."

Anytime someone edged too close to the subject of concussion, Owen had three standard responses, *that* one prime among them. She'd come to despise it. Because she'd detected a hint of hesitancy as though healthy fear had made a valiant effort to rise above the din of ridiculousness and talk sense into him.

Could he hear it?

Would he try?

"But do *you* love it?"

"What's not to love?"

"That it could kill you."

"A risk I take every time I drive my car."

"An activity you've relegated to Jude."

"It gives him purpose. Income."

He wasn't budging.

A white-hot heat sizzled inside her.

"It's your health, your future at stake. What more evidence do you need to lay this down than what you see in your own father? Can you not consider those who care about you, namely me?" Fuming, she jabbed a thumb at her chest.

"It's what I do."

The second response she'd hated.

"You'd been warned by medical, Owen, and didn't care enough to tell me."

He glanced away. His profile hardened. A ticked jumped along his jaw.

"I figured it wouldn't matter." He returned a level stare. "Love endures all things, right?"

"But you're more than football. Get out while you can. Invest in your foundation, your kids—Eli, for crying out loud. If ever he needed a hero in his life, it's now."

"Heroes don't give up."

"Retiring from football isn't giving up. You've seen the documentaries of others who've gone before you. It's the most admirable, courageous, and sacrificial thing you can do."

"Maybe I just don't have the strength to do it."

"Then ask God for it."

He expelled a jagged breath and raked a hand through his slicked hair. "As I said, you'll get used to it."

She'd already admitted to God she didn't want to live life alone and could commit to caring for him whatever the future held—so long as he walked away. Now.

But the insufferable man wouldn't relent.

She utterly refused to let the dawn of his grin, the pull of endearing eyes, work its magic on her. Stiffly, she waved her hands and took several more steps back. "No, Owen, I won't."

His gaze stilled, and his grin slackened. "We make a great team. Strength in numbers. Team Walker."

There he went, casting a vision, reeling her in, his demeanor playful and luring.

He advanced and eliminated the distance. Winked.

Pray, don't fall, stupid heart!

Fearful he'd enfold her to him, she placed a hand on his chest. "Owen, I respect your passion to play. But I can't continue to watch you hurt yourself. If you refuse to give it up, we can't be together."

Storm clouds rumpled over his forehead. "I'm not retiring."

In staunch refusal, he'd snapped the head off the one tiny bit of hope and peace she'd nurtured about a happily ever after. With him.

Because for Serenity, there'd be no one else.

Owen's declaration spiraled around Serenity's heart and threatened to squeeze the life out of it. Her thoughts raced in a frenzied effort to find order. This required a response. She had none.

"I want us to be together," he said, voice lush and heady. "In the spring, I could help you out again."

With barely a glance, he directed an arm toward the still, hollowed bakery.

Bullheaded *and blind* jock.

His gaze held a rigorous intent to prod response. When she didn't answer, he took her hands in his and massaged them. "I seriously think you and me could make a go of things."

"I watched my dad persist in his goals and die doing it. The autopsy revealed he'd suffered dehydration and likely became dizzy while up on Moreland's roof the day he slipped off it."

"It's what I do, Seren." Words bobbed at his throat as if Harvey's repetitive phrase during Owen's formative years had lodged there, originating from his brain's neural network. He tightened his squeeze. "I love who I am with you. I love everything about you."

His voice was ripe with need, desire, and intensity. He stroked her hair, knowing exactly where to touch and how much pressure to apply. Not too rough, not too gentle. Just right.

Enough to make a soupy batter out of her resolve. But in fairness, he'd spoken from an uninformed place. "You wouldn't say that if you really knew me."

His greatest disappointment.

A sizzle of frustration marked his words. "Dang it, Seren, why can't you see how amazing you are?"

The truth shrugged out of its cloak, took center stage, and demanded a voice. "When I was in the fifth grade, I told my parents I'd been awarded a certificate from the teacher to say I was the most special student the in class."

A tilt of his head suggested she'd elicited intrigue. Or struggled to care.

"I lied."

Swallowed in his shadow, she tipped her chin to meet his stare. A pained gaze claimed his angular features. The lines around his eyes lengthened.

"The truth was that *everyone* got a certificate. When my parents found out I'd lied, they made me apologize."

He gave a sympathetic grin and opened his arms to her. She let them swallow her.

He planted a sympathy kiss on her head. His sweet, warm breath drizzled over her like threads of sugary icing. His scent of fresh shower, power, and masculinity soaked into her pores.

Stop liking this!

"You don't need a certificate to tell you're special, Seren."

At that, the towering, muscled guy managed to hold her gaze in a deadlock. Made her forget how laughable it was to consider—

"I want us together as a family. Forever," he said in forceful seriousness.

Was becoming deaf a sign of traumatic brain injury?

Time to strip the veneer.

A heavy exhale blistered her lungs. The truth burned like acid when it left her lips. "I can't have kids, Owen."

The hunger in his eyes froze above a waning, strained grin. He recoiled, and his forehead pinched to a "V," deep enough to hold a small coin between his brows.

Disappointment claimed his features and clawed at her heart. Fear salted the wound.

Her stomach roiled at the effect her pronouncement had on him.

He hooked a searing gaze on her. "You mean you don't want kids?"

"No, I want a house full of them—just like you do. But I can't."

"That's not possible, Seren."

She wrenched her hands inside moist palms. "It *is* possible. I have MRKH, an extremely rare disorder where the uterus fails to develop. In many cases, it's missing altogether. So, I can't have kids."

God, don't make me say it again. Ever.

Owen's stance shifted like he fought the urge to run. The awkward twitch of his head went to shaking violently, refusing to ingest the bitter reality.

"But you can get that fixed, can't you?" Begging marked his tone.

Irritation festered beneath a layer of shame. "Not everything that's wrong with a body can be fixed."

The blackness of funnel clouds gathered in his eyes. "For months now, I'd built a relationship with you based on a false reality—" He turned away, speaking into the moist night, fumbling to find a place for his gaze to land. "One where we'd be together and ..." Numbly, he turned back and swept a palm in her direction. "You'd be the mother of my kids."

"I tried to tell you, Owen, but every time I brought up the idea of adoption, you refused to accept it."

"There's nothing wrong with not wanting to adopt."

"That's true. It isn't for everyone, which I've learned includes you. I get that. It just means I'm not your girl."

Oh, the shredding of her heart ... bleeding ... nearly drained of courage. *Leave me. Don't go!*

"You knew how much this meant to me, Serenity."

At the granite, formal tone, shame tugged her chin to her chest—misted her vision. She dragged her lower lip over her teeth, breathing rapid and shallow. Her missing parts created an unnavigable space between them. "I was afraid you'd walk away."

"Why'd you lead me to believe something that wasn't true?"

She jerked her glance back up at him. "Why'd you refuse to tell me you've had doctors—and your father, for crying out loud—urge you to quit based on crystal clear medical evidence?"

"This is all so confusing," Owen growled low, looking like he needed to hit something. He tunneled a hand through his hair, gathering it in clenched fists. "I can't believe this. God, really?"

He turned attention skyward as though seeking help beyond her—or his—ability to produce a miracle.

The agony had grown beyond her ability to bear. Her lids shuddered to a close. The pavement turned to quicksand.

"Look at me, Serenity."

She made herself pull her gaze from the pavement and look directly at him. She struggled to breathe at the sight of his hauntingly cold stare. His flawlessly chiseled chest, form-fitted inside a black T-shirt, heaved like he'd endured a two-a-day. His cheeks were aflame, and his eyes reddened.

A low rumble of thunder rattled. Raindrops spat on her cheeks and stung her arms. Lamplights blurred through a haze of tears. She swallowed hard, unable to free the clog in her throat.

This felt worse than she'd imagined, the primary reason she'd avoided it.

"I'm not sure our being together is a good thing anymore." His tone dropped ruthlessly low. Strained, definitive, and edgy.

A hideous silence fell between them and broadened the distance to miles.

"Because I can't have kids."

"Yeah. Or ... no." His arm fell limp against his side. "I don't know." His mouth stretched into a grim line. "This is hard to take."

That wasn't brain injury talking. It was the raw and unfiltered utterance of his soul.

His unwieldy, empty stare had said the thing her heart feared worst. His admission slammed her—body and soul—to the ground.

She didn't measure up. He'd deemed her uniqueness undesirable.

What a fool she'd been for fantasizing this exchange so differently, dusting it with a sugary hope that he'd see nothing of flaws and imperfection.

Serenity was no longer special.

Something is wrong with me.

Rain gathered strength, soaked her hair, and pelted her shirt. She ran palms along her wet arms to smooth the pop of chill bumps.

"Gah, Seren. I had envisioned us working at your bakery after I retired."

A billion years from now. Debilitated and wheelchair-bound, barely able to form sentences, posing a danger to her. And for the love of butter and sugar, he still hadn't registered that his vision—and its utilities—had been cut off.

"My infertility makes that an impossibility." She delivered the evocative statement with a level tone, inviting swift rebuttal. But when he gave his head a sluggishly slow shake, the verdict was clear.

He couldn't—or wouldn't—love her as she was.

To cauterize emotional hemorrhage, she gathered the facts associated with loving someone who bore all the signs and symptoms of CTE. She elevated her voice above the rain and drowned out the rubbery sound of loss. "Well, I guess that's it. Good luck with your career. I'll be seeing—or, rather, hearing about you."

Rain stabbed at her face, and tears dribbled down her cheeks. She turned in a hard pivot and hastened to her car.

"Wait, Seren," he called at her back.

Desperation—and possibly remorse—tinged his entreaty. She swiped at her cheeks and turned to face him, taking a final look at the golden brown and green hue of his eyes set inside his "beloved of all women" face.

Desire whooshed in and reignited determination greater than when she'd clandestinely watched him play in college and daydreamed of what his future would be like—wishing she could be a part of it. But now, she'd tasted the vial of incurable heartache, and it brought her dangerously close to ...

"I love you, Seren."

That.

"That's sweet, Owen."

No, cupcakes are sweet. She, on the other hand, was dumb. *Incurably, insufferably dumb.* A tongue-tied bakery girl in the presence of the star athlete now staring at her with searching, reddened eyes.

He returned a reticent smile. "Just give me time to think this through."

Time enough to cut a girl to pieces, mark her damaged goods, then pull out the Walker playbook for how games are won in overtime.

"What's to think through, Owen? You want what I can't give. It's pretty straightforward, even for a guy whose brain isn't firing on all circuits."

"You can't hold this against me." A tender ferocity marked his tone. "I've been upfront with you about what I wanted. You never told me you can't have kids."

Rain plinked above her non-answer.

"Look, I took a hard hit tonight. Eli's sick. And I need you." His words hung on his bobbing throat. He squeezed his eyes shut and raised his fingers to his temple, massaging it. He glanced away, placed a splayed hand low at his waist, then turned back to her. A speck of light caught in his misty gaze. "They've benched me. I'm on IR. And I can't walk this alone."

"You've got your family. Your fans."

"I need you, Seren."

"I'm no good for you, Owen."

He stiffened.

"I'll decide what's good for me." His tone was conflicted, pleading, and fierce. All trace of remorse now evaporated to nothing.

"Your insistence on playing despite months of growing contraindications makes me question your ability to discern what's good for you. I refuse to be another decision you make and then regret."

"I've got discernment enough to question whether it's really *my* limitations or yours that's got you spooked."

In a sentence, he'd turned the tables. "I'm not spooked about my limitations."

"Then stay with me."

She stepped back. "I can't replicate little Walker boys and girls." But oh, how very badly she'd wanted to.

She registered defeat in his expression before his chin fell to his chest.

To think she held the power to take down this giant of a man with her refusal to let him inside her heart tasted wickedly delicious. His injury had been her injury. He'd arrived on the playing field of her heart, tromped all over it.

Tough go of things—three-time Defensive Player of the Year.

The urge to fall to her knees and sob mounted. She squared her shoulders against it. "This is a game even you can't win."

She unleashed a huge breath of bitter relief at the finality.

Leaving him in the mess they'd made, she sloshed through puddles—away from her lifeless bakery toward her car. But if so relieved, why was her heart wrenching into twisted knots, threatening to splinter?

Chapter Eighteen

During the third night after the breakup, peace still eluded Owen. She hadn't returned his calls or his texts. The silence fired like lightning rods in his head.

Eventually, mental and physical exhaustion allowed minimal dozing. The following Sunday, during the early midnight hour, he jolted awake and clutched his pillow like he'd completed the tackle.

No. He'd held the celestial creature of his dreams close to his chest, keeping her safe. The light of his love for her defeating the dark of her insecurity.

Street light reached through his bedroom window and fell over the wall at a downward angle. He begged for daybreak. Sitting upright, he fumbled for his cell.

4:23 a.m.

His shoulders lagged in exhale. Hands clasped behind his head, he sank into his pillow. His neck and back were drenched.

"Eight more hours," he moaned.

After the fateful game, Ross requested that Owen come visit Eli.

ROSS: Temozolomide is making Eli sick. Any chance you could get him out of the house for a little while?

OWEN: I can be there Sunday. 1:00 okay?

ROSS: That's great. Thanks, Owen. Praying for you.

The void of time stretched ahead of him on an indistinct horizon. Is this what it'd be like for a washed-up player? Plagued by nothingness. Useless and forgotten in the annals of history? No longer the golden boy of the NFL?

Where's the playbook for how to function out of uniform, for recovery after he'd been blindsided by Serenity's counterplay? Fake in the opposite direction?

Gainer for her. Loss for him.

"Seren, Seren, Seren ..." Repeating her name brought solace. He grasped at her blurred image before it faded. She'd been the source of strength he needed to walk Eli through the most difficult challenge this kid would ever face. Now he'd have to put on his game face and reassure Eli everything would be okay when he didn't believe it for himself.

Ambling to the bathroom, Owen pressed his knuckles to the counter and glared at his reflection. Arms bowed, a disjointed image stared back. "Who are you, Owen Walker. Really. Who are you?"

Mid-morning finally delivered relief. Owen called Ross's cell and talked to Eli. "Cupcakes at The Pear Tree?"

"Nah. That'd make me throw up."

The kid's lack of appetite eliminated most of their favorite eating spots.

"Can we go to that big white house where the fundraiser was? The one that has the cool history?"

"Moreland?"

"Yeah."

And so it was. He made arrangements with Everley for a visit. She welcomed them and shared that Gabe had gone sailing with his dad on Lake Verret, west of Napoleonville.

Just inside Moreland's threshold, he took Everley in an easy hug. Her tone and body language suggested she knew nothing of his and Serenity's breakup. She turned to shake Eli's hand. "Welcome back."

"Thanks." Awe filtered into Eli's gaze at the chandelier blinking above his head.

"It's against doctor's orders, but I've been working in the office." Everley massaged her sides near her lower back. "Feel free to sit on the porch and enjoy some lemonade and refreshments. Make yourselves at home."

Owen raised a staying hand. "Please don't go to any trouble."

"It's no problem at all. We've hired help."

Stepping gingerly, she ushered them to a warm and refurbished kitchen through the adjoining walk-in pantry that led to an adjoining screen porch behind the south wing. "Refreshments will be out shortly." She smiled and went back inside.

Seated on one of two cushioned, white rockers, Eli's feet dangled. "You should have asked Serenity to come along."

"You asked for me."

"You're hedging. Where's she at?"

"Probably the bakery."

"It's Sunday. Bakery's closed."

"Remember." Owen tapped at his temple and clucked his tongue. "Investigations?"

"It doesn't take a PI to conclude the obvious."

A rebel grin twitched on one side of Eli's mouth. Owen exerted effort to hide a disconcerted expression.

The screen door screeched open.

Lettie appeared. Her gnarled fingers curled around a serving tray that held two glasses, apple slices, grapes, a variety of crackers, and what smelled of pear jam.

"Hey there, sweet lady." He rose and leaned in to take her bony frame in a gentle embrace. "The Kings ought to recruit you. You work harder than an ox, the bakery *and* Moreland?"

That toothy smile he loved disappeared. She set the tray on a glass-top table and ran her hands down the front of her apron. "Naw, sir. Miz Serenity closed it up the end of August."

The bad news slashed his heart. "What? Why?"

"Couldn't pay Mista Maurice what she owed."

The Pear Tree ... closed? What more hadn't Serenity told him? Three nights ago, he'd stood right there, stating his case, adding to her misery.

Eli's stare burned along his cheek.

Jaw clenched and ticking, Owen tamped down emotion. "I had no idea."

"You just leave the tray for me to pick up when you boys is finished."

"Thanks. Uh, good to see you, Lettie."

Her lids lowered as if in reverence to the dead. She nodded slowly and went back inside.

"That's an epic bummer," Eli said. "Wonder why Serenity didn't tell you."

Owen planted his elbows on his knees and steepled his fingers. He dipped his chin to hide a smoldering gaze in the shadow of his ball cap. "Great question, Sergeant Billings."

Eli fingered an apple and bit into it. "Maybe she didn't want the news to distract you from the game."

"I'd have helped her. Given her rent money. Done anything."

"She seems to be the kind of girl that wants to prove she can do things for herself."

Like save a dying establishment?

"It's not your money she wants anyway."

Owen concentrated his gaze on the young sleuth. "What does she want?"

"Girls are big on undivided devotion."

"You speak from experience?" He jibed if only to deflect heartache and crush the fear he'd not loved Serenity well. At least not the way God loved—without conditions.

Sacrificially.

Dang.

Seriousness dimmed the angelic nature of Eli's freckled face. "Seeing you go down Thursday really scared me." He wrenched the armrests. "Especially when they hauled you into the locker room."

"There was no hauling. I walked."

"Yeah. Like a player who got hit *real* bad. Anyway, imagine what that did to her."

Serenity again.

You're not gonna quit over this, are you, son?

No, sir, Dad. Never.

That's the Walker spirit.

Throughout his time with the Rams, he'd received several texts from Dad to that effect. Held to an impossible standard, his heart had been sectioned like a pie, Serenity getting one slice of the whole. Almighty God got less than that when, really, he should have all of it.

An undivided heart.

But it would take strength beyond himself to tell Dad he wanted to give it up for the girl he loved.

"It sucks to see my parents suffer because of this cancer thing I can't control. But for you, it's not too late to cut your losses."

Wisdom rustled, dividing bone from marrow—lie from truth.

"At the press conference, Coach Wagner said they were going to give it a week to decide, see how you do in practice," Eli said.

Melting ice clinked inside Owen's glass. He stared at the scarred flooring beneath his shoes, ordered his words, then raised his head. "It's very likely I'll be put on IR."

Great move, Walker. A fact entrusted to a select few in the upper echelon now divulged to a twelve-year-old—and, in a moment of desperation, to Serenity.

"I love the game too much and chose to ignore warnings."

"Why'd you ignore them?"

"It's part of the game. I'm paid to play. I've got youth who look up to me, an obligation to use my platform to help others succeed."

"Football isn't the reason I'm your number one fan."

Owen jerked a glance at Eli.

"It's the stuff on the inside. The agency that drives you to do community service things and give kids like me a chance. You treat me like I'm yours."

He tousled Eli's silky hair. "I'd die for you, kid, you know that?"

"No rush to prove your sincerity." Eli gave a crooked grin, popped a grape into his mouth, and chomped on it. Then his gaze went glassy. "Anyways, looks like I'm gonna die before you do."

Owen could no more deny medical facts than stop the flow of the Mississippi with his hands.

A breeze whistled past the screen door, rustling through the nearby grove of trees. The scent of cinnamon wafted from the tray. He took several bites of an apple slice and eased into the rocker, letting the sweet juice coat his tongue. "The subject of dying makes me thankful for heaven."

Eli picked at some flaking paint on the armrest. "I just hope I've scored enough points to get in."

It'd never occurred to Owen to talk to Eli about matters of faith. Arlene and Ross freely professed a belief in God and were actively involved in a church. He'd assumed—wrongly—Eli knew God's plan of salvation.

"Does your church teach that crazy doctrine?" Owen said.

"I wouldn't know. As soon as old Preacher Broussard starts talking, my mind wanders to sports and stuff."

"Do your parents talk to you about their faith?"

"Sometimes. I mean, Dad prays before we eat. Mom goes to a woman's Bible study every week."

Eli's understanding of salvation through Jesus was not unlike Owen's at one time. Weak and ineffective.

"Heaven can't be acquired through good behavior. Even if it was, no one is capable of scoring enough points."

"I can't figure any other way to get there."

"You just ask." A remarkably weak volley. Owen scrounged his memory to four years ago when Pastor Crawford skillfully layered phrasing like icing on a cupcake until Owen couldn't resist taking a bite. It'd given his heart the rest it needed in his war against a supreme being who'd allowed Mom's death, the victim of a head-on collision on her way to his state championship game. But if he'd known the reason she'd never made it to the stands, he'd not have performed at the level he did that night.

God was good.

God is good.

The Way, the Truth, and the Life.

"Everyone is born with sin. It's the reason we think wrong thoughts and do bad things. The reason our bodies fail and we—"

"Get sick?"

Fist to his mouth, he cleared his throat and nodded. "The penalty for our sin is death, but God offers us forgiveness through the death and resurrection of his son, Jesus, who committed no penalties. Does that make sense?"

"Yes, but what's that got to do with me?"

Closing in. Don't let me fumble this.

"When you confess your belief in what Jesus did for you, he secures your place in heaven. He gives you faith to believe when you ask in prayer." He rubbed clammy palms together. "Faith is a free gift, or else we'd all boast about what we did to earn it."

"Like that Super Bowl ring you're wearing."

Owen thumbed the bulky metal on the third finger of his right hand and laughed low.

"Think of it this way, Eli. We've all been diagnosed with sin. Jesus is the cure."

Eli nodded readily and glugged lemonade, chomping on an ice cube.

"You want to pray now ... together ... and ask Jesus's forgiveness?"

A stream of lemonade trickled off Eli's chin. He swiped it off with the back of his hand, set his glass down, and situated himself in his rocker. "I guess so."

Owen covered Eli's hands with one of his own and bowed his head. After each segment of the prayer, rookie as it was, Eli repeated after Owen. He inhaled Eli's whispered amen, his lungs expanding in humble satisfaction.

One more soul adopted into the family of Believers.

Arlene's words in the hospital came to mind.

"We were always afraid Eli would somehow feel less valuable when he learned he wasn't biologically ours. But we've always viewed him like God views us ... adopted children through Jesus Christ."

Stony beliefs overshadowed by ignorance were now bright with truth, pliable, and reassuring.

Brown eyes, clear and pure, Eli's youthful, merry laugh bubbled out. "I just thought of something. You're natural-born to your mom and dad, but I was adopted. Now we're both adopted by God, which makes us brothers."

Owen wrapped an arm around Eli's shoulders and tugged him close. "You're amazing, you know that?"

"Yeah. I do."

Eli plucked another grape and bored a sharpened gaze into Owen. "When are you gonna ask Serenity to marry you?"

"How'd we go from Jesus to Serenity?"

Eli's brows inched high, waiting.

His heart jackhammered. "We, uh, broke up."

"Why?" Eli snapped.

Owen shrank. "Things weren't what I thought they were."

To think he'd considered retiring for Serenity's sake when she'd withheld a truth that'd rivaled any hit he'd suffered.

"Tell me you didn't mess this up. She's the one good thing you got going right now."

"Lessons in tact, kid." He jabbed a finger at Eli. "That's what you need."

"You're hedging."

"She kept a secret from me. Said she couldn't have kids. And, God knows, I don't want to—"

A holy hand pinched his lips shut. His heart, a stone. He brought the rocker to a halt, gripping the armrests.

"Don't want to what?" Eli's question was a scalpel excising Owen's thoughts.

He released a blustery sigh. "We want different things. It takes someone pretty special to commit to a guy who might end up like Dad."

"All right, here's the winning play I think you need to make, so listen up." Authority marked Eli's tone, juxtaposed with his thin frame. "Man up and tell your dad you want to quit, announce it to the world in a sappy YouTube video or at an affiliate cable network studio, then go after the girl. The two of you could then get married and go open up a bakery somewhere."

That butt-ugly gingerbread house in town. On one of their dates, Serenity shared the photo, confessed she loved it, and cast a vision. He'd made no space in his brain for it.

Trepidation zinged down Owen's spine, reason and desire an immiscible mixture. A ball of pain worked its way to the side of his head.

"Clearly, you're still conflicted. Let's look at this from a different angle." Eli arranged the cinnamon shaker beside the tray. "Say that's Serenity." He set a grape on the top and pointed to it. "She's like the QB with the ball, the one you're after."

Eli moved Owen's glass to block the cinnamon shaker and tapped the glass. "That's the offensive lineman, attempting man-to-man coverage, blocking your advance to what you want—freedom from fear of telling your dad you're done."

Huddling close, Owen propped his chin in his palm and concentrated his attention.

Eli raised Owen's glass. "Now, this is you. You make it successfully past the dad obstacle." He maneuvered the glass with a *swish* past Eli's empty glass, set it on its side, and closed in on the shaker. "But now you've got a triple-team threat, running interference—" He guarded the cinnamon by way of the saltshaker and two crackers, forming a tight lineup. "Making your retirement public."

Dread pricked over Owen's limbs like an ice bath.

Eli moved Owen's glass through the make-shift, three-man offense, nudging it against the shaker. With flair, he plopped the grape into the glass, touched the rim to the shaker with a *ding*, and sounded a prolonged *swaaaak!*

"Now you're free to walk away from the game and win the heart of the girl you love."

Yep. Investigations. Law school. United States President. Worldwide leader.

"And if God is as powerful as you say, Owen, there's nothing to fear. Not even death."

Chapter Nineteen

Bereft. That was a word, wasn't it? Owen remembered hearing it at a funeral once.

And more nightmares.

The opening in the dome of the stadium framed a black ink sky. The hydraulic slats closed, creaking loudly before they slammed shut. Lights went out. Seats emptied. Disillusioned fans stomped out like angry bears.

The earth shook underfoot.

A multi-layered helmet engineered to mitigate collisions, reduce the trauma of impact, and muffle outside sound was incapable of protecting him against his greatest opponent.

Fear.

In a furious huff, he shot out of bed. The moist sheet clung to his bare back. He tugged on a fresh pair of boxers, mopped his forehead with the crook of his arm, and paced. Dizziness crawled inside his skull like fingers grasping at neural circuitry, crimping nerve endings. Maybe he should call Pastor Donovan on the coast. Though two hours behind, he'd remembered the pastor to be an early riser.

"I'm desperate for time with God before the day hits," he'd said.

Owen fired up the Bible app on his phone and returned to where he'd left off a few weeks ago. John, chapter fifteen. As he paced, the soothing bass voice wrapped reassurance around wounded places.

"This is my commandment, that you love one another as I have loved you."

He listened again.

Eli's gameplay barreled through his memory.

Tell Dad.

Tell the world.

Get the girl.

If Owen was going to retire of his own volition, it ought to be out of obedience to God, not to win Serenity's heart. He was pretty certain this move was an act of obedience. Because nothing about it would be easy.

But to suffer was to know the heart of God.

When the curtain was drawn on Owen's career, the public would expect him to turn to sports reporting, the narrow road offered to guys like him. How would he be perceived if he went for his dreams and did something unconventional like open a bakery?

With some reservation, he'd visited Bakery World mid-summer. Reason being he'd wanted to study the competition. Found it vanilla. Nothing but a commercial, cookie-cutter company that had, for a brief couple of months, benefited from his stock purchases until—at Owen's directive—Nina sold the shares.

He—no, Seren and he—managed to surpass what the multi-level chain offered. The distinct difference between costly, exquisite wine and a three-dollar bottle of sangria.

Following last week's humiliating defeat, he could no longer break through the strength of conviction. But he'd want Dad's blessing.

"That's about as likely as being handed the ball by the opposition after the snap, but Lord, I'm prepared to ask."

Already busted up the night of their break up, he'd had to endure Dad's repetitive mantra at Ben's. "Don't let this set you back. Bumps and dings are part of the game."

Setbacks that included the loss of his girl.

"God, no matter the fallout, I'll do it." *Just make Dad accept my decision.*

A wicked headache prodded Owen to enlist Jude to drive him to Tuesday morning's practice. The loyal companion kept silent, his years of service enabling him to discern what was razzing Owen without interrogation.

When Jude shut off the engine, Owen's heart thumped in his chest. He set his elbow on the window ledge and shifted a pitiful glance at Jude, whose firm resolve infused strength. A man who'd fearlessly entered war zones.

"I have your back."

Owen nodded and called Serenity.

No answer.

He left a message. "Hey, Seren. Uh, I just wanted to let you know I've made a decision ... something really tough ... and I'd like to talk through it with you first. If you get this message in the next hour or so, call me. Please. I'm sorry how things ended between us. If nothing else, just, you know, pray for me to be brave. Bye."

I love you.

McNamara's soft practice drills hardly justified a shower before Owen left to take Dad to his 4:00 doctor's appointment. Coach's response to him cutting out of practice early hadn't carried the same gravity as in years past. In greater measure, his usefulness to the team was drying up. And he refused to keep the sidelines warm wearing full gear, watching the game clock tick—upholding the belief he'd be the magic bullet when truth was, last Thursday's hit had drawn a line in the sand.

The brief stint at The Pear Tree showed him he had more to offer. If it meant hanging up his cleats and trusting God with the next steps, he'd do it.

The neurologist's findings were as expected. Dad's symptoms had progressed, his memory caught in a widening mesh of yesterday and today, wound around a ball of confusion. Given the right trigger, he'd go from sappy sentimental to wildly aggressive.

At Dad's house, Owen took their plated po' boys and fries to the lumpy sofa and sat. Beside him, Dad sank slowly into his designated chair, shoving it back to rest his legs. He locked a vacant, weary gaze on the ceiling.

Owen glanced at the broken window. Only the panes were whole and clear, the frame solid and white. He'd forgotten to call Gabe to see about restoring it. "When did you get Gabe to fix the window?"

Dad's gaze went glassy and bemused. He shook his head and squinted at the window. "I didn't. Maybe it fixed itself."

A thundering, divine presence moved over the room. Above the whir of the refrigerator, a beat of quiet sounded, quickly overrun by the blare of a coach's whistle—reruns of Dad in college when Harvey Walker had become a household name.

Owen glanced at the lighted curio cabinet filled with memorabilia—football trophies and the jersey that Dad wore during his first Pro Bowl game. Number 99 was stitched in gold across black nylon. They'd won that game, but he'd lost his career fighting for it. And here he sat, presently confused and serene but potentially volatile.

Mom had been spared seeing the love of her life transform into a mangled network of mental chemistry that fired every which way like a ballplayer fighting for the endzone.

"I remember that season." Dad tapped a finger in the air. "Was targeted for the draft. And the rest, as they say, is history." A bass, throaty laugh jerked his upper body.

He dragged his gaze to Owen. "What'd you want to tell me, son?"

Owen hadn't said much of anything since they arrived. Certainly hadn't mentioned the explosive question that took the form of a grenade in his throat. Capturing Dad's lucid moments was like looking for the pocket on offense. When it formed, he needed to break through.

The smell of remoulade sauce and fried shrimp soured his stomach. He dragged his fries through a pool of ketchup.

A stiff smile fit Dad's mouth. "I'm not so far gone that I don't recognize that look. The one where you've got something on your mind but can't bring yourself to say it."

Read him like a playbook.

"I'll get the party started." Dad adjusted himself in the recliner. "How've you been feeling since you got dinged?"

Bereft. Gutted. Aimless.

"Not too bad. Just dizziness and headaches. Nothing that doesn't come with the league."

One side of Dad's mouth quirked up. He shook his head slowly like a forensic pathologist. "You're having nightmares that keep you up at night and forgetting where you put your keys. You purchased a luxury car for the thrill of driving it, yet you pay for escort service for fear you'll forget directions. You get all sappy when you see a kitty stuck in a tree, and the idea of a kid suffering shreds you to bits."

Owen squeezed his hand around his sub. He winced at the burn of Dad's gaze boring into his cheek.

Dad's inner coach surfaced. He spoke with authority and drive, and his hands gestured in a circular motion.

"You have no clue what your next steps should be. You're caught between what you really want and what you feel obligated to."

Stomach roiling, he draped a napkin over his sub to bury the smell of seafood.

The leather recliner crinkled as Dad twisted harder at the waist. "Your old man is getting close."

His cheeks puffed at a labored sigh.

"You've lost sight of why you're playing anymore, though you refuse to release your grip on the gridiron for fear of becoming inconsequential because you've been on everyone's radar for so long it's unbearable to imagine life any other way."

Nervously, his heel bobbed. He ran palms along the side stripe of his track pants. "I'm on IR, Dad. Out for the season."

"And you're pressured to keep it all under wraps—so news doesn't leak to other teams."

He nodded.

"You've become nothing but a team trophy that sits pretty but has no power. They refuse to give you up but won't let you play. It's a kicker, for sure."

"I've still got two more years in my contract."

"Might ought to consider listening to medical wisdom, son, and spare what's left of you for those you love. For too long, I believed my mule-headed brain could take the hits. Apparently not."

"What?"

"My headaches, sleeplessness, mood swings, depression. It doesn't take a medical degree for a guy to know when he's going down CTE's unrecoverable road. Of course, they can't give an affirmative diagnosis without an autopsy." Dad strained a stare. "I thought I'd wait."

Easy laughter thinned the somber veil shrouding the room.

"Doctors aren't always right."

"Yes, but the great physician hasn't misdiagnosed a person since the days of Adam. The big league can make a guy mighty arrogant, Owen. God had to cleanse me from all that."

The truth rippled over the parts of Owen's brain that hadn't been crushed and seeped into his heart.

With a start, Dad shot out of his recliner and hollered over the sports commentator. "Stupid ref, the guy clearly impeded Lamont's ability to snag the ball." He swung a fist in a swift arc across his chest. Stiffening arms at his side, he stepped within inches of the screen. "Pass interference, you morons! Make the call!"

In a blink, Dad paused, went lax, and turned a pitiful gaze at Owen. "See that? Listless one minute, a fire-breathing dragon the next. No one's safe. The only—and I mean *only*—blessing of losing your mom was knowing that she'd not have to live with this."

"Aw, c'mon, Dad. She'd love you no matter what. Even at your worst."

For better or worse.

"Guess we'll never know." He hitched a shoulder and returned to his chair. "So, you gonna quit?"

For the first time, the petulant question held a tinge of pleading. Absent threat or condemnation. And for the first time, it offered an open door.

A choice.

"You all but threatened me not to quit, even as recent as last Thursday. Now you're urging me off the field?"

"Owen, a father tells his prodigy the best he knows with what he's been given at the time. Years past, I shrank my view of what matters down to one little thing. Football. Your mom, on the other hand, worked her darndest to expand you and Derek's horizons. I didn't want you to see beyond the game because, in my day, a guy was a sissy if he sat out over a head ding. Now we got former players speaking out, the institution of a concussion protocol. God allowed me to be roughed up in my body to humble my insides. Suffering does that."

A veil of melancholy washed through Owen. Fear skittered along his spine. The future—an endless stretch of yardage with no way to reach the endzone.

"You're a powerful machine on the gridiron, son. A fearsome mechanism of destruction with deadly, unsurpassed moves. A lightning rod. A muscular matrix of brutal force ..."

Where was this leading?

Dad rolled forward and fixed a weighty gaze on Owen. "The problem is not that people think a player can walk on water. It's that *he's* convinced himself he can. But a bunch of muscle wrapped around an arrogant man is a perfect waste of physiology." In a rare wave of clarity, Dad had spoken intelligently and smoothly, his bangled thoughts a serene lake.

"In or out of uniform, you're still the same as when I first held all ten pounds, twenty-four inches of you in my palm."

Dad muttered vile objections at the ref again, then lasered his attention back on Owen. "Took me a while to realize it, but we're not ballplayers. We're children of God." His eyes began to mist. "You aren't what you do, son. I love you no matter what."

Sheesh. Had Dad really gone off the deep end? Or ... had God answered Owen's prayer?

"As for the bakery gig, you always did favor being in the kitchen with your mother. You've got business smarts to operate a place like that. Where others have the vision, you know how to execute."

Serenity? She was the visionary in need of an executor.

"I don't think I've ever seen you more satisfied than in recent months, son. Not even after you snagged the ball midair, ran it sixty yards for a touchdown."

It'd been eighty yards. But no matter. His heart inched closer to what it needed to hear. "I figured you'd say that a person with my athletic ability had no business doing something like that."

"At one time, I would have, but I'm calling an audible, son. Now's your time to do something else."

There were financial benefits for Owen to be denied clearance. His contract still entitled him to $1.2 million this season and another $600 thousand if the concussion ended his career. If he didn't retire and had his agent scout another team to consider signing him, they'd have to take the risk into consideration. Recovering from the hits was taking longer each time.

He stroked the stubble on his chin. "You really think I should go for it?"

Dad swept up a palm and shrugged. "You're a big guy who likes to bake. Pity the fool who tries to razz you for it."

All this—spoken by a man who, despite mental degeneration, had seen things—God-sized, deeply spiritual things and spoke divine, spirit-breathed truth. One who, while crumbling physically, demonstrated God's ability to heal and restore.

Dad spoke through the side of his mouth and gave Owen a slanted glance. "Make sure to take the bakery girl along with you. She's pretty and has a good head on her shoulders. Just like your momma."

"I lost her, too."

The remote crashed to the floor. Ire flashed in Dad's steel gray eyes.

"She … she broke up with me."

Hardest hit to date.

Dad's expression turned brutally grim, the look of a coach glaring at a star player who'd run the wrong direction.

"She claims she can't live with my refusal to quit the game."

"But you don't believe it."

"I think she's using that as a defense against the fact that she can't have kids."

Dad tapped his chin the way he did in high school when strategizing the right play. "Darn shame."

"I picked her because I thought she was the one."

"She's not a draft choice, son. Sounds like you're placing conditions on a girl when you haven't got a leg to stand on. You either love her in full or release her to another guy who will."

A virulent possessiveness reared inside at the idea of her in the arms of someone else. Serenity wasn't his to possess. She was his to love exactly the way God had designed her.

"You love her."

"With all my heart."

"That's impossible," Dad guffawed. "Most of your heart loves Owen."

The scathing rebuke shredded his insides.

Owen opened his mouth and clamped it shut. He worked his lower lip between his teeth.

"You told her you love her?"

"Yes. But I don't think she believes me."

"You didn't tell America you're a good ballplayer. You demonstrated it. She'll believe you when she sees it."

With that, the famed Harvey Walker reclaimed the remote, settled back into his recliner, and worked up a sweat, shouting obscenities at the ref.

Chapter Twenty

Serenity hadn't talked to Owen since their breakup a week ago. Seven agonizing days that felt like a million forevers. She'd gotten his texts and repeatedly listened to his tender message about needing courage to do a hard thing.

As asked, she'd prayed for him because God could meet Owen's greatest need. It just wouldn't include her.

Her heart begged to know the nature of his struggle. She ached to listen to every word of it. To linger in his arms like before while he stroked her hair and included her in his ramblings about what his future might look like.

Making a couple out of them.

After all, Owen had been the one and only guy she ever dared to allow into private spaces where she'd shared pieces of her dark moment—the need of a little girl for assurance she'd not been a disappointment. A guy with widespread notoriety who, to Serenity, was reachable and real when they were together. He offered acceptance and strength and said she was his refuge from the pressure to perform. A place off the grid where he could free his mind to explore life after football which, she'd falsely presumed, included her bakery.

A guy who, until he learned of her one crucial limitation, had celebrated her uniqueness.

During the summer, she'd planted more and more of Owen into her heart, letting his charm and ingenuity till the soil a bit. In favor of letting love grow, the truth of her inability to bear children had burrowed deep, further from the light. And when it sprang out of Serenity's mouth, it had to have brutalized his ego. Since that night, the anger she'd harbored against him began to thaw and nurture humility.

"I love you, Owen Walker. Always will. I wish you the very best."

Meandering through the French Quarter, its scent heady with cuisine, history, and revelry, Serenity developed a hankering for pastry. Aside from Café du Monde or The Pear Tree, where *did* a girl go for quality baked goods? Bakery World was only five blocks to the northeast.

Dare she?

Pride hissed. She denied its power. Because, apparently, her competition had something special.

The ease of parking was the first clue to Bakery World's success. Serenity paused inside the entrance and gazed around the interior. Plain, ordinary white walls held mass-produced posters with glorified images of pastries—none of which matched the offerings inside the glass showcase.

A sparse, self-serve coffee bar with two urns and creamer pitchers sat to the left of a gray, waist-high countertop. The world's most crucial wake-up beverage had been treated as an afterthought. Beside it, racks of sprinkled doughnuts, twists, muffins, and frosted cupcakes wore saccharine smiles.

She fidgeted with the neck of her T-shirt and muttered, "Dreadful. Unimpressive."

Within the eating area, familiar faces of former clientele caught her attention. Among them sat Mrs. Beasley—a faithful former patron—perched at a slightly tilted table.

Her eyes suddenly dipped beneath the brim of a floppy hat. Going for anonymous, nibbling at an *ugly* domed muffin.

A dull pastry that mocked the poster's promise on the wall behind her.

Out of respect for management, Serenity placed an order—a small coffee and plain vanilla cupcake that looked several days old and like it'd been frosted by a toddler. Nodding her thanks, she paid the moderate sum of $4.50 and sat at a two-person, tippy table against the opposite wall.

The door swung open. She turned to see Brooke.

Ouch.

Their gazes collided, Brooke's eyes rounding in stunned surprise like an adolescent caught sneaking through the window after curfew. Her brows drooped over a crimped smile that held a hard mixture of pity and angst.

She walked over. "Hey." The breezy greeting was an admirable attempt to appear as though this encounter wasn't supremely awkward. "I was just about to pick the kids up from school, and I, you know, they really love the sprinkle doughnuts here and—"

Serenity cupped Brooke's elbows and gave them a gentle squeeze. "It's okay. It's cheaper here and ..." She shrugged. "We never offered doughnuts."

A whoosh of air left Brooke's lungs. "We sure missed you at dinner after the game."

The game to end all.

"Sorry I haven't called you," Brooke said. "Since school started, it's been crazy around the O'Brien household adjusting to strict schedules."

"No doubt. Can you sit a minute?"

"Sure." Brooke sat opposite Serenity, the table tipping Brooke's direction when she set her purse on it. "I hate that you had to close up."

A moan shuddered through her chest as she sipped lukewarm coffee from a standard cup through a standard lid.

The Pear Tree had offered so much more than cheap products and easy parking. It had ambiance and art and color and jazz and ... Owen ... and fragrance and custom-made, hand-baked pastries and ... Owen—for four sweet months.

Squinting through a mental fog, peering through mist, she paused to remember the things she'd incorporated to give life to the place. But like a mother, when her child is sick, she'd done all she could to revive it.

Owen. He'd been its oxygen mask.

Why hadn't The Pear Tree been appreciated beyond the blessed stretch of eight years? Seated in a reproducible establishment offering common products at affordable prices, she had her answer. When presented with a choice, the public had determined her unique establishment ... meh.

Which meant she was meh.

Love my bakery, love me. Hate my bakery, hate me.

Serenity peeled the casing from the cupcake, took a bite, and shivered in disgust. "How is it that my mom left Moreland to my older sister—who'd seen no value in the historic treasure—while I chased after a dream to open a bakery and harnessed the social media savvy to make a go of it? And here I sit, eating an altogether stale and crappy cupcake because my place was outclassed by ..." She darted a scathing glance around, then leaned in and whisper-shouted. "one that's epically mediocre."

Brooke sounded an empathetic moan.

The greatest heartache of all she'd left unspoken, tucked in shadows of insecurity. It was that she'd loved only one man on the planet. And with that one man, she'd wanted children—lots of them.

Had she been wrong to break up? Would time heal enough to enable him to process her infertility and see the beauty of adoption?

Was that too impossible a thing to ask, God?

"Did you hear back from Bryan J. Carlyle about the recipe contest?" Brooke shifted in her chair—her gaze ripe with anticipation.

"Serenity's Special wasn't chosen."

Brooke gave a wan grin.

"I got an impersonal email with verbiage stating how they'd received hundreds of entries and appreciated my participation, the product was—" She made quotes in the air. "nice."

"That's ridiculous. Your cupcake is far from nice."

"I read no further than 'Unfortunately.'"

"Oh, Serenity, I'm so sorry." Brooke shook her head slowly, then perked up, her eyes flashing merriment. "Remember the lady who'd traveled over an hour to The Pear Tree because her friends had raved about it and ordered a dozen cupcakes for her grandkids in New Orleans?"

She remembered. That was sweet.

"And that stuffed shirt CEO, Warren Murdock, ordered his staff to purchase a box of cupcakes for their weekly board meetings?"

She'd remembered that, too. He'd preferred Walker's Big Hits but graciously accepted hers when she'd explained he'd taken the secret recipe with him when he left.

But it was his recipe. He owned the right to conceal his secret when he returned to the game.

It took Brooke's recall for Serenity to remember her original recipe *was* special to a handful of souls. Wasn't that satisfying enough?

Yes, it was.

Thank you, Jesus.

Ever since she could remember, Serenity had wanted to leave her fingerprints on the world and for people to say that it was good that God created a girl named Serenity Chapelle Lewis who'd established a trendy bakery, a filling station of joy unmatched by the competition. And, like her bakery, she'd wanted to be considered entirely distinct, a girl whose design was intentional and beautiful and purposeful.

Because, really, her limitations weren't in any way flawed or incomplete. And if she embraced them, nothing would be impossible for her.

Peace would, at long last, be her constant companion.

A wisp of spiritual truth drifted into her mind, floated to her heart, and breathed life.

All of you, pleases all of Me.

A subtle undercurrent of euphoria washed Serenity's cheeks in warmth—and just as quickly turned frosty when the front door of Bakery World slung open and held the unmistakable form of Owen Walker.

The guy who was out of her league. Whom she loved.

Effortlessly, he turned her direction as though he'd felt her presence, sensed where she'd be—the superior quality of a star player who could zero in on who to tackle.

An unmistakable hush expanded within the common area. Patrons turned in their seats. Murmurs and subtle gasps rippled over tables.

He'd hidden his eyes behind reflective shades, his bronze-brown hair tucked beneath a ball cap. In one fluid motion, he removed his shades and tucked them inside the neck of his baby blue golf shirt. The soft one. A favorite of hers ... cool and satiny against her skin when she'd snuggled up to it, trying to match the rise and fall of his husky breathing.

A mix of reticence and delight rang in his expression. Lines deepened aside his haggard, granite eyes. His hands fell loosely arced at his side, and tension ripped along the tendons of his arms. She could feel tremors going through him as he crossed over. His shoulders rose in an inhale.

"I saw your car out front," he said, breaking her stare. He trailed a gaze at Brooke. "Hey, Brooke."

"Hi, Owen."

After a minimal nod, Brooke glanced at her cell, released a tiny gasp, and stood. "The kids. I almost forgot." She snatched the box of pitifully original doughnuts. "I've gotta go. We'll catch up later, Serenity."

Owen returned Brooke's wave and watched her skip-walk out the door. He drew a cautious glance back to Serenity, tucked a hand in his pocket, and motioned toward the vacated seat. "Can I sit?"

To tamp down a slew of nerves, she chuckled and stood. "It'd break."

His simple, melodic laugh was like bliss. She'd missed their playful banter and games of one-upmanship.

The reality that he'd gone beyond mere help months ago to pursue a dating relationship pooled like a creamy confection in her middle. It was as if he viewed her as a wildly intriguing, unchartered topography that he desired to explore. This one man who possessed a delicious set of dimples when he smiled had confessed his love for her. When she considered it for more than two seconds, it'd rocked the earth beneath her feet ... like it did just then, inhaling his scent of sandalwood, strength, and happy endings.

Don't inhale.

Security and ardor sparked in his softened gaze. The look ... yes, *that* one ... he'd reserved only for her still held seductive power. Desire churned and simmered.

The walls closed in and swallowed her air supply.

"You've already created a stir among inquiring minds, most of whom look like female trout pulled from the water, so we'd better take this party outside."

Some party. It felt more like a funeral reception—or an inquisition. After their breakup, she was emotionally raw and defenseless in his presence, quite certain her soul couldn't withstand a barrage of questions. Given his training, he had to know the effect his dominance had on the opposition. She was, after all, the one who'd ended things.

Utilizing athletic grace, he turned to the gaping stargazers and blessed them with his killer smile before scuttling ahead of Serenity to open the door for her. A hint of desire to impress rang in his body language, his brows angled and hopeful.

What if he hadn't chased after her to win the fight or to ravage her with accusations? What if he merely sought understanding? Needed to be understood?

Restoration at best.

A modest glow of sunlight shouldered through a cottony haze of clouds. They stood facing each other outside the entrance. Nerves nibbled at her spine. She clasped trembling, moist hands—if for no other reason than to offset any thoughts he may have had about claiming them.

"Your bakery, Seren. I had no idea."

Painful silence clamored.

His woeful gaze begged for an explanation.

"I didn't tell you."

"You've mastered that move."

"How'd you find out?"

"Lettie. At Eli's request, I took him over to Moreland last Sunday. Said she's working there now."

God's provision. She tossed up a quick prayer of thanks.

"First, I learn you can't have kids." Censure infused his tone. "Then the bakery. Why couldn't you trust me with that?"

Inquisition, here we go.

"For all the bravery I possess, I didn't have enough to risk losing you over something I can't fix."

"There's more."

She thumbed her ear. His ability to read her unspooled her resolve. If God had ever given thought to making the two of them into a couple, she'd have to own up to that which had been buried deep inside her soul. For years, she'd refused to confess to anyone outside Everley and Mom. Now, she'd been cornered. "I was afraid you'd think I wasn't enough."

A wince claimed the sculpted planes of his face as though her words tasted of turpentine. He gave his head a twitchy shake. "I never walked away, Seren."

"You hesitated."

"It hit me hard."

This from the three-time Defensive Player of the Year?

"I've watched you take hits for over ten years." *Closely.* "I'd naively hoped ... somehow ... that, once I told you the truth, you'd be indifferent to it." Early on—following the unforgettable soccer field kiss—she'd fantasized often about how she wanted this exchange to go.

"I want to have kids with you," he'd say.

"All right, well, is it okay if I can't?" she'd ask.

"Sure. No problem."

"You cool with adoption?"

And sweetening their exchange, he'd profess, "Anything so long as I can have you, Seren."

On this drab pavement, outside an equally drab establishment—none of their conversation played out as she'd scripted it. But for all his hesitation that awful day, she remained dumbfounded by his attraction to her. The steadfastness with which he'd held her, his determination to claim her heart.

If what Owen Walker wanted most was not possible, why'd he bother?

"I just wish you'd been upfront with me from the beginning. I don't want to be lied to by the girl I love."

Again, he'd confessed his love, this time marked by ardent fervor, his gesturing hands hinting at desperation.

Confounded situation.

"I thought I'd made it clear how I feel about you, Seren."

She steadied her stance and gathered courage. "Kissing a girl could suggest love. It's not proof of it."

He flinched like she'd swung a battle-ax at him. But he wasted no seconds to regroup at the line of scrimmage. "I promise you, Seren. I've never kissed a girl like I've kissed you. Never felt what I feel when I'm with you." A subtle fury, thickly coated in desire, soaked his tone. He took two steps closer as though intent on breaking through an impenetrable barrier. His chest heaved in shallow, hot breaths. "Never *wanted* a girl like I want you nor proclaimed love to another girl. You're the first one I ever trusted with my vulnerabilities, a safe place to be real. You know the Owen Walker behind the uniform. The only girl who could offer a future, an alternative to football ..." His throat bobbed, eyes misting. "a family."

Millions of women before Serenity had probably ached to hear Owen profess his love. Some may have given all of themselves for a shot at it. Yet—she dared believe—he'd made his choice clear. Which only complicated the underlying problem.

"See. Right there. I *can't* offer you what you want. A family you have every right to enjoy." She crossed her arms and gripped her elbows in her palms to keep her heart from popping out of her chest.

Within his engulfing shadow, she leaned back and tipped her chin to study his expression. "You wanted what you believed was true of me, Owen. Once you learned what was beneath the surface, you retreated."

"Your deceit was disrespectful."

Valid argument. Because for a man, respect was oxygen. When in short supply, his soul died.

"And I felt …" He drew out an elongated sigh.

Don't say it.

"Dis—"

"Disappointed?"

Disappointment, thy name is Serenity.

The truth knifed at her heart, twisted all around.

"*Felt* disappointed," he shot back.

Disquiet and confusion thundered above the rumble of a nearby delivery truck.

Tears sprang. Emotion strangled. She coughed at the burn of exhaust.

"All I asked for was time to think. But I never left you, Seren." His voice was ruthlessly level, gaze flinty and grave. His jaw ticked. "Never."

Sorrow ringed his eyes red.

Her heart thundered in rabid rhythm. A fresh well of tears blurred her vision. Oh, good gracious, this magnificent, tender warrior of a man! The shame she'd carried over her inadequacy lacerated his pride, lanced his heart, and shredded his dignity.

He pressed his fingers into his pockets. His lips pinched into a thin line. A scrutinizing gaze prickled along her skin. "Hear me now, please, Seren. I accept you as you are and as Christ accepts me." His words rasped out. "The question is ..."

And here was the kicker.

"Can you love a guy with battered parts?"

Chapter Twenty-One

Endless quiet ping-ponged between Owen and Serenity. The question he asked would either be the nail in the coffin or that which set them on a course of figuring out how to navigate their differences. He'd give her all the time she needed to answer. In football, timing was crucial. Games were lost due to impulsive moves, forcing a rush.

"Maybe I'll ask if Bakery World is hiring," she finally said, masterfully deflecting his question with appalling nonsense.

Her pitiful expression suggested she needed rescue.

Because, *uh-uh*. "Wrong move, Seren."

He hated the picture of this beautiful, creative creature—who smelled of roses and sugar and held a blistering inner resolve—to be relegated to a uniform of an ugly brown T-shirt bearing the logo of a nationwide chain.

"I need a job."

"This isn't your place. This is a mass-produced, run-of-the-mill bakery. It's not you." He moved a back-handed gesture toward the siding.

One side of her mouth hitched. She shrugged, projecting helplessness. "People prefer it. A fully functioning body made up of many functioning parts, capable of limitless reproduction."

At the subtext, a breakable sorrow filled her gaze, misting now. Chin quivering, she jerked a glance away and sniffed—fighting with the fury of a locomotive to hold herself together, it appeared. And he'd done it. He'd wrecked her.

Instinct surged down to his feet. The massive defender considered coverage. He moved his focus off the backfield, seizing the opportunity to lunge for the girl who'd gotten herself turned around and risked making a lousy play. She stood on one side of the neutral zone, wide open ... within his grasp. It'd be easy to clutch her to his chest and kiss some sense into her. Chase after her heart.

You're losing her, Walker.

Encroachment would only earn him a penalty. She wasn't a game he had to win.

"Despite all the effort and investment I'd put into The Pear Tree, involving a big personality like you, I couldn't keep it going on my own." The sheen of sunlight caught her gemstone eyes and encircled them in white gold. "But I get that. No one's interested in unique."

Take position—on the line of scrimmage. He broke into the neutral zone, drew her chin his direction, and fixed his gaze. "God is. He made you."

She didn't wince or wrinkle her nose in disdain. Or pop a weak little fist across his upper arm in frustration. Cautiously, she stood there as he watched her mental gears turn, looking like she'd really needed to hear that. An easy nod suggested she'd listened. Maybe savored his words like a ravenous orphan who hadn't had a good meal in a very long time.

"The biggest problem isn't that you were born with some crazy whatever-you-call-it condition. It's that you've forgotten your worth."

No thanks to him.

Her shoulders drew up in inhale. Yearning moved across her graceful features. She swallowed hard as flecks of sun-kissed light dotted her misty gaze.

Eye on the pocket, Walker.

Spirit-breathed words sprang to his tongue, squeezing past a boulder of emotion in his throat.

"I'd like to think God could use me somehow ... to help you remember."

A cautious smile fit the playful curve of her lips, glossy and colored pink to match her shoelaces. What had his sentiment done to her heart?

Even this late in the game, the odds were stacked against him, but he prayed it healed her wound. Because the girl—all of her—mattered more than football.

With no more than a rapid nod, Serenity claimed a sudden need to be somewhere and left Owen standing on the pavement. She walked backward to her car in dragging steps. The exertion to refrain from blocking her retreat nearly buckled his knees. He kept his gaze on her until she turned and faded from view.

Desperation to chase after her and beg for an answer fired hot.

Could she love a guy with broken parts?

But love didn't demand. It pursued but didn't insist on its own way. If she wanted him, she'd find him.

"God, take care of the bakery girl." An easy wind brushed past, caught his throaty petition, and whisked it heavenward.

A few more days of soft practice, and Owen could have tugged off his helmet and chucked it into the stands. He felt like a lion trapped in the forest, stripped of his crown. Impotent among the pride despite a showcase of trophies. He wasn't up for contract negotiation, and his agent insisted he stick it out.

"Even with my agenting finesse, I don't think I could arrange a deal lucrative enough for another team to take you. Your best play is to let the dust settle and wait this one out."

After Owen showered, he dressed in black track pants and a USMC T-shirt he'd borrowed from Jude. A vicarious move to slip into the skin of someone in another vocation.

Moisture beaded along his neck and back, breaths shallowed by intense disquiet. In front of his locker, he sank to the bench. Leaning forward, he lowered his forehead to his palms and grasped his wet hair. Teammates patted him on the shoulder as they passed. "Miss you on the gridiron, Walker."

Spare the pity, guys.

For a couple days after his conversation with Dad, Owen's steps had been lighter, and the weight of fear and guilt lifted. But they'd turned to lead after the exchange with Serenity.

The need to be alone on a ball field overwhelmed him. To feel the turf and allow the expanse of a stadium to envelop him—body, soul, and mind.

To make peace with the game.

He contacted Oscar Simmons, the varsity football coach at Destrehan High School, home of the Fighting Wildcats and the onetime host location of his football camp during City Park restoration from Hurricane Katrina. Not at all unlike the field where Dad had poked at Owen's psyche in high school like a branding iron ...

"Listen to me, son," Dad had snarled. "You're a Walker, and Walkers play football. Now, get back on your feet, keep your eyes off the backfield, and let's run this again".

At the mention of Owen's name, Coach Simmons granted access.

"Here's the deal, coach. I don't want any cameras or media. I'll need complete privacy for about an hour."

"Take all the time you need. Practice isn't until 3:30. I'll even unlock the athletic complex if you'd like to get a workout in."

"That won't be necessary. Thanks."

A long stretch of jagged clouds hovered over a shrinking cityscape as Owen motored southwest toward the winding Mississippi where Destrehan High School sat east of its banks. Coach Simmons met him at the gate that opened to a 5000-seat, multi-purpose stadium. A burnt orange running track encircled the field.

Just as the smell of fresh turf sniped at his determination, the burly coach took Owen's hand in a fierce grip and nodded beneath a red ball cap. The gate screeched when Coach opened it.

"The field is yours."

Coach turned toward the school bearing the gimpy gait of a former athlete in his team sweatpants and T-shirt stretched over a growing paunch.

The realization that Serenity wasn't the perfect package she'd led him to believe soured Owen's stomach. It took the hammer of Dad's wisdom—forged from hardship, the advancing work of grace—and the discipline of listening to his Bible app to realign his understanding of what it looked like to love a person.

Love wasn't a feeling. It had to be authenticated by action.

While we were still sinners, Christ died for us.

It required sacrifice.

It meant exerting effort to assure the object of his love—Serenity—was secure in that knowledge.

It meant firming his resolve when tackled by disappointment.

At its root, love was a matter of the heart.

Claiming a place in the endzone, Owen felt the light of God's presence wash over him. Fragmented thoughts and found order.

"God—" His address to the Almighty came out raspy. "I've spent my entire career chasing down the opposition and made millions doing it. But I've crushed the girl I love."

Owen's hesitation had shaken Serenity's trust in his ability to love well. He'd had no right to exact an unachievable standard on her when he couldn't offer the same.

"Owen Lane Walker, Hypocrite of the Year."

He'd either love her in full, no matter what, or walk away, leaving her free to create beauty in the world apart from him.

But if he walked away, his heart would have no place to land. Because the alternative was to keep holding onto a season in his life that'd reached its expiration and miss out on a new and promising season ahead—the opportunity to extend the reach of his sports camps and give more charitably. Fight for Eli throughout chemo treatments.

For years, he'd determined to be the one to choose when or if he'd call it quits. But what he'd really done was hide behind his fear that fans only loved the image they had of him. To give up football meant he'd no longer allow the game or his fans to define his identity. He could walk away now because he knew who he was apart from it. And though he didn't know what challenges tomorrow held, he could trust God's good purpose in it.

Slowly, he took a knee, opened his palms, and tipped his chin. Storm clouds floated in and shadowed the field. Raindrops dotted his head—his cheeks. "I've been an arrogant man. Forgive me. Thank you for your love, for the game of football—and what it's allowed me to do for kids and communities. Thank you for making Seren exactly the way she is. Help her know she's loved—all of her. Please help her get back on her feet so she can continue to bless others. Even if it means ..." A clap of thunder ripped through the charcoal sky. Drilling rain moved in sheets over the field. "I can't be a part of it."

The words burned Owen's tongue and seared his insides. Made the agony of two-a-days seem like a country stroll. He doubled over, palms flattened on the ground, and lowered his forehead to the prickling grass. Heated breaths wrenched his lungs. Tears pooled and beat against his eyes, a fierce contender against his stubborn will.

Cry it out, Walker.

Rain sluiced down his back and soaked his shirt, his entire body awash in God's presence. He welcomed it— the cathartic, cleansing rain slicking over the stubborn grip he had on earthly things and backward thinking. The strength of the wind ground his arrogance to dust and swept it away.

His upper body chugged against the mounting urge to sob. Tears fell over splayed hands, mingled with the earthy scent of rain and earth. They rose in waves, crashed against his soul, and spilled out for several minutes.

A lifetime of toxic emotion drained out of him.

Emptied of self, a rush of holy strength overtook his body. He sucked a cleansing breath into his lungs. The experience fortified his resolve to do the one thing he'd believed he could outrun.

Retire.

After several minutes, Owen sat on his heels.

"God, I give it all to you. Take the game, the recognition, the stats. I'm not Owen Lane Walker, number ninety-one of the New Orleans Kings, son of Harvey Walker. I'm your adopted son. Use me as you will."

A distant crash of thunder murmured. The sun broke through and lined pillowed clouds in white light. The rain slowed as he stood on soaked feet inside soggy shoes. His shirt clung to his skin, and his knees were stained in mud.

But he felt clean on the inside.

From his vantage point, the chalk lines bordering one hundred yards faded.

A gap opened.

Having traded his cleats for those of a commoner, he raced out of the endzone toward the sideline.

God had seen fit for Owen to retire long before he thought he was ready. But bearing up under the strain, he'd come out a winner.

Which brought him back to the next move in Coach Eli's playbook.

Tell the world.

In football, everything had always come naturally to Owen. There was something innate about being in full gear that'd enabled him to perform at such an exceptionally high level for so long. Football had been perfectly suited for the way God designed him. But it didn't come with a manual for how to tell the staff and teammates his season had come to an end.

Responses from Kings' owner Gerald Godfrey, the GM Hank Mahoney, and Coaches Wagner and McNamara in the sacred space of the linebacker room at Mercedes-Benz stadium were brutal at best. "You've still got plenty of yardage left," Coach Wagner said. He wore a strained smile to mask the undercurrent of angst. The same one he wore on the Super Bowl sidelines when they were at the mercy of a missed field goal by the opponent to clench the win.

"You're darn near immortal, Walker. No way we're cutting you." Gerald Godfrey shot from his chair—nearly toppling it as he spun away—and thrust hands into his pockets.

"You sure about this?" Coach McNamara's husky question conveyed measurable concern and compassion. As the defensive coach, he'd had an exclusive front-row seat to the toll football had taken on Owen's body. His spirit. His joy.

"Very." *Before I chicken out.*

The hallowed room clamored in thunderous silence.

Threat and a tinge of mocking smile gathered in Godfrey's steel gray gaze. "You tell Harve yet?"

Years after retirement and Dad still lingered in the minds of notables in the league.

"He urged me to. Gave me his blessing."

A guffaw sounded among the naysayers.

Godfrey slapped a hand on his knee. "That's a miracle."

"It is, actually." *An answer to prayer.*

"What about Caplin?" Godfrey said. "He'll hate you."

He answered with a shrug. The lineup of white-washed faces stared back. An ache for this turbulent meeting to end festered beneath his skin.

Finally, General Manager, Hank Mahoney, spoke. "Owen, you're the best thing that's ever happened to the team. It's been a great ride. But I respect your decision and know you well enough that it hasn't come easy." He drew a sluggish glance at the rest and directed a nod at Coach Wagner. "Once retirement papers are filed, we'll look at the roster, bring some guys in to fill the position, and arrange a press conference."

Godfrey sounded a disparaging scowl. Disenfranchisement climbed into his gaze, shifting into rabid fury. He gripped the back of a chair and swung it against the wall, leaving a golf ball-sized hole. The chair tumbled and crashed to the floor.

Owen fired to his feet to dodge the fray. The legs of his chair screeched over the floor.

"You're paying for that, Godfrey," Coach barked.

With his gaze steeled on Coach, Godfrey lanced a finger at Owen. "Take it out of his salary."

Far from a peaceful parting—but Owen had completed the play. Relief circuited through his chest at Godfrey's hasty exit and enabled deeper breaths. He shook hands with the remaining three.

A mixture of elation and misery churned. Nausea bubbled in his stomach. His temples throbbed, and his head spun. He teetered, caught himself with a hand to the wall, leaned forward, and coughed.

Refusing eye contact, he dashed down the hallway to the locker room and hurled his lunch in the sink.

Yep. Not immortal.

Motoring his Bentley along Luling Bridge, he draped an arm out his open window and let the road take him with no clear destination. An airy solace and weightlessness urged him onward. Soft shafts of sunlight winked through lazy clouds in a dusty blue sky. He breathed in the leafy smell of autumn and lakeside grasses. Cool air brushed his arm, whipped his hair, and swept over his face.

As expected, Tommy welcomed the news with the calm and sensitivity of a soaked Siamese cat. "You worried about what people will think being on IR? Word hasn't leaked to the league that I'm aware of."

"I'm filing for retirement."

"You can't," he sneered, voice jittery. The sound of agitated steps and rifling papers were likely symptoms of nicotine withdrawal. "You've still got two years on that contract. If you make this move now, that's a butt load of dead money against the salary cap. Tough this out."

"My body—and my contract—says I can. I've made myself clear."

"Which means I've lost a client."

"You've got twenty-two by my last count. Still the league's leading agency, holding the record for representing the greatest number of first-round draft picks. I won't be missed."

"Like the engine on a Boeing 747 won't be missed."

Silence gained agonizing yardage.

"This isn't my first rodeo, Owen. Benched players become restless. They begin to believe they're washed up and are no good to the team. Pride gets damaged, fear takes hold, and they turn in their gear. But then there's you—a blue-chip player that an agent can only hope to represent. You darn near walk on water."

On the trail of a disquieting laugh, Owen heard nervous pacing, Tommy's desperate attempt to string the right words together.

"You're not just a number on a roster. Twenty years in this business, and you, Walker, remain my best find to date."

"Cap, I'm filing papers by day's end. I'll arrange for a private production company to record the announcement. Secure the creatives who'd filmed Moreland's restoration in Napoleonville a couple years back."

"Okay, seriously. I'm beginning to believe you *do* have brain damage. Did you hear a word I said?"

"All of it."

"Then why are you doing this? And, sheesh, Napoleonville?" A dog yelped in the background as if he'd given the poor thing a swift kick. "You're the engine that makes the Kings run."

"Which has broken down."

"Things break, but that's football. You're supposed to love this stuff."

I love Serenity more.

"It's time, Cap. *Past* time. I'm choosing to hang on to whatever I have left of my future."

"It's not like it was in the beginning when you had suitors clamoring for a piece of you. As to your future, I haven't lined up any sportscasting or, let's say, medical insurance sales gigs."

"Not interested."

Tommy's frustration blustered like an early winter wind and was just as icy. "No one will buy into Owen Walker outside of uniform. It won't work."

"I can bake."

A derisive laugh. "And I can paint by number. But you don't see me giving up a lucrative job to sell paintings."

"Plenty of games have been won on unconventional plays. I'm ready to shake things up. Do what I really enjoy."

"Yeah, but baking?" Another metallic laugh, this one digging under Owen's skin. "Sounds like a sissy move if you ask me."

"Say that to my face, Caplin."

Silence, a nervous cough, and a froggy laugh—probably patting his pocket for a cigarette. "All right, now. Just calm down, Owen, my main man. Let's think this through."

"I've already thought this through. So much so that my head hurts."

"Nothing new there, champ. Listen, here's what I'll do. I hear Brad Worthington at Top Team Sports is on his way out as co-anchor. Let me give the producer a call and arrange for an interview. Formality, of course. They'd be crazy not to take you."

That scrambling again. If Cap had committed to quitting smoking, this call might be what broke another attempt at abstinence.

"I appreciate it, Tommy. But I'm looking to do something totally different." Unique and very Serenity-like. "I've thought about opening up a bakery." And pray he could co-own the establishment with the girl he loved.

"What part of stepping in to help that damsel in distress has mangled your thinking?" Exasperation amplified. "What about the sports camps—and the foundation, for crying out loud?"

"Nothing changes about that. In fact, I'll have more time to devote to it and grow it. Nina will still handle scheduling, registration, oversee financials, acquire funding, and whatever else she does." Which, it pained him to admit, he really didn't know.

"You really do have a screw loose, you know that?"

A tick of silence. The force of a hard sigh.

"Couldn't you just consider toughing out the season and make the end of next year your big exit? Give us time to secure media backing?"

Temptation taunted. Inadequacy hissed.

"No."

"You ought to at least give your fans an opportunity to grieve this loss. Maybe they'll hate you less." Tommy's voice rang with derision.

Eli's timely wisdom landed on Owen's tongue. "If people only loved me as a football player, I never really gained their loyalty in the first place."

Chapter Twenty-Two

How did a girl frame her response to what amounted to a tortuously unfair question? Owen had served up an authentic declaration of devoted love infused with the blissful romanticism of 'till death do us part' and slathered it in a challenge.

This was a matter for Everley, who, at present, was still relegated to bed rest.

Heaven help her, a professionally minded woman who craved routine and order, now a month away from delivering two precious baby boys who carried their daddy's DNA and would turn her right side up world topsy-turvy.

As Serenity saw it, Everley's bed rest restriction held no inconvenience for a woman confined, as it were, inside a beautifully restored historical treasure. Moreland was a priceless home that'd charmed inhabitants and honored guests for over one hundred fifty years.

In the mid-80s, Momma said Moreland had hosted Cora Lindenberg, the Oscar-nominated actress and leading lady of *Until We See Tomorrow*. It turned out that Cora shared Momma's passion for architecture, art, and old homes. Two years ago, Everley's story came across the roving eye of MidDay Media. Under the contract, the production company filmed on location—the heiress, her contractor, and the restoration—to create a sizzle reel to pitch a series idea to a network. But when Everley chose Gabe over a lucrative project, the deal fell through.

Moreland was partial to none, welcoming to all.

And thanks to divine intervention, in good repair and fit to live in.

Serenity gave Everley a call. "Hey, Evers."

"Hi, Serenity."

"I hear the TV. Binge-watching *Fixed Up Right*?"

"Guilty. But, in my defense, it's kept my sanity while doing the books."

"Sorry to disrupt that happy task, but I'm headed over to visit. Want anything?"

"All these food commercials have me craving sweets."

Don't say doughnuts.

"I'd give anything for some of your cupcakes."

Thank you, Jesus.

"Your wish is my command. I'll bring the ingredients and whip them up in your kitchen. See you soon."

The lanky, minimally traveled highway into Napoleonville cut through acres of field grasses and sugar cane. Patchworks of nothingness to the eye of the misguided. A mellow autumn sun hung among cream puff clouds. The drive slowed the spin of Serenity's thoughts from confusion to solitude.

A few miles ahead of the community of Napoleonville, Serenity slowed to take in the impressive pitch of Moreland's roof as it rose to the level of the bordering fringed treetops.

At the top of the drive, she shut off her engine. In the shadow of the looming architectural wonder, fluted columns rose in welcome. She loved and understood old houses—a heroine who could breathe life into them.

The longing to own Moreland still niggled a bit, a structure that'd once been deemed worthless when matched against polished counterparts. But restored with working parts, it held more than adequate room to grow a family.

Thoughts of Owen and his confession of love intruded. Had her dreaming of a thousand tomorrows with him. Then again, she'd always been dreaming, rising above the pain and limitations of reality. Ideas shared with Momma were sometimes met with a grim smile. While stroking Serenity's hair, she'd bob her head in an amiable, slow tilt and fit a high-on-love hippie look to her face like she'd gone on a mental LSD trip. A product of the Woodstock era, Momma should not have had to struggle to connect with Serenity's uniqueness.

"How'd you paint those beautiful flowers, Momma?" young Serenity had wondered.

"I use the medium of the invisible image in my mind's eye to create what is visible," Momma had said. "The way God spoke everything into existence when he created the masterpiece we call the world."

"Am I a masterpiece?"

"Hand me that paintbrush over there, would you, sweetie?"

Once upon a time, fear of risk made Everley fiercely unwilling to dream. Mama's objective to pry Everley out of her coffin of risk-averse living had been a rousing success.

Today said inheritance was worth ... well, a lot.

A sack of ingredients in hand, Serenity stepped inside Moreland's grand entry. Pale chandelier light dotted the gleaming pinewood flooring. Moreland contained family heirlooms and antiques and smelled of sanded cedar, dust, and history—a perfect mix of old and new. Imaginings of the past echoed in Serenity's mind ... the ping of china teacups and the clatter and buzz of ongoing repair. Family banter, impending war, husband and wife ...

"Making babies."

Serenity brought ingredients to the kitchen and then skirted the mahogany railing to find Everley in her room, sitting upright. Her belly protruded beneath a thick white duvet. The room was awash in hazy sunlight. In the cozy sitting area, a three-wick candle that smelled of roses and patchouli flickered on a leather-topped drum table between two armchairs.

Hand on a remote, a bowl of grapes on the lamp table beside her bed, Everley held the picture of a graceful, privileged princess.

All that was missing was Prince Bellevue, who'd busied himself with restoration efforts in Napoleonville—a community that could *really* use a bakery.

"Hey, Evers."

She turned, yawned, and gave a weary smile. "I want cupcakes. Let's go to the kitchen." She drew her bare, creamy feet to the floorboards and stood. Faltered slightly, slipped a hand beneath her belly, and plunked back down.

Serenity wagged a finger. "I refuse to be the reason you go into early labor."

"Listen, Sis. This is my house, my kitchen, and I want you to bake cupcakes for me to consume. So, help a girl out and walk me downstairs."

"You're supposed to be on—"

A stiff hand clamped Serenity's mouth shut.

Evers offered a crooked elbow. "You're worth the risk of early labor."

"I'm in love with the new and improved, post-Gabe version of you, Evers."

Before Moreland came into play, Everley would have refused to deter from sense and reason. The softened, contemplative planes of her face ignited her red hair, resulting in an altogether indomitable and forthright heiress.

On the descent into the kitchen, the smell of home-cooked southern fare overtook the undertone of musty air and aged wood.

Pulling a stool from the island, Everley eased into it while Serenity gathered ingredients for vanilla cupcakes and cream cheese frosting and arranged them on a stained cement surface.

"Lettie left before you called. Said to tell you hello, and that she misses you."

"I miss her, too. Especially her pear tree jam."

Everley leaned into the lip of the island and crossed her arms. A musing sound rumbled in her chest. "How you find your way around a kitchen astounds me. You're so good at this."

"Creating original food mixtures is relaxing. It's good for the soul. Gives me peace."

"Well, Mom and Dad *did* name you after Europe's most iconic chapel."

"And they named *you* after a constellation."

"Because they conceived me in a tent with a gaping hole in the top and became entranced by Orion while camping on the Appalachian Trail."

Serenity laughed while measuring flour. One cup, two cups. She tipped it into the bowl and then stilled her mixing. "Makes me wonder how they came up with my name."

"The trip to Paris, remember? When Mom was in her first trimester, pregnant with you, she and Brooke's mom Bonnie Sue took an impulsive trip to Europe. She said she'd fallen in love with Sainte Chapelle."

A place of worship. Peace. Serenity.

Over the measured portion of sugar, she cracked eggs against the lip of the bowl. She took a fork and whisked the eggs to a gentle foam. Her lids shuddered in recall.

"Mom told me I kicked and squirmed a lot when I was inside her."

"She must have sensed you weren't at peace. Naming you after a sacred place was meant to remind you that God delights to dwell in you."

The thought ribboned over her soul. Discontent tied it in a knot. She gave Everley a sharp look. "What is it about God that makes him want to dwell in a place that's so messed up?"

"Because he formed you."

She took the muffin tin and slapped it on the counter. "Limited, Evers. He made me limited."

"But you're not. That's like saying that there are *only* three primary colors."

"There are."

"What if a writer lamented that they couldn't possibly write a book because there were *only* twenty-six letters in the alphabet?"

"For a logical girl, you make no sense."

"Serenity, we aren't limited because we have limitations but because we haven't embraced them. Think about it. There's no end to the colors that could come from mixtures of red, yellow, and blue. And you, Sis, possess a virtual warehouse full of romance novels."

Fuel for the imagination, the dreamer.

Incertitude wrenched her gut and collided with the vehemence in Everley's countenance. Taking the pithy statement, she turned to the oven to preset the temperature and turned back.

"You don't disdain your cupcakes if they have air pockets or come out dry or crumbly. Lack sweetness or zing."

"No." *My babies.* "But they're not products I can sell." Serenity peeled the paper from a stick of butter and a block of cream cheese. Oily residue slicked over her fingers. "No one would want them."

"Owen would."

"He'll eat anything." She enfolded the wet ingredients into the dry and stirred to create a moistened, fragrant batter.

"It's obvious he loves you."

Her mouth tightened around the rise of a smile. A sugary pink emotion tickled her ribs. "He said as much. And I love him."

Sweeter together.

Everley gave her head a probing tilt. "Have you told him yet?"

The hum of the refrigerator registered over the thumping of her heart, the heated kitchen an inferno. She dumped the sugar onto the block of butter and set the mixer to cream.

"It's on my to-do list."

"Move it to the top."

"I already told him I can't have kids—which is confession enough and basically lowers my stock value." The truth scratched at her heart like a rusty metal spatula on a baking sheet.

"And he still loves you."

She nodded weakly and arranged casings in the muffin pan. Gingerly, she portioned batter into each.

"Then it's evident he's had a change of heart. As for children, the two of you can work through that."

One final scoop, two-thirds full.

"Who are you really trying to protect here?"

"Maybe I don't want to be known as the girl who married Owen Walker and became his shadow. It threatens my need to be my own person. Set apart and unconventional."

"Owen doesn't rob you of uniqueness. He adds greater depth to it. Tell him you love him and see where that takes you."

"I've officially fallen out of love with the new and

improved version of you."

"She's here to stay."

Fear snaked around her throat and squeezed.

Everley leaned elbows on the island and targeted her gaze. Her voice swooped low. "Please don't make my same mistake and let Dad's accident keep you from risking your heart in love. Or the fact that you lied about the teacher awarding you the special student certificate."

Her heart lurched. She shot Everley the side-eye and flattened her palms on the cold surface. "Mom and Dad told you about that?"

One shoulder hitched in a shrug. "I overheard them talking."

Serenity huffed. "Nosey."

"Remember when you chastised me for almost letting Gabe slip through my fingers?"

Hopeless romantic, she remembered it well. Still shuddered at the angry roar of Gabe's truck as it rumbled from the curb. Because Everley's fear of spontaneity had threatened to rob her of the one great love she'd ever know. The idea of Everley narrowly missing out on Gabe ... the tiny humans that grew inside her now ... robbing Serenity of being an aunt ... convulsed through her chest in waves.

Everley took Serenity's hand in hers. "Now I'm telling you. Time to tackle Owen Walker."

Sorrow slashed at her ribs. Moisture pooled in her eyes. Her chin quivered as she wrestled against collapse and fought to maintain control. "But what if he regrets his decision and grows tired of me?"

"Will you grow tired of him if he becomes increasingly symptomatic?"

Cool, vented air rippled along her skin. "I couldn't, no," she rasped out, head shaking rapidly. "That would be hypocritical."

Nothing of the unfailing love God had demonstrated.

"Then I see two very incomplete people who are, one, very much in love, and two, perfectly suited for one another."

Serenity sniffed back emotion and laughed low. "You and numbers."

What Serenity had believed were incongruent beings who had no business being together—her the weaker link—seemed to fit nicely and framed an emergent, hazy image of a whole.

Owen's weighty statement shouted over her thoughts. The one he'd left like a ticking bomb at her feet, now threatening to detonate.

The question is, can you love a guy with battered parts?

"Promise me you'll call him, Sis. Today. Tell him you love him."

Breaking Everley's imploring, green-eyed stare, Serenity opened the oven door and slid the muffin tin into place.

Heat slicked across her cheeks and melted her resolve as the oven door rasped shut. If Owen wasn't yet able to retire—in his own time, in his own way—who was she to control when or how he'd experience a satisfying end to his career?

Over the past few months, she'd watched numerous videos of players who'd made the excruciating decision. None of them smiled. None of them loved their decision. None expressed enthusiasm about staring down an unknown future. Some teared up. Because crying did, in fact, occur in football.

Whether rehearsed and private or filmed live in a studio, their angst was palpable. All bore the anguish of restraining emotion evidenced by hard ripples over their muscular bodies that'd exhausted efficacy to the game.

I love you, Seren.

The tantalizing reverb suffused white-hot heat all over again.

"I see you mulling," Everley said.

She nodded slowly, the heat of the oven at her back. Her gaze went distant again.

If Owen truly wanted her, she could no longer deny him access to her heart nor wedge an unfair standard between them. Football was perfectly suited to his stamina, power, and lust for intensity and enabled him to provide entertainment for millions.

She was one of those millions.

He chose her. Kissed her breathless.

She absolutely could—and did—love a guy with broken parts who refused to quit. Welcomed it.

"How'd I become blind to my hypocrisy—exacting conditions on him while refusing to abide any conditions on me?"

"Love makes people do stupid things."

Serenity illuminated the oven and peered at her cupcakes through the glass.

Maybe her confession would loosen her fear and deliver the peace that'd slipped from her hands like a stick of butter at room temperature.

"No matter how Owen—or anyone for that matter—views us, we're made in the image of God, a pleasing and purposeful design. He delights in the work of His hands."

Like her cupcakes.

Like Eli.

Like Owen.

A flustered sigh left her lungs. "I need work."

Everley blinked a few times and flitted her gaze away in momentary thought, then opened her palms in invitation.

"Work here. Bless our guests with your pastry-making magnificence."

"Really?" she squeaked out.

"Absolutely." She adjusted herself on the stool. "It doesn't solve my woefully inadequate event planning capability, but your vision will be a plus."

"I'd really love that, Evers."

"We couldn't pay much, but Lettie would welcome you to take over the baking."

Consideration had her drumming fingernails on the counter.

"You could even move into one of the upstairs bedrooms."

"And take care of my darling nephews while you work in the office, play hostess to guests."

"Listen, if their disposition is anything like their father, you and Owen can adopt them."

Their laughs mingled and wafted throughout the delicious smell of the kitchen.

A kaleidoscope of color painted Serenity's thoughts with peace and trust, creating a beautiful, sugary sweet tomorrow. She considered God's purpose in the relational roadblock she'd come to. Wondered at the way he'd engineered circumstances to intersect Owen's life with hers and whether or not their relationship would be fleeting or … forever.

Tell him. *Today.*

"You know what I want?" Serenity tipped her chin, taut with intention.

Neck craned, Evers strained her gaze over Serenity's shoulder. "To burn my cupcakes?"

With a whoosh, Serenity spun to the oven and checked to see her cupcakes nestled and golden but not quite ready.

Setting the timer for five more minutes, she turned back, heaving a relieved exhale. "Good save, Evers. Now, back to what I want."

"Besides being married to Owen?" Elbows on the ledge, Everley lowered her chin to interlaced hands, a smirk to upend the fiercest warrior. "Go ahead, I'm listening."

A giggle betrayed the attempt at annoyance.

"Your whole countenance lights up at the mention of his name, Sis."

And she felt it—deep inside her soul. Ethereal and magical and right. *Carrying me away.*

"Yes, maybe marrying that impossibly gorgeous man has crossed my mind." *A million times.* "But what I also want is that house."

"The French Victorian?"

"That's the one." At first sight, it held her spellbound. Its potential wrapped her in a blanket of historic charm. "It needs me. It wants to be a bakery and serve the community. To offer them a unique experience." She palmed her heart. "I can feel it."

"If I hadn't believed a house could talk, I'd say you were crazy." Everley paused to circle her gaze around the fully functional, restored kitchen rife with the rich patina of priceless history. "But here I sit, enveloped in evidence to the contrary."

Envy slithered and began its hissing. This time though, Serenity stomped on its head and celebrated her sister's joy. "—shared by Prince Charming."

At that, Ever's gaze went all dreamy.

Serenity snapped a finger at Everley, who blinked out of a romantic haze. "On the way over, I noticed the house is under Gabe's listing, Bellevue Realty."

"Which tells me you drove a few miles past Moreland into Napoleonville to see it before you got here."

"For the sake of my sanity, dispense with the logic for just a millisecond, would you?"

"I'd sooner die."

"My point is, Evers, I saw that my brother-in-law owns the real estate I want."

"It's sat vacant for several years. To serve the purpose you have in mind, Gabe would have to do far more to convert it to commercial use."

"Remember, Moreland had been abandoned before Mom and Dad bought it. It wanted to be a bed and breakfast, grace the covers of travel magazines, and draw artisans and history buffs—and one Hollywood actress—from all over the world. Almost launched a cable network series. Now, look at her. She smiled when I drove up, you know."

"Gabe has listed it for twice what he paid."

"Where you've always seen a wall, I see a door. Where you've seen impossible, I see possible."

A notification on her sports app pinged breaking news. Serenity squinted and blinked. "Tommy Caplin, former agent to Owen Walker, says the unstoppable defensive end plans to announce his retirement. Details at 5 CST."

Jaw unhinged, her head spun in a free fall of disbelief. Her cell slipped from her loosened grip, plunged into the remaining batter, and sank below the surface. Wavering, she sucked in a jagged breath and dragged her gaze to Everley. "Impossible."

Chapter Twenty-Three

Owen replayed the fantasy. He'd take Tommy by the scruff of his neck, press his back to the wall, and force answers.

No doubt his former agent had a part in leaking Owen's decision to cable news anchors. Maybe pressed by sports analysts looking to edge their counterparts in a televised delivery, begging to know the story behind the story.

Did the rogue piece of news reach Seren?

Mental fatigue from a week's worth of insomnia fogged his thoughts. Created a mess of difficulty performing fundamental tasks—tying his laces, checking his mail, and scheduling grocery delivery. His stomach churned. He swung the pantry door open. A hollowed, darkened space stared back—save those pre-packaged, store-bought poppy seed muffins.

"Jude could use those for projectiles."

He slammed the door shut. Framed certificates rattled along the wall.

But one thing was clear. He hated life without her.

Seren.

Maybe Caplin's misjudgment was good. It'd afforded him a softer way for the world to prep for full disclosure.

In the interim, Owen turned his attention to the lovable, intelligent, and gangly kid named Eli. Someone he never imagined he'd be sharing a sleeve of saltines with and sipping from a juice box, fishing for trout at St. Tammany Parish pier on Lake Pontchartrain. Certainly not how he'd envisioned the day after breaking news to the coaching staff and league managers.

But before his commitment to Serenity and The Pear Tree, he hadn't tuned into much of anything that wasn't green, measured in yards, set apart by hash marks, and encased in cheering fans.

Tucked beneath the I-10 Twin Span Bridge, a segment of the wooden pier stretched crosswise. The U-bend at each end was capped by a small, raised roof. Interstate traffic hummed overhead, the air moist and reedy. Water slurped at solid concrete pilings.

A favorite family spot for locals, the pier was constructed from parts reclaimed after Hurricane Katrina had ripped the original inter-coastal passage and fractured the bridge into small segments.

Old parts made new.

With the spawning bridge in his periphery, Owen slung his rod over the slanted railing even with his hips.

"How's chemo going?" His beefy shadow engulfed Eli, who stood beside him.

Owen's gift of a black and gold knit Kings cap crowned Eli's round, freckled face. "Well, I puked my breakfast this morning." He tugged off the cap. Several golden strands floated into the water, gentle ripples carrying them elsewhere. "Losing some hair, as you can see, but otherwise, I'm okay."

Ordinarily, he'd tousle those wavy locks but couldn't bear to loosen the fragile remnants. "I admire your courage. You're a real fighter."

Eli slipped his head into the cap, tugging it to cover prominent ears. "That stands to reason. I've made a good study of you through the years." A toothy and glorious smile radiated warmth over Owen's soul. Eli's bold—but futile—attempt to jab his ribs roused a laugh.

A common kid who'd been remarkably impacted by his career.

"Where are we on gameplay for retirement?" Eli's tone rang with authority and demanded answers.

Owen scrubbed a hand down his jaw that held a day's worth of bristle. "I've changed my mind."

Eli twisted at the waist, sparks for eyes. "What?" He nearly lost his pole to the water below.

Owen snatched it and turned a wry glance at him. "I've decided you have a far better future as a head coach than a private investigator."

"Ah. Funny." Eli reclaimed the rod, dimples deepening.

"Seriously. Your bark is equal to your bite. Once you reach age, I'll see you get the right connections. You'd be an ideal replacement for Coach Wagner."

The side of Eli's mouth curled upward, matching the smile in his voice before he went all businesslike. "Now, the three-part play."

"Told Dad, then my brother Derek and his wife Marianne, a social media influencer. That should earn me extra points. I shared my decision with the owner, GM, and coaches. Got my agent to file paperwork who then, I suspect, leaked my intent to networks." He released a blustery sigh of indignation.

"I see you're still breathing. Next, the world."

An immensely large world that included Seren. For days, he'd ached to talk to her about this. Because she deserved to know and would have just the right thing to say. Like the sun, her smile would break through malignant cloud cover and chase it away.

Promising something sweet and solid and beautiful.

Bubbles formed at Owen's line. Circles rippled over the movement of iridescent trout beneath the surface. He tugged, felt resistance, then yanked on the pole and reeled in the line.

Nothing.

"How do we envision this, Coach Billings?" Owen cast the lure again, this time with a muscled effort to let it find choppy water. "Call a press conference or arrange something with just me in a studio?"

Eli let his pole lag over the water's surface. His expression lacked the unwavering studied gaze of a fisherman intent on snagging a catch. "Definitely do it on your own but film it outside. Somewhere on your turf, expressing thanks, saying goodbye to the game."

Emotion hitched. Eli coughed past it. "People like that stuff. It shows this wasn't an easy decision. A pre-recording gives you the advantage of thinking up your reasons ahead of time and keeps you from looking stupid in front of the press."

"When your chemo and all this is behind you, I'll pay for law school."

Eli shrugged off the compliment, keeping to business. "Maybe you could film out front of where Serenity's bakery used to be. Let people get a glimpse of what you'd like to start up with your dream girl."

"It's already got another tenant. A tea and spice shop."

"What a waste of real estate." Flecked by the sun, his chocolate eyes leveled over the water like he was assessing the O-line.

"That'd be presumptuous. I'm not sure Serenity wants me in her life."

"Trust me, she does, and you're not one to fear the obstacles on the line of scrimmage. But we gotta tell the world first."

A trout swished below the surface, swirling near Owen's line. Then a bite. He yanked the pole and reeled in a sizable catch.

Dangling midair, the hooked trout thrashed and twisted.

"Too small." Owen released and tossed it into the water that swirled above its swishing descent.

A fresh wave of enthusiasm marked Eli's tone. "Let's think of some really cool place that'd work for you and Serenity."

"There is no me and Serenity."

"Like I said, there is. Put on your thinking cap."

Owen shut his eyes and conjured the images Serenity had shared of the house she'd wanted in Napoleonville, a few miles west of Moreland. Near family.

"Beneath the rough exterior, it's really adorable," she'd said. "I can just see this place being outfitted as a bakery to service people of Assumption Parish. The closest bakery is an hour north, has unimpressive ratings, and very few offerings. Everley could order products for her guests rather than arrange delivery from the Quarter."

She had seen what he needed her help to see.

Replaying the interaction in his mind, he registered the exuberance in her tone. The night she'd mentioned the house—on the wings of his hint at a future together—he'd done an online search of the area. That piece of real estate could be an ideal location to establish a bakery. Write the next chapter in the autobiography of Owen Walker's life apart from the game. A means to silence football's tortuous taunt ... *You are nothing without me.*

Visions surfaced of a front porch with lacquered shutters to frame the windows. Football memorabilia to greet clientele, a flatscreen in one corner.

A whistle blew in his head. This was *her* dream.

What would it say if he brandished his financial prowess and swiped the place out from under her, choosing, in effect, love of self over love that sacrificed for the good of another?

Nowhere on the planet could he open a bakery or embark on any venture without the girl he loved to manage it with him. The source of its sweetness and the one his heart loved.

Beautiful, flawless. *Made for me.*

If he bought the place, nothing would be gained if he didn't offer it to her free and clear and release her to float like a butterfly so she could do her thing. Yes, that was the thing to do.

Bless her outright—with no conditions. And let her go.

The satellite image of Napoleonville proper depicted a library, schools, a smattering of churches, a hardware and general store, a courthouse, a police department and jailhouse, a post office, and an antique store called Vestiges of the Past.

It had no bakery.

She'd said so a few times. He hadn't listened.

A finger snap jerked his attention back to the present. He turned to collide with Eli's impish grin. "A mere mention of her name, and you go all lovesick on me."

"I haven't talked to her in two days." The day he'd left his heart in a puddle at her feet.

Eli bobbed his pole carelessly. Gaze leveled over the horizon, his interest in catching fish waning.

"I told Seren I loved her and gave her an opening to reciprocate. No matter how well I execute the next steps, she may still refuse."

"And sometimes a lucky QB slipped past your grip no matter how good your execution. But you never left the game. I used to wonder if you'd still play even if you knew you'd lose in the end." For the duration of Eli's poignant oratory, he chopped the weathered railing a few times with the side of his hand. He turned a fixed gaze on Owen. "You would never quit during a crucial moment when you know your involvement could alter the outcome."

Puffy clouds marched in easy strides across the sky and cast shadows over the water's slate-blue surface. A gentle wind tugged at his jacket and brushed against his face. The Spirit's kiss.

Pure love meant sacrifice. Serenity and her dreams weren't meant to hide in shadows. The beautiful bakery girl needed a place where she could thrive and serve. A smiling wildflower—brought into the sunlight to stand out from the rest.

And she needed to be reminded of her worth, an affirmation delivered by one selfish—redeemed—jerk.

Even if it meant he'd not be welcome to share her dream.

Love as I have loved you.

"According to that sports devotional you gave me—which is pretty cool, by the way—your job is to make the play and trust God with the outcome." Securing the pole between his knees, Eli gestured with animated hands. "Love isn't about winning or losing. It's about growing closer to God when things are tough."

He gave Eli's thin shoulders a playful shove. "You'd also make an excellent film producer." Or a pastor.

No matter. The kid would always be Eli Billings—an amazing and wise and wonderful *adopted* child who'd befriended his hero, now a washed-up athlete in want of a new direction.

When Owen called Gabe, the screech and whir of equipment sounded through the phone.

"Hello," Gabe shouted above the shrill blade chewing through wood.

"Gabe, it's Owen."

"Hey there, big guy." Paused machinery quieted to a softening purr. "How are you?"

"Pretty good."

"How's your Dad's house?"

"It's great, thanks. Dad, not so much."

"Sorry to hear that."

"Same for me and Derek, but it comes with the game."

He'd let pride drive his decisions for so long that it churned the pot roast and potatoes in his stomach from last night's dinner at Eli's house.

"I failed to thank you for fixing Dad's window."

"I'm not following."

"Dad doesn't remember how it happened, but my guess is that it was his angry response to a bad call during a game."

"And he broke the window?"

"Yes. And you ... or your crew ... repaired it."

"Not I, friend."

Divine presence surged beneath Owen's skin. He shivered, leaving the mystery alone.

"Hold up a second, Owen." Gabe's voice went muffled. "Dad, would you hand me that jack plane to your left? Yep. Thank you, sir." Gabe returned. "What's on your mind?"

"Are you familiar with a Victorian-looking house a few miles from Moreland? Somewhere near Napoleonville's main square?"

"The one with turquoise shutters?"

"I think so, yeah."

"I'm standing across the street from it. Only one of its kind. Unmistakable beauty. Great potential, worn by time."

"Who owns it?"

"I do. Dad and I are doing business as Bellevue Realty."

"That's awesome, man. Congrats. Well, Serenity favors it and wants to convert it into a bakery. I'd like to buy it for her."

"Serenity?"

"I love her like crazy, Gabe." A thunderous silence exploded and set his heart to thud. "Is it even fair for me to expect her to love me back?"

"No, not fair. But to my way of thinking, it's not right to deny her the right to refuse."

Peace coursed through in gentle, soothing waves. Eye on the goal. "Would I have you and Everley's blessing?"

"If a guy has a house full of awards but hasn't won the heart of the girl he loves, I say that makes him a loser. Consider yourself blessed."

Gratitude surged, emboldened his purpose.

"But, the thing is, the house is under contract." Gabe's tone wilted.

No! He'd waited too long. Hesitated, overthought. Made the wrong play.

He scrubbed a hand down his face. "Then I'll buy it from them, offer double the value. Money, as you know, is no object."

"It's seen better days, dated in the late 1800s, and, of course, I'd have to discuss this with the buyers. But there's plenty of space for clientele on the main level, a kitchen in the back, and living quarters on the second level. All that'd be missing is a business permit and signage to welcome folks. It'd certainly be a win-win for both of us."

Gabe's enthusiasm was contagious, a hard-wired genteel nature and deal-making capability the bedrock of his success.

"I'd like to buy it outright, sign it over to Seren. No strings attached. Do my part to assure she knows how special she is."

Cherished, honored, and precious. Worth the high price God had paid for her. Created exactly the way he intended. But Only God knew if Owen's fumbled relational move earlier in the game would result in the greatest loss of a lifetime.

"The buyers are old money, a couple in their sixties. Art dealers, history buffs. It's doubtful they'll be willing to part with it, but I'll ask."

Make the play. Trust me with the outcome.

"Thanks. And I'd also like to get our families and friends involved when I hand it over, surprise her somehow."

"Count on me for surprises. I know Serenity is helping Brooke plan a baby shower over at Moreland for Everley this Saturday. If my buyers relent—and that's a big if—we could stage something at the front end, figure a way to get Serenity over there."

"I admire your thinking, man."

"So do I," he laughed.

"Oh, and one more thing, Gabe." Emotion knotted at Owen's throat. He coughed hard. "I need the name of the big kahuna who filmed Moreland's restoration."

"The one Everley permitted to film Moreland's restoration until she listened to reason, fell in love with me, and fired his butt?"

"That's the one."

"Alex Coleman. Why?"

"I want to hire him to film my retirement announcement."

The tsunami of uncertainty in Gabe's labored breathing wobbled his stance. He could feel Gabe's brows knit together and his nostrils flare—a sure sign Gabe had been challenged or was overwrought with concern. "You're giving it up?"

"A little late on the tackle, but yeah." Somehow the admittance buoyed him, expanding his lung capacity. He'd no longer trudge through a career bearing the weight of false identity. Driven by eternal purpose and intention now, he'd developed a confident stride and set his mind on things money can't buy.

Things that last.

Over the phone with Alex Coleman, Owen detailed his vision. An LA native, Alex had followed Owen's career closely and grieved when he'd signed with the Kings.

"Sure hate to hear that," Alex said. "Hate worse you're asking me to film it. Kind of like being chosen to put nails in Jesus's hands and feet, you know?"

"But that all turned out in everyone's favor, so ... the film gig? Are you available?"

"I'm honored you'd ask, especially since I'm working independently, but for a project that sounds like it'd come to only a few minutes, you could get someone to capture this with a cell. Spare the expense."

"A decision of this magnitude demands excellence. I've researched your previous work with MidDay and viewed projects on your website, White Horse Entertainment. You game?"

"Sure, sure. But, uh, why not the linebacker room at Mercedes-Benz stadium? Invite all the bigwigs, AP, and local cable news. Toss in a few sports-camp kids—win over your audience. Something people expect?"

"I'm doing this out of obedience, not to score points."

In full surrender, Alex agreed to Owen's terms, awaited his decision on location, and committed to having edits and layovers done within a week. He'd contact major sports networks and cable affiliates to air the pre-recorded announcement the following Tuesday evening.

For a sliver of a second, he'd considered filming in front of the gingerbread house, hinting at his new direction, but the buyers hadn't yet relented. That and Coach Billings shot the idea down.

"I think you need to pick a stadium for this," Eli said.

"The Benz?"

"Nah. Too predictable and impersonal."

"Wildcat High football field?"

"Works for me."

Owen gave Eli a high five, then contacted Coach Simmons to make arrangements and communicated his decision to Alex. Since it was Eli's suggestion to take his final play to the gridiron, it made sense to include the young sage. He brought Dad along, too—for moral support and to provide a visual aid to superglue his cleats to the ground.

Following a day's rain, Wildcat field held a gauzy heat and smelled of damp earth. The horizon held a burn of amber beneath a clear sky. Owen positioned a camp chair in the endzone, Eli, a sentry, at his side. His muddy brown eyes were shaded by a Kings ball cap. Dad maintained a safe distance, his gaze clear and steady over the last hour.

God, may he stay that way.

Alex traipsed over the turf in tennis shoes, dark denim, and a ball cap. His T-shirt promoted White Horse Entertainment, the full-scale media company he'd established last year.

At the ten, Alex shook Harvey's hand and then crossed into the endzone, pumping Owen's hand in a presumptuous 'we-go-way-back' manner. He proceeded to circle the field, tipped an assessing gaze toward the sky, and directed his camera guy, Josiah, to arrange the boom mic and lighting. He bent to shake Eli's hand. "Didn't know you had a kid, Owen. Looks just like you."

"He's one of my sports-camp kids, here for moral support."

In case I tuck tail and run.

Alex straightened. Questions rang in his gaze before he broke into producer mode. "We'll frame this using low-angle shots in medium close-up, vary the angles. I want to capture sequences to suggest power and evoke emotion. We'll use auxiliary light to soften shadows or if we start to lose the sun."

Alex fastened a lavalier mic to the ribbed neckline of Owen's white shirt and stepped back. He rounded the camera, slipped a headset over his cap, adjusted the lens, and nodded at Josiah.

"We ready?" Alex said.

Owen turned a wary glance at Dad, the crusty old coach who'd kept clear of camera angle. He wound his arms tightly at his chest and parted his feet. With his lids drawn, Dad nodded slowly. Eli stood in Dad's looming shadow, his confident smile cheering Owen on.

At Josiah's thumbs-up, Alex raised three fingers, steadied a scrutinizing gaze, and stepped back. "We're a go in three, two, one—"

Heat balled in Owen's stomach and thudded in his chest. He barely glanced at his prepared speech.

"Recording," Alex mouthed, his brows winged.

Fist to his mouth, he coughed past the hiss of angst.

"In football, one mistake, one decision, can change everything. Every catch, drop, loss, and injury is meant to teach something. Until this last concussion, I'd been unwilling to listen and refused to walk away. I'd disregarded clear warnings from medical professionals and ... those I love."

Emotion chugged up. He snapped his finger and gritted his teeth in hard clench until it passed. "At some point, I'd placed football and the image it afforded me above more important things. For me, life apart from football wasn't an option."

A serene stillness settled over the field and stretched long. Peace nestled into fissures throughout his body. Tasted sweet.

Alex and Josiah's subtle gestures faded from the forefront of his thoughts.

"The NFL circle of life tells us the day will come when we'll need to retire, but there are those like me who struggle to accept the truth. It wasn't that my fans believed I could walk on water. It was that I believed I could."

Assume the throne of God.

He shifted an imperceptible gaze at Dad, who graced him with a nod.

"Given that, I'm formally announcing my retirement from football for the good of the game and my teammates." He drew a numb gaze to the paper, then glanced back at the camera. "I can no longer play my fast, intense, physical game without risking further injury. I'm grateful to the entire organization, the coaching staff, teammates, and fans who've supported me over the years. To Donovan Crawford, chaplain for the Rams, who introduced me to a faith in God that's carried me through tough times and reminded me to give all glory to God for my achievements."

To Serenity Lewis, the reason he understood and had experienced the unmerited love of God.

A cool wind whisked through the stadium and swept up the seats—delivering the smell of cleansing rain, fresh turf, and a promising future.

His hand fisted. He tapped it to his chest. "I love the game of football with everything I've got, but it's something I did." He splayed his fingers. "It's not who I am. It's given me resources to pour into kids who want a shot at pursuing their dreams and discovering their strengths. If I've impacted even one life, helped grow them into the man or woman God created them to be, all the hits and losses are worth it."

Dad's countenance lifted in a pleased grin and held an uncanny radiance—a reward superior to another Super Bowl ring.

Introspection had Owen in a stifling pause. He searched past the camera lens, looked into Serenity's soul, and prayed she'd hear his heart. He conjured her face framed by vanilla blonde hair and eyes like an endless summer sky reflecting a meadow covered in purple roses. Crumpling the papers, he abandoned the rest of his speech. Words afresh landed on his tongue.

Voice bold and forceful, born of adversity.

"My biggest regret is that my decision to keep playing has hurt someone I love very much. I pray God will restore what I've trampled."

Lips pressed in anguish, he momentarily lowered his head and released an extended breath. Heat rushed to his feet before he captured the camera again. Still searching ... now, begging God to heal her heart.

Dread seeped in. That raw, flesh-torn feeling when, on rare occasions, he'd let the QB slip into open space, outrun him. His gut twisted in regret. His retirement may have brought the bitter end of much more than the game he loved.

Strength sapped—the sting of moisture crawled to his eyes. He waved off Alex and gave Josiah a quick nod. "That's ... that's it. I'm done."

Chapter Twenty-Four

Serenity gave a small yelp, bounded down the stairs, two at a time, and jogged weightlessly back to her car.

A momentary loss of spatial awareness was to blame for waves of light-headedness. Engine idling on Moreland's drive, she took her cell in trembling hands. "Just once more."

That made twenty times she'd listened to the video.

At the power-packed conclusion of Owen's announcement, she pressed fingers to her smiling lips and then tapped a loose fist against her chest. The fact that he'd made the epic announcement apart from the studio spotlight communicated volumes. The way he'd held himself conveyed a rare mixture of a cool pro athlete— all together comfortable in front of a camera—and a guy who'd taken extra measures with his appearance as though dreadfully afraid of rebuff.

Undeniably, something in Owen had changed. For the better. It added splendor to his smile, the gaze of a man resigned to part ways with the field and accept a new direction, open to God's leading.

Raw, unadulterated surrender.

Back home, she lounged on the sofa and blinked rapidly. Her mouth went dry, and her skin tingled. "I bet I missed something. I'd better watch this again. Just once more ..."

To his résumé of handsome and generous and intelligent, Serenity included vulnerable transparency. An aphrodisiac to a girl who'd spent the better part of her life wondering at her value, hesitant to let people in.

Lids shuddering closed, she summoned the smell of his fresh, sporty scent.

"My decision to stay in the game hurt someone I love very much. I pray God will restore what I've trampled."

Her throat constricted in a strained whisper. "And I love you very much, Owen Walker."

Explosive on the field and expressive in his thoughts, he wasn't one to bottle up emotion. He's admitted to verbally processing well past midnight on several occasions. Nothing of his delivery smacked of manipulation, a ruse to get her to admit her shortsightedness.

Three days had passed since Owen's news busted through the sports fan stratosphere. She should have devoted the sole of her time and attention to preparing for Everley's baby shower set for Saturday afternoon. But if gold medals were awarded for the greatest frequency of replays, she'd have earned one.

Sending Owen a text was hardly the way to communicate sympathy for what had to be an immensely difficult decision. But his monumental announcement—amassing viewers by the millisecond—had her scrambling to string sentences together.

SERENITY: I saw it. I know that was difficult.

OWEN: Very.

SERENITY: Future plans?

OWEN: Make it up to you?

An olive branch. A rush of pinkish, sugar-coated desire chilled her skin.

Apparently, he hadn't despised her too badly for her staunch refusal to respond to his overtures. That was good.

SERENITY: Hosting a baby shower at Moreland tomorrow at 2. Could we talk after?

The simple thumbs-up emoji drizzled anticipation over her insides, making the 24-hour wait equal to infinity.

Later that afternoon, she worked meticulously in Moreland's grand dining hall in the north wing to arrange floral centerpieces on linen-draped, circular tables.

Everley waddled in, smelling of delicate gardenia. Her giddiness added to the soothing fragrance of white roses, carnations, delphinium, and eucalyptus. She trekked her gaze over Momma's antique buffet to the tables. A glow of expectant motherhood smoothed her features. "It's beautiful, Sis."

"I'm so happy you love it. Only the best for you, Gabe, and my nephews."

Serenity continued to maneuver and rearrange to create the look she wanted.

Giving her design a nod, Serenity pivoted to face Everley. "What I'm thinking is, we'll socialize, eat refreshments, and open gifts in here, then move the party outside on the lawn for punch and cupcakes. Speaking of, I want to show you the super cute decorations I came up with. They're in the kitchen."

She followed Everley into the grand entry past the staircase, through the south wing dining hall that adjoined a plush and sunny front parlor.

Halting mid-stride, she spun, and belly-bumped Everley, who faltered.

"Are you trying to send me into early labor?"

"Sorry, no. It's just … I wish I'd … I should have told him I loved him sooner."

Sentiment rose in Everley's gaze. She assumed her big sister posture that never failed to coax Serenity to spill.

"Telling him now will only seem like it's in response to his announcement—like my love is contrived and conditional." The very thing she hated. That which God had driven out of her. It'd been self-defense to slay the dragon of heartbreak before it slew her.

Entering the parlor from the grand entry, Gabe rapped on the wood. He smelled of cedar chips and looked like he'd stepped out of an ad for preserving the past in his jeans, boots, and plaid shirt. He carried the redolence of an industrious entrepreneur and wore his call to historical house restoration like a second skin.

He leaned in to kiss Everley, smiled against her lips, and whispered something that roused an infectious giggle and caused her cheeks to flame in a blush of love.

Finding herself a voyeur, Serenity redirected her attention to her cell and scrolled through images of cupcake designs and bakery storefronts.

Gabe widened his arms at his side. "Sold the house, babe."

Serenity pocketed her cell. "What house?"

He darted a conspiratorial gaze at Everley, then shifted it back to her. "The French Victorian."

"The one I want?"

"Yep."

Spoken like he'd sold her hamster or something.

Mouth agape, she steadied herself.

"The buyer paid double what I intended to list it for." Amidst this awful news, Gabe demonstrated no shortage of malignant gloating and commenced smiling.

Frosty reserve glazed her tongue. "You didn't think to let me know first?"

"Could you have paid for it?"

"You know I couldn't, but it would have eased the blow to have had a heads up that someone had their eye on it. Maybe I could have figured something out." She started figuring. "Attempted to secure a loan, swung negotiations in my favor, or maybe bluffed a counter-offer."

Set up a lemonade stand and sold cupcakes. *Anything.*

At his soul-pestering silence, frustration sizzled. "Who bought it?"

The two conspirators exchanged tentative stares.

"Owen."

"What?" she spewed. "You sold my house to that ... to him?"

"I did."

Sorrow oozed beneath her skin. Hot rage coursed through her limbs. She shook her head to dislodge the insult. "That unconscionable creep! He stole it right out from under me."

"Calm thyself, Serenity." One side of Gabe's mouth tipped in mirth, enjoying her predicament at her expense. "Maybe it isn't what you think."

"It's exactly what I think. Owen's retirement is only a segue to start a bakery of his own and sell his Walker Big Hits, sacking me in the process."

"Or maybe it *isn't* what you think," Everley added, her voice controlled and slow. A concerted effort to douse the flames licking Serenity's spine.

Stupid, stupid heart.

Moisture blurred her vision. Why'd she ever allow herself to believe she could catch—and hold—the eye of Owen Walker? That he'd love her for who she was, dignify her dreams?

That he really meant what he'd said?

To think she'd forgiven him for having trampled her—*his* words, not hers. But apt.

For now, she'd nurse her sour attitude until after tomorrow's shower and extend an olive branch of her own. Let him grovel at her feet and explain why he'd thought nothing of pummeling her dignity a second time.

Because he'd gone on to tackle a new venture, taking her coveted property and leaving her out of it.

"I've no time to take a two-by-four to his head right now. Brooke confirmed there will be twenty-five guests here tomorrow, and I've got three dozen cupcakes to bake."

"Looking forward to it, spitfire." Gabe kissed Everley and left the parlor by way of the adjoining dining room.

The following morning, Serenity's kitchen was filled with the sweet scent of cupcakes and frosting and one faithful friend.

Brooke held a cupcake in her palm and rotated it. "These are absolutely adorable, Serenity. Love the tiny little blue fondant baby feet on each of them."

Weeks back, Serenity researched a fun adaptation to Everley's request for Serenity's Special recipe. Using white cake rather than double fudge, she topped each with the traditional chocolate-covered cherry cordial but piped blue-tinted buttercream frosting around it. She made fondant, tinted it powder blue, pressed it into tiny baby feet molds, and adorned the frosting with the fondant.

She lingered a pleased glance over the little darlings that sat tucked in prepared boxes. "Mmm. Better than I'd imagined."

Brooke tugged off her apron. "Let's go. Now."

She roved a glance around her kitchen and peered into the handled totes and sealed containers. "You sure we got everything? Plates, napkins, balloons, the rubber duckies to float atop Blue Hawaiian punch?"

"Yes." Brooke jerked a head toward the door.

"You sure you ordered a *blue* balloon bouquet?"

"Yes, yes. Now, let's go."

Suspicion piqued. "Since when do you care about punctuality?"

"People can change." A winsome grin softened Brooke's frazzled expression.

Guests were due to arrive at Moreland in two hours, and Serenity's nerves jangled. She'd taken multiple treks between the outside tables and the kitchen.

Had she remembered everything? Would there be enough? Would her product be deemed acceptable? Were the flowers still smiling?

Would the experience be special?

God, do you delight in me?

In the kitchen, she peered over Lettie's shoulder while the dear woman worked nimble fingers to prepare pear tarts, finger sandwiches, and a fruit tray.

Turning a stare at Serenity, Lettie cupped her cheeks with weathered hands, shifted her gaze as if reading Serenity's thoughts, and delivered her soulful, alto rendition of the classic hymn. "When peace like a river attendeth my ways or sorrow be filling up my days, Miz Serenity's gonna sing it be well, it be well with my soul."

And it was. For now.

Outside, she made quick work of arranging her cupcake babies on a floral rim, tiered stand while Brooke prepared the punch. She set the stand on an elongated table under a canopy. The crisp, dry weather was ideal for celebrating new life, answers to prayer, and the love of friends and family.

A gentle, cool breeze blessed the day and rustled a melody through the trees.

From the front door, Gabe and Everley wandered over. Sunlight gilded her russet strands in streaks of rose gold.

She wore a stretch knit red dress with cuff sleeves, dangle earrings, and beaded sandals—the picture of maternal tranquility and exuberant expectancy. "This is all so very beautiful, Sis. I feel honored."

"Celebrating you makes me happy, Evers."

"Perfect day for new beginnings," Gabe added.

At the sound of incoming text, Gabe retrieved his cell and lifted his gaze. Moments later, the whipping thrum of a helicopter hovered. The midday sun provided backlight for the robust aircraft.

Serenity gasped when the pilot made an easy landing along the west side grove. Branches bent to the powerful sweep of wind spawned by spinning blades.

She peered long and spit a wry response. "A chopper? At a baby shower?"

A raven-haired pilot whose eyes were concealed by reflective shades unfolded from the side. He strode over the lawn in the direction where she stood beside Brooke, Everley, and Gabe. Outfitted in utility pants and a snug olive-green shirt, he presented crisp, clean, and purposeful—the makings of *somebody's* Prince Charming right there.

When he neared, she recognized the unmistakable cool bearing of Owen's driver—the stalwart Marine, Major not-so-smiley Jude Buchanan.

Jude gave a sharp nod to the three, who returned silent greetings and secretive smiles, all of them. He pivoted to Serenity and raised his voice above the roar of the chopper. "Hello, ma'am. I've been asked to escort you into Napoleonville proper."

A stone's throw.

"The *Marines* sent you?"

"No, ma'am. Owen Walker."

Her lids flickered in haughty disbelief. "Right."

Jude didn't flinch. Trained to focus on and carry out his mission, lasering his eye on the target, apparently.

Brooke poked Serenity on the arm. "Listen. If a guy looking like *that* was assigned by the man I loved to escort me somewhere, I wouldn't hesitate."

Turning a conflicted gaze at Everley, Serenity begged direction.

Everley threw an arm over the lawn, emerald gaze aflame. "Get on that chopper, Sis."

"I've got no time for a joy ride, Evers. Have you forgotten the shower? The reason I'm here and you're here—guests expected to arrive in—"

"You're to be returned at 1300 hours, ma'am. An hour out from the pre-scheduled event."

Owen had taken care enough to know she'd never consent if it meant missing Ever's big day. She seared the three conspirators with a scowl and gave Jude a nod of surrender. No matter his accomplishments in battle, he'd duly succeeded in commanding her attention.

"Listen up, Major. I'm only consenting to his wishes so I can give him a piece of my mind."

"Yes, ma'am."

And was that a smirk she'd detected on the fearsome soldier before he turned to escort her to that hulking chopper?

Fastened inside, headset snug against her ears, her stomach lurched when Jude lifted the whipping craft. Below her, Moreland shrank to a tiny white pebble.

After a two-minute ride, he deftly lowered the helicopter to a smooth landing in a spacious vacant lot across from ... the French Victorian.

Her house.

No, Owen's house.

Still lovely, forlorn—in want of loving arms and a dusting of sugar and the breath of life.

Jude returned a text and then turned to her. "Stand by, ma'am."

When he unfolded from the helicopter, she sat immobilized in her seat until he eased her out on her side. Following his lead, she jogged beneath the whipping blades over to a crumbling curb several yards from the front of the house, where he stopped abruptly. "Good day, ma'am."

Through a narrowed gaze, she trailed Jude's retreat as he piloted up and out of sight.

Taking the reticent steps of a mom who'd abandoned her child, Serenity's stare locked on the flaking, turquoise shutters aside sad windows. She panned a gaze along the spindled wraparound porch, which held Owen's dominating frame.

The structure shrank to a doll house against his presence.

For a nanosecond, sympathy zipped through her for what his decision cost, the burden of an uncertain tomorrow. But then again, wasn't she standing on his big, bright, and beautiful tomorrow, a trampled bystander to his happy new life?

The air held the heady scent of roses. Hundreds of lavender petals graced the steps. More lay strewn over the lawn and, she now realized, beneath her feet.

A complicated flower. Appreciated for its beauty and fragrance, the complexities of its design and uniqueness were easily overlooked.

"I thought all girls loved red roses," Owen had said.

"I'm different that way," she'd said.

Uncommon. Rarely a prime selection.

She stooped to claim a petal and rubbed its silken texture between her fingers. A serene quiet whispered over her soul. She sniffed the delicate fragrance, heart slowing its rhythm.

"Thanks for coming out." Owen's easy-going confidence held an attractive vulnerability. Suddenly, she'd forgotten how enraged she was.

Her voice muscled past a rampart of discomfort. "Not like I had a choice. I mean, you did send a United States Marine to escort me here." Maintaining the guise of irritation was futile against her treasonous grin.

"Decorated war vet, I trust Jude with my life. And yours."

She tamped down a rustle of nerves. "Surely you didn't snatch me from a long-anticipated baby shower to regale me with the meritorious conduct of a Marine."

He tweaked a smile and shook his head. "Uh-uh."

Schoolboy charm claimed his mouth. His chin sported a perfect smattering of day-old auburn whiskers. A delicious, whisky-hued shadow colored his jaw.

You're mad, remember? Red hot, blazing mad.

Or maybe just red hot, hopelessly faint with love.

Paired with jeans and white athletic shoes, his charcoal blue shirt stretched across his oft-photographed chest, inside which was the tender heart of a darn persistent and generous man. A slaying combination of heat, compassion, and admiration quaked through her.

He advanced a step. Sunlight glazed the outline of his body.

Her breath hitched at the tremor of ecstasy that'd circled down her spine. Such foolishness to enter his arena. But what was she going to do, turn around and run?

And really, at this moment, there was no other place on the entire planet she'd rather be—and stay—than right here.

Mad, remember?

Okay, she'd play nice first, then strike him with a two-by-four.

He delivered a small, wickedly powerful smile to rival the muscles cording up his arms. Those two massive limbs—strength she'd desperately missed—parted in an invitation to narrow the distance. Hope and angst gathered in his winsome gaze.

Curiosity had her edging toward the bottom step. Because no matter his reason for swiping her dream house, there was still that little bit she'd wanted to convey ... should have already conveyed ... that she, in great measure, loved him and would dare to accept him as is.

Like a house in rough shape that needed someone to take a chance on it.

Stepping in casual swagger mid-way down the steps, he bent and offered a hand.

She took it. The power in his clutch short-circuited reason.

A tense silence ensued.

Within the shadowed, crumbling porch, she freed her hand, arms now useless appendages. She entwined them to keep her heart from leaping out of her chest. "Your retirement speech. That was nice, what you said."

"I meant it."

His gaze drifted down her front. Shivers popped along her skin as he drew it back, appraising her as though admiring art.

"Seren, I've looked at you through the wrong set of lenses, created in my mind what an ideal family should look like. The truth is—a family is one man and one woman. Home is wherever they're together. And you're the most amazing woman I've ever met. I need you to know that I love you for who and what you are."

When I consider your heavens, Lord, the work of your fingers, the moon and the stars …

"I have no right to place blame, Owen. You were right. I knew what you wanted—a desire to carry on the Walker legacy. But I kept my inabilities from you for fear you couldn't … wouldn't love me—"

"Unconditionally."

"Yes, that."

A huge breath fell out of him. He swallowed hard. "Until recently, your fear was justified. Now it's not."

Her defenses died a slow death. A warm air breezed over her lungs, and a sugary sweet desire coated her insides.

"Maybe we ought to drop the penalties we've stacked against each other then," he said.

The warmth of his sincerity opened the petals of her heart. The ache underfoot sought rain of redemption. This might do it.

But first—"Why'd you bring me here, Owen? You could have called."

Who am I that Owen would bother with me?

"My decision to retire means nothing unless I know you and I are okay. I needed to see in your face that you've forgiven me for how I let the game come between us."

"I forgive you. Will you forgive my disrespect?"

"Forgiven." The angular planes of his face tensed as though preparing an oratory. "You've got this crazy ability to make me feel safe about admitting my struggle—everything football demands I ignore for the good of the team. Now I see endless possibilities that, before you, were limited to a hundred-yard playing field. My future may be an ugly one, but I'm not ashamed of it, and it no longer scares me."

His raw confession ticked in agonizing beats along her spine. Deafening silence rattled between them.

"I've been cruel. I've been stupid. I've been selfish. I've been …" He folded his arms and widened his stance. "You're welcome to stop me."

"Why would I? Your stats are spot on," she smirked.

He quirked a grin. "You'd make a supreme offensive lineman."

"You're up for the challenge."

Enveloped in his shadow, she risked being lured by his charm. "How'd you figure meeting on the property that—as I learned yesterday—now belongs to you was a good strategy to mend what's been broken?"

"It's not my house."

She seared him with a look. "You bought it."

"For you." Gently, he unfurled her hand and placed a bronze key in it, the metal cool against her palm. He curled her fingers over it and cupped the whole of his mammoth hand over hers. Sealing something inside her.

Lips parted in wonderment, she tilted her stare up at him. "M-me?"

Just shy of the heavenly beings, crowned with glory and honor…

Slowly, he released her hand. "The house is in your name. Free and clear. No conditions."

"I'm … I'm …"

"Happy?" His lifted brow tugged the desired response.

"Over the moon." Cliché and emotionally flat, but emotionally rich, fresh, and pithy responses went missing.

Her throat tightened, and her vision blurred. The whirl of elation nearly buckled her knees. Painful caution seized her thoughts. A sudden whoosh of inhibition infused her soul and colored it gray. "But I don't want it, Owen."

A hint of agony and righteous fury snuffed the light he'd held in his eyes. He retreated like she'd slapped him, tone strident. "Why?"

She startled at the eruption of shrill whistles and whoops. From behind the house, a precious pack of friends and family appeared—Everley and Gabe, followed by sweet Lettie, who held a bobbing bouquet of pearlescent lavender balloons.

Rounding the opposite side, Arlene and Ross and Eli, his smiling face crowned in a knit cap. Next, Brooke, Justin, Derek, Marianne, and a slow-going Harvey Walker—who made his way to the lower step and thrust a thumbs-up at Owen.

"Perfectly executed, everyone. Just like we'd practiced. But, uh ..." Owen's voice dropped to barely audible. He massaged the back of his neck and plodded over the lawn to join them. His shoulders sagged as he tucked fingers in his front pockets. "Seren doesn't want the house."

A stiff silence churned in threatening waves.

Putting her red hair to good use, Everley tromped near the porch and seared Serenity with a smoldering glare. "Are you crazy?"

"Relax, Evers," she laughed. "I'm totally taking the house." She skipped down the rickety steps and fixed her gaze on Owen. "But I don't want the house unless you come with it."

His brows shot up over a gaze that shifted in a rabid left-right movement over hers.

"What good is a dream come true without the one who makes it sweet?" The one whose grand gesture this fine day needed more than a pathetic thank you.

"Seren, that's not what this is about. Really, I just wanted to give you—"

"Walker, if you think I'm going to take this house, turn it into a bakery, and leave you out of it, you really do have brain damage."

"Don't you need time to think this through?"

"I've been thinking this through since your jumbo cupcakes outclassed mine and sales soared."

Okay, really, long before that.

A cheeky smile inched his lips. "True to the name, they were a Big Hit."

That elicited a chuckle.

"Refuse the offer if you will, Walker, but anyone who goes into business with me must have your exact same capabilities and be able to take my vision and make magic happen."

That wolfish grin again. Dots of sunlight played in his glistening eyes, flecked them in gold. He trekked a whimsical gaze at the house and back to her. "Someone looking for new direction?"

"Particularly a big, retired someone."

"Who can bake like nobody's business?"

"Definitely a plus. Minus the cocky attitude."

Eager whispers rustled around them. In mock contemplation, he rubbed his thumb and forefinger along that delicious stubble dusting his chin, his scent of musk and irresistibility nearly stealing her breath. "I guess I could be persuaded to partner up with you."

"It's a little unorthodox, you know. I mean, a former pro ballplayer in a pink apron."

"I think it's a sweet matchup."

Far beyond sweet.

"Seren, you're like that one book among millions that's worth reading over and over and over."

"Sounds like you've traded football for the sport of sappy analogies to win a girl's heart."

A rogue smile—feathery and possessive enough to make a girl swallow her chewing gum—drew along the sides of his mouth, and suddenly her breaths went shallow and rapid.

He prowled forward. "I see it's working."

Playfully, she inched backward. "I thought you gave up football."

Closer. "I may have a few plays left in me." Purpose mounted in his ravenous gaze, voice husky and intentional.

"Who am I kidding, Seren? It's you I want. The two of us together for the duration."

He scored on directness.

Anguish pinched the space between her brows. Reality slowed the speed of a euphoric free fall and burned on her tongue. "What about kids, Owen? Honoring your mom's memory?"

"Let Derek and Marianne figure it out." He tossed a sidelong glance at the two, Derek returning a sharp nod.

"What if you regret your decision?"

Gravity claimed his expression. "I will never, ever tire of you, Seren. Never."

Passion pounded in her chest. She claimed his gaze—clouded with need—and voiced the thing she'd uttered in agonizing silence for years. "I love you, Owen."

Collective sniffs and murmurs and tongue clucks surrounded her.

An incomprehensible, ethereal peace whooshed in fierce waves, twirling sweet grace like cotton candy.

Taking her face in his hands, Owen angled down and kissed her, setting her ablaze. Moving over her mouth in delicious, fiery pressure. Crushing and hungry. He worked his kisses in indulgent, resolute strokes.

A new man who'd discovered who he was off the field, able to see himself through the eyes of God.

"Seren ..." he whispered, pulling back. In one fluid movement, he lowered to one knee, expectant stare unwavering. "Will you marry me?"

At the splendor of his smile, she brought palms to her blazing hot cheeks and nodded rapidly. A pathetic "Yes" squeaked out. A second time, louder in case he hadn't heard. "Yes."

He stood, tugged her close, and took her mouth in another hard, feverish kiss worthy of the hall of fame.

Whistled cheers and hearty claps sounded aside them.

Hands about his neck and chest heaving, she attempted to make an utterance. "Before we make this engagement official, I need to tell you something."

"What's that?" he said in a hoarse whisper.

"My doctor said there's a promising surgery for cases of MRKH similar to mine that've resulted in successful conception. She said numerous married couples have enjoyed full-term, healthy babies."

He tickled her neck in kisses and roved his mouth along her jaw.

Kids, Walker. Good grief, was the man listening? Because, at present, he seemed far more interested in kisses, drawing her to an inescapable hold.

She flattened her palms to his chest and captured his gaze. "There is one little caveat we'd need to agree to."

"What's that?"

"After the surgery, it would require frequent attempts to conceive."

Ah, the glorious Owen Walker smile. "I'm nothing if not a team player."

In his embrace, her chest heated to an inferno.

He leaned in and hovered his lips over hers. A gush of pink warmth oozed into her pores.

Derek gave a strident cough and stepped in to wave at them. "Hate to break this up, but we *are* still here."

Serenity and Owen turned to the happy onlookers. She swayed in dizziness. He gripped her hand.

"And my cooler is packed with a couple dozen cupcakes to sweeten the occasion," Brooke said.

"Which has turned out to be a double doozy of a celebration." Lettie steepled wrinkled hands and held them to her mouth.

Marianne feverishly recorded the happy occasion on her cell.

"All this kissing is making me sicker than chemo." Eli stuck out his tongue and placed a hand on his middle.

Satiny laughter ribboned over the group.

Owen engulfed Eli in a gentle hug and lifted him off his feet. "Sure do love you, kid."

He beamed. "Told you she'd say yes."

"Good call, Coach Billings." Owen lowered Eli, who raised his palm and clapped Owen's hand in a high five.

Gabe took Owen's hand in a hard shake and slapped his shoulder. "Welcome to the family, my brother."

Everley bracketed Serenity's arms. "Your Prince has come."

"Yes, he—"

Eyes flaring, Everley sucked in a sharp breath and cupped her hands beneath her abdomen, doubling over. "Uh-oh."

Gabe angled his stare. "You okay, babe?"

"My water just broke."

"But the baby shower? Guests will be arriving soon," Serenity said with a whine.

"There *is* no baby shower, Sis," Everley managed to puff out, bending lower, wincing.

"Sorry, Serenity," Brooke said. "The food and decorations are really an after party—just for us—a big ruse for celebrating Owen's gift of the house to you. The proposal was frosting on the cupcake."

Everley shrieked and elbowed Gabe's ribs with a sharp jab.

"Gotta go, folks. The Bellevue boys are breaking free." Beneath the canopy of silky blue sky, he scooped her expectant body into his arms and jogged to his truck.

"Drive safe, Gabe," Serenity called over the roar of his engine. "You're transporting very special cargo!"

Owen tugged her to his side. "You're very special."

Her heart lifted. "Must run in the family."

When Owen turned her to face him and kissed her, the world and its insufficiencies fell away, a sweet peace holding her heart fast in the arms of a dream come true.

About the Author

Mary A. Felkins is an inspirational romance author, blogger, and contributor to writer's blogs and inspirational publications. She and her husband Bruce live in the magnificent foothills of North Carolina. They have four young adult children. She is a member of ACFW (American Christian Fiction Writers) and My Book Therapy.

Her purpose in writing is to reclaim God's intention and motivation when he created the world —to enable readers to know his heart and experience his love.

The unmerited gift of a large, unopened bag of Peanut M&Ms or an episode of Fixer Upper will lure her from her writer's desk. A surprise appearance by her teen idol, Donny Osmond, would also do the trick, although she'd likely pass out.

If, upon introduction, she likes your first or last name, expect to see it show up in one of her novels.

To receive Mary's story-style devotions via email, along with quarterly author newsletter offering book-related giveaways, subscribe on her website www.maryfelkins. com/blog

The Heart of Moreland Manor Series

You Are
the Reason

The Heart of
Moreland Manor
Book 1

MARY A. FELKINS